GATEWAYS RETRO SCIENCE FICTION

HOW TO WRITE GREAT SCIENCE FICTION

GATEWAYS RETRO SCIENCE FICTION

HOW TO WRITE GREAT SCIENCE FICTION

WORKING JOURNAL

AND BEST-KNOWN CLASSICS

BY HORACE L. GOLD

GATEWAYS BOOKS AND TAPES

NEVADA CITY, CALIFORNIA

Some material in this book has appeared in its present form
or earlier textual versions in
THE OLD DIE RICH AND OTHER SCIENCE FICTION STORIES
edited by H.L. Gold (Dennis Dobson, London 1965)

Gateways Books and Tapes
P.O. Box 370
Nevada City, CA 95959
1-800-869 0658
http://www.gatewaysbooksandtapes.com

Library of Congress Cataloging-in-Publication Data

Gold, H. L. (Horace Leonard), 1914-
[Old die rich]
How to write great science fiction : working journal and best-known classics / by Horace L. Gold.
p. cm. -- (Gateways retro science fiction ; 1)
Originally published as: The old die rich. New York : Crown Publishers, c1955. With new foreword.
ISBN 0-89556-126-3 (alk. paper) -- ISBN 0-89556-125-5 (pbk. : alk.paper) -- ISBN 0-89556-127-1 (limited deluxe fine art ed. : alk. paper)
1. Science fiction, Canadian. 2. Science fiction--Authorship. I.Title. II. Series.
PR9199.3.G5975 O43 2002 808.3'876--dc21
2002004658

CONTENTS

INTRODUCTION

Before the Second World War, Horace worked for *Action* and *National Comics;* he and his writing partner Ken Crossen were among the highest paid strip writers in the world.

Then Horace was drafted, and this story is developed further in Horace's "Gold on Gold".

After the war, Horace returned to New York City where he landed a job editing a girlie magazine called *Girls GALore*.

It was moderately received, but it was early for *Playboy's* market, and the day of the pin-up magazine hadn't yet arrived.

Girls GALore didn't live up to market saturation expectations, and Lombi asked him to come up with another idea for an American market magazine, which he did; actually, two names for sci-fi 'zines:

Galaxy, *If* and a fantasy bimonthly called *Beyond*, which regrettably lasted only a few issues. A little study of the contents page from the *Girls GALore* reveals two interesting facts: One, the editorial and publishing staff for *Girls GALore* and *Galaxy Magazine* are the same. Two, the publishing address for *Girls GALore* happens to be the home address (505 East 14th Street, NY, NY) of soon to be editor for *Galaxy Magazine* Horace L. Gold.

Just think, if the T&A *Girls GALore* had made a more immediate financial splash we may never have seen the great sci-fi published by transmogrified *Galaxy*.

E. J. Gold

THE GREAT AMERICAN HOAX—Author's Foreword

Once a hoax has been established, it becomes the next worst thing to immortal. Years ago, for example, I reported—with a straight face, as befits the telling of a whopper—that parents bought their children baby alligators, which soon outgrew bowl, sink and bathtub and were flushed into the New York sewer system, where they flourished on the warmth and abundant food. Now the publicity department of that estimable system has a printed form refuting the "fact" that refuses to die.

But confession doesn't kill hoaxes. H.L. Mencken spent 20 minutes inventing, and a lifetime disowning, the story that winter bathing was illegal in colonial Boston, yet you still keep encountering it.

Every year, too, someone will declare that Jules Verne described the periscope so accurately that the subsequent inventor of it was denied a patent. It's not so.

Neither is the ever-repeated complaint of professional fans that today's science fiction is lacking in science. This charge is much more elderly than you might think, going back to the late 19th century, when Verne, the elderly engineer of sf, bitterly attacked young upstart H.G. Wells, the basic researcher of sf, for not having Science in his fiction.

There is room in this field for both kinds of writers, of course. But Verne lived to see most of his work become obsolete while Wells, with a handful of novels and a few dozen shorter stories, originated very many themes of modern sf. Serious people are working on Wells's antigravity, which Verne denounced as fantasy, but who is working on Verne's spaceship shot out of an enormous cannon, not to mention such funny ideas of his as clockwork machine guns and underwater bikes?

This division of scientists and authors into basic researchers and engineers is a practical one. Insisting on either to the exclusion of the other is not practical.

Naturally the engineer authors have more success in forecasting, working as they do on applications of existing knowledge. SF is glad to accept applause for such successes, but forecasting is not the primary function of sf. If it were, we'd have stories about the perfect clothes hanger and the like, exclusively.

To paraphrase a phrase-monger, the idea is the hero of sf. Here are some examples:

It's a commonplace statement that da Vinci invented the auto, airplane and air conditioning. Lacking motive power, he used what was available—springs and sails, human and animal muscle power. They were not good enough, though nothing was cheaper, and da Vinci, stuck fast to the knowledge of his time, as his followers were to theirs and we to ours, could not envision electricity and the internal combustion engine. Even if he had, how well could he have described them, much less worked out the math and metallurgy, the chemistry, physics and geology—the great number of disciplines that produce and move these everyday wonders? Could he then have gone a step further and predicted how these wonders pollute the air and water, the extinction of whole species of life, the forced migration from farm too small to be machine-worked to the city strangling with people and machines, the paving of more and more of our land so more and more vehicles can go murderously from one congested city to another?

Thomas More's Utopia had telephones, generations before they were invented. Instead of electric wires, however, he used something that the science of his day considered workable: hollow tubes. Just imagine what a tangle that would be!

Perhaps you remember Baron Münchausen's tale of the Russian winter being so cold that it froze voices, which were heard when spring came. Nobody believed him, of course. Yet we freeze voices all the time, and music as well, and do not have to wait till spring to hear them.

George Washington's passionate plan to link up the vast new United States with an equally vast network of canals seemed entirely reasonable to his contemporaries, and it was pushed even more fervently a couple of decades later, when the Louisiana Purchase doubled the size of the infant country. The most optimistic citizens estimated that it would take 25 generations—until 2400 A.D.—to tame and colonize the additional 1,000,000 square miles. At that moment, in England and in New Jersey, two inventors were developing the steam locomotive.

Just about that time, the King, having inspected Faraday's laboratory, asked: "Of what earthly use, Sir, are all these toys?" Faraday replied: "Of what earthly use, Sire, is a newborn baby?" Within their lifetimes, Faraday and Volta saw more progress than in the millennia since electrical phenomena were first observed. Yet even they could not foresee, however dimly, the civilization built by electricity.

Malthus predicted that population growth would always outstrip food production. It's hard to say which would astonish him more, a world of three billion people or a nation that bribes farmers to prevent glut. A doomsman, he'd no doubt point to the underfed parts of the globe, and, tragically, he would be right. But they could support their populations with modern methods—and huge areas of the world, like the interiors of South America, Africa, Australia, even Canada, are desperately underpopulated.

Berlioz was considered mad because he scored his music for thousands of voices and instruments, believing that the resulting sound would be that many times louder. It wouldn't. But how was he to suspect that a neighbor, with just the touch of a heavy hand on a small dial, could drive us out of our homes with a volume that Berlioz could only dream of?

Coming down almost to the present—to 1957, in fact—we sf writers casually had spaceships built by updated Wright brothers, never knowing that only a world power—and a big, rich one at that—could put a man on the Moon by spending so much of its treasure for so long a time.

For that matter, whatever became of the spaceships we wrote about so knowingly, shiny on one side to reflect heat, black on the other to absorb it?

If you date back as far as I do—I sold my first story (at a very early age) in 1934—you may remember a greatly respected author suggesting that we develop "science secretaries" to cue in people of one science with the knowledge of another. Luckily, before the planet had to be scoured for such phenomenal minds, computers came along—lots of them, improving all the time, with memory banks able to hold all the sciences of all of mankind—and retrieval time in microseconds.

What point am I trying to make? Just this: that the idea is the message both in science and science fiction, and that explaining future discoveries in terms of current knowledge must always prove as laughable as the examples I've given.

But that must not stop the ideasters. Their job is to get the idea written and published and read.

In sf, that means presenting it entertainingly. And I submit that doubletalking characters in and out of time machines, starships and other standard themes of sf are not entertaining. For of what earthly use, dear critics of modern sf, are repetitions of tired old analogies that even now sound as hollow as telephone tubes, formulas and equations taken from textbooks and detailed just as thrillingly—while the reader is impatiently saying: "Okay, okay, so you've got robots (or androids or espers or whatever)—now what's the story?"

Certainly I exempt the fresh new idea, which comes along more often than sf is credited with and needs explanation, or even "explanation"—but with two reservations: a) it should be woven into the story instead of dumped in a lump in the reader's lap; b) it should be taken for granted when, or if, it becomes a standard sf theme.

That's not much to ask, is it?

— H. L. Gold

To My Mother and the Memory of My Father

THE OLD DIE RICH

"YOU AGAIN, WELDON," the Medical Examiner said wearily. I nodded pleasantly and looked around the shabby room with a feeling of hopeful eagerness. Maybe this time, I thought, I'd get the answer. I had the same sensation I always had in these places—the quavery senile despair at being closed in a room with the single shaky chair, tottering bureau, dim bulb hanging from the ceiling, the flaking metal bed.

There was a woman on the bed, an old woman with white hair thin enough to show the tight-drawn scalp, her face and body so emaciated that the flesh between the bones formed parchment pockets. The M.E. was going over her as if she were a side of beef that he had to put a federal grade stamp on, grumbling meanwhile about me and Sergeant Lou Pape, who had brought me here.

"When are you going to stop taking Weldon around to these cases, Sergeant?" the M.E. demanded in annoyance. "Damned actor and his morbid curiosity!"

For the first time, Lou was stung into defending me. "Mr. Weldon is a friend of mine—I used to be an actor, too, before I joined the force—and he's a follower of Stanislavsky."

The beat cop who'd reported the D.O.A. whipped around at the door. "A Red?"

I let Lou Pape explain what the Stanislavsky method of acting was, while I sat down on the one chair and tried to apply it. Stanislavsky was the great pre-Revolution Russian stage director whose idea was that actors had to think and feel like the characters they portrayed so they could *be* them. A Stanislavskian works out everything about a character right up to the point where a play starts—where he was born, when, his relationship with his parents, education, childhood, adolescence, maturity, attitudes toward men, women, sex, money, success, including incidents. The play itself is just an extension of the life history created by the actor.

How does that tie in with the old woman who had died? Well, I'd had the cockeyed kind of luck to go bald at twenty-five and I'd been playing old men ever since. I had them down pretty well—it's not just a matter of shuffling around all hunched over and talking in a high cracked voice, which is cornball acting, but learning what old people are like inside—and these cases I talked Lou Pape into taking me on were studies in senility. I wanted to understand them, know what made them do what they did, *feel* the compulsion that drove them to it.

The old woman on the bed, for instance, had $32,000 in five bank accounts . . . and she'd died of starvation.

You've come across such cases in the news, at least a dozen a year, and wondered who they were and why they did it. But you read the items, thought about them for a little while, and then forgot them. My interest was professional; I made my living playing old people and I had to know as much about them as I could.

That's how it started off, at any rate. But the more cases I investigated, the less sense they made to me, until finally they were practically an obsession.

Look, they almost always have around $30,000 pinned to their underwear, hidden in mattresses, or parked in the bank, yet they starve themselves to death. If I could understand them, I could write a play or have one written; I might really make a name for myself, even get a Hollywood contract, maybe, if I could act them as they should be acted.

So I sat there in the lone chair, trying to reconstruct the character of the old woman who had died rather than spend a single cent of her $32,000 for food.

"Malnutrition induced by senile psychosis," the M.E. said, writing out the death certificate. He turned to me. "There's no mystery to it, Weldon. They starve because they're less afraid of death than digging into their savings."

I'd been imagining myself growing weak from hunger and trying to decide that I ought to eat even if it cost me something. I came out of it and said, "That's what you keep telling me."

"I keep hoping it'll convince you so you won't come around any more. What are the chances, Weldon?"

"Depends. I will when I'm sure you're right. I'm not."

He shrugged disgustedly, ordered the wicker basket from the meat wagon and had the old woman carried out. He and the beat cop left with the basket team. He could at least have said good-by. He never did, though.

A fat lot I cared about his attitude or dogmatic medical opinion. Getting inside this character was more important. The setting should have helped; it was depressing, rank with the feel of solitary desperation and needless death.

Lou Pape stood looking out the one dirty window, waiting patiently for me. I let my joints stiffen as if they were thirty years older and more worn out than they were, and empathized myself into a dilemma between getting still weaker from hunger and drawing a little money out of the bank.

I worked at it for half an hour or so with the deep concentration you acquire when you use the Stanislavsky method. Then I gave up.

"The M.E. is wrong, Lou," I said. "It doesn't feel right."

Lou turned around from the window. He'd stood there all that time without once coughing or scratching or doing anything else that might have distracted me. "He knows his business, Mark."

"But he doesn't know old people."

"What is it you don't get?" he prompted, helping me dig my way through a characterization like the trained Stanislavskian he was—and still would have been if he hadn't gotten so sick of the insecurity of acting that he'd become a cop. "Can't money be more important to a psychotic than eating?"

"Sure," I agreed. "Up to a point. Undereating, yes. Actual starvation, no."

"Why not?"

"You and the M.E. think it's easy to starve to death. It isn't. Not when you can buy day-old bread at the bakeries, soup bones for about a nickel a pound, wilted vegetables that groceries are glad to get rid of. Anybody who's willing to eat that stuff can stay alive on nearly nothing a day. Nearly nothing, Lou, and hunger is a damned potent instinct. I can understand hating to spend even those few cents. I can't see going without food altogether."

He took out a cigarette; he hadn't until then because he didn't want to interrupt my concentration. "Maybe they get too weak to go out after old bread and meat bones and wilted vegetables."

"It still doesn't figure." I got up off the shaky chair, my joints now really stiff from sitting in it. "Do you know how long it takes to die of starvation?"

"That depends on age, health, amount of activity —"

"Nuts!" I said. "It would take weeks!"

"So it takes weeks. Where's the problem—if there is one?"

I lit the pipe I'd learned to smoke instead of cigarettes—old men seem to use pipes more than anything else, though maybe it'll be different in the next generation. More cigarette smokers now, you see, and they'd stick to the habit unless the doctor ordered them to cut it out.

"Did you ever try starving for weeks. Lou?" I asked.

"No. Did you?"

"In a way. All these cases you've been taking me on for the last couple of years—I've tried to be them. But let's say it's possible to die of starvation when you have thousands of dollars put away. Let's say you don't think of scrounging off food stores or working out a way of freeloading or hitting soup lines. Let's say you stay in your room and slowly starve to death."

He slowly picked a fleck of tobacco off his lip and flicked it away, his sharp black eyes poking holes in the situation I'd built up for him. But he wasn't ready to say anything yet.

"There's charity," I went on, "relief—except for those who have their dough in banks, where it can be checked on—old age pension, panhandling, cadging off neighbors."

He said, "We know these cases are hermits. They don't make contact with anybody."

"Even when they're starting to get real hungry?"

"You've got something, Mark, but that's the wrong tack," he said thoughtfully. "The point is that *they* don't have to make contact; other people know them or about them. Somebody would check after a few days or a week—the janitor, the landlord, someone in the house or the neighborhood."

"So they'd be found before they died."

"You'd think so, wouldn't you?" he agreed reluctantly. "They don't generally have friends, and the relatives are usually so distant, they hardly know these old people and whether they're alive or not. Maybe that's what threw us off. But you don't need friends and relatives to start wondering, and investigate when you haven't shown up for a while." He lifted his head and looked at me. "What does that prove, Mark?"

"That there's something wrong with these cases. I want to find out what."

I got Lou to take me down to Headquarters, where he let me see the bankbooks the old woman had left.

"She took damned good care of them," I said. "They look almost new."

"Wouldn't you take damned good care of the most important thing in the world to you?" he asked. "You've seen the hoards of money the others leave. Same thing."

I peered closely at the earliest entry, April 23, 1907, $150. My eyes aren't that bad; I was peering at the ink. It was dark, unfaded. I pointed it out to Lou.

"From not being exposed to daylight much," he said. "They don't haul out the bankbooks or money very often, I guess."

"And that adds up for you? I can see them being psychotics all their lives . . . but not *senile* psychotics. "

"They hoarded, Mark. That adds up for me."

"Funny," I said, watching him maneuver his cigarette as if he loved the feel of it, drawing the smoke down and letting it out in plumes of different shapes, from rings to slender streams. What a living he could make doing cigarette commercials on TV! "I can see *you* turn into one of these cases, Lou."

He looked startled for a second, but then crushed out the butt carefully so he could watch it instead of me. "Yeah?" How so?"

"You've been too scared by poverty to take a chance. You know you could do all right acting, but you don't dare give up this crummy job. Carry that far enough and you try to stop spending money, then cut out eating, and finally wind up dead of starvation in a cheap room."

"Me? I'd never get that scared of being broke!"

"At the age of seventy or eighty?"

"Especially then! I'd probably tear loose for a while and then buy into a home for the aged."

I wanted to grin, but I didn't. He'd proved my point. He'd also shown that he was as bothered by these old people as I was.

"Tell me, Lou. If somebody kept you from dying, would you give him any dough for it, even if you were a senile psychotic?"

I could see him using the Stanislavsky method to feel his way to the answer. He shook his head. "Not while I was alive. Will it, maybe, not give it."

"How would that be as a motive?"

He leaned against a metal filing cabinet. "No good. Mark. You know what a hell of a time we have tracking down relatives to give the money to, because these people don't leave wills. The few relatives we find are always surprised when they get their inheritance—most of them hardly remember dear old who-ever-it-was that died and left it to them. All the other estates eventually go to the State treasury, unclaimed."

"Well, it was an idea."

I opened the oldest bankbook again. "Anybody ever think of testing the ink, Lou?"

"What for? The banks' records always check. These aren't forgeries, if that's what you're thinking."

"I don't know what I'm thinking," I admitted. "But I'd like to turn a chemist loose on this for a little while."

"Look, Mark, there's a lot I'm willing to do for you, and I think I've done plenty, but there's a limit —"

I let him explain why he couldn't let me borrow the book and then waited while he figured out how it could be done and did it. He was still grumbling when he helped me pick a chemist out of the telephone directory and went along to the lab with me.

"But don't get any wrong notions," he said on the way. "I have to protect State property, that's all, because I signed for it and I'm responsible."

"Sure, sure," I agreed, to humor him. "If you're not curious, why not just wait outside for me?"

He gave me one of those white-tooth grins that he had no right to deprive women audiences of. "I could do that, but I'd rather see you make a sap of yourself."

I turned the bankbook over to the chemist and we waited for the report. When it came, it had to be translated.

The ink was typical of those used fifty years ago. Lou Pape gave me a jab in the ribs at that. But then the chemist said that, according to the amount of oxidation, it seemed fresh enough to be only a few months or years old, and it was Lou's turn to get jabbed. Lou pushed him about the aging, asking if it couldn't be the result of unusually good care. The chemist couldn't say—that depended on the kind of care; an airtight compartment, perhaps, filled with one of the inert gases, or a vacuum. They hadn't been kept that way, of course, so Lou looked as baffled as I felt.

He took the bankbook and we went out to the street.

"See what I mean?" I asked quietly, not wanting to rub it in.

"I see something, but I don't know what. Do you?"

"I wish I could say yes. It doesn't make any more sense than anything else about these cases."

"What do you do next?"

"Damned if I know. There are thousands of old people in the city. Only a few of them take this way out. I have to try to find them before they do."

"If they're loaded, they won't say so, Mark, and there's no way of telling them from those who are down and out."

I rubbed my pipe disgruntledly against the side of my nose to oil it. "Ain't this a beaut of a problem? I wish I liked problems. I hate them."

Lou had to get back on duty. I had nowhere to go and nothing to do except worry my way through this tangle. He headed back to Headquarters and I went over to the park and sat in the sun, warming myself and trying to think like a senile psychotic who would rather die of starvation than spend a few cents for food.

I didn't get anywhere, naturally. There are too many ways of beating starvation, too many chances of being found before it's too late.

And the fresh ink, over half a century old . . .

I took to hanging around banks, hoping I'd see someone come in with an old bankbook that had fresh ink from fifty years before. Lou was some help there—he convinced the guards and tellers that I wasn't an old-looking guy casing the place for a gang, and even got the tellers to watch out for particularly dark ink in ancient bankbooks.

I stuck at it for a month, although there were a few stage calls that didn't turn out right, and one radio and two TV parts, which did and kept me going. I was almost glad the stage parts hadn't been given to me; they'd have interrupted my outside work.

After a month without a thing turning up at the banks, though, I went back to my two rooms in the theatrical hotel one night, tired and discouraged, and I found Lou there. I expected him to give me another talk on dropping the whole thing; he'd been doing that for a couple of weeks now, every time we got together. I felt too low to put up an argument. But Lou was holding back his excitement—acting like a cop, you know, instead of projecting his feelings—and he couldn't haul me out to his car as fast as he probably wanted me to go.

"Been trying to get in touch with you all day, Mark. Some old guy was found wandering around, dazed and suffering from malnutrition, with $17,000 in cash inside the lining of his jacket."

"*Alive*?" I asked, shocked right into eagerness again.

"Just barely. They're trying intravenous feeding to pull him through. I don't think he'll make it."

"For God's sake, let's get there before he conks out!"

Lou raced me to the City Hospital and up to the ward. There was a scrawny old man in a bed, nothing but a papery skin stretched thin over a face like a skull and a body like a Halloween skeleton, shivering as if he was cold. I knew it wasn't the cold. The medics were injecting a heart stimulant into him and he was vibrating like a rattletrap car racing over a gravel road.

"Who are you?" I practically yelled, grabbing his skinny arm. "What happened to you?"

He went on shaking with his eyes closed and his mouth open.

"Ah, hell!" I said, disgusted. "He's in a coma."

"He might start talking," Lou told me. "I fixed it up so you can sit here and listen in case he does."

"So I can listen to delirious ravings, you mean."

Lou got me a chair and put it next to the bed. "What are you kicking about? This is the first live one you've seen, isn't it? That ought to be good enough for you." He looked as annoyed as a director. "Besides, you can get biographical data out of delirium that you'd never get if he was conscious."

He was right, of course. Not only data, but attitudes, wishes, resentments that would normally be repressed. I wasn't thinking of acting at the moment, though. Here was somebody who could tell me what I wanted to know . . . only he couldn't talk.

Lou went to the door. "Good luck," he said and went out.

I sat down and stared at the old man, *willing* him to talk. I don't have to ask if you've ever done that; everybody has. You keep thinking over and over, getting more and more tense, "Talk, damn you, *talk*!" until you find that every muscle in your body is a fist and your jaws are aching because you've been clenching your teeth so hard. You might just as well not bother, but once in a while a coincidence makes you think you've done it. Like now.

The old man sort of came to. That is, he opened his eyes and looked around without seeing anything, or it was so far away and long ago that nobody else could see what he saw.

I hunched forward on the chair and willed harder than ever. Nothing happened. He stared at the ceiling and through and beyond me. Then he closed his eyes again and I slumped back, defeated and bitter—but that was when he began talking.

There were a couple of women, though they might have been little girls in his childhood, and he had his troubles with them. He was praying for a toy train, a roadster, to pass his tests, to keep from being fired, to be less lonely, and back to toys again. He hated his father, and his mother was too busy with church bazaars and such to pay much attention to him. There was a sister: she died when he was a kid. He was glad she died, hoping maybe now his mother would notice him, but he was also filled with guilt because he was glad. Then somebody, he felt, was trying to shove him out of his job.

The intravenous feeding kept dripping into his vein and he went on rambling. After ten or fifteen minutes of it, he fell asleep. I felt so disappointed that I could have slapped him awake, only it wouldn't have done any good. Smoking would have helped me relax, but it wasn't allowed, and I didn't dare go outside for one, for fear he might revive again and this time come up to the present.

"Broke!" he suddenly shrieked, trying to sit up.

I pushed him down gently, and he went on in frightful terror, "Old and poor, nowhere to go, nobody wants me, can't make a living, read the ads every day, no jobs for old men."

He blurted through weeks, months, years—I don't know—of fear and despair. And finally he came to something that made his face glow like a radium dial.

"An ad. No experience needed. Good salary." His face got dark and awful. All he added was "El Greco," or something that sounded like it, and then he went into terminal breathing.

I rang for the nurse and she went for the doctor. I couldn't stand the long moments when the old man's chest stopped moving, the abrupt frantic gulps of air followed by no breath at all. I wanted to get away from it, but I had to wait for whatever more he might say.

It didn't come. His eyes fogged and rolled up and he stopped taking those spasmodic strangling breaths. The nurse came back with the doctor, who felt his pulse and shook his head. She pulled the blanket over the old man's face.

I left, feeling sick. I'd learned things I already knew about hate and love and fear and hope and frustration. There was an ad in it somewhere, but I had no way of telling if it had been years ago or recently. And a name that sounded like "El Greco." That was a Spanish painter of four-five hundred years ago. Had the old guy been remembering a picture he'd seen?

No, he'd come up at least close to the present. The ad seemed to solve his problem about being broke. But what about the $17,000 that had been found in the lining of his jacket? He hadn't mentioned that. Of course, being a senile psychotic, he could have considered himself broke even with that amount of money. None coming in, you see.

That didn't add up, either. His was the terror of being old and jobless. If he'd had money, he would have figured how to make it last, and that would have come through in one way or another.

There was the ad, there was his hope, and there was this El Greco. A Greek restaurant, maybe, where he might have been bumming his meals.

But where did the $17,000 fit in?

Lou Pape was too fed up with the whole thing to discuss it with me. He just gave me the weary eye and said, "You're riding this too hard, Mark. The guy was talking from fever. How do I know what figures and what doesn't when I'm dealing with insanity or delirium?"

"But you admit there's plenty about these cases that doesn't figure?"

"Sure. Did you take a look at the condition the world is in lately? Why should these old people be any exception?"

I couldn't blame him. He'd pulled me in on the cases with plenty of trouble to himself, just to do me a favor. Now he was fed up. I guess it wasn't even that—he thought I was ruining myself, at least financially and maybe worse, by trying to run down the problem. He said he'd be glad to see me any time and gas about anything or help me with whatever might be bothering me, if he could, but not these cases any more. He told me to lay off them, and then he left me on my own.

I don't know what he could have done, actually. I didn't need him to go through the want ads with me, which I was doing every day, figuring there might be something in the ravings about an ad. I spent more time than I liked checking those slanted at old people, only to find they were supposed to become messengers and such.

One brought me to an old brownstone five-story house in the East 80's. I got on line with the rest of the applicants—there were men and women, all decrepit, all looking badly in need of money—and waited my turn. My face was lined with collodion wrinkles and I wore an antique shiny suit and rundown shoes. I didn't look more prosperous or any younger than they did.

I finally came up to the woman who was doing the interviewing. She sat behind a plain office desk down in the main floor hall, with a pile of application cards in front of her and a ball-point pen in one strong, slender hand. She had red hair with gold lights in it and eyes so pale blue that they would have seemed the same color as the whites if she'd been on the stage. Her face would have been beautiful except for her rigid control of expression; she smiled abruptly, shut it off just like that, looked me over with all the impersonality and penetration of an X-ray from the soles to the bald head, exactly as she'd done with the others. But that skin! If it was as perfect as that all over her slim, stiffly erect, proudly shaped body, she had no business off the stage!

"Name, address, previous occupation, social security number?" she asked in a voice with good clarity, resonance and diction. She wrote it all down while I gave the information to her. Then she asked me for references, and I mentioned Sergeant Lou Pape. "Fine," she said. "We'll get in touch with you if anything comes up. Don't call us—we'll call you."

I hung around to see who'd be picked. There was only one, an old man, two ahead of me in the line, who had no social security number, no references, not even any relatives or friends she could have checked up on him with.

Damn! *Of course* that was what she wanted! Hadn't all the starvation cases been people without social security, references, either no friends and relatives or those they'd lost track of?

I'd pulled a blooper, but how was I to know until too late?

Well, there was a way of making it right.

When it was good and dark that evening, I stood on the corner and watched the lights in the brownstone house. The ones on the first two floors went out, leaving only those on the third and fourth. Closed for the day . . . or open for business?

I got into a building a few doors down by pushing a button and waiting until the buzzer answered, then racing up to the roof while some man yelled down the stairs to find out who was there. I crossed the tops of the two houses between and went down the fire escape.

It wasn't easy, though not as tough as you might imagine. The fact is that I'm a whole year younger than Lou Pape, even if I could play his grandpa professionally. I still have muscles left and I used them to get down the fire escape at the rear of the house.

The fourth-floor room I looked into had some kind of wire mesh cage and some hooded machinery. Nobody there.

The third floor room was the redhead's. She was coming out of the bathroom with a terry cloth bathrobe and a towel turban on when I looked in. She slid the robe off and began dusting herself with powder. That skin *did* cover her.

She turned and moved toward a vanity against the wall that I was on the other side of. The next thing I knew, the window was flung up and she had a gun on me.

"Come right in—Mr. Weldon, isn't it?" she said in that completely controlled voice of hers. One day her control would crack, I thought irrelevantly, and the pieces would be found from Dallas to North Carolina. "I had an idea you seemed more curious than was justified by a help-wanted ad."

"A man my age doesn't get to see many pretty girls," I told her, making my own voice crack pathetically in a senile whinny.

She motioned me into the room. When I was inside, I saw a light over the window blinking red. It stopped the moment I was in the room. A silent burglar alarm.

She let her pale blue eyes wash insolently over me. "A man your age can see all the pretty girls he wants to. You're not old."

"And you use a rinse," I retorted.

She ignored it. "I specifically advertised for old people. Why did you apply?"

It happened so abruptly that I hadn't had a chance to use the Stanislavsky method to *feel* old in the presence of a beautiful nude woman. I don't even know if it would have worked. Nothing's perfect.

"I needed a job awful bad," I answered sullenly, knowing it sounded like an ad lib.

She smiled with more contempt than humor. "You had a job, Mr. Weldon. You were very busy trying to find out why senile psychotics starve themselves to death."

"How did you know that?" I asked, startled.

"A little investigation of my own. I also happen to know you didn't tell your friend Sergeant Pape that you were going to be here tonight."

That was a fact, too. I hadn't felt sure enough that I'd found the answer to call him about it. Looking at the gun in her steady hand, I was sorry I hadn't.

"But you did find out I own this building, that my name is May Roberts, and that I'm the daughter of the late Dr. Anthony Roberts, the physicist," she continued. "Is there anything else you want me to tell you about yourself?"

"I know enough already. I'm more interested in you and the starvation cases. If you weren't connected with them, you wouldn't have known I was investigating them."

"That's obvious, isn't it?" She reached for a cigarette on the vanity and used a lighter with her free hand. The big mirror gave me another view of her lovely body, but that was beginning to interest me less than the gun. I thought of making a grab for it. There was too much distance between us, though, and she knew better than to take her eyes off me while she was lighting up. "I'm not afraid of professional detectives, Mr. Weldon. They deal only with facts and every one of them will draw the same conclusions from a given set of circumstances. I don't like amateurs. They guess too much. They don't stick to reality. "The result"—her pale eyes chilled and her shapely mouth went hard—"is that they are likely to get too close to the truth."

I wanted to smoke myself, but I wasn't willing to make a move toward the pipe in my jacket. "I may be close to the truth, Miss Roberts, but I don't know what the devil it is. I still don't know how you're tied in with the senile psychotics or why they starve with all that money. You could let me go and I wouldn't have a thing on you."

She glanced down at herself and laughed for real for the first time. "You wouldn't, would you? On the other hand, you know where I'm working from and could nag Sergeant Pape into getting a search warrant. It wouldn't incriminate me, but it would be inconvenient. I don't care to be inconvenienced."

"Which means what?"

"You want to find out my connection with senile psychotics. I intend to show you."

"How?"

She gestured dangerously with the gun. "Turn your face to the wall and stay that way while I get dressed. Make one attempt to turn around before I tell you to and I'll shoot you. You're guilty of house-breaking, you know. It would be a little inconvenient for me to have an investigation . . . but not as inconvenient as for you."

I faced the wall, feeling my stomach braid itself into a tight, painful knot of fear. Of what, I didn't know yet, only that old people who had something to do with her died of starvation. I wasn't old, but that didn't seem very comforting. She was the most frigid, calculating, *deadly* woman I'd ever met. That alone was enough to scare hell out of me. And there was the problem of what she was capable of.

Hearing the sounds of her dressing behind me, I wanted to lunge around and rush her, taking a chance that she might be too busy pulling on girdle or reaching back to fasten a bra to have the gun in her hand. It was a suicidal impulse and I gave it up instantly. Other women might compulsively finish concealing themselves before snatching up the gun. Not her.

"All right," she said at last.

I faced her. She was wearing coveralls that, if anything, emphasized the curves of her figure. She had a sort of babushka that covered her red hair and kept it in place—the kind of thing women workers used to wear in factories during the war. She had looked lethal with nothing on but a gun and a hard expression. She looked like a sentence of execution now.

"Open that door, turn to the right and go upstairs," she told me, indicating directions with the gun.

I went. It was the longest, most anxious short walk I've ever taken. She ordered me to open a door on the fourth floor, and we were inside the room I'd seen from the fire escape. The mesh cage seemed like a torture chamber to me, the hooded motors designed to shoot an agonizing current through my emaciating body.

"You're going to do to me what you did to the old man you hired today?" I probed, hoping for an answer that would really answer.

She flipped on the switch that started the motors and there was a shrill, menacing whine. The wire mesh of the cage began blurring oddly, as if vibrating like the tines of a tuning fork.

"You've been an unexpected nuisance, Weldon," she said above the motors. "I never thought you'd get this far. But as long as you have, we might as well both benefit by it."

"Benefit?" I repeated. "*Both* of us?"

She opened the drawer of a work table and pulled out a stack of envelopes held with a rubber band. She put the stack at the other edge of the table.

"Would you rather have all cash or bank accounts or both?'

My heart began to beat. *She was where the money came from!*

"You trying to tell me you're a philanthropist?" I demanded.

"Business is philanthropy, in a way," she answered calmly. "You need money and I need your services. To that extent, we're doing each other a favor. I think you'll find that the favor I'm going to do for you is a pretty considerable one. Would you mind picking up the envelopes on the table?"

I took the stack and stared at the top envelope. "May 15, 1931," I read aloud, and looked suspiciously at her. "What's this for?"

"I don't think it's something that can be explained. At least it's never been possible before and I doubt if it would be now. I'm assuming you want both cash and bank accounts. Is that right?"

"Well, yes. Only —"

"We'll discuss it later." She looked along a row of shelves against one wall, searching the labels on the stacks of bundles there. She drew one out and pushed it toward me. "Please open that and put on the things you'll find inside."

I tore open the bundle. It contained a very plain business suit, black shoes, shirt, tie and a hat with a narrow brim.

"Are these supposed to be my burial clothes?"

"I asked you to put them on," she said. "If you want me to make that a command, I'll do it."

I looked at the gun and I looked at the clothes and then for some shelter I could change behind. There wasn't any.

She smiled. "You didn't seem concerned about my modesty. I don't see why your own should bother you. Get dressed!"

I obeyed, my mind anxiously chasing one possibility after another, all of them ending up with my death. I got into the other things and felt even more uncomfortable. They were all only an approximate fit: the shoes a little too tight and pointed, the collar of the shirt too stiffly starched and too high under my chin, the gray suit too narrow at the shoulder and the ankles. I wished I had a mirror to see myself in. I felt like an ultra-conservative Wall Street broker and I was sure I resembled one.

"All right," she said. "Put the envelopes in your inside pocket. You'll find instructions on each. Follow them carefully."

"I don't get it!" I protested.

"You will. Now step into the mesh cage. Use the envelopes in the order they're arranged in."

"But what's this all about?"

"I can tell you just one thing, Mr. Weldon—don't try to escape. It can't be done. Your other questions will answer themselves if you follow the instructions on the envelopes."

She had the gun in her hand. I went into the mesh cage, not knowing what to expect and yet too afraid of her to refuse. I didn't want to wind up dead of starvation, no matter how much money she might have given me—but I didn't want to get shot, either.

She closed the mesh gate and pushed the switch as far as it would go. The motors screamed as they picked up speed; the mesh cage vibrated more swiftly; I could see her through it as if there were nothing between us.

And then I couldn't see her at all.

I was outside a bank on a sunny day in spring.

My fear evaporated instantly—I'd escaped somehow!

But then a couple of realizations slapped me from each side. It was day instead of night. I was out on the street and not in her brownstone house.

Even the season had changed!

Dazed, I stared at the people passing by. They looked like characters in a TV movie, the women wearing long dresses and flowerpot hats, their faces made up with petulant rosebud mouths and bright blotches of rouge; the men in hard straw hats, suits with narrow shoulders, plain black or brown shoes—the same kind of clothes I was wearing.

The rumble of traffic in the street caught me next. Cars with square bodies, tubular radiators . .

For a moment, I let terror soak through me. Then I remembered the mesh cage and the motors. May Roberts could have given me electro-shock, kept me under long enough for the season to change, or taken me south and left me on a street in daylight.

But this was a street in New York. I recognized it, though some of the buildings seemed changed, the people dressed more shabbily.

Shrewd stage setting? Hypnosis?

That was it, of course! She'd hypnotized me. . .

Except that a subject under hypnosis doesn't know he's been hypnotized.

Completely confused, I took out the stack of envelopes I'd put in my pocket. I was supposed to have both cash and a bank account, and I was outside a bank. She obviously wanted me to go in, so I did. I handed the top envelope to the teller.

He hauled $150 out of it and looked at me as if that was enough to buy and sell the bank. He asked me if I had an account there. I didn't. He took me over to an officer of the bank, a fellow with a Hoover collar and a John Gilbert mustache, who signed me up more cordially than I'd been treated in years.

I walked out to the street, gaping at the entry in the bankbook he'd handed me. My pulse was jumping lumpily, my lungs refusing to work right, my head doing a Hopi rain dance.

The date he'd stamped was May 15, 1931.

I didn't know which I was more afraid of—being stranded, middle-aged, in the worst of the depression, or being yanked back to that brownstone house. I had only an instant to realize that I was a kid in high school uptown right at that moment. Then the whole scene vanished as fast as blinking and I was outside another bank somewhere else in the city.

The date on the envelope was may 29th and it was still 1931. I made a $75 deposit there, then $100 in another place a few days later, and so forth, spending only a few minutes each time and going forward anywhere from a couple of days to almost a month.

Every now and then, I had a stamped, addressed envelope to mail at a corner box. They were addressed to different stock brokers and when I got one open before mailing it and took a look inside, it turned out to be an order to buy a few hundred shares of stock in a soft drink company in the name of Dr. Anthony Roberts. I hadn't remembered the price of the shares being that low. The last time I'd seen the quotation, it was more than five times as much as it was then. I was making dough myself, but I was doing even better for May Roberts.

A few times I had to stay around for an hour or so. There was the night I found myself in a flashy speakeasy with two envelopes that I was to bet the contents of, according to the instructions on the outside. It was June 21, 1932, and I had to bet on Jack Sharkey to take the heavyweight title away from Max Schmeling.

The place was serious and quiet—no more than three women, a couple of bartenders, and the rest male customers, including two cops, huddling up close to the radio. An affable character was taking bets. He gave me a wise little smile when I put the money down on Sharkey.

"Well, it's a pleasure to do business with a man who wants an

American to win," he said, "and the hell with the smart dough, eh?"

"Yeah," I said, and tried to smile back, but so much of the smart money was going on Schmeling that I wondered if May Roberts hadn't made a mistake. I couldn't remember who had won. "You know what J.P. Morgan said—don't sell America short."

"I'll take a buck for my share," said a sour guy who barely managed to stand. "Lousy grass growing in the lousy streets, nobody working, no future, nothing!"

"We'll come out if it okay," I told him confidently.

He snorted into his gin. "Not in our lifetime, Mac. It'd take a miracle to put this country on its feet again. I don't believe in miracles." He put his scowling face up close to mine and breathed blearily and belligerently at me. "Do you?"

"Shut up, Gus," one of the bartenders said. "The fight's starting."

I had some tough moments and a lot of bad Scotch, listening. It went the whole fifteen rounds, Sharkey won, and I was in almost as bad shape as Gus, who'd passed out halfway through the battle. All I can recall is the affable character handing over a big roll and saying, "Lucky for me more guys don't sell America short," and trying to separate the money into the right amounts and put them into the right envelopes, while stumbling out the door, when everything changed and I was outside a bank again.

I thought, "My God, what a hangover cure!" I was as sober as if I hadn't had a drink, when I made that deposit.

There were more envelopes to mail and more deposits to make and bets to put down on Singing Wood in 1933 at Belmont Park and Max Baer over Primo Carnera, and then Cavalcade at Churchill Downs in 1934, and James Braddock over Baer in 1935, and a big daily double payoff, Wanoah-Arakay at Tropical Park, and so on, skipping through the years like a flat stone over water, touching here and there for a few minutes to an hour at a time. I kept the envelopes for May Roberts and myself in different pockets and the bankbooks in another. The envelopes were beginning to bulge and the deposits and accrued interest were something to watch grow.

The whole thing, in fact, was so exciting that it was early October of 1938—a total of maybe four or five hours subjectively—before I realized what she had me doing. I wasn't thinking much about the fact that I was time traveling or how she did it I accepted that, though the sensation in some ways was creepy, like raising the dead. My father and mother, for instance, were still alive in 1938. If I could break away from whatever it was that kept pulling me jumpily through time, I could go and see them.

The thought attracted me enough to make me shake badly with intent, yet pumped dread through me. I wanted so damned badly to see them again and I didn't dare. I couldn't . . .

Why couldn't I?

Maybe the machine covered only the area around the various banks, speakeasies, bars and horse parlors. If I could get out of the area, whatever it might be, I could avoid coming back to whatever May Roberts had lined up for me.

Because, naturally, I knew now what I was doing: I was making deposits and winning sure bets just as the "senile psychotics" had done. The ink on their bankbooks and bills was fresh because it was fresh; it wasn't given a chance to oxidize —at the rate I was going, I'd be back to my own time in another few hours or so, with $15,000 or better in deposits, compound interest and cash.

If I'd been around seventy, you see, she could have sent me back to the beginning of the century with the same amount of money, which would have accumulated to something like $30,000.

Get it now?

I did. And I felt sick and frightened.

The old people had died of starvation somehow with all that dough in cash or banks. I didn't give a hang if the time travel was responsible, or something else was. I wasn't going to be found dead in my hotel and have Lou Pape curse my corpse because I'd been borrowing from him when, since 1931, I'd had a little fortune put away. He'd call me a premature senile psychotic and he'd be right, from his point of view, not knowing the truth.

Rather than make the deposit in October, 1938, I grabbed a battered old cab and told the driver to step on it. When I showed him the $10 bill that was in it for him, he squashed down the gas pedal. In 1938, $10 was real money.

We got a mile away from the bank and the driver looked at me in the rear-view mirror.

"How far you want to go, mister?"

My teeth were together so hard that I had to unclench them before I could answer, "As far away as we can get."

"Cops after you?"

"No, but somebody is. Don't be surprised at anything that happens, no matter what it is."

"You mean like getting shot at?" he asked worriedly, slowing down.

"You're not in any danger, friend. I am. Relax and step on it again."

I wondered if she could still reach me, this far from the bank, and handed the guy the bill. No justice sticking him for the ride in case she should. He pushed the pedal down even harder than he had been doing before.

We must have been close to three miles away when I blinked and was standing outside the first bank I'd seen in 1931.

I don't know what the cab driver thought when I vanished out of his hack. He probably figured I'd opened the door and jumped while he wasn't looking. Maybe he even went back and searched for a body splashed all over the street.

Well, it would have been a hopeless hunt. I was a week ahead.

I gave up and drearily made my deposit. The one from early October that I'd missed. I put in with this one.

There was no way to escape the babe with the beautiful hard face, gorgeous warm body and plans for me that all seemed to add up to death. I didn't try any more. I went on making deposits, mailing orders to her stock brokers, and putting down bets that couldn't miss because they were all past history.

I don't even remember what the last one was, a fight or a race. I hung around the bar that had long ago replaced the speakeasy, until the inevitable payoff, got myself a hamburger and headed out the door. All the envelopes I was supposed to use were gone and I felt shaky, knowing that the next place I'd see was the room with the wire mesh cage and the hooded motors.

It was.

She was on the other side of the cage, and I had five bankbooks and envelopes filled with cash amounting to more than $15,000, but all I could think of was that I was hungry and something had happened to the hamburger while I was traveling through time. I must have fallen and dropped it, because my hand was covered with dust or dirt. I brushed it off and quickly felt my face and pulled up my sleeves to look at my arms.

"Very smart," I said, "but I'm nowhere near emaciation."

"What made you think you would be?" she asked.

"Because the others always were."

She cut the motors to idling speed and the vibrating mesh slowed down. I glared at her through it. God, she was lovely—as lovely as an ice sculpture! The kind of face you'd love to kiss and slap, kiss and slap. . .

"You came here with a preconceived notion, Mr. Weldon. I'm a businesswoman, not a monster. I like to think there's even a good deal of the altruist in me. I could hire only young people, but the old ones have more trouble finding work. And you've seen for yourself how I provide nest eggs for them they'd otherwise never have."

"And take care of yourself at the same time."

"That's the businesswoman in me. I need money to operate."

"So do old people. Only they die and you don't."

She opened the gate and invited me out. "I make mistakes occasionally. I sometimes pick men and women who prove to be too old to stand the strain. I try not to let it happen, but they need money and work so badly that they don't always tell the truth about their age and state of health."

"You could take those who have social security cards and references."

"But those who don't have any are in worse need!" She paused. "You probably think I want only the money you and they bring back, that it's merely some sort of profit-making scheme. It isn't."

"You mean the idea is not just to buildup a fortune for you with a cut for whoever helps you do it?"

"I said I need money to operate, Mr. Weldon, and this method serves. But there are other purposes, much more important. What you have gone through is —basic training, you might say. You know now that it's possible to travel through time, and what it's like. The initial shock, in other words, is gone and you're better equipped to do something for me in another era."

"Something else?" I stared at her puzzledly. "What else could you want?"

"Let's have dinner first. You must be hungry."

I was, and that reminded me: "I bought a hamburger just before you brought me back. I don't know what happened to it. My hand was dirty and the hamburger was gone, as if I'd fallen somehow and dropped it and got dirt on my hand."

She looked worriedly at the hand, probably afraid I'd cut it and disqualified myself. I could understand that; you never know what kind of diseases can be picked up in different times, because I remember reading somewhere that germs keep changing according to conditions. Right now, for instance, strains of bacteria are becoming resistant to antibiotics. I knew her concern wasn't really from me, but it was pleasant all the same.

"That could be the explanation, I suppose," she said. "The truth is that I've never taken a time voyage—somebody has to operate the controls in the present—so I can't say it's possible or impossible to fall. It must be, since you did. Perhaps the wrench back from the past was too violent and you slipped just before you returned."

She led me down to an ornate dining room, where the table had been set for two. The food was waiting on the table, steaming and smelling tasty. Nobody was around to serve us. She pointed out a chair to me and we sat down and began eating. I was a little nervous at first, afraid there might be something in the food, but it tasted fine and nothing happened after I swallowed a little and waited for some effect.

"You did try to escape the time tractor beam, didn't you, Mr. Weldon?" she asked. I didn't have to answer; she knew. "That's a mistaken notion of how it functions. The control beam doesn't cover *area*; it covers *era*. You could have flown to any part of the world and the beam would still have brought you back. Do I make myself clear?"

She did. Too bloody clear. I waited for the rest.

"I assume you've already formed an opinion of me," she went on. "A rather unflattering one, I imagine."

"'Bitch' is the cleanest word I can find. But a clever one. Anybody who can invent a time machine would have to be a genius."

"I didn't invent it. My father did—Dr. Anthony Roberts—using the funds you and others helped me provide him with." Her face grew soft and tender. "My father was a wonderful man, a great man, but he was called a crackpot. He was kept from teaching or working anywhere. It was just as well, I suppose, though he was too hurt to think so; he had more leisure to develop the time machine. He could have used it to extort repayment from mankind for his humiliation, but he didn't. He used it to help mankind."

"Like how?" I goaded.

"It doesn't matter, Mr. Weldon. You're determined to hate me and consider me a liar. Nothing I tell you can change that."

She was right about the first part—I hadn't dared let myself do anything except hate and fear her—but she was wrong about the second. I remembered thinking how Lou Pape would have felt if I had died of starvation with over $15,000, after borrowing from him all the time between jobs. Not knowing how I got it, he'd have been sore, thinking I'd played him for a patsy. What I'm trying to say is that Lou wouldn't have had enough information to judge me. I didn't have enough information yet, either, to judge her.

"What do you want me to do?" I asked warily.

"Everybody but one person was sent into the past on specific errands—to save art treasures and relics that would otherwise have been lost to humanity."

"Not because the things might be worth a lot of dough?" I said nastily.

"You've already seen that I can get all the money I want. There were upheavals in the past—great fires, wars, revolutions, vandalism—and I had my associates save things that would have been destroyed. Oh, beautiful things, Mr. Weldon! The world would have been so much poorer without them!"

"El Greco, for instance?" I asked, remembering the raving old man who had been found wandering with $17,000 in his coat lining.

"El Greco, too. Several paintings that had been lost for centuries." She became more brisk and efficient-seeming. "Except for the one man I mentioned, I concentrated on the past—the future is too completely unknown to us. And there's an additional reason why I tentatively explored it only once. But the one person who went there discovered something that would be of immense value to the world."

"What happened to *him*?"

She looked regretful "He was too old. He survived just long enough to tell me that the future has something we need. It's a metal box, small enough to carry, that could supply this whole city with power to run its industries and light its homes and streets!"

"Sounds good. Who'd you say benefits if I get it?"

"We share the profits equally, of course. But it must be understood that we sell the power so cheaply that everybody can afford it."

"I'm not arguing. What's the other reason you didn't bother with the future?"

"You can't bring anything from the future to the present that doesn't exist right now. I won't go into the theory, but it should be obvious that nothing can exist before it exists. You can't bring the box I want, only the technical data to build one."

"Technical data? I'm an actor, not a scientist."

"You'll have pens and weatherproof notebooks to copy it down in."

I couldn't make up my mind about her. I've already said she was beautiful, which always prejudices a man in a woman's favor, but I couldn't forget the starvation cases. They hadn't shared anything but malnutrition, useless money and death. Then again, maybe her explanation was a good one, that she wanted to help those who needed help most and some of them lied about their age and physical condition because they wanted the jobs so badly. All I knew about were those who had died. How did I know there weren't others—a lot more of them than the fatal cases, perhaps—who came through all right and were able to enjoy their little fortunes?

And there was her story about saving the treasures of the past and wanting to provide power at really low cost. She was right about one thing; she didn't need any of that to make money with; her method was plenty good enough, using the actual records of the past to invest in stocks, bet on sports—all sure gambles.

But those starvation cases . . .

"Do I get any guarantees?" I demanded.

She looked annoyed. "I'll need you for the data. You'll need me to turn it into manufacture. Is that enough of a guarantee?"

"No. Do I come out of this alive?"

"Mr. Weldon, please use some logic. I'm the one who's taking the risk. I've already given you more money than you've ever had at one time in your life. Part of my motive was to pay for services about to be rendered. Mostly, it was to give you experience in traveling through time."

"And to prove to me that I can't run out," I added.

"That happens to be a necessary attribute of the machine. I couldn't very well move you about through time unless it worked that way. If you'd look at my point of view, you'd see that I lose my investment if you don't bring back the data. I can't withdraw your money, you realize."

"I don't know what to think," I said, dissatisfied with myself because I couldn't find out what, if anything, was wrong with the deal. "I'll get you the data for the power box if it's at all possible and then we'll see what happens."

Finished eating, we went upstairs and I got into the cage.

She closed the circuit. The motors screamed. The mesh blurred.

And I was in a world I never knew.

You'd call it a city, I suppose; there were enough buildings to make it one. But no city ever had so much greenery. It wasn't just tree-lined streets, like Unter den Linden in Berlin, or islands covered with shrubbery, like Park Avenue in New York. The grass and trees and shrubs grew around every building, separating them from each other by wide lawns. The buildings were more glass—or what looked like glass—than anything else. A few of the windows were opaque against the sun, but I couldn't see any shades or blinds. Some kind of polarizing glass or plastic?

I felt uneasy being there, but it was a thrill just the same, to be alive in the future when I and everybody who lived in my day were supposed to be dead.

The air smelled like the country. There was no foul gas boiling from the teardrop cars on the glass-level road. They were made of transparent plastic clear around and from top to bottom, and they moved along at a fair clip, but more smoothly than swiftly. If I hadn't seen the airship overhead, I wouldn't have known it was there. It flew silently, a graceful ball without wings, seeming to be borne by the wind from one horizon to the other, except that no wind ever moved that fast.

One car stopped nearby and someone shouted, "Here we are!" Several people leaped out and headed for me.

I didn't think. I ran. I crossed the lawn and ducked into the nearest building and dodged through long, smoothly walled, shadowlessly lit corridors until I found a door that would open. I slammed it shut and locked it. Then, panting, I fell into a soft chair that seemed to form itself around my body, and felt like kicking myself for the bloody idiot I was.

What in hell had I run for? They couldn't have known who I was. If I'd arrived in a time when people wore togas or bathing suits, there would have been some reason for singling me out, but they had all had clothes just like ours—suits and shirts and ties for the men, a dress and high heels for the one woman with them. I felt somewhat disappointed that clothes hadn't changed any, but it worked out to my advantage; I wouldn't be so conspicuous.

Yes why should anyone have yelled "Here we are!" unless. . . No, they must have thought I was somebody else. I didn't figure any other way. I had run because it was my first startled reaction and probably because I knew I was there on what might be considered illegal business; if I succeeded, some poor inventor would be done out of his royalties.

I wished I hadn't run. Besides its making me feel like a scared fool, I was sweaty, out of breath. Playing old men doesn't make climbing down fire escapes much tougher than it should be, but it doesn't exactly make a sprinter out of you—not by several lungfuls.

I sat there, breathing hard and trying to guess what next. I had no more idea of where to go for what I wanted than an ancient Egyptian set down in the middle of Times Square with instructions to sneak a mummy out of the Metropolitan Museum. I didn't even have that much information. I didn't know any part of the city, how it was laid out, or where to get the data that May Roberts had sent me for.

I opened the door quietly and looked both ways before going out. After losing myself in the cross-connecting corridors a few times, I finally came to an outside door. I stopped, tense, trying to get my courage. My inclination was to slip, sneak or dart out, but I made myself walk away like a decent, innocent citizen. That was one disguise they'd never be able to crack. All I had to do was act as if I belonged to that time and place and who would know the difference?

There were other people walking as if they were in no hurry to get anywhere. I slowed down to their speed, but I wished wistfully that there was a crowd to dive into and get lost.

A man dropped into step and said politely, "I beg your pardon. Are you a stranger in town?"

I almost halted in alarm, but that might have been a give-away. "What makes you think so?" I asked, forcing myself to keep at the same easy pace.

"I—didn't recognize your face and I thought—"

"It's a big city," I said coldly. "You can't know everyone."

"If there's anything I can do to help—"

I told him there wasn't and left him standing there. It was plain common sense, I had decided quickly while he was talking to me, not to take any risks by admitting anything. I might have been dumped into a police state or the country could have been at war without my knowing it, or maybe they were suspicious of strangers. For one reason or another, ranging from vagrancy to espionage, I could be pulled in, tortured, executed, God knows what. The place looked peaceful enough, but that didn't prove a thing.

I went on walking, looking for something I couldn't be sure existed, in a city I was completely unfamiliar with, in a time when I had no right to be alive. It wasn't just a matter of getting the information she wanted. I'd have been satisfied to hang around until she pulled me back without the data.

But then what would happen? Maybe the starvation cases were people who had failed her! For that matter, she could shoot me and send the remains anywhere in time to get rid of the evidence.

Damn it, I didn't know if she was better or worse than I'd supposed, but I wasn't going to take any chances. I had to bring her what she wanted.

There was a sign up ahead. It read: TO SHOPPING CENTER. The arrow pointed along the road. When I came to a fork and wondered which way to go, there was another sign, then another pointing to still more farther on.

I followed them to the middle of the city, a big square with a park in the center and shops of all kinds rimming it. The only shop I was interested in said: ELECTRICAL APPLIANCES.

I went in.

A neat young salesman came up and politely asked me if he could do anything for me. I sounded stupid even to myself, but I said,

"No, thanks, I'd just like to do a little browsing," and gave a silly nervous laugh. Me, an actor, behaving like a frightened yokel! I felt ashamed of myself.

He tried not to look surprised, but he didn't really succeed. Somebody else came in, though, for which I was grateful, and he left me alone to look around.

I don't know if I can get my feelings across to you. It's a situation that nobody would ever expect to find himself in, so it isn't easy to tell what it's like. But I've got to try.

Let's stick with the ancient Egyptian I mentioned a while back, the one ordered to sneak a mummy out of the Metropolitan Museum. Maybe that'll make it clearer.

The poor guy has no money he can use, naturally, and no idea of what New York's transportation system is like where the museum is, how to get there, what visitors to a museum do and say, the regulations he might unwittingly break, how much an ordinary citizen is supposed to know about which customs and such. Now add the possible danger that he might be slapped into jail or an insane asylum if he makes a mistake and you've got a rough notion of the spot I felt I was in. Being able to speak English doesn't make much difference; not knowing what's regarded as right and wrong, and the unknown consequences, are enough to panic anybody.

That doesn't make it clear enough.

Well, look, take the electrical appliances in that store; that might give you an idea of the situation and the way it affected me.

The appliances must have been as familiar to the people of that time as toasters and TV sets and lamps are to us. But the things didn't make a bit of sense to me . . . any more than our appliances would to an ancient Egyptian. Can you imagine him trying to figure out what those items are for and how they work?

Here are some gadgets you can puzzle over:

There was a light fixture that you put against any part of a wall—no screws, no cement, no wires, even—and it held there and lit up, and it stayed lit no matter where you moved it on the wall. Talk about pin-up lamps . . . this was really it!

Then I came across something that looked like an ashtray with a blue electric shimmer obscuring the bottom of the bowl. I lit my pipe—others I'd passed had been smoking, so I knew it was safe to do the same—and flicked in the match. It disappeared. I don't mean it was swirled into some hidden compartment. It vanished. I emptied the pipe into the ashtray and that went, too. Looking around to make sure nobody was watching, I dredged some coins out of my pocket and let them drop into the tray. They were gone. Not a particle of them was left. A disintegrator? I haven't got the slightest idea.

There were little mirror boxes with three tiny dials on the front of each. I turned the dials on one—it was like using three dial telephones at the same time—and a pretty girl's face popped onto the mirror surface and looked expectantly at me.

"Yes?" she said, and waited for me to answer.

"I—uh—wrong number, I guess," I answered, putting the box down in a hurry and going to the other side of the shop because I didn't have even a dim notion how to turn it off.

The thing I was looking for was on a counter—a tinted metal box no bigger than a suitcase, with a lipped hole on top and small undisguised verniers in front. I didn't know I'd found it, actually, until I twisted a vernier and every light in the store suddenly glared and the salesman came rushing over and politely moved me aside to shut it off.

"We don't want to burn out every appliance in the place, do we?" he asked quietly.

"I just wanted to see if it worked all right," I said, still shaking slightly. It could have blown up or electrocuted me, for all I knew.

"But they always work," he said.

"Ah—always?"

"Of course. The principle is simple and there are no parts to get worn out, so they last indefinitely." He suddenly smiled as if he'd just caught the gist. "Oh, you were joking! Naturally—everybody learns about the Dynapack in primary education. You were interested in acquiring one?"

"No, no. The—the old one is good enough. I was just—well, you know, interested in knowing if the new models are much different or better than the old ones."

"But there haven't been any new models since 2073," he said. "Can you think of a reason why there should be?"

"I—guess not," I stammered. "But you never can tell."

"You can with Dynapacks," he said, and he would have gone on if I hadn't lost my nerve and mumbled my way out of the store as fast as I could.

You want to know why? He'd asked me if I wanted to "acquire" a Dynapack, not buy one. I didn't know what "acquire" meant in that society. It could be anything from saving up coupons to winning whatever you wanted at some kind of lottery, or maybe working up the right number of labor units on the job—in which case he'd want to know where I was employed and the equivalent of social security and similar information, which I naturally didn't have—or it could just be fancy sales talk for buying.

I couldn't guess, and I didn't care to expose myself any more than I had already. And my blunder about the Dynapack working and the new models was nothing to make me feel at all easier.

Lord, the uncertainties and hazards of being in a world you don't know anything about! Daydreaming about visiting another age may be pleasant, but the reality is something else again.

"Wait a minute, friend!" I heard the salesman call out behind me.

I looked back as casually, I hoped, as the pedestrians who heard him. He was walking quickly toward me with a very worried expression on his face. I stepped up my own pace as unobtrusively as possible, trying to keep a lot of people between us, meanwhile praying that they'd think I was just somebody who was late for an appointment. The salesman didn't break into a run or yell for the cops, but I couldn't be sure he wouldn't.

As soon as I came to a corner, I turned it and ran like hell. There was a sort of alley down the block. I jumped into it, found a basement door and stayed inside, pressed against the wall, quivering with tension and sucking air like a swimmer who'd stayed underwater too long.

Even after I got my wind back, I wasn't anxious to go out. The place could have been cordoned off, with the police, the army and the navy all cooperating to nab me.

What made me think so? Not a thing except remembering how puzzled our ancient Egyptian would have been if he got arrested in the subway for something somebody did casually and without punishment in his own time—spitting! I could have done something just as innocent, as far as you and I are concerned, that this era would consider a misdemeanor or a major crime. And in what age was ignorance of the law ever an excuse?

Instead of going back out, I prowled carefully into the building. It was strangely silent and deserted. I couldn't understand why until I came to a lavatory. There were little commodes and wash basins that came up to barely above my knees. The place was a school. Naturally it was deserted—the kids were through for the day.

I could feel the tension dissolve in me like a ramrod of ice melting, no longer keeping my back and neck stiff and taut. There probably wasn't a better place in the city for me to hide.

A primary school!

The salesman had said to me, "Everybody learns about the Dynapack in primary education."

Going through the school was eerie, like visiting a familiar childhood scene that had been distorted by time into something almost totally unrecognizable.

There were no blackboards, teacher's big desk, children's little desks, inkwells, pointers, globes or books. Yet it was a school. The small fixtures in the lavatory downstairs had told me that, and so did the miniature chairs drawn neatly under the low, vividly painted tables in the various schoolrooms. A large comfortable chair was evidently where the teacher sat when not wandering around among the pupils.

In front of each chair, firmly attached to the table, was a box with a screen, and both sides of the box held spools of wire on blunt little spindles. The spools had large, clear numbers on them. Near the teacher's chair was a compact case with more spools on spindles, and there was a large screen on the inside wall, opposite the enormous windows.

I went into one of the rooms and sat down in the teacher's chair, wondering how I was going to find out about the Dynapack. I felt like an archeologist guessing at the functions of strange relics he'd found in a dead city.

Sitting in the chair was like sitting on a column of air that let me sit upright or slump as I chose. One of the arms had a row of buttons. I pressed one and waited nervously to find out if I'd done something that would get me into trouble.

Concealed lights in the ceiling and walls began glowing, getting brighter, while the room gradually turned dark. I glanced around bewilderedly to see why, because it was still daylight.

The windows seemed to be sliding slightly, very slowly, and as they slid, the sunlight was damped out. I grinned, thinking of my ancient Egyptian would make of that. I knew there were two sheets of polarizing glass, probably with a vacuum between to keep out the cold and the heat, and the lights in the room were beautifully synchronized with the polarized sliding glass.

I wasn't doing so badly. The rest of the objects might not be too hard to figure out.

The spools in the case alongside the teacher's chair could be wire recordings. I looked for something to play them with, but there was no sign of a playback machine. I tried to lift a spool off a spindle. It wouldn't come off.

Hah! The wire led down the spindle to the base of the box, holding the spool in place. That meant the spools could be played right in that position. But what started them playing?

I hunted over the box minutely. Every part of it was featureless—no dials, switches or any unfamiliar counterparts. I even tried moving my hands over it, figuring it might be like a terminal, and spoke to it in different shades of command, because it could have been built to respond to vocal orders. Nothing happened.

Remember the Poe story that shows the best place to hide something is right out in the open, which is the last place anyone would look? Well, these things weren't manufactured to baffle people, any more than our devices generally are. But it's only by trying everything that somebody who didn't know what a switch is would start up a vacuum cleaner, say, or light a big chandelier from a wall clear across the room.

I'd pressed every inch of the box, hoping some part of it might act as a switch, and I finally touched one of the spindles. The spool immediately began spinning at a very low speed and the screen on the wall opposite the window glowed into life.

"The history of the exploration of the Solar System," said an announcer's deep voice, "is one of the most adventuresome in mankind's long list of achievements. Beginning with the crude rockets developed during World War II . . ."

There were newsreel shots of V-1 and V-2 being blasted from their takeoff ramps and a montage of later experimental models. I wished I could see how it all turned out, but I was afraid to waste the time watching. At any moment, I might hear the footsteps of a guard or janitor or whoever tended buildings then.

I pushed the spindle again. It checked the spool, which rewound swiftly and silently, and stopped itself when the rewinding was finished. I tried another. A nightmare underwater scene appeared.

"With the aid of energy screens," said another voice, "the oceans of the world were completely charted by the year 2027 . . ."

I turned it off, then another on developments in medicine, one on architecture, one on history, the geography of such places as the interior of South America and Africa that were—or are—unknown today, and I was getting frantic, starting the wonderful wire films that held full-frequency sound and pictures in absolutely faithful color, and shutting them off hastily when I discovered they didn't have what I was looking for.

They were courses for children, but they all contained information that our scientists are still groping for . . . and I couldn't chance watching one all the way through!

I was frustratedly switching off a film on psychology when a female voice said from the door, "May I help you?"

I snapped around to face her in sudden fright. She was young and slim and slight, but she could scream loud enough to get help. Judging by the way she was looking at me, outwardly polite and yet visibly nervous, that scream would be coming at any second.

"I must have wandered in here by mistake," I said, and pushed past her to the corridor, where I began running back the way I had come.

"But you don't understand!" she cried after me. "I really want to help —"

Yeah, help, I thought, pounding toward the street door. A gag right out of that psychology film, probably—get the patient to hold still, humor him, until you can get somebody to put him where he belongs. That's what one of our teachers would do, provided she wasn't too scared to think straight, if she found an old-looking guy thumbing frenziedly through the textbooks in a grammar school classroom.

When I came to the outside door, I stopped. I had no way of knowing whether she'd given out an alarm, or how she might have done it, but the obvious place to find me would be out on the street, dodging for cover somewhere.

I pushed the door open and let it slam shut, hoping she'd hear it upstairs. Then I found a door, sneaked it open and went silently down the steps.

In the basement, I looked for a furnace or coal bin or a fuel tank to hide behind, but there weren't any. I don't know how they got their heat in the winter or cooled the building in the summer. Probably some central atomic plant that took care of the whole city, piping in the heat or coolant in underground conduits that were led up through the walls, because there weren't even any pipes visible.

I hunched into the darkest corner I could find and hoped they wouldn't look for me there.

By the time night came, hunger drove me out of the school, but I did it warily, making sure nobody was in sight.

The streets of the shopping center were more or less deserted. There was no sign of a restaurant. I was so empty that I felt dizzy as I hunted for one. But then a shocking realization made me halt on the sidewalk and sweat with horror.

Even if there had been a restaurant, what would I have used for money?

Now I got the whole foul picture. She had sent old people back through time on errands like mine . . . and they'd starved to death because they couldn't buy food!

No, that wasn't right. I remembered what I had told Lou Pape: anybody who gets hungry enough can always find a truck garden or a food store to rob.

Only . . . I hadn't seen a truck garden or food store anywhere in this city.

And . . . I thought about people in the past having their hands cut off for stealing a loaf of bread.

This civilization didn't look as if it went in for such drastic punishments, assuming I could find a loaf of bread to steal. But neither did most of the civilizations that practiced those barbarisms.

I was more tired, hungry and scared than I'd ever believed a human being could get. Lost, completely lost in a totally alien world, but one in which I could still be killed or starve to death . . . and God knew what was waiting for me in my own time in case I came back without the information she wanted.

Or maybe even if I came back with it!

That suspicion made up my mind for me. Whatever happened to me now couldn't be worse than what she might do. At least I didn't have to starve.

I stopped a man in the street. I let several others go by before picking him deliberately because he was middle-aged, had a kindly face, and was smaller than me, so I could slug him and run if he raised a row.

"Look, friend," I told him, "I'm just passing through town —"

"Ah?" he said pleasantly.

"—And I seem to have mislaid —" No, that was dangerous. I'd been about to say I'd mislaid my wallet, but I still didn't know whether they used money in this era. He waited with a patient, friendly smile while I decided just how to put it. "The fact is that I haven't eaten all day and I wonder if you could help me get a meal."

He said in the most neighborly voice imaginable, "I'll be glad to do anything I can, Mr. Weldon."

My entire face seemed to drop open. "You—you called me —"

"Mr. Weldon," he repeated, still looking up at me with that neighborly smile. "Mark Weldon, isn't it? From the twentieth century?"

I tried to answer, but my throat had tightened up worse than on any opening night I'd ever had to live through. I nodded, wondering terrifiedly what was going on.

"Please relax," he said persuasively. "You're not in any danger whatever. We offer you our utmost hospitality. Our time, you might say, is our time."

"You know who I am," I managed to get out through my constricted glottis. "I've been doing all this running and ducking and hiding for nothing."

He shrugged sympathetically. "Everyone in the city was instructed to help you, but you were so nervous that we were afraid to alarm you with a direct approach. Every time we tried to, as a matter of fact, you vanished into one place or another. We didn't follow for fear of the effect on you. We had to wait until you came voluntarily to us."

My brain was racing again and getting nowhere. Part of it was dizziness from hunger, but only part. The rest was plain frightened confusion.

They knew who I was. They'd been expecting me. They probably even knew what I was after.

And they wanted to help!

"Let's not go into explanations now," he said, "although I'd like to smooth away the bewilderment and fear on your face. But you need to be fed first. Then we'll call in the others and —"

I pulled back. "What others? How do I know you're not setting up something for me that I'll wish I hadn't gotten into?"

"Before you approached me, Mr. Weldon, you first had to decide that we represented no greater menace than May Roberts. Please believe me, we don't."

So he knew about that, too!

"All right, I'll take my chances," I gave in resignedly. "Where does a guy find a place to eat in this city?"

It was a handsome restaurant with soft light coming from three-dimensional, full-color nature murals that I might mistakenly have walked into if I'd been alone, they looked so much like gardens and forests and plains. It was no wonder I couldn't find a restaurant or food store or truck garden anywhere—food came up through the pneumatic chutes in each building, I'd been told on the way over, grown in hydroponic tanks in cities that specialized in agriculture, and those who wanted to eat "out" could drop into the restaurant each building had. Every city had its own function. This one was for people in the arts. I liked that.

There was a glowing menu on the table with buttons alongside the various selections. I looked starvingly at the items, trying to decide which I wanted most. I picked oysters, onion soup, breast of guinea hen under plexiglas and was hunting for the tastiest and most recognizable dessert when the pleasant little guy shook his head regretfully and emphatically.

"I'm afraid you can't eat any of those foods, Mr. Weldon," he said in a sad voice. "We'll explain why in a moment."

A waiter and the manager came over. They obviously didn't want to stare at me, but they couldn't help it. I couldn't blame them. I'd have stared at somebody from George Washington's time, which is about what I must have represented to them.

"Will you please arrange to have the special food for Mr. Weldon delivered here immediately?" the little guy asked.

Every restaurant has been standing by for this, Mr. Carr," said the manager. "It's on its way. Prepared, of course—it's been ready since he first arrived."

"Fine," said the little guy, Carr. "It can't be too soon. He's very hungry."

I glanced around and noticed for the first time that there was nobody else in the restaurant. It was past the dinner hour, but, even so, there are always late diners. We had the place all to ourselves and it bothered me. They could have ganged up on me . . .

But they didn't. A light gong sounded, and the waiter and manager hurried over to a slot of a door and brought out a couple of trays loaded with covered dishes.

"Your dinner, Mr. Weldon," the manager said, putting the plates in front of me and removing the lids.

I stared down at the food.

"This," I told them angrily, "is a hell of a trick to play on a starving man!"

They all looked unhappy.

"Mashed dehydrated potatoes, canned meat and canned vegetables," Carr replied. "Not very appetizing, I know, but I'm afraid it's all we can allow you to eat."

I took the cover off the dessert dish.

"Dried fruits!" I said in disgust.

"Rather excessively dried, I'm sorry to say," the manager agreed mournfully.

I sipped the blue stuff in a glass and almost spat it out. "Powdered milk! Are these things what you people have to live on?"

"No, our diet is quite varied," Carr said in embarrassment. "But we unfortunately can't give you any of the foods we normally eat ourselves."

"And why in blazes not?"

"Please eat, Mr. Weldon," Carr begged with frantic earnestness. "There's so much to explain—this part of it, of course—and it would be best if you heard it on a full stomach."

I was famished enough to get the stuff down, which wasn't easy; uninviting as it looked, it tasted still worse.

When I was through, Carr pushed several buttons on the glowing menu. Dishes came up from an opening in the center of the table and he showed me the luscious foods they contained.

"Given your choice," he said, "you'd have preferred them to what you have eaten. Isn't that so, Mr. Weldon?"

"You bet I would!" I answered, sore because I hadn't been given that choice.

"And you would have died like the pathetic old people you were investigating," said a voice behind me.

I turned around, startled. Several men and women had come in while I'd been eating, their footsteps as silent as cats on a rug. I looked blankly from them to Carr and back again.

"These are the clothes we ordinarily wear," Carr said. "An eighteenth century motif, as you can see—updated knee breeches and shirt waists, modified stock for the men, the daring low bodices of that era, the full skirts treated in a modern way by using sheer materials for the women, bright colors and sheens, buckled shoes of spun synthetics. Very gay, very ornamental, very comfortable, and thoroughly suitable to our time."

"But everybody I saw was dressed like me!" I protested.

"Only to keep you from feeling more conspicuous and anxious than you already were. It was quite a project, I can tell you—your styles varied so greatly from decade to decade, especially those for women—and the materials were a genuine problem; they'd gone out of existence long ago. We had the textile and tailoring cities working a full six months to clothe the inhabitants of this city, including, of course, the children. Everybody had to be clad as your contemporaries were, because we knew only that you would arrive in this vicinity, not where you might wander through the city."

"There was one small difference you didn't notice," added a handsome mature woman. "You were the only man in a gray suit. We had a full description of what you were wearing, you see, and we made sure nobody else was dressed that way. Naturally, everyone knew who you were, and so we were kept informed of your movements."

"What for?" I demanded in alarm. "What's this all about?"

Pulling up chairs, they sat down, looking to me like a witchcraft jury from some old painting.

"I'm Leo Blundell," said a tall man in plum-and-gold clothes. "As chairman of—of the Mark Weldon Committee, it's my responsibility to handle this project correctly."

"Project?"

"To make certain that history is fulfilled, I have to tell you as much as you must know."

"I wish *somebody* would!"

"Very well, let me begin by telling you much of what you undoubtedly know already. In a sense, you are more a victim of Dr. Anthony Roberts than his daughter. Roberts was a brilliant physicist, but because of his eccentric behavior, he was ridiculed for his theories and hated for his arrogance. He was an almost perfect example of self-defeat, the way in which a man will hamper his career and wreck his happiness, and then blame the world for his failure and misery. To get back to his connection with you, however, he invented a time machine—unfortunately, its secret has since been lost and never rediscovered—and used it for antisocial purposes. When he died, his daughter May carried on his work. It was she who sent you to this time to learn the principle by which the Dynapack operates. She was a thoroughly ruthless woman."

"Are you sure?" I asked uneasily.

"Quite sure."

"I know a number of old people died after she sent them on errands through time, but she said they'd lied about their age and health."

"One would expect her to say that," a woman put in cuttingly.

Blundell turned to her and shook his head. "Let Mr. Weldon clarify his feelings about her, Rhoda. They are obviously very mixed."

"They are," I admitted. "She seemed hard, the first time I saw her, when I answered her ad, but she could have been just acting businesslike. I mean she had a lot of people to pick from and she had to be impersonal and make certain she had the right one. The next time—I hope you don't know about that—it was really my fault for breaking into her room. I really had a lot of admiration for the way she handled the situation."

"Go on," Carr encouraged me.

"And I can't complain about the deal she gave me. Sure, she came out ahead on the money I bet and invested for her. But I did all right myself—I was richer than I'd ever been in my life—and she gave that money to me before I even did anything to earn it!"

"Besides which," somebody else said, "she offered you half of the profits on the Dynapack."

I looked around at the faces for signs of hostility. I saw none. That was surprising. I'd come from the past to steal something from them and they weren't angry. Well, no, it wasn't really stealing. I wouldn't be depriving them of the Dynapack. It just would have been invented before it was supposed to be.

"She did," I said. "Though I wouldn't call that part of it philanthropy. She needed me for the data and I needed her to manufacture the things."

"And she was a very beautiful woman," Blundell added.

I squirmed a bit. "Yes."

"Mr. Weldon, we know a good deal about her from notes that have come down to us among her private papers. She had a safety deposit box under a false name. I won't tell you the name; it was not discovered until many years later, and we will not voluntarily meddle with the past."

I sat up and listened sharply. "So that's how you knew who I was and what I'd be wearing and what I came for! You even knew when and where I'd arrive!"

"Correct," Blundell said.

"What else do you know?"

"That you suspected her of being responsible for the deaths of many old people by starvation. Your suspicion was justified, except that her father had caused all those that occurred before 1947, when she took over after his own death. All but two people were sent into the past. Roberts was curious about the future, of course, but he did not want to waste a victim on a trip that would probably be fruitless. In the past, you understand, he knew precisely what he was after. The future was completely unknown territory."

"But she took the chance," I said.

"If you can call deliberate murder taking a chance, yes. One man arrived in 2094, over fifty years ago. The other was yourself. The first one, as you know, died of malnutrition when he was brought back to your era."

"And what happened to me?" I asked, jittering.

"You will not die. We intend to make sure of that. All the other victims—I presume you're interested in their errands?"

"I think I know, but I'd like to find out just the same."

"They were sent to the past to buy or steal treasures of various sorts—art, sculpture, jewelry, fabulously valuable manuscripts and books, anything that had great scarcity value."

"That's not possible," I objected. "She had all the money she wanted. Any time she needed more, all she had to do was send somebody back to put down bets and buy stocks that she knew were winners. She had the records, didn't she? There was no way she or her father could lose!"

He moved his shoulders in a plum-and-gold shrug. "Most of the treasures they accumulated were for acquisition's sake—and for the sake of vengeance for the way they believed Dr. Roberts had been treated. When there were unusual expenses, such as replacing the very costly parts of the time machine, that required more than they could produce in ready cash, both Roberts and his daughter 'discovered' these treasures."

He waited while I digested the miserable meal and the disturbing information he had given me. I thought I'd found a loophole in his explanation: "You said people were sent back to the past to *buy* treasures, besides stealing them."

"I did," he agreed. "They were provided with currency of whatever era they were to visit."

I felt my forehead wrinkle up as my theory fell apart. "Then they could buy food. Why should they have died of malnutrition?"

"Because, as May Roberts herself told you, nothing can exist before it exists. Neither can anything exist after it is out of existence. If you returned with a Dynapack, for example, it would revert to a lump of various metals, because that was what it was in your period. But let me give you a more personal instance. Do you remember coming back from your first trip with dust on your hand?"

"Yes. I must have fallen."

"On one hand? No, Mr. Weldon. May Roberts was greatly upset by the incident; she was afraid you would realize why the hamburger had turned to dust—and why the old people died of starvation. All of them, not just a few."

He paused, giving me a chance to understand what he had just said. I did, with a sick shock.

"If I ate your food," I said shakily, "I'd feel satisfied until I was returned to my own time. But the food wouldn't go along with me!"

Blundell nodded gravely. "And so you, too, would die of malnutrition. The foods we have given you existed in your era. We were very careful of that, so careful that many of them probably were stored years before you left your time. We regret that they are not very palatable, but a least we are positive they will go back with you. You will be as healthy when you arrive in the past as when you left.

"Incidentally, she made you change your clothes for the same reason—they had been made in 1930. She had clothing from every era she wanted visited and chose old people who would fit them best. Otherwise, you see, they'd have arrived naked."

I began to shake as if I were as old as I'd pretended to be on the stage. "She's going to pull me back! If I don't bring her the information about the Dynapack, she'll shoot me!"

"That, Mr. Weldon, is our problem," Blundell said, putting his hand comfortingly on my arm to calm me.

"Your problem? I'm the one who'll get shot, not you!"

"But we know in complete detail what will happen when you are returned to the twentieth century."

I pulled my arm away and grabbed his. "You know that? Tell me!"

"I'm sorry, Mr. Weldon. If we tell you what you did, you might think of some alternate action, and there is no knowing what the result would be."

"But I didn't get shot or die of malnutrition?"

"That much we can tell you. Neither."

They all stood up, so bright and attractive in their colorful clothes that I felt like a shirt-sleeved stagehand who'd wandered in on a costume play.

"You will be returned in a month, according to the notes May Roberts left. She gave you plenty of time to get the data, you see. We propose to make that month an enjoyable one for you. The resources of our city—and any others you care to visit—are at your disposal. We wish you to take full advantage of them."

"And the Dynapack?"

"Let us worry about that. We want you to have a good time while you are our guest."

I did.

It was the most wonderful month of my life.

The mesh cage blurred around me. I could see May Roberts through it, her hand just leaving the switch. She was as beautiful as ever, but I saw beneath her beauty the vengeful, vicious creature her father's bitterness had turned her into; Blundell and Carr had let me read some of her notes, and I knew. I wished I could have spent the rest of my years in the future, instead of having to come back to this.

She came over and opened the gate, smiling like an angel welcoming a bright new soul. Then her eyes traveled startledly over me and her smile almost dropped off. But she held it firmly in place.

She had to, while she asked, "Do you have the notes I sent you for?"

"Right here," I said.

I reached into my breast pocket and brought out a stubby automatic and shot her through the right arm. Her closed hand opened and a little derringer clanked on the floor. She gaped at me with an expression of horrified surprise that should have been recorded permanently; it would have served as a model for generations of actors and actresses.

"You—brought back a weapon!" she gasped. "You shot me!" She stared vacantly at her bleeding arm and then at my automatic. "But you can't—bring anything back from the future. And you aren't—dying from malnutrition."

She said it all in a voice shocked into toneless wonder.

"The food I ate and this gun are from the present," I said. "The people of the future knew I was coming. They gave me food that wouldn't vanish from my cells when I returned. They also gave me the gun instead of the plans for the Dynapack."

"And you took it?" she screamed at me. "You idiot! I'd have shared the profits honestly with you. You'd have been worth millions!"

"With acute malnutrition," I amended. "I like it better this way, thanks—poor, but alive. Or relatively poor, I should say, because you've been very generous and I appreciate it."

"By shooting me!"

"I hated to puncture that lovely arm, but it wasn't as painful as starving or getting shot myself. Now if you don't mind—or even if you do—it's your turn to get into the cage, Miss Roberts."

She tried to grab the derringer on the floor with her left hand.

"Don't bother," I said quietly. "You can't reach it before a bullet reaches you."

She straightened up, staring at me for the first time with terror in her eyes.

"What are you going to do to me?" she whispered.

"I could kill you as easily as you could have killed me. Kill you and send your body into some other era. How many dozens of deaths were you responsible for? The law couldn't convict you of them, but I can. And I couldn't be convicted, either."

She put her hand on the wound. Blood seeped through her fingers as she lifted her chin at me.

"I won't beg for my life, Weldon, if that's what you want. I could offer you a partnership, but I'm not really in a position to offer it, am I?"

She was magnificent, terrifyingly intelligent, brave clear through … and deadlier than a plague. I had to remember that.

"Into the cage," I said. "I have some friends in the future who have plans for you. I won't tell you what they are, of course; you didn't tell me what I'd go through, did you? Give my friends my fondest regards. If I can manage it, I'll visit them—and you."

She backed warily into the cage. It would have been pleasant to kiss those wonderful lips good-by. I'd thought about them for a whole month, wanting them and loathing them at the same time.

It would have been like kissing a coral snake. I knew it and I concentrated on shutting the gate on her.

"You'd like to be rich, wouldn't you, Weldon?" she asked through the mesh.

"I can be," I said. "I have the machine. I can send people into the past or future and make myself a pile of dough. Only I'd give them food to take along. I wouldn't kill them off to keep the secret to myself. Anything else on your mind?"

"You want me," she stated.

I didn't argue.

"You could have me."

"Just long enough to get my throat slit or brains blown out. I don't want anything that much."

I rammed the switch closed.

The mesh cage blurred and she was gone. Her blood was on the floor, but she was gone into the future I had just come from.

That was when the reaction hit me. I'd escaped starvation and her gun, but I wasn't a hero and the release of tension flipped my stomach over and unhinged my knees.

Shaking badly, I stumbled through the big, empty house until I found a phone.

Lou Pape got there so quickly that I still hadn't gotten over the tremors, in spite of a bottle of brandy I dug out of a credenza, maybe because the date on the label, 1763, gave me a new case of shivers.

I could see the worry on Lou's face vanish when he assured himself that I was all right. It came back again, though, when I told him what had happened. He didn't believe any of it, naturally. I guess I hadn't really expected him to.

"If I didn't know you, Mark," he said, shaking his big, dark head unhappily, "I'd send you over to Bellevue for observation. Even knowing you, maybe that's what I ought to do."

"All right, let's see if there's any proof," I suggested tiredly. "From what I was told, there ought to be plenty."

We searched the house clear down to the basement, where he stood with his face slack.

"Christ!" he breathed. "The annex to the Metropolitan Museum!"

The basement ran the length and breadth of the house and was twice as high as an average room, and the whole glittering place was crammed with paintings in rich, heavy frames, statuettes, books, manuscripts, goblets and ewers and jewelry made of gold and huge gems, and tapestries in brilliant color ... and everything was as bright and sparkling and new as the day it was made, which was almost true of a lot of it.

"The dame was loaded and she was an art collector, that's all," Lou said. "You can't tell me that screwy story of yours. She was a collector and she knew where to find things."

"She certainly did," I agreed.

"What did you do with her?"

"I told you. I shot her through the arm before she could shoot me and I sent her into the future."

He took me by the front of the jacket. "You killed her, Mark. You wanted all this stuff for yourself, so you knocked her off and got rid of her body somehow."

"Why don't you go back to acting, where you belong, Lou, and leave sleuthing to people who know how?" I asked, too worn to pull his hands loose. "Would I kill her and call you up to get right over here? Wouldn't I have sneaked these things out first? Or more likely I'd have sneaked them out, hidden them and nobody—including you—would know I'd ever been here. Come on, use your head."

"That's easy. You lost your nerve."

"I'm not even losing my patience."

He pushed me away savagely. "If you killed her for this stuff or because of that crazy yarn you gave me, I'm a cop and you're no friend. You're just a plain killer I happened to have known once, and I'll make sure you fry."

"You always did have a taste for that kind of dialogue. Go ahead and wrap me up in an airtight case, have them throw the book at me, send me up the river, put me in the hot squat. But you'll have to do the proving, not me."

He headed for the stairs. "I will. And don't try to make a break or I'll plug you as if I never saw you before."

He put in a call at the phone upstairs. I didn't give a particular damn who it was he'd called. I was too relieved that I hadn't killed May Roberts; destroying anything that beautiful, however evil, would have stayed with me the rest of my life. There was another reason for my relief—if I'd killed her and left the evidence for Lou to find, he'd never help me. No, that's not quite so; he'd probably have tried to get me to plead insanity on the basis of my unbelievable explanation.

But most of all, I couldn't get rid of the look on her face when I'd shot her through the arm, the arm that was so wonderful to look at and that had held a murderous little gun to greet me with.

She was in the future now. She wouldn't be executed by them; they regarded crime as an illness, and they'd treat her with their marvelously advanced therapy and she'd become a useful, contented citizen, living out her existence in an era that had given me more happiness than I'd ever had.

I sat and tried to stupefy myself with brandy that should long ago have dried to brick-hardness, while Lou Pape stood at the door with his hand near his holster and glared at me. He didn't take his eyes off me until somebody name Prof. Jeremiah Aaronson came in and was introduced briefly and flatly to me. Then Lou took him upstairs.

It was minutes before I realized what they were going to do. I ran up after them.

I was just in time to see Aaronson carefully take the housing off the hooded motors, and leap back suddenly from the fury of lightning sparks.

The whole machine fused while we watched helplessly—motors, switches, panel and mesh cage. They flashed blindingly and blew apart and melted together in a charred and molten pile.

"Rigged," Aaronson said in the tone of a bitter curse. "Set to short if it was tampered with. I wouldn't be surprised if there were incendiaries placed at strategic spots. Nothing else could have made a mess like this."

He finally glanced down at his hand and saw it was scorched. He hissed with the realization of pain, blew on the burn, shook it in the air to cool it, and pulled a handkerchief out of his back pocket by reaching all the way around the rear for it with his left hand.

Lou looked worriedly at the heap of cooling slag. "Can you make any sense of it, Prof.?" he asked.

"Can you?" Aaronson retorted. "Melt down a microtome of any other piece of machinery you're unfamiliar with, and see if you can identify it when it looks like this."

He went out, wrapping his hand in the handkerchief.

Lou kicked glumly at a piece of twisted tubing. "Aaronson is a top physicist, Mark. I was hoping he'd make enough out of the machine to—ah, hell, I wanted to believe you! I couldn't. I still can't. Now we'll have to dig through the house to find her body."

"You won't find it or the secret of the machine," I answered miserably. "I told you they said the secret would be lost. This is how. Now I'll never be able to visit the future again. I'll never see them or

May Roberts. They'll straighten her out, get rid of her hate and vindictiveness, and it won't do me a damned bit of good because the machine is gone and she's generations ahead of me."

He turned to me puzzledly. "You're not afraid to have us dig for her body, Mark?"

"Tear the place apart if you want."

"We'll have to," he said. "I'm calling Homicide."

"Call in the Marines. Call in anybody you like."

"You'll have to stay in my custody until we're through."

I shrugged. "As long as you leave me alone while you're doing your digging, I don't give a hand if I'm under arrest for suspicion of murder. I've got to do some straightening out. I wish the people in the future could take on the job—they could do it faster and better than I can—but some nice, peaceful quiet would help."

He didn't touch me or say a word to me as we waited for the squad to arrive. I sat in the chair and shut out first him and then the men with their sounding hammers and crowbars and all the rest.

She'd been ruthless and callous, and she'd murdered old people with no more pity than a wolf among a herd of helpless sheep.

But Blundell and Carr had told me that she was as much a victim as the oldsters who'd died of starvation with the riches she'd given them still untouched, on deposit in the banks or stuffed into hiding places or pinned to their shabby clothes. She needed treatment for the illness her father had inflicted on her. But even he, they'd said, had been suffering from a severe emotional disturbance and proper care could have made a great and honored scientist out of him.

They'd told me the truth and made me hate her, and they'd told me their viewpoint and made that hatred impossible.

I was here, in the present, without her. The machine was gone. Yearning over something I couldn't change would destroy me. I had no right to destroy myself. Nobody did, they'd told me, and nobody who reconciles himself to the fact that some situations just are impossible to work out ever could.

I'd realized that when the squad packed up and left and Lou Pape came over to where I was sitting.

"You knew we wouldn't find her," he said.

"That's what I kept telling you."

"Where is she?"

"In Port Said, exotic hellhole of the world, where she's dancing in veils for the depraved—"

"Cut out the kidding! Where is she?"

"What's the difference, Lou? She's not here, is she?"

"That doesn't mean she can't be somewhere else, dead."

"She's not dead. You don't have to believe me about anything else, just that."

He hauled me out of the chair and stared hard at my face. "You aren't lying," he said. "I know you well enough to know you're not."

"All right, then."

"But you're a damned fool to think a dish like that would have any part of you. I don't mean you're nothing a woman would go for, but she's more fang than female. You'd have to be richer and better-looking than her, for one thing -"

"Not after my friends get through with her. She'll know a good man when she sees one and I'd be what she wants." I slid my hand over my naked scalp. "With a head of hair, I'd look my real age, which happens to be a year younger than you, if you remember. She'd go for me—they checked our emotional quotients and we'd be a natural together. The only thing was that I was bald. They could have grown hair on my head, which would have taken care of that, and then we'd have gotten together like gin and tonic."

Lou arched his black eyebrows at me. "They really could grow hair on you?"

"Sure. Now you want to know why I didn't let them." I glanced out the window at the smoky city. "That's why. They couldn't tell me if I'd ever get back to the future. I wasn't taking any chances. As long as there was a possibility that I'd be stranded in my own time, I wasn't going to lose my livelihood. Which reminds me, you have anything else to do here?"

"There'll be a guard stationed around the house and all her holdings and art will be taken over until she comes back—"

"She won't."

"— or is declared legally dead."

"And me?" I broke in.

"We can't hold you without proof of murder."

"Good enough. Then let's get out of here."

"I have to go back on duty," he objected.

"Not any more. I've got over $15,000 in cash and deposits—enough to finance you and me."

"Enough to kill her for."

"Enough to finance you and me," I repeated doggedly. "I told you I had the money before she sent me into the future —"

"All right, all right," he interrupted. "Let's not go into that again. We couldn't find a body, so you're free. Now what's this about financing the two of us?"

I put my fingers around his arm and steered him out to the street.

"This city has never had a worse cop than you," I said.

"Why? Because you're an actor, not a cop. You're going back to acting, Lou. This money will keep us both going until we get a break."

He gave me the slit-eyed look he'd picked up in line of duty. "That wouldn't be a bribe, would it?"

"Call it a kind of memorial to a lot of poor, innocent old people and a sick, tormented woman."

We walked along in silence out in the clean sunshine. It was our silence; the sleek cars and burly trucks made their noise and the pedestrians added their gabble, but a good Stanislavsky actor like Lou wouldn't notice that. Neither would I, ordinarily, but I was giving him a chance to work his way through this situation.

"I won't hand you a lie, Mark," he said finally. "I never stopped wanting to act. I'll take your deal on two considerations."

"All right, what are they?"

"That whatever I take off you is strictly a loan."

"No argument. What's the other?"

He had an unlit cigarette almost to his lips. He held it there while he said: "That any time you come across a case of an old person who died of starvation with $30,000 stashed away somewhere, you turn fast to the theatrical page and not tell me or even think about it."

"I don't have to agree to that."

He lowered the cigarette, stopped and turned to me. "You mean it's no deal?"

"Not that," I said. "I mean there won't be any more of those cases. Between knowing that and both of us back acting again, I'm satisfied. You don't have to believe me. Nobody has to."

He lit up and blew out a pretty plume, fine and slow and straight, which would have televised like a million in the bank. Then he grinned. "You wouldn't want to bet on that, would you?"

"Not with a friend. I do all my sure-thing betting with bookies."

"Then make a token bet," he said. "One buck that somebody dies of starvation with a big poke within a year."

I took the bet. I took the dollar a year later.

JOURNAL NOTES
The Old Die Rich

Theme:
Newspaper reports of old people dead of malnutrition, leaving lot of cash or bank deposits or both. Amount most often mentioned, $32,000; smallest, $17,000 on wandering man found dying—something go wrong somewhere? Psychiatric explanation, senile psychosis, undoubtedly right, but no story. Ignore it, find reason that will make one.

Possibilities:
Experiments by researcher into aging process? Attempt at alien invasion? War weapon being tested? Ironic twist of buying life-force for cash? Time travel? Only last two explain the money without putting hammerlock on reader's intelligence. Buying life-force for cash would be O. Henry payoff; why waste potentially big idea on a one-punch story? That leaves time travel.

Development:
The deposits and bank notes date back as much as fifty years—time travel takes care of that. But when is payment made and how come malnutrition? If at end of service, silly gesture to pay a corpse or dying person. Must be a con, then—earning the fee is both payment in advance and training for real reason for time travel. (Also why the antagonist sends others instead of going personally; better than old line about having to operate the machine.) Malnutrition must be by-product of time travel, known and exploited deliberately by antagonist, unknown by victim. Food is the crux. Not given money of era, so can't buy food? Doesn't make sense—antagonist wouldn't risk failure that way. What happens to food? Well, it decomposes. It also doesn't exist before it exists. Explore that both ways—nothing can exist before it exists or after it decomposes. That explains the whole thing: payment in advance as basic training in time travel, service rendered, death by malnutrition conveniently shuts victims' mouths.

Editorial Comment:
The characters, excluding the female antagonist (whom I picked to

heighten the conflict), were people I knew from my youth, when I was vastly interested in the theater and inevitably encountered the Stanislavsky method. The hero's obsession with the deaths of these senile psychotics is believable and convincing, unless you've never met Stanislavskians. Given a problem of characterization, they're bulldogs; they hang on relentlessly until they have what they are seeking. The Peeping Tom incident may seem dragged in for sensationalism, but it was really meant to highlight the deadliness of the antagonist ... any woman who would grab a gun instead of a girdle is nobody to fool around with. The strongest plot points are the walking chase, the frustration of not being able to note knowledge that present-day scientists would give their corneas for, the twist on the walking chase, and the hate for what the antagonist has done being canceled out by understanding of why she did it.

One question you might ask, if you ask that kind of question, is: who does magic happen to? King's sons, yes; goatherds, and virtuous maidens, certainly; sometimes nowadays, writers, honeymooners, melancholy fellows in boarding houses, and of course Mad Scientists. That, at any rate, was the way it was up to the first issue of UNKNOWN, in March, 1939. Readers who stopped shuddering after finishing Eric Frank Russell's Sinister Barrier, the lead story, discovered a new kind of hero, or straight man, for fantasy in Greenberg the concessionaire, who learned the importance of H_2O *the hard way.*

TROUBLE WITH WATER

GREENBERG DID NOT DESERVE his surroundings. He was the first fisherman of the season, which guaranteed him a fine catch; he sat in a dry boat—one without a single leak—far out on a lake that was ruffled only enough to agitate his artificial fly. The sun was warm, the air was cool; he sat comfortably on a cushion; he had brought a hearty lunch; and two bottles of beer hung over the stern in the cold water.

Any other man would have been soaked with joy to be fishing on such a splendid day. Normally, Greenberg himself would have been ecstatic, but instead of relaxing and waiting for a nibble, he was plagued by worries.

This short, slightly gross, definitely bald, eminently respectable businessman lived a gypsy life. During the summer he lived in a hotel with kitchen privileges in Rockaway; winters he lived in a hotel with kitchen privileges in Florida, and in both places he operated concessions. For years now, rain had fallen on schedule every week end, and there had been storms and floods on Decoration Day, July 4th and Labor Day. He did not love his life, but it was a way of making a living.

He closed his eyes and groaned. If he had only had a son instead of his Rosie! Then things would have been mighty different—

For one thing, a son could run the hot dog and hamburger griddle, Esther could draw beer, and he would make soft drinks. There would be small difference in the profits, Greenberg admitted to himself; but at least those profits could be put aside for old age, instead of toward a dowry for his miserably ugly, dumpy, pitifully eager Rosie.

"All right—so what do I care if she don't get married?" he had cried to his wife a thousand times. "I'll support her. Other men can set up boys in candy stores with soda fountains that have only two spigots. Why should I have to give a boy a regular International Casino?"

"May your tongue rot in your head, you no-good piker!" she would scream. "It ain't right for a girl to be an old maid. If we have to die in the poor-house, I'll get my poor Rosie a husband. Every penny we don't need for living goes to her dowry!"

Greenberg did not hate his daughter, nor did he blame her for his misfortunes; yet, because of her, he was fishing with a broken rod that he had to tape together.

That morning his wife opened her eyes and saw him packing his equipment. She instantly came awake. "Go ahead!" she shrilled—speaking in a conversational tone was not one of her accomplishments—"Go fishing, you loafer! Leave me here alone. I can connect the beer pipes and the gas for soda water. I can buy ice cream, frankfurters, rolls, sirup, and watch the gas and electric men at the same time. Go ahead—go fishing!"

"I ordered everything," he mumbled soothingly. "The gas and electric won't be turned on today. I only wanted to go fishing—it's my last chance. Tomorrow we open the concession. Tell the truth, Esther, can I go fishing after we open?"

"I don't care about that. Am I your wife or ain't I, that you should go ordering everything without asking me—"

He defended his actions. It was a tactical mistake. While she was still in bed, he should have picked up his equipment and left. By the time the argument got around to Rosie's dowry, she stood facing him.

"For myself I don't care," she yelled. "What kind of a monster are you that you can go fishing while your daughter eats her heart out? And on a day like this yet! You should only have to make supper and dress Rosie up. A lot you care that a nice boy is coming to supper tonight and maybe take Rosie out, you no-good father, you!"

From that point it was only one hot protest and a shrill curse to find himself clutching half a broken rod, with the other half being flung at his head.

Now he sat in his beautifully dry boat on an excellent game lake far out on Long Island, desperately aware that any average fish might collapse his taped rod.

What else could he expect? He had missed his train; he had had to wait for the boathouse proprietor; his favorite dry fly was missing; and, since morning, not a fish struck at the bait. Not a single fish!

And it was getting late. He had no more patience. He ripped the cap off a bottle of beer and drank it, in order to gain courage to change his fly for a less sporting bloodworm. It hurt him, but he wanted a fish.

The hook and the squirming worm sank. Before it came to rest, he felt a nibble. He sucked in his breath exultantly and snapped the hook deep into the fish's mouth. Sometimes, he thought philosophically, they just won't take artificial bait. He reeled in slowly.

"Oh, Lord," he prayed, "a dollar for charity—just don't let the rod bend in half where I taped it!"

It was sagging dangerously. He looked at it unhappily and raised his ante to five dollars; even at that price it looked impossible. He dipped his rod into the water, parallel with the line, to remove the strain. He was glad no one could see him do it. The line reeled in without a fight.

"Have I—God forbid!—got an eel or something not kosher?" he mumbled. "A plague on you—why don't you fight?"

He did not really care what it was—even an eel—anything at all.

He pulled in a long, pointed, brimless green hat.

For a moment he glared at it. His mouth hardened. Then, viciously, he yanked the hat off the hook, threw it on the floor and trampled on it. He rubbed his hands together in anguish.

"All day I fish," he wailed, "two dollars for train fare, a dollar for a boat, a quarter for bait, a new rod I got to buy—and a five-dollar-mortgage charity has got on me. For what? For you, you hat, you!"

Our in the water an extremely civil voice asked politely: "May I have my hat, please?"

Greenberg glowered up. He saw a little man come swimming vigorously through the water toward him: small arms crossed with enormous dignity, vast ears on a pointed face propelling him quite rapidly and efficiently. With serious determination he drove through the water, and, at the starboard rail, his amazing ears kept him stationary while he looked gravely at Greenberg.

"You are stamping on my hat," he pointed out without anger.

To Greenberg this was highly unimportant. "With the ears you're swimming," he grinned in a superior way. "Do you look funny!"

"How else could I swim?" the little man asked politely.

"With the arms and legs, like a regular human being, of course."

"But I am not a human being. I am a water gnome, a relative of the more common mining gnome. I cannot swim with my arms, because they must be crossed to give an appearance of dignity suitable to a water gnome; and my feet are used for writing and holding things. On the other hand, my ears are perfectly adapted for propulsion in water. Consequently, I employ them for that purpose. But please, my hat—there are several matters requiring my immediate attention, and I must not waste time."

Greenberg's unpleasant attitude toward the remarkably civil gnome is easily understandable. He had found someone he could feel superior to, and, by insulting him, his depressed ego could expand. The water gnome certainly looked inoffensive enough, being only two feet tall.

"What you got that's so important to do, Big Ears?" he asked nastily.

Greenberg hoped the gnome would be offended. He was not, since his ears, to him, were perfectly normal, just as you would not be insulted if a member of a race of atrophied beings were to call you "Big Muscles." You might even feel flattered.

"I really must hurry," the gnome said, almost anxiously. "But if I have to answer your questions in order to get back my hat—we are engaged in restocking the Eastern waters with fish. Last year there was quite a drain. The bureau of fisheries is cooperating with us to some extent, but, of course, we cannot depend too much on them. Until the population rises to normal, every fish has instructions not to nibble."

Greenberg allowed himself a smile, an annoyingly skeptical smile.

"My main work," the gnome went on resignedly, "is control of the rainfall over the Eastern seaboard. Our fact-finding committee, which is scientifically situated in the meteorological center of the continent, coordinates the rainfall needs of the entire continent; and when they determine the amount of rain needed in particular spots of the East, I make it rain to that extent. Now may I have my hat, please?"

Greenberg laughed coarsely. "The first lie was big enough—about telling the fish not to bite. You make it rain like I'm President of the United States!" He bent toward the gnome slyly. "How's about proof?"

"Certainly, if you insist." The gnome raised his patient, triangular face toward a particularly clear blue spot in the sky, a trifle to one side of Greenberg. "Watch that bit of the sky."

Greenberg looked up humorously. Even when a small dark cloud rapidly formed in the previously clear spot, his grin remained broad. It could have been coincidental. But then large drops of undeniable rain fell over a twenty-foot circle; and Greenberg's mocking grin shrank and grew sour.

He glared hatred at the gnome, finally convinced. "So you're the dirty crook who makes it rain on week-ends!"

"Usually on week-ends during the summer," the gnome admitted. "Ninety-two percent of water consumption is on weekdays. Obviously we must replace that water. The week-ends, of course, are the logical time."

"But, you thief!" Greenberg cried hysterically, "you murderer! What do you care what you do to my concession with your rain? It ain't bad enough business would be rotten even without rain, you got to make floods!"

"I'm sorry," the gnome replied, untouched by Greenberg's rhetoric. "We do not create rainfall for the benefit of men. We are here to protect the fish.

"Now please give me my hat. I have wasted enough time, when I should be preparing the extremely heavy rain needed for this coming week-end."

Greenberg jumped to his feet in the unsteady boat. "Rain this week-end—when I can maybe make a profit for a change! A lot you care if you ruin business. May you and your fish die a horrible, lingering death."

And he furiously ripped the green hat to pieces and hurled them at the gnome.

"I'm really sorry you did that," the little fellow said calmly, his huge ears treading water without the slightest increase of pace to indicate his anger. "We Little Folk have no tempers to lose. Nevertheless, occasionally we find it necessary to discipline certain of your people, in order to retain our dignity. I am not malignant; but, since you hate water and those who live in it, water and those who live in it will keep away from you."

With his arms still folded in great dignity, the tiny water gnome flipped his vast ears and disappeared in a neat surface dive.

Greenberg glowered at the spreading circles of waves. He did not grasp the gnome's final restraining order; he did not even attempt to interpret it. Instead he glared angrily out of the corner of his eye at the phenomenal circle of rain that fell from a perfectly clear sky. The gnome must have remembered it at length, for a moment later the rain stopped. Like shutting off a faucet, Greenberg unwillingly thought.

"Good-by, week-end business," he growled. "If Esther finds out I got into an argument with the guy who makes it rain—"

He made an underhand cast, hoping for just one fish. The line flew out over the water; then the hook arched upward and came to rest several inches above the surface, hanging quite steadily and without support in the air.

"Well, go down in the water, damn you!" Greenberg said viciously, and he swished his rod back and forth to pull the hook down from its ridiculous levitation. It refused.

Muttering something incoherent about being hanged before he'd give in, Greenberg hurled his useless rod at the water. By this time he was not surprised when it hovered in the air above the lake. He merely glanced red-eyed at it, tossed out the remains of the gnome's hat, and snatched up the oars.

When he pulled back on them to row to land, they did not touch the water—naturally. Instead they flashed unimpeded through the air, and Greenberg tumbled into the bow.

"A-ha!" he grated. "Here's where the trouble begins." He bent over the side. As he had suspected, the keel floated a remarkable distance above the lake.

By rowing against the air, he moved with maddening slowness toward shore, like a medieval conception of a flying machine. His main concern was that no one should see him in his humiliating position.

At the hotel he tried to sneak past the kitchen to the bathroom. He knew that Esther waited to curse him for fishing the day before opening, but more especially on the very day that a nice boy was coming to see her Rosie. If he could dress in a hurry, she might have less to say—

"Oh, there you are, you good-for-nothing!"

He froze to a halt.

"Look at you!" she screamed shrilly. "Filthy—you stink from fish!"

"I didn't catch anything, darling," he protested timidly.

"You stink anyhow. Go take a bath, may you drown in it! Get dressed in two minutes or less, and entertain the boy when he gets here. Hurry!"

He locked himself in, happy to escape her voice, started the water in the tub, and stripped from the waist up. A hot bath, he hoped, would rid him of his depressed feeling.

First, no fish; now, rain on week-ends! What would Esther say—if she knew, of course. And, of course, he would not tell her.

"Let myself in for a lifetime of curses!" he sneered. "Ha!"

He clamped a new blade into his razor, opened the tube of shaving cream, and stared objectively at the mirror. The dominant feature of the soft, chubby face that stared back was its ugly black stubble; but he set his stubborn chin and glowered. He really looked quite fierce and indomitable. Unfortunately, Esther never saw his face in that uncharacteristic pose, otherwise she would speak more softly.

"Herman Greenberg never gives in!" he whispered between savagely hardened lips. "Rain on week-ends, no fish—anything he wants; a lot I care! Believe me, he'll come crawling to me before I go to him."

He gradually became aware that his shaving brush was not getting wet. When he looked down and saw the water dividing into streams that flowed around it, his determined face slipped and grew desperately anxious. He tried to trap the water—by catching it in his cupped hands, by creeping up on it from behind, as if it were some shy animal, and shoving his brush at it—but it broke and ran away from his touch. Then he jammed his palm against the faucet. Defeated, he heard it gurgle back down the pipe, probably as far as the main.

"What do I do now?" he groaned. "Will Esther give it to me if I don't take a shave! But how? ... I can't shave without water."

Glumly, he shut off the bath, undressed and stepped into the tub. He lay down to soak. It took a moment of horrified stupor to realize that he was completely dry and that he lay in a waterless bathtub. The water, in one surge of revulsion, had swept out onto the floor.

"Herman, stop splashing!" his wife yelled. "I just washed that floor. If I find one little puddle I'll murder you!"

Greenberg surveyed the instep-deep pool over the bathroom floor. "Yes, my love," he croaked unhappily.

With an inadequate washrag he chased the elusive water, hoping to mop it all up before it could seep through to the apartment below. His washrag remained dry, however, and he knew that the ceiling underneath was dripping. The water was still on the floor.

In despair, he sat on the edge of the bathtub. For some time he sat in silence. Then his wife banged on the door, urging him to come out. He started and dressed moodily.

When he sneaked out and shut the bathroom door tightly on the flood inside, he was extremely dirty and his face was raw where he had experimentally attempted to shave with a dry razor.

"Rosie!" he called in a hoarse whisper. "Sh! Where's mamma?"

His daughter sat on the studio couch and applied nail-polish to her stubby fingers. "You look terrible," she said in a conversational tone. "Aren't you going to shave?"

He recoiled at the sound of her voice, which, to him, roared out like a siren. "Quiet, Rosie! Sh!" And for further emphasis, he shoved his lips out against a warning finger. He heard his wife striding heavily around the kitchen. "Rosie," he cooed, "I'll give you a dollar if you'll mop up the water I spilled in the bathroom."

"I can't papa," she stated firmly. "I'm all dressed."

"Two dollars, Rosie—all right, two and a half, you blackmailer."

He flinched when he heard her gasp in the bathroom; but, when she came out with soaked shoes, he fled downstairs. He wandered aimlessly toward the village.

Now he was in for it, he thought; screams from Esther, tears from Rosie—plus a new pair of shoes for Rosie and two and a half dollars. It would be worse, though, if he could not get rid of his whiskers—

Rubbing the tender spots where his dry razor had raked his face, he mused blankly at a drugstore window. He saw nothing to help him, but he went inside anyhow and stood hopefully at the drug counter. A face peered at him through a space scratched in the wall case mirror, and the druggist came out. A nice-looking, intelligent fellow, Greenberg saw at a glance.

"What you got for shaving that I can use without water?' he asked.

"Skin irritation, eh?" the pharmacist replied. "I got something very good for that."

"No. It's just— Well, I don't like to shave with water."

The druggist seemed disappointed. "Well, I got brushless shaving cream." Then he brightened. "But I got an electric razor—much better."

"How much?" Greenberg asked cautiously.

"Only fifteen dollars, and it lasts a lifetime."

"Give me the shaving cream," Greenberg said coldly.

With the tactical science of a military expert, he walked around until some time after dark. Only then did he go back to the hotel, to wait outside. It was after seven, he was getting hungry, and the people who entered the hotel he knew as permanent summer guests. At last a stranger passed him and ran up the stairs.

Greenberg hesitated for a moment. The stranger was scarcely a boy, as Esther had definitely termed him, but Greenberg reasoned that her term was merely wish-fulfillment, and he jauntily ran up behind him.

He allowed a few minutes to pass, for the man to introduce himself and let Esther and Rosie don their company manners. Then, secure in the knowledge that there would be no scene until the guest left, he entered.

He waded through a hostile atmosphere, urbanely shook hands with Sammie Katz, who was a doctor—probably, Greenberg thought shrewdly, in search of an office—and excused himself.

In the bathroom he carefully read the direction for using brushless shaving cream. He felt less confident when he realized that he had to wash his face thoroughly with soap and water, but without benefit of either, he spread the cream on, patted it, and waited for his beard to soften. It did not, as he discovered while shaving. He wiped his face dry. The towel was sticky and black, with whiskers suspended in paste, and, for that, he knew, there would be more hell to pay. He shrugged resignedly. He would have to spend fifteen dollars for an electric razor after all; this foolishness was costing him a fortune!

That they were waiting for him before beginning supper, was, he knew, only a gesture for the sake of company. Without changing her hard, brilliant smile, Esther whispered: "Wait! I'll get you later—"

He smiled back, his tortured, slashed face creasing painfully. All that could be changed by his being enormously pleasant to Rosie's young man. If he could slip Sammie a few dollars—more expense, he groaned—to take Rosie out, Esther would forgive everything.

He was too engaged in beaming and putting Sammie at ease to think of what would happen after he ate caviar canapes. Under other circumstances Greenberg would have been repulsed by Sammie's ultra-professional waxed mustache—an offensively small, pointed thing—and his commercial attitude toward poor Rosie; but Greenberg regarded him as a potential savior.

"You open an office yet, Doctor Katz?"

"Not yet. You know how things are. Anyhow, call me Sammie."

Greenberg recognized the gambit with satisfaction, since it seemed to please Esther so much. At one stroke Sammie had ingratiated himself and begun bargaining negotiations.

Without another word, Greenberg lifted his spoon to attack the soup. It would be easy to snare this eager doctor. A doctor! No wonder Esther and Rosie were so puffed with joy.

In the proper company way, he pushed his spoon away from him. The soup spilled onto the tablecloth.

"Not so hard, you dope," Esther hissed.

He drew the spoon toward him. The soup leaped off it like a live thing and splashed over him—turning, just before contact, to fall on the floor. He gulped and pushed the bowl away. This time the soup poured over the side of the plate and lay in a huge puddle on the table.

"I didn't want any soup anyhow," he said in a horrible attempt at levity. Lucky for him, he thought wildly, that Sammie was there to pacify Esther with his smooth college talk—not a bad fellow, Sammie, in spite of his mustache; he'd come in handy at times.

Greenberg lapsed into a paralysis of fear. He was thirsty after having eaten the caviar, which beats herring any time as a thirst raiser. But the knowledge that he could not touch water without having it recoil and perhaps spill, made his thirst a monumental craving. He attacked the problem cunningly.

The others were talking rapidly and rather hysterically. He waited until his courage was equal to his thirst; then he leaned over the table with a glass in his hand. "Sammie, do you mind—a little water, huh?"

Sammie poured from a pitcher while Esther watched for more of his tricks. It was to be expected, but still he was shocked when the water exploded out of the glass directly at Sammie's only suit.

"If you'll excuse me," Sammie said angrily, "I don't like to eat with lunatics."

And he left, though Esther cried and begged him to stay. Rosie was too stunned to move. But when the door closed, Greenberg raised his agonized eyes to watch his wife stalk murderously toward him.

Greenberg stood on the boardwalk outside his concession and glared blearily at the peaceful, blue, highly unpleasant ocean. He wondered what would happen if he started at the edge of the water and strode out. He could probably walk right to Europe on dry land.

It was early—much too early for business—and he was tired. Neither he nor Esther had slept; and it was practically certain that the neighbors hadn't either. But above all he was incredibly thirsty.

In a spirit of experimentation, he mixed a soda. Of course its high water content made it slop onto the floor. For breakfast he had surreptitiously tried fruit juice and coffee, without success.

With his tongue dry to the point of furriness, he sat weakly on a boardwalk bench in front of his concession. It was Friday morning, which meant that the day was clear, with a promise of intense heat. Had it been Saturday, it naturally would have been raining.

"This year," he moaned, "I'll be wiped out. If I can't mix sodas, why should beer stay in a glass for me? I thought I could hire a boy for ten dollars a week to run the hot-dog griddle; I could make sodas, and Esther could draw beer. All I can do is make hot dogs, Esther can still draw beer; but twenty or maybe twenty-five a week I got to pay a sodaman. I won't even come out square—a fortune I'll lose!"

The situation really was desperate. Concessions depend on too many factors to be anything but capriciously profitable.

His throat was fiery and his soft brown eyes held a fierce glaze when the gas and electric were turned on, the beer pipes connected, the tank of carbon dioxide hitched to the pump, and the refrigerator started.

Gradually, the beach was filling with bathers. Greenberg writhed on his bench and envied them. They could swim and drink without having liquids draw away from them as if in horror. They were not thirsty—

And then he saw his first customers approach. His business experience was that morning customers buy only soft drinks. In a mad haste he put up the shutters and fled to the hotel.

"Esther!" he cried. "I got to tell you! I can't stand it—"

Threateningly, his wife held her broom like a baseball bat. "Go back to the concession, you crazy fool. Ain't you done enough already?'

He could not be hurt more than he had been. For once he did not cringe. "You got to help me, Esther."

"Why didn't you shave, you no-good bum? Is that any way—"

"That's what I got to tell you. Yesterday I got into an argument with a water gnome—"

"A what? Esther looked at him suspiciously.

"A water gnome," he babbled in a rush of words. "A little man so high, with big ears that he swims with, and he makes it rain—"

"Herman!" she screamed. "Stop that nonsense. You're crazy!"

Greenberg pounded his forehead with his fist. "I ain't crazy. Look, Esther. Come with me into the kitchen."

She followed him readily enough, but her attitude made him feel more helpless and alone than ever. With her fists on her plump hips and her feet set wide, she cautiously watched him try to fill a glass of water.

"Don't you see?" he wailed. "It won't go in the glass. It spills over. It runs away from me."

She was puzzled. "What happened to you?"

Brokenly, Greenberg told of his encounter with the water gnome, leaving out no single degrading detail. "And now I can't touch water," he ended. "I can't drink it. I can't make sodas. On top of it all, I got such a thirst, it's killing me."

Esther's reaction was instantaneous. She threw her arms around him, drew his head down to her shoulder, and patted him comfortingly as if he were a child. "Herman, my poor Herman!" she breathed tenderly. "What did we ever do to deserve such a curse?"

"What shall I do, Esther?" he cried helplessly.

She held him at arm's length. "You got to go to a doctor," she said firmly. "How long can you go without drinking? Without water you'll die. Maybe sometimes I am a little hard on you, but you know I love you—"

"I know, mamma," he sighed. "But how can a doctor help me?"

"Am I a doctor that I should know? Go anyhow. What can you lose?"

He hesitated. "I need fifteen dollars for an electric razor," he said in a low, weak voice.

"So?" she replied. "If you got to, you got to. Go, darling. I'll take care of the concession."

Greenberg no longer felt deserted and alone. He walked almost confidently to a doctor's office. Manfully, he explained his symptoms. The doctor listened with professional sympathy, until Greenberg reached his description of the water gnome.

Then his eyes glittered and narrowed. "I know just the thing for you, Mr. Greenberg," he interrupted. "Sit there until I come back."

Greenberg sat quietly. He even permitted himself a surge of hope. But it seemed only a moment later that he was vaguely conscious of a siren screaming toward him; and then he was overwhelmed by the doctor and two interns who pounced on him and tried to squeeze him into a bag.

He resisted, of course. He was terrified enough to punch wildly. "What are you doing to me?" he shrieked. "Don't put that thing on me!"

"Easy now," the doctor soothed. "Everything will be all right."

It was on that humiliating scene that the policeman, required by law to accompany public ambulances, appeared. "What's up?" he asked.

"Don't stand there, you fathead," an intern shouted. "This man's crazy. Help us get him into this strait jacket."

But the policeman approached indecisively. "Take it easy, Mr. Greenberg. They ain't gonna hurt you while I'm here. What's it all about?"

"Mike!" Greenberg cried, and clung to his protector's sleeve. "They think I'm crazy—"

"Of course he's crazy," the doctor stated. "He came in here with a fantastic yarn about a water gnome putting a curse on him."

"What kind of a curse, Mr. Greenberg?" Mike asked cautiously.

"I got into an argument with the water gnome who makes it rain and takes care of the fish," Greenberg blurted. "I tore up his hat. Now he won't let water touch me. I can't drink, or anything—"

The doctor nodded. "There you are. Absolutely insane."

"Shut up." For a long moment Mike stared curiously at Greenberg. Then: "Did any of you scientists think of testing him? Here, Mr. Greenberg." He poured water into a paper cup and held it out.

Greenberg moved to take it. The water backed up against the cup's far lip; when he took it in his hand, the water shot out into the air.

"Crazy, is he?" Mike asked with heavy irony. "I guess you don't know there's things like gnomes and elves. Come with me, Mr. Greenberg."

They went out together and walked toward the boardwalk. Greenberg told Mike the entire story and explained how, besides being so uncomfortable to him personally, it would ruin him financially.

"Well, doctors can't help you," Mike said at length. "What do they know about the Little Folk? And I can't say I blame you for sassing the gnome. You ain't Irish or you'd have spoke with more respect to him. Anyhow, you're thirsty. Can't you drink anything?"

"Not a thing," Greenberg said mournfully.

They entered the concession. A single glance told Greenberg that business was very quiet, but even that could not lower his feelings more than they already were. Esther clutched him as soon as she saw them.

"Well?" she asked anxiously.

Greenberg shrugged in despair. "Nothing. He thought I was crazy."

Mike stared at the bar. Memory seemed to struggle behind his reflective eyes. "Sure," he said after a long pause. "Did you try beer, Mr. Greenberg? When I was a boy my old mother told me all about elves and gnomes and the rest of the Little Folk. She knew them, all right. They don't touch alcohol, you know. Try drawing a glass of beer—"

Greenberg trudged obediently behind the bar and held a glass under the spigot. Suddenly his despondent face brightened. Beer creamed into the glass—and stayed there! Mike and Esther grinned at each other as Greenberg threw back his head and furiously drank.

"Mike!" he crowed. "I'm saved. You got to drink with me!"

"Well—" Mike protested feebly.

By late afternoon, Esther had to close the concession and take her husband and Mike to the hotel.

The following day, being Saturday, brought a flood of rain. Greenberg nursed an imposing hang-over that was constantly aggravated by his having to drink beer in order to satisfy his recurring thirst. He thought of forbidden icebags and alkaline drinks in an agony of longing.

"I can't stand it!" he groaned. "Beer for breakfast—phooey!"

"It's better than nothing," Esther said fatalistically.

"So help me, I don't know if it is. But, darling, you ain't mad at me on account of Sammie, are you?"

She smiled gently. "Poo! Talk dowry and he'll come back quick."

"That's what I thought. But what am I going to do about my curse?"

Cheerfully, Mike furled an umbrella and strode in with a little old woman, whom he introduced as his mother. Greenberg enviously saw evidence of the effectiveness of icebags and alkaline drinks, for Mike had been just as high as he the day before.

"Mike told me about you and the gnome," the old lady said. "Now I know the Little Folk well, and I don't hold you to blame for insulting him, seeing you never met a gnome before. But I suppose you want to get rid of your curse. Are you repentant?"

Greenberg shuddered. "Beer for breakfast! Can you ask?"

"Well, just you go to this lake and give the gnome proof."

"What kind of proof?" Greenberg asked eagerly.

"Bring him sugar. The Little Folk love the stuff—"

Greenberg beamed. "Did you hear that, Esther? I'll get a barrel—"

"They love sugar, but they can't eat it," the old lady broke in. "It melts in water. You got to figure out a way so it won't. Then the little gentleman'll know you're repentant for real."

"A-ha!" Greenberg cried. "I knew there was a catch!"

There was a sympathetic silence while his agitated mind attacked the problem from all angles. Then the old lady said in awe: "The minute I saw your place I knew Mike had told the truth. I never seen a sight like it in my life—rain coming down, like the flood, everywhere else; but all around this place, in a big circle, it's dry as a bone!"

While Greenberg scarcely heard her, Mike nodded and Esther seemed peculiarly interested in the phenomenon. When he admitted defeat and came out of his reflected stupor, he was alone in the concession, with only a vague memory of Esther's saying she would not be back for several hours.

"What am I going to do?" he muttered. "Sugar that won't melt—" He drew a glass of beer and drank it thoughtfully. "Particular they got to be yet. Ain't it good enough if I bring simple sirup—that's sweet."

He pottered about the place, looking for something to do. He could not polish the fountain on the bar, and the few frankfurters boiling on the griddle probably would go to waste. The floor had already been swept. So he sat uneasily and worried his problem.

"Monday, no matter what," he resolved, "I go to the lake. It don't pay to go tomorrow. I'll only catch a cold because it'll rain."

At last Esther returned, smiling in a strange way. She was extremely gentle, tender and thoughtful; and for that he was appreciative. But that night and all day Sunday he understood the reason for her happiness.

She had spread word that, while it rained in every other place all over town, their concession was miraculously dry. So, besides a headache that made his body throb in rhythm to its vast pulse, Greenberg had to work like six men satisfying the crowd who mobbed the place to see the miracle and enjoy the dry warmth.

How much they took in will never be known. Greenberg made it a practice not to discuss such personal matters. But it is quite definite that not even in 1929 had he done so well over a single week-end.

Very early Monday morning he was dressing quietly, not to disturb his wife. Esther, however, raised herself on her elbow and looked at him doubtfully.

"Herman," she called softly, "do you really have to go?"

He turned, puzzled. "What do you mean—do I have to go?"

"Well—" She hesitated. Then: "Couldn't you wait until the end of the season, Herman, darling?"

He staggered back a step, his face working in horror. "What kind of an idea is that for my own wife to have?" he croaked. "Beer I have to drink instead of water. How can I stand it? Do you think I like beer? I can't wash myself. Already people don't like to stand near me; and how will they act at the end of the season? I go around looking like a bum because my beard is too tough for an electric razor, and I'm all the time drunk—the first Greenberg to be a drunkard. I want to be respected—"

"I know, Herman, darling," she sighed. "But I thought for the sake of our Rosie— Such a business we've never done like we did this week-end. If it rains every Saturday and Sunday, but not on our concession, we'll make a fortune!"

"Esther!" Herman cried, shocked. "Doesn't my health mean anything?"

"Of course, darling. Only I thought maybe you could stand it for—"

He snatched his hat, tie and jacket, and slammed the door. Outside, though, he stood indeterminedly. He could hear his wife crying, and he realized that, if he succeeded in getting the gnome to remove the curse, he would forfeit an opportunity to make a great deal of money.

He finished dressing more slowly. Esther was right, to a certain extent. If he could tolerate his waterless condition—

"No!" he gritted decisively. "Already my friends avoid me. It isn't right that a respectable man like me should always be drunk and not take a bath. So we'll make less money. Money isn't everything—"

And with great determination he went to the lake.

But that evening, before going home, Mike walked out of his way to stop in at the concession. He found Greenberg sitting on a chair, his head in his hands, and his body rocking slowly in anguish.

"What is it, Mr. Greenberg?" he asked gently.

Greenberg looked up. His eyes were dazed. "Oh, you, Mike," he said blankly. Then his gaze cleared, grew more intelligent, and he stood up and led Mike to the bar. Silently, they drank beer. "I went to the lake today," he said hollowly. "I walked all around it hollering like mad. The gnome didn't stick his head out of the water once."

"I know," Mike nodded sadly. "They're busy all the time."

Greenberg spread his hands imploringly. "So what can I do? I can't write him a letter or send him a telegram; he ain't got a door to knock on or a bell for me to ring. How do I get him to come up and talk?"

His shoulders sagged. "Here, Mike. Have a cigar. You been a real good friend, but I guess we're licked."

They stood in an awkward silence. Finally Mike blurted: "Real hot, today. A regular scorcher."

"Yeah. Esther says business was pretty good, if it keeps up."

Mike fumbled at the Cellophane wrapper. Greenberg said: "Anyhow, suppose I did talk to the gnome. What about the sugar?"

The silence dragged itself out, became tense and uncomfortable. Mike was distinctly embarrassed. His brusque nature was not adapted for comforting discouraged friends. With immense concentration he rolled the cigar between his fingers and listened for a rustle.

"Day like this's hell on cigars," he mumbled, for the sake of conversation. "Dries them like nobody's business. This one ain't, though."

"Yeah," Greenberg said abstractedly. "Cellophane keeps them—"

They looked suddenly at each other, their faces clean of expression.

"Holy smoke!" Mike yelled.

"Cellophane on sugar!" Greenberg choked out.

"Yeah," Mike whispered in awe. "I'll switch my day off with Joe, and I'll go to the lake with you tomorrow. I'll call for you early."

Greenberg pressed his hand, too strangled by emotion for speech. When Esther came to relieve him, he left her at the concession with only the inexperienced griddle boy to assist her, while he searched the village for cubes of sugar wrapped in Cellophane.

The sun had scarcely risen when Mike reached the hotel, but Greenberg had long been dressed and stood on the porch waiting impatiently. Mike was genuinely anxious for his friend. Greenberg staggered along toward the station, his eyes almost crossed with the pain of a terrific hang-over.

They stopped at a cafeteria for breakfast. Mike ordered orange juice, bacon and eggs, and coffee half-and-half. When he heard the order, Greenberg had to gag down a lump in his throat.

"What'll you have?" the counterman asked.

Greenberg flushed. "Beer," he said hoarsely.

"You kidding me?" Greenberg shook his head, unable to speak. "Want anything with it? Cereal, pie, toast—"

"Just beer." And he forced himself to swallow it. "So help me," he hissed at Mike, "another beer for breakfast will kill me!"

"I know how it is," Mike said around a mouthful of food.

On the train they attempted to make plans. But they were faced by a phenomenon that neither had encountered before, and so they got nowhere. They walked glumly to the lake, fully aware that they would have to employ the empirical method of discarding tactics that did not work.

"How about a boat?" Mike suggested.

"It won't stay in the water with me in it. And you can't row it."

"Well, what'll we do then?"

Greenberg bit his lip and stared at the beautiful blue lake. There the gnome lived, so near to them. "Go through the woods along the shore, and holler like hell. I'll go the opposite way. We'll pass each other and meet at the boathouse. If the gnome comes up, yell for me."

"O.K.," Mike said, not very confidently.

The lake was quite large and they walked slowly around it, pausing often to get the proper stance for particularly emphatic shouts. But two hours later, when they stood opposite each other with the full diameter of the lake between them, Greenberg heard Mike's hoarse voice: "Hey, gnome!"

"Hey, gnome!" Greenberg yelled. "Come on up!"

An hour later they crossed paths. They were tired, discouraged, and their throats burned; and only fishermen disturbed the lake's surface.

"The hell with this," Mike said. "It ain't doing any good. Let's go back to the boathouse."

"What'll we do?" Greenberg rasped. "I can't give up!"

They trudged back around the lake, shouting half-heartedly. At the boathouse, Greenberg had to admit that he was beaten. The boathouse owner marched threateningly toward him.

"Why don't you maniacs get away from here?" he barked. "What's the idea of hollering and scaring away the fish? The guys are sore—"

"We're not going to holler any more," Greenberg said. "It's no use."

When they bought beer and Mike, on an impulse, hired a boat, the owner cooled off with amazing rapidity, and went off to unpack bait.

"What did you get a boat for?" Greenberg asked. "I can't ride in it."

"You're not going to. You're gonna walk."

"Around the lake again?" Greenberg cried.

"Nope. Look, Mr. Greenberg. Maybe the gnome can't hear us through all that water. Gnomes ain't hardhearted. If he heard us and thought you were sorry, he'd take his curse off you in a jiffy."

"Maybe." Greenberg was not convinced. "So where do I come in?"

"The way I figure it, some way or other you push water away, but the water pushes you away just as hard. Anyhow, I hope so. If it does, you can walk on the lake." As he spoke, Mike had been lifting large stones and dumping them on the bottom of the boat. "Give me a hand with these."

Any activity, however useless, was better than none, Greenberg felt. He helped Mike fill the boat until just the gunwales were above water. Then Mike got in and shoved off.

"Come on," Mike said. "Try to walk on the water."

Greenberg hesitated. "Suppose I can't?"

"Nothing'll happen to you. You can't get wet; so you won't drown."

The logic of Mike's statement reassured Greenberg. He stepped out boldly. He experienced a peculiar sense of accomplishment when the water hastily retreated under his feet into pressure bowls, and an unseen, powerful force buoyed him upright across the lake's surface. Though his footing was not too secure, with care he was able to walk quite swiftly.

"Now what?" he asked, almost happily.

Mike had kept pace with him in the boat. He shipped his oars and passed Greenberg a rock. "We'll drop them all over the lake—make it damned noisy down there and upset the place. That'll get him up."

They were more hopeful now, and their comments, "Here's one that'll wake him," and "I'll hit him right on the noodle with this one," served to cheer them still further. And less than half the rocks had been dropped when Greenberg halted, a boulder in his hands. Something inside him wrapped itself tightly around his heart and his jaw dropped.

Mike followed his awed, joyful gaze. To himself, Mike had to admit that the gnome, propelling himself through the water with his ears, arms folded in tremendous dignity, was a funny sight.

"Must you drop rocks and disturb us at our work?" the gnome asked.

Greenberg gulped. "I'm sorry, Mr. Gnome," he said nervously. "I couldn't get you to come up by yelling."

The gnome looked at him. "Oh. You are the mortal who was disciplined. Why did you return?"

"To tell you that I'm sorry, and I won't insult you again."

"Have you proof of your sincerity?" the gnome asked quietly.

Greenberg fished furiously in his pocket and brought out a handful of sugar wrapped in Cellophane, which he tremblingly handed to the gnome.

"Ah, very clever, indeed," the little man said, unwrapping a cube and popping it eagerly into his mouth. "Long time since I've had some."

A moment later Greenberg spluttered and floundered under the surface. Even if Mike had not caught his jacket and helped him up, he could almost have enjoyed the sensation of being able to drown.

Journal Notes
Trouble with Water

Theme:
Walking in dismal rain toward editorial conference, me without an idea in my head ... worried sub-vocalization sticks in groove of old song about walking between raindrops. Feeling of elation—how about a man whom water won't touch?

Possibilities:
Just one—experiment goes blooey; inverted ionization ought to account more or less reasonably for the phenomenon. Editor John Campbell vetoes, unbelievably wants a pure fantasy with maybe a water gnome to put a curse on the protagonist. Good reason needed, but that's my job, not his. (It should have been a water sprite, but neither of us discovered that till later.) Now why would he want pure fantasy when he's putting out a science fiction magazine? Who knows? That's his business, not mine. All right, a supernatural curse. But why, and how is it gotten rid of?

Development:
The two big problems are finding someone to whom the curse would be a real disaster instead of an inconvenience, and using that to goad him into forcing the water gnome to put the curse on him. Water-supply engineer? Obvious and dull. Sea captain? Equally obvious and a ranting nuisance. Avoid obviousness and use frustration of a quietly desperate sort rather than rage; if possible, throw in a gain of some kind that will give the curse a backhanded advantage as well as the overt disadvantage. The gnome controls rainfall, makes it pour on weekends because water consumption is greatest during the week—the latter true, the former seemingly true. Who would be angriest at that arrangement? A boardwalk concessionaire, of course; he depends on week-end business and would also be furiously helpless if he couldn't touch water. Give him a family, including ugly daughter who needs dowry, to emphasize his financial problem. Gimmick needed to remove curse, but not too hard to find—something soluble in water that gnomes yearn for (sugar?) and wrap it in cellophane.

Certainly sugar. Advantage is that protagonist's concession, being the only dry one on the boardwalk, is making money for a change. He's begged to live with the curse for a while, but can't because of thirst and non-bathing and non-shaving. (The Little People don't touch alcohol, so he can drink beer, which makes his degradation even worse.)

Editorial Comments:
The story was written with love for the people involved, including the nagging wife whose ill-temper is really a form of affection, and the daughter and cop—though I'm afraid he comes a bit close to vaudeville caricature. When I learned that the story was considered a howler, I was aghast and outraged. But it taught me a powerful lesson—really good humor is based on tragedy. If it isn't, the result is comedy, which isn't the same thing by several light-years. Comedy is a manufactured product; humor grows, nourished by love, compassion and admiration, which is why I have a special affection for this story.

NO CHARGE FOR ALTERATIONS

IF THERE WAS ONE THING Dr. Kalmar hated, and there were many, it was having a new assistant fresh from a medical school on Earth. They always wanted to change things. They never realized that a planet develops its own techniques to meet its own requirements, which are seldom similar to those of any other world. Dr. Kalmar never got along with his assistants and he didn't expect to get along with this young Dr. Hoyt who was coming in on the transfer ship from Vega.

Dr. Kalmar had been trained on Earth himself, of course, but he wistfully remembered how he had revered Dr. Lowell when he had been Lowell's assistant. He'd known that his own green learning was no match for Dr. Lowell's wisdom and experience after thirty years on Deneb, and he had avidly accepted his lessons.

Why, he grumbled to himself on his way to the spaceport to meet the unknown whippersnapper, why didn't Earth turn out young doctors the way it used to? They ought to have the arrogance knocked out of them before they left medical school. That's what must have happened to him, because his attitude had certainly been humble when he landed.

The spaceport was jammed, naturally. Ship arrivals were infrequent enough to bring everybody from all over the planet who was not on duty at the farms, mines, factories, freight and passenger jets and all the rest of the busy activities of this comparatively new colony. They brought their lunches and families and stood around to watch. Dr. Kalmar went to the platform.

The ship sat down on a mushroom of fire that swiftly became a flaming pancake and then was squashed out of existence.

"I'm waiting for a shipment of livestock," enthused the man standing next to Dr. Kalmar.

"You're lucky," the doctor said. "They can't talk back."

The man looked at him sympathetically. "Meeting a female?"

"Gabbier and more annoying," said Dr. Kalmar, but he didn't elaborate and the man, with the courtesy of the frontier, did not pry for an explanation.

Livestock and freight came down on one elevator and passengers came down another. Slidewalks carried the cargo to Sterilization and travelers to the greeting platform. Dr. Kalmar felt his shoulders droop. The man with the medical bag had to be Dr. Hoyt and he was even more brisk, erect and muscular than Dr. Kalmar had expected, with a superior and inquisitive look that made the last assistant, unbearable as he'd been, seem as tractable as one of the arriving cows.

Dr. Hoyt spotted him instantly and came striding over to grab his hand in a grip like an ore-crusher. "You're Dr. Kalmar. Glad to know you. I'm sure we'll get along fine together. Miserable trip. Had to change ships four times to get here. Hope the food's better than shipboard slop. Got a nice hospital to work in? Do I live in or not?"

Dr. Kalmar was grudgingly forced to say rapidly, "Right. Likewise. I hope so. Too bad. Suits us. I think so. In."

He got Dr. Hoyt into a jetcab and told the driver to make time back to the hospital. Appointments were piling up while he had to make the courtesy trip out to the spaceport, which was another nuisance. Now he'd have all of those and a talkative assistant who'd want to know the reasons for everything.

"Pretty barren," said Dr. Hoyt, looking out the window at the vegetationless ground below. "Why's that?"

He'd known he was going to Deneb, Dr. Kalmar thought angrily. The least he could have done was read up on the place. *He* had.

"It's an Earth-type planet," Dr. Kalmar said in a blunt voice, "except that life never developed on it. We had to bring everything—benign germ cultures, seed, animals, fish, insects—a whole ecology. Our farms are close to the cities. Too wasteful of freight to move them out very far. Another few centuries and we'll have a *real* population, millions of people instead of the 20,000 we have now in a couple of dozen settlements around this world. Then we'll have the whole place a nice shade of green."

"City boy myself," said Dr. Hoyt. "Hate the country. Hydroponics and synthetic meat—that's the answer."

"For Earth. It'll be a long time before we get that crowded here on Deneb."

"Deneb," the young doctor repeated, dissatisfied. "That's the name of the star. You mean to tell me the planet has the same name?"

"Most solar systems have only one Earth-type planet. It saves a lot of trouble to just call that planet Deneb, Vega or whatever."

"Is *that* clutch of shacks the *city*?" exclaimed Dr. Hoyt.

"Denebia," said Dr. Kalmar, beginning to enjoy himself finally.

"Why, you could lose it in a suburb of Bosyorkdelphia!"

"That monstrosity that used to be New York, Pennsylvania,

Connecticut, Rhode Island and Massachusetts? I wouldn't want to."

He was pleased when Dr. Hoyt sank into stunned silence. If luck was with him, that stupefaction might last the whole day. It seemed as though it might, for the sight of the modest little hospital was too much for the youngster who had just come from the mammoth health factories of Earth.

Dr. Hoyt revived somewhat when he saw the patients waiting in the scantily furnished outer room, but Dr. Kalmar said, "Better get yourself settled," and opened a door for his immature colleague.

"But there's only one bed in this room," Dr. Hoyt objected. "You must have made a mistake."

Dr. Kalmar, recalling the crowded cubicles of Earth, gave out a proud little dry laugh. "You're on Deneb now, boy. Here you'll have to get used to spaciousness. We like elbow room."

The young doctor went in hesitantly, leaving the door open for a fast escape in case an error had been made. Dr. Kalmar had done the same when he'd arrived nine years ago. Judging by his own experience, it would take Dr. Hoyt a full six months to get used to having a room all to himself. There would be plenty of time to start showing him the ropes tomorrow, and in the meantime there were the backed-up appointments to be taken care of.

Dr. Kalmar went to his office and had his nurse, Miss Dupont, send in the first patient.

It was a girl of seventeen, Avis Emery, who had been brought by her parents. She sat sullenly, dark-haired, too daintily pretty and delicately shapely for a frontier world like this, while Mr. Emery put the file from Social Control on the doctor's desk.

"We're farmers—" the man began.

Dr. Kalmar interrupted, "The information is in the summary. Avis is to be assigned her mate next year, but she wants to go to Earth and become a nightclub singer. She refuses to marry a boy who'd be able to help around the farm, and she won't work on it herself."

He looked up severely at the parents. "This is your own fault, you know. You pampered her. Farm labor is too valuable for pampering. We can't afford it."

"You can blame me, Doc," said Mr. Emery miserably. "She's such a pretty little thing—I couldn't work her the way Sue and I work ourselves."

"And then she started getting notions," Mrs. Emery added, giving her husband a vicious glare. Dr. Kalmar could imagine the nights of argument and accusation before they were at last forced to go for medical help to solve their self-created problem. "Singing in nightclubs back on Earth, marrying a billionaire, living in a sky yacht!"

"Avis," said Dr. Kalmar gently. "You know it's not that easy, don't you? There are lots and lots of pretty girls on Earth and very few billionaires. If you did get a job singing in a nightclub, you know you'd have to do some unpleasant things because there's so much competition for customers. Things like strip-teasing, drinking at the tables and going out with whoever the owner tells you to."

The girl's face grew animated for the first time. "Well, sure! Why do you think I want to go?"

"And you don't love Deneb and your farm?"

"I hate both of them!"

"But you realize that we must have food. Doesn't it make you feel important to grow more food so we can increase our population?"

"No! Why should I care? I want to go to Earth!"

Dr. Kalmar shook his head regretfully. He pushed a button on his desk. It was connected to a gravity generator directly under the girl's chair. Four gravities suddenly pushed her down into it and a hypodermic needle jabbed her swiftly with a hypnotic drug. She slumped. He released the button and the artificial gravity abated, but she remained dazed and relaxed.

"You're not going to hurt her, are you, Doc?" Mr. Emery begged.

"Certainly not. But I suppose you know Social Control's orders."

They nodded, the husband gloomily, the wife with a single sharp jerk of her head.

"You go right ahead and do it," she said. "I'm sick of working my fingers to the bone while she primps and preens and talks all the time about going to Earth."

"Come, Avis," Dr. Kalmar said in a low, commanding voice.

She stood up, blank-faced, and followed him out to the Ego Alter room. He closed the door, sat her down in the insulated seat next to the control console, put the wired plastic helmet on her and adjusted it to fit her skull snugly.

Running his finger down the treatment sheet of her Social Control file, he set the dials according to its instructions. The psychic areas to be reduced were sex drive, competitiveness and imagination, while the areas of reproductive urge and cooperation were to be intensified. He regulated the individual timers and sent the varying charge through her brain.

There was no reaction, no convulsion, no distortion of features. She sat there as if nothing had happened, but her personality had changed as completely as though she had been retrained from birth.

Miss Dupont came in without knocking. She knew, of course,

that any patient in the Ego Alter room would be incapable of being disturbed.

"Rephysical, Dr. Kalmar?" she asked.

"I'm afraid so. Will you prepare her, please?"

The nurse removed the girl's clothes. There was no resistance.

"Such a lovely body," she said. "It's a shame."

He shrugged. "Until we have enough people and farms and industries, Miss Dupont, we'll just have to get used to altering people to fit the needs of our society. I'm sure you understand that."

"Yes, but it still seems a shame. Bodies like that don't grow on trees."

He gently moved the girl into the Rephysical Chamber. "They grow in this machine, though. As soon as we can afford it, which ought to be only a few hundred years from now, we can make any woman look like this, or even better."

"And don't forget the men," Miss Dupont said as he started the mitogenetic generator. "We could use some Adonises around here."

"We'll have them," he assured her.

"Somebody will. None of us'll live that long."

Working like a sculptor with a cathode in one hand and an anode in the other, Dr. Kalmar began reshaping the girl who stood fixedly in the boxlike chamber. The flesh fled from the cathode and chased after the anode as he broadened the fine nose, thickened the mobile lips, squared the slender jaw and drew out carefully the delicately arched orbital ridges.

"I'll leave the curl in her hair," he said. "Every woman needs at least one feature she can be proud of."

"You're telling me," Miss Dupont replied.

"Synthetic tissue, please."

She drew out a tube with a variable nozzle and started working just ahead of him. A spray of high-velocity cells shot through the girl's smooth skin at the neck, shoulders, breasts, hips and legs, forming shapeless lumps that he guided into cords and muscles. The slim figure quickly broadened, grew brawny and competent-looking, the body of a woman who could breed phenomenally while farming alongside her man.

Dr. Kalmar racked up the instruments and helped Miss Dupont dress the girl in coveralls and sandals. He felt the pride of craftsmanship when he found that the clothing supplied for her by Social Control exactly fitted her. He injected an antidote to the hypnotic and gave her the standard test for emotional response as her expressionless face cleared to placidity.

"Do you know where you are, Avis?"

"Yes. Ego Alter and Rephysical."

"What have we done to you?"

"Changed me to fit my environment."

"Do you resent being changed?"

"No." She paused and looked worried. "Who's taking care of the crops while I'm here?"

"They can wait till you and your parents get back, Avis. Let's show them the change, shall we?"

"All right," she said. "I think they'll be proud of me. This is how they always wanted me to be."

"And you?"

"Oh, I feel much better. As if I don't have to try so hard."

"I'm glad, Avis. Miss Dupont, better have a sedative ready when her father sees her. I think he'll need it."

"And her mother?" asked the nurse practically.

"She'll probably want a drink to celebrate. Give her one."

Dr. Kalmar's prognosis was correct, only it didn't go far enough. His young assistant from Earth had come scooting out of his disquietingly large quarters and was jittering in the office when they entered.

"Is *that* the pretty girl who was waiting when we came in?" he yelped in outrage. "What have you done to her?"

Dr. Kalmar gave the sedative to him instead of Mr. Emery, who was shocked, but had known in advance what to expect. Miss Dupont prepared another sedative quickly, gave Mrs. Emery a celebration drink and moved the family toward the door.

"She looks fine, Doctor," the mother said happily. "Avis ought to be a big help around the house and farm from now on."

"I'm sure she will," he said.

"But she was so lovely!" wept Mr. Emery, though in a rapidly becalming voice as the sedative took effect.

The door closed behind them.

"You ought to be reported to the Medical Association back on Earth!" Dr. Hoyt said angrily. "Ruining a girl's looks like that!"

Dr. Kalmar sighed. He had hoped to be able to put off this orientation lecture until the following day, when there wouldn't be so many patients jamming his appointment book.

"All right, let's get it over with. First, I was also trained on Earth and know how Ego Alter and Rephysical are used there: Ego Alter to remove psychic blocks so people can compete better, and Rephysical so they'll be more attractive. Second, we're not under the jurisdiction of Earth's Medical Association. Third, we'd damn well better not be, because our problems and solutions aren't the same at all."

"You'd have been jailed for spoiling that girl's chances of a good marriage!"

"I didn't," Dr. Kalmar said quietly. "I improved them."

"You did nothing of the—" Dr. Hoyt stopped. "Improved? How?"

"I keep telling you this is a frontier world and you keep acting as if you understand, but you don't. Look, a family is an economic liability on Earth; it consumes without producing. That's why girls have so much trouble finding husbands there. Out here it's different. A family is an asset—if every member in it is willing to work."

"But a pretty girl like that can always get by."

"No Denebian can afford to marry a pretty girl. It's too risky. She can't work as hard as we do and still take care of her looks. And he'd worry about her constantly, which would cut into his efficiency. By having me make her a merely attractive girl in a wholesome, hearty way, Social Control guarantees more than just a marriage for her—it guarantees a contented married life."

"Sweating away on a farm," Dr. Hoyt said.

"Now that her anti-social strivings are gone, she'll realize that Deneb needs farmers instead of nightclub singers. She'll take pride in being a good worker, she'll raise as many children as she'll be capable of bearing, and she'll have a good husband and a prosperous farm. That wouldn't have satisfied her before. It will now. And she's better for it and so is Deneb."

Dr. Hoyt shook his head. "It's all upside down."

"You'll get used to it. Why not take today off and explore Denebia? You need a rest after all those months in space."

"Maybe I will," said Dr. Hoyt vaguely, slightly anesthetized.

"Good." Dr. Kalmar buzzed for Miss Dupont. "Send in the next patient, please. Oh, and Dr. Hoyt is taking the day off."

But the young assistant was stunned into staying by the huge size of the Social Control file that was carried by the next patient, Mr. Fallon, and his wife.

"I know just what you're thinking, Dr. Kalmar!" cried Mrs. Fallon distractedly, but with a nervously bright smile. "Those awful Fallons again! I don't blame you a bit, but—"

As a matter of fact, that was exactly what Dr. Kalmar was thinking, plus the defeated feeling that they were all he needed to make the day complete.

"Good Lord, what's in all those files?" Dr. Hoyt exclaimed.

Dr. Kalmar could have explained, but he didn't feel up to it.

Mr. Fallon, a wispy, shyly affable, poetic-looking chap, did it for him. "Papers," he said.

"I know that, but why so many?" Dr. Hoyt asked impatiently.

Miss Dupont seemed wryly amused as she watched his consternation.

"I guess you might say it's because I can't make my mind up," confessed Mrs. Fallon with an uneasy giggle. She was a big woman who might have gurgled over a collection of toy dogs on Earth, but here she was a freight checker and her husband was a statistician in the Department of Supply, though on Earth he might have been anything from a composer to a social worker. "No matter how often we rephysical Harry, I always get tired of his looks in a few months."

"And how often has that been done?" Dr. Hoyt demanded.

"I think it's eleven times. Isn't that right, dear?"

"No, sweet," said Mr. Fallon. "Thirteen."

Dr. Kalmar could have interrupted, but he considered it wiser to let his assistant learn the hard way. Miss Dupont was enjoying it too much to interfere.

"We've made him tall and we've made him short, skinny, fat, bulging with muscle, red hair, black hair, blond hair, gray hair—I don't know, just about everything in the book," said Mrs. Fallon, "and I simply can't seem to find one I'd like for keeps."

"Then why the devil don't you get another husband?"

Mrs. Fallon looked shocked. "Why, he was assigned to me!"

"Dr. Hoyt just came from Earth," Dr. Kalmar cut in at last, before a brawl could start. "He's not familiar with our methods."

"Let's hear the cockeyed reason," Dr. Hoyt said resignedly.

"We keep our population balanced," said Dr. Kalmar. "Too many of either sex creates tension, hostility, loss of efficiency; look at Earth if you want proof. We can't risk even a little of that, so we use prenatal sex control to keep them nearly equal."

"There's a wife for every man," Mr. Fallon put in genially, "and a husband for every woman. Works out fine."

"With no surplus," Dr. Kalmar added. "There are no floaters to allow the kind of marital moving day you have on Earth, where so many just up and shift over to new mates. We get ours for life. That's where Ego Alter and Rephysical come in."

"You mean people bring in their mates to have them done over?"

"If they're not satisfied and if the mates agree to be changed."

"I don't mind," said Mr. Fallon virtuously. "I figure Mabel will decide what she wants one of these changes, and then we can settle down and be happy with each other."

"But what about you?" asked Dr. Hoyt, bewildered. "Don't you want her changed?"

"Oh, no. I like her fine just as she is."

"You see now how it works?" Dr. Kalmar asked. "We can't have a variety of mates, but we can have all the variety we want in one mate. It comes to the same thing, as far as I can see, and causes much less confusion, especially since we need stable relationships."

Dr. Hoyt was striving heroically to stay indignant in spite of the sedative. "And do many ask to have their mates changed?"

"I guess we're a sort of record, aren't we?" Mr. Fallon boasted.

"I guess you are," agreed Dr. Kalmar. "And now, Dr. Hoyt, if there aren't any more questions, I'd like to proceed with this couple."

Dr. Hoyt stretched his eyes wide to keep them open. "It's all screwy to me, but it's none of my business. As soon as I finish my internship, I'm heading back to Earth, where things make sense, so I don't have to understand this mishmash you call a planet. Need help?"

"If you'd find out what Mrs. Fallon has in mind this time, it would let me run the patients through a lot faster."

"How would they feel about it?" Dr. Hoyt asked.

"It's all right with me," Mr. Fallon said amiably. "I'm pretty used to this, you know."

"But what are we going to make you look like, Harry?" his wife fretted. "I felt very jealous of other women when you were handsome and I didn't like you just ordinary-looking."

"Why not go through the model book with Dr. Hoyt?" suggested Dr. Kalmar. "There are still some types you haven't tried."

"There *are*?" she asked in gratified astonishment. "Would you mind very much, Dr. Hoyt?"

"Glad to," he said.

Miss Dupont brought out the model book for him, and he and Mrs. Fallon studied the facial and physical types that were very explicitly illustrated there in three-dimensional full color. Mr. Fallon, contentedly working out math problems on a sheet of paper, left the choice entirely to her.

Meanwhile, Dr. Kalmar and Miss Dupont swiftly took care of a succession of other patients, raising the tolerance level of frustration in a watchmaker, replating the acne-pitted skin of a sensitive youth, restoring a finger lost in a machine-shop accident, and building up good-natured aggression in an ore miner whose productivity had slumped.

Mrs. Fallon still hadn't decided when the last patient had been taken care of. She said unhappily, "I don't know. I simply absolutely don't know. Couldn't you suggest *something*, Dr. Hoyt?"

"Wouldn't be ethical," he told her bluntly. "Not allowed to."

Dr. Kalmar, checking the Social Control papers with Miss Dupont, wondered if he should interfere. It would lower confidence in Dr. Hoyt, which meant that people would insist on Dr. Kalmar's treating them. Then, instead of having an assistant to remove some of the load, he'd have to do the work of two men. He decided to let the young doctor handle it.

But Dr. Hoyt stood up in exasperation, slammed the book shut, and said, "Mrs. Fallon, if you know what you want, I'll be glad to oblige. But I'm not a telepath—"

"Is there anything I can do?" Dr. Kalmar interrupted quickly, before his assistant could create any more damage.

"He doesn't have to get huffy," Mrs. Fallon said indignantly. "All I asked for was a suggestion or two."

"Insult my wife, will he?" Mr. Fallon belligerently added.

"It's my fault," Dr. Kalmar said. "Dr. Hoyt just got in today from Earth and he's tired and he naturally doesn't understand all our ways yet—"

"*Yet*?" Dr. Hoyt repeated in disgust. "What makes you think I'll ever—"

"And I shouldn't have burdened him with this problem until he's had a chance to rest up and look around," Dr. Kalmar continued in a slightly louder voice. "Now, let's see if we can't settle this problem before closing time, eh?"

The Fallons subsided, Dr. Hoyt watched with a sarcastic eye, though he kept silent as Dr. Kalmar and Miss Dupont, working as a shrewd team, gave them the suggestion they had been looking for. It was all done very smoothly, so smoothly that Dr. Kalmar felt professional pride because even his stiff-necked assistant was unable to detect the fact that it was a suggestion.

Dr. Kalmar got Mrs. Fallon to reminisce about the alterations her husband had undergone, and Miss Dupont promptly agreed with her when she explained why each had been unsatisfactory. It took some time, but he eventually brought her back to what Mr. Fallon had looked like when she'd first married him.

"Now, isn't that the strangest thing?" she said, puzzled. "I can't remember. Can you, dear?"

"It's a little mixed up," Mr. Fallon admitted. "Let's see, I know I was taller and I think I had a long, thin face—"

"Oh, we don't have to guess," Dr. Kalmar said. "Nurse, we have the information on file, don't we?"

"Yes, Doctor," she said, and instantly produced a photograph. They evidently thought it was merely filing efficiency; they hadn't noticed her searching for the picture quietly while Dr. Kalmar had been leading them on. He had, in fact, delayed asking her until she'd nodded to indicate that she had found it.

Mr. Fallon frowned as if he'd recognized the face but couldn't remember the name. His wife gave a little shriek of admiration.

"Why, Harry, you looked perfectly wonderful!"

"Those deep dimples made shaving pretty hard," he recalled.

"But they're *darling*! Why did you ever let me change you?"

"Because I wanted you to be happy, sweet."

It was as simple as that—a bit of practical psychology based on knowledge of the patients. Dr. Kalmar wished wistfully that old Dr. Lowell had been there to observe. He would have approved, which might have made up for Dr. Hoyt's unpleasant expression.

"I hope this is the one you want," Dr. Kalmar said as he took them to the front door after the rephysical.

"Goodness, I hope so!" Mrs. Fallon exclaimed. She looked fondly at her husband, and this time had to look up to see his face. "I'm almost *positive* this is what I want Harry to be."

"Well, if it isn't, sweet," Mr. Fallon said, "we'll try something else. I don't mind as long as it makes you happy."

They closed the door behind them, leaving the hospital empty of all but the small staff.

"They're crazy!" Dr. Hoyt exploded. "He's not the one we should be changing. That idiotic female needs a good Ego Alter!"

"He hasn't asked for it," Dr. Kalmar pointed out patiently.

"Then he ought to!"

"That's his decision, isn't it? There's such a thing as ethics, you know."

"I've never seen anything more insane than the way you work," snapped Dr. Hoyt. "I can't wait to finish my stretch here and go home."

He stamped out, weaving slightly because of the sedative.

"Well, what do you think of our assistant?" asked Dr. Kalmar.

"He's cute," Miss Dupont said irrelevantly.

Dr. Kalmar glowered at her. He'd forgotten that she was due to have a mate assigned to her this year.

Routine at the hospital was anything but routine. Dr. Hoyt barely kept from yelping each time someone was treated, and his help was given so unwillingly that Dr. Kalmar, sweating under a double load and with Dr. Hoyt to argue with at the same time, was all for putting him on the ship and asking Earth for another intern. But Miss Dupont talked him out of it.

For no discernible reason other than loneliness, Dr. Hoyt was taking her out. She was pleased, even though he crabbed constantly about the shabby-looking clothes she wore, which were typical of Deneb, and the way they fitted her.

Either the two of them didn't talk shop, or she had no influence with him—his criticism and impatience grew sharper each week.

It bothered Dr. Kalmar more than he thought it should, and much more than Mrs. Kalmar wanted it to. She was a pleasant little woman who liked things as they were, which was why Dr. Kalmar had hesitated all this while to ask her to undergo a slight rephysical; he would have preferred her a little taller, more filled out, her slight wrinkles deleted and, while he was thinking about it, he wished she'd let him give her space-black hair instead of her indeterminately blondish mop. But he'd rather have her as she was than peevish, so he had never mentioned it.

"Don't let the boy upset you," she said. "It's only that he's so young and inexperienced. You can't expect him to adjust quickly to a new environment and a whole new medical orientation."

"But that's just what annoys me! Why, I used to hang onto every word of Dr. Lowell's when I came here! I never thought I knew better than he did."

"Well, dear, you're you and Dr. Lowell is Dr. Lowell and Dr. Hoyt is Dr. Hoyt."

He tried to think of an answer and couldn't. "I suppose so."

"Maybe you'd feel better if you spoke to Dr. Lowell about it."

"What could he do? This is really an internal problem that I should work out with Dr. Hoyt. I can't involve Dr. Lowell in it."

But it became intolerable when there was a young girl who wanted to be a boy and Dr. Kalmar and Dr. Hoyt got into the worst battle yet. Naturally, she had to be given an Ego Alter to make her happy about being a girl, whereas Dr. Hoyt argued that she should be allowed to be a boy if that was what she wanted. Dr. Kalmar explained angrily once more that the sexes were closely balanced and Dr. Hoyt quoted the rule of personal choice. It was applicable on Earth, but not on Deneb, Dr. Kalmar retorted, to which Dr. Hoyt snorted something about playing God.

Dr. Kalmar confessed harshly to his wife that she was right. He had to bring old Dr. Lowell into the situation; it was out of Dr. Kalmar's control and was keeping the hospital in a turmoil. It was time for Dr. Lowell to inspect the hospital, the job he had taken in place of actual retirement. Dr. Kalmar needed help from Miss Dupont to bring the problem out into the open. But she became unexpectedly obstinate.

"I won't hurt Leo's career," she explained flatly.

Dr. Kalmar gave her a vacant look. "Leo?"

She blushed. "Dr. Hoyt. He's honestly trying to understand, but he finds it so different from Earth. Practically everything we do here is in reverse."

"But so is our environment, Miss Dupont. Earth is overcrowded and Deneb is underpopulated, so of course our methods would be the opposite of Earth's. He has to be made to see that we must solve our problems our own way."

She studied his face suspiciously. "That's all you want?"

"Certainly. Damn it, do you think I want him fired and sent back to Earth before his internship's up? I know it would hurt his record. Besides, I need an assistant—but not one I have to bicker with every time I make a move."

"Well, in that case—"

"Good girl. All you have to do is help me hold off the cases he'd argue about until Dr. Lowell gets here." He stared down glumly at his hands, which were gripping each other tightly. "God knows I'm no diplomat. Dr. Lowell is. He convinced me easily enough when I came here. Maybe he can do the same with Dr. Hoyt."

"Oh, I hope he can," Miss Dupont said earnestly. "I want so much to have you and Leo work together in harmony."

He glanced up, curious. "Why?"

"Because I'm in love with him."

He found himself nodding bitterly. Having Dr. Hoyt go back to Earth wouldn't be a fraction as bad as Miss Dupont leaving with him. So now there was something else to worry about.

Dr. Lowell came bouncing out of the jetcab a few days later. "The hospital better be spotless!" he called out jovially, paying off the hackie. "I'm in a mean mood. Liable to suspend everybody."

There was a strange lift to Dr. Kalmar's spirits as the old man entered the office. He wished without hope that he could inspire the same sort of reverence and respect. Impossible, of course. Dr. Lowell was great; he himself was nothing more than competent.

Dr. Kalmar introduced his young assistant to the old man.

"Young and strong," Dr. Lowell approved. "That's what we need on Deneb. Skill is important, but health and youth even more so."

"For those who stay," said Dr. Hoyt frostily. "I'm not."

Dr. Kalmar felt himself quiver with rage. The wet-nosed pup couldn't talk to Dr. Lowell like that!

But Dr. Lowell was saying cheerily, "You seem to have made up your mind to go back. No matter. Some decisions are like eggshells—made only to be broken. I hope that's what you'll do with yours."

"Not a chance," Dr. Hoyt said. He didn't take the arrogant expression off his face even when Miss Dupont looked at him pleadingly.

"Then I say let's signal the next ship—" Dr. Kalmar began.

Dr. Lowell cut in quickly, "You two have patients to attend to, I see. Don't worry about me. I know my way around this poor little wretch of a building. Not much like Earth hospitals, is it?" He headed for the medical supply room, adding just before he went in, "A lot can be said for small installations. The personal touch, you know."

Dr. Kalmar enviously realized how deftly the old man had put the youngster in his place, whereas he would have stood there and slugged it out verbally. Lord, if he could only acquire that awesome wisdom!

"Well, back to work," he said, trying to imitate the cheeriness at least.

"Sure, let's ruin some more lives," Dr. Hoyt almost snarled.

"Leo, *please*!" whispered Miss Dupont imploringly.

Five minutes later the two doctors were furiously arguing over a very old man who had been sent by Social Control to have his eyesight strengthened.

"You have no right to let anybody dodder around like this!" Dr. Hoyt yelled. "What in hell is Rephysical for if not for such cases?"

"You probably think we ought to make him look like twenty-five again," Dr. Kalmar yelled back. "If that's all you've learned working here—"

"Now, now," said Dr. Lowell soothingly. He'd come in unnoticed by either of the men. "Dr. Hoyt is right, of course. We would like to make old people young and some day we'll be able to afford it. But not for some time to come."

"Why not?" Dr. Hoyt demanded in a lower tone, visibly flattered by Dr. Lowell's seemingly taking his side.

"Rephysical can't actually make anyone young. It can only give the outward appearance of youth and replace obviously diseased parts. But an old body is an old organism; it has to break down eventually. If we give it more vigor than it can endure, it breaks down too soon, much sooner than if we let it age normally. That represents economic loss as well as a humanitarian one."

"I don't follow you," Dr. Hoyt said bewilderedly.

"Well, our patient used to be a machinist. A good one. Now he's only able to be an oiler. A good one, too, when you improve his eyesight. He can go on doing that for years, performing a useful function. But he'd wear himself out in no time as a machinist again if you de-aged him."

"Is that supposed to make sense?"

"It does," said Dr. Lowell, "for Deneb."

Dr. Hoyt wanted to continue the discussion, but Dr. Lowell was already on his way to inspect another part of the hospital. Grumbling, the young man helped chart the optical nerves that had to be replaced and measure the new curve of the retinas ordered by Social Control.

But he fought just as strenuously over other cases, especially a retired freight-jet pilot who had to have his reflexes slowed down so he could become a contented meteorologist. Whenever there was a loud disagreement of this sort, Dr. Lowell was there to mediate calmly.

At the end of the day, Dr. Kalmar was emotionally exhausted. He said as he and Dr. Lowell were washing up. "The kid's hopeless. I thought you could straighten him out—God knows I couldn't—but he'll never see why we have to work the way we do."

"What do you suggest?" Dr. Lowell asked through a towel.

"Send him back to Earth. Get an intern who's more malleable."

Dr. Lowell tossed the towel into the sterilizer. "Can't be done. We're expanding so fast all over the Galaxy that Earth can't train and ship out enough doctors for the new colonies. If we sent him back, I don't know when we'd get another."

Dr. Kalmar swallowed. "You mean it's him or nobody?"

"Afraid so."

"But he'll never fit in on Deneb!"

"You did," Dr. Lowell said.

Dr. Kalmar tried to smile modestly. "I realized immediately how little I knew and how much more experience you had. I was willing to learn. Why, I used to listen to you and watch you work and try to see your reasons for doing things—"

"You think so?" asked Dr. Lowell.

Dr. Kalmar glanced at him in astonishment. "You know I did. I still do, for that matter."

"When you landed on Deneb," said Dr. Lowell, "you were the most stubborn, opinionated young ass I'd ever met."

Dr. Kalmar's smile became an appreciative grin. "Damn, I wish I had that light touch of yours!"

"You were so dogmatic and argumentative that Dr. Hoyt is a suggestible schoolboy in comparison."

"Well, you don't have to go that far," Dr. Kalmar said. "I get what you're driving at—every intern needs orientation and I should be more patient and understanding."

"Then you don't follow me at all," stated Dr. Lowell. "Invite Dr. Hoyt, Miss Dupont and me to your house for dinner tonight and maybe you'll get a better idea of what I mean."

"Anything for a free meal, eh?"

"And to keep a doctor here on Deneb that we'd lose otherwise."

"Implying that I can't do it."

"Isn't that the decision you'd come to?"

"Yes, I guess it is," Dr. Kalmar confessed. "All right, how about dinner at my house tonight? I'll round up the other two and call Harriet so she'll expect us."

"Delighted to come," said Dr. Lowell. "Nice of you to ask me."

Miss Dupont was elated at the invitation and Dr. Hoyt said he had nothing else to do anyway. On the videophone Mrs. Kalmar was dismayed for a moment, until Dr. Lowell told her to put through an emergency order to Central Commissary and he'd verify it.

That was when Dr. Kalmar realized how serious the old man was. On a raw planet where crises were everyday routine, a situation had to be catastrophe before it could be called an emergency.

Dinner on Deneb was the same as anywhere else in the Galaxy. To free women for other work, food was delivered weekly in cooked form. A special messenger from Central Commissary had brought the emergency rations and Mrs. Kalmar had simply punctured the self-heat cartridges and put the servings in front of each guest; the containers were disposable plates and came with single-use plastic utensils. No garbage, no preparation, no cleaning up afterward, except to toss them all into the converter furnace. Dr. Hoyt was still not accustomed to wholly grown foods; he'd been raised on synthetics, of course, which were the staples on Earth.

"Well, that was good," said Dr. Lowell, getting up from the table with his round little belly comfortably expanded. "Now, let's have a few drinks before we start a professional bull session. Where do you keep your liquor? I'd like to mix my special so Dr. Hoyt can see we colonials are not so provincial."

"Good Lord, I haven't had your special for years!" exclaimed Dr. Kalmar. "Since about the time I came to Deneb, in fact."

"That's why it's a special. Reserved for state occasions, such as arrivals of colleagues from our dear old home planet."

"Oh, you don't have to go to all that bother," said Dr. Hoyt. "You'd have to make it twice—once now and once when I leave."

"That won't be for quite a while, will it?" Miss Dupont asked anxiously.

"As soon as I finish my internship. No more alien worlds for me. I like Earth."

Mrs. Kalmar got him to talk about it, which was much easier than getting him to stop, while Dr. Kalmar showed the old man where the liquor stock and fixings were kept. Watching him mix the ingredients with a chemist's care, Dr. Kalmar felt a glow of nostalgia. He recalled the celebration at Dr. Lowell's house, several months after he had come from Earth, when he'd enjoyed himself so much that he'd passed out. It was one of the pleasanter memories of his start on Deneb.

"Can't mix them all in a single batch," Dr. Lowell explained, bringing the drinks over one at a time as he finished preparing them. "Mrs. Kalmar ... Miss Dupont...our gracious host, Dr. Kalmar ... and now Dr. Hoyt and myself." He lifted his glass at Dr. Hoyt. "Welcome to our latest associate—product, like ourselves, of the great medical schools of Earth. It's a forlorn hope, but may he learn as much from us about our peculiar methods as we learn from him about the latest terrestrial advances."

Dr. Hoyt, smiling as if he didn't think it possible, stood up when they'd downed their toast to him. "To Earth," he said. "May I get back in record time." He gulped it, said, "Delicious—for a colonial drink," and froze with his smile as fixed as if it had been painted on.

"Leo!" Miss Dupont cried, and shook him, but he stayed frozen.

"The man's allergic to alcohol!" said Dr. Kalmar, astonished.

"Do something!" Mrs. Kalmar begged. "Don't let him stand there like that! He—he looks like a petrified man!"

"Don't get panicky," said Dr. Lowell in a quiet, confident voice. "That's when you passed out, Dr. Kalmar. Right after your first taste of my special."

"But *we* haven't," Dr. Kalmar objected.

"Naturally. Your drinks weren't drugged."

"Drugged?" shrieked Miss Dupont. "You doped him?"

"That's rather obvious, isn't it?"

"But—what for?" Dr. Kalmar stammered.

"Same reason I slipped you a mickey not long after you got here. We can't take any chances that he'll ship back to Earth. You see?"

"I don't," raged Miss Dupont. "I think it's a cheap, dirty, foul trick and it won't work, either. You can't *keep* him drugged."

"I don't like you talking to Dr. Lowell like that," said Dr. Kalmar indignantly.

"You should be the last one to object," Mrs. Kalmar pointed out. "He said he drugged you, too."

"I know," Dr. Kalmar said blankly. "I don't understand—"

"You will," promised Dr. Lowell. "Just come along and don't interfere. Better give him the order; it'll keep things straighter."

Mrs. Kalmar was grimly disapproving and Miss Dupont was close to hysteria. Only Dr. Kalmar retained his awed respect for Dr. Lowell. If the old man said it was all right, it was, even if he couldn't see the reason.

"Go ahead," urged Dr. Lowell.

"Dr. Hoyt!"

"Yes, Dr. Kalmar?"

"You will come with us!"

"Yes, Dr. Kalmar."

Dr. Lowell took them back to the hospital.

"Now what?" asked Dr. Kalmar.

"You actually don't know?" Miss Dupont demanded. "He wants to put Leo through the Ego Alter."

"That's absurd," Dr. Kalmar said angrily, "and an outright slander. Dr. Lowell wouldn't consider such a thing—the boy didn't ask for it and it wasn't authorized by Social Control."

Dr. Lowell smiled genially and opened the door to the Ego Alter room. "I hate to disillusion you, Dr. Kalmar. That's exactly what I have in mind—the same thing I did to you."

"That's absurd," Dr. Kalmar repeated, but with less conviction and more confusion than before.

"It worked. Tell him to sit down."

Dr. Kalmar did, and automatically fitted the wired plastic helmet to Dr. Hoyt's head.

"You can't!" cried Miss Dupont as he reached for the dials on the control console. "It's not fair!"

"Let's not get involved in a discussion on ethics," Dr. Lowell said. "Deneb can't afford to lose him; we need every doctor we have. If he goes back to Earth, it may be years before we get a replacement."

"But you can't do it without his consent!"

"There's time for that later," the old man grinned. "Keep his eyes on you, Dr. Kalmar, while you build up his father image. Cut down on hostility, aggression and power drive. Boost social responsibility and adventurousness. But make sure he's looking at you constantly."

"I won't allow it," said Mrs. Kalmar flatly. "You won't make my husband violate his oath."

"I did it to him, didn't I?" Dr. Lowell replied jovially. "It got you a husband."

Miss Dupont grabbed at Dr. Kalmar's hand, but he had already turned on the current.

"Anything else?" he asked.

"Well, he has to get married, of course," Dr. Lowell said. "Let him look at Miss Dupont—she's scheduled for this year, isn't she?—while you give him a shot of mating urge. Now, wipe out the memory of this incident and put him on a joy jag. We can validate that by liquoring him up afterward. When you're finished, bring him to."

Dr. Hoyt came out of it almost with a whoop. He lurched out of the insulated seat, stared at Miss Dupont for a moment with eyes that almost glittered, and seized and kissed her.

"My goodness!" she gasped.

"Now, what were you saying about ethics?" Dr. Lowell asked.

There was no answer. Both Miss Dupont and Mrs. Kalmar had frozen.

"You drugged them, too?" Dr. Kalmar weakly wanted to know."

"A bit slower-acting," admitted the old man. "All you have to do with them is wipe out the last half hour. Don't want any witnesses to an unethical act, you know. Oh, and put them on a jag also."

Dr. Kalmar followed instructions.

Finished, they left the three uproariously drunk in the waiting room and went to wash up. Dr. Kalmar went along bewilderedly. The old man was as unconcerned as if he did this sort of thing daily.

"I was as arrogant and belligerent as this squirt was?"

"Worse," Dr. Lowell said. "He was willing to finish out his internship. You weren't. Still worried about the ethics?"

"Yes. Naturally."

"All right, apply some logic, then. Are you happier on Deneb than you'd have been on Earth?"

"Well, certainly. I'd have been lucky to get a job doctoring in a summer camp. I wouldn't trade a roomy planet like this for the jammed cubicles of Earth. And I like our methods better than terrestrial dogma. But those are my preferences. I can't inflict them on anybody else."

"The hell they were your preferences. You bickered more about our methods and longed more loudly for the tenements of Earth than this lad ever did. All it took was a slight Ego Alter and you have a happier life than you would have had. Right?"

Dr. Kalmar felt his tension ease. If the old man said it was right, it was. He became momentarily resentful when he realized that that reaction had been installed by Dr. Lowell, but then he smiled. It really was right. A bit arbitrary, perhaps, but for the good of Dr. Hoyt and Deneb in the long run, just as it had been for himself.

"Look," he said, drying his arms. "I've been wanting my wife to go through a slight rephysical."

"Why don't you ask her?"

"The fact is that I'm afraid she'll think I'm dissatisfied and I don't want her to get resentful."

"Maybe she'd like you to do some changing, too."

"What for? I'm all right."

"She probably feels the same way about herself."

"But all I want are a few changes in her. She's as high as a space pilot now. It would be a cinch to—"

Dr. Lowell flung down the towel and gave him an outraged glare. "There's such a thing as professional ethics, Dr. Kalmar!"

"But you—"

"That's different. It was a social decision, not a selfish one. If you ask her and she agrees, that's up to her. But you can't take advantage of her in an egocentric, arbitrary way. You just try it and I'll have you sent back to Earth."

Dr. Kalmar felt his knees grow weak in alarm. "No, no. It's not that important. Just an insignificant kind of wish."

And it was, he discovered when they went out to the waiting room. Unused to jags, Mrs. Kalmar was more affectionate than she'd been since they were first married; he'd have to remember to go on them periodically with her. Miss Dupont, unwilling to budge out of Dr. Hoyt's tight arms, had glassily joyous eyes. Dr. Hoyt didn't let her go until he caught sight of Dr. Kalmar.

"Greatest doctor I ever met," he said enthusiastically. "Won'ful planet, Deneb. Just wanna marry Miss Dupont, stay here and learn at your feet. Okay?"

Dr. Kalmar's glance at the old man was no less worshipful. "It couldn't be okayer," he said.

JOURNAL NOTES
No Charge for Alterations

Theme:
Adaptation to an underpopulated outworld can't possibly be the same as adaptation to an overcrowded Earth; it must be almost exactly the reverse. But colonists can't make the adaptation themselves if it means physical as well as psychological changes. No slow psychoanalysis or gradual building muscles—can't spare the time. Medicine has to step in and do it quickly. Unreasonable? No, over 90 percent of all prescriptions written today couldn't have been filled just ten years ago; only logic that medicine must advance even more swiftly as major discoveries open whole new fields of research and therapy.

Possibilities:
Adaptation of colonizing party to hostile new planet? Too fast and melodramatic, no chance to play up characterization and get a twisty plot. That calls for a partly developed world where techniques of adaptation have been worked out. Contrast with young doctor fresh out of terrestrial medical school, where methods are just the opposite. Build conflict on the contrast.

Development:
Middle-aged doctor committed to the logical needs of a planet that can't spare any possible worker. Young terrestrial doctor opposed violently to everything that contradicts his training. Need mediator—old, retired doctor who taught middle-aged one everything and is all but revered by him. (Use adaptation gadget for surprise payoff.) Love interest to strengthen battle—pleasant but not gorgeous nurse in love with young doctor, not requited, gadget resolves. (Personal problem of middle-aged doctor: wants wife to undergo treatment, doesn't dare ask her, tries to get old doctor to use same trickery, is stiffly rebuffed in topper to surprise payoff.)

Editorial Comments:
The characters come off, but are subsidiary to the theme itself, which is supported by dramatically integrated logic. This is the toughest part of writing science fiction. Anybody can stop narration

dead to explain something the reader has to know in order to understand the story—when I first began writing, back in 1934, I once did it for *two full* pages cribbed from a biochemistry textbook, and that was by no means the record—but modern science fiction demands and gets its necessary information woven in so that it advances instead of retards the action. In this story, the young doctor fights for his terrestrial training, the middle-aged doctor is committed to colonial goals that are just the reverse of Earth's, the old doctor calmly and realistically shows that this about-face of conditioning can't be achieved without ruthless reconditioning—and the heated data is as important dramatically as any other plot element. That process of integration takes real work, but, Lordy, is it ever worth the trouble!

DON'T TAKE IT TO HEART

MEN WHO COME INTO A SHOE STORE are usually meek and apologetic, which may explain why Eliot Grundy had remained head salesman at Footfitter Shoes for over twenty-five years. A small, fussy man with glinting eyeglasses and white hair combed flatly and precisely over a growing bald spot, he had a surprisingly big, authoritative voice. When he announced bluntly that a customer ought to take a certain shoe, that shoe was as good as bought.

Mr. Cahill liked to watch Grundy sell, and he especially liked to show Saturday extras how it was done. Mr. Cahill was the store manager, had been since two years before Grundy came there, but he knew he couldn't, as he put it, hold a candle to Grundy's masterful selling.

"Now watch this," he said one day to a salesman named Barnes, who, as a matter of fact, never made the grade. "That gentleman wants a wingtip shoe in cordovan leather. Listen to Grundy handle him."

"It bites in front," the customer complained, standing up and flexing the shoe several times. "Could you put in a bite pad?"

"I could," Grundy said in his astonishing voice. "But I won't."

"Huh?" asked the customer and Barnes, both startled.

"If that's what the guy wants," Barnes continued to Mr. Cahill, "why shouldn't Grundy fix up the bite for him?"

"He knows what he's doing," said Mr. Cahill. "Listen."

"I don't get it," the customer said bewilderedly. "If you charge for bite pads, that's okay."

Grundy hitched forward on his salesman's stool. "Not with me. Here, sit down." He lifted the customer's left ankle while the man was still standing, dumping him into a seat, then unfaced the shoe swiftly and shoved it hard against the sole of his foot. "All right now, let's see why it bites. Did you ever think of asking yourself that question? Shoes don't bite without a reason, you know. If they do, it's because *the last is all wrong for the foot.*"

The customer swallowed uneasily. "It is?"

"Wingtips are too narrow for you. See how this shoe tapers to a point?" He stopped and glinted his eyeglasses at the man. "Your feet don't come to a point, do they?"

"Well, no—"

"And cordovan is as hard and stiff a leather as there is. You have sensitive feet, don't you?"

"Well, yes—"

Mr. Cahill turned to Barnes with a smile of pride in craftsmanship. "There you are. The sale's wrapped up."

But it wasn't. The customer allowed Grundy to try on a pair that he thought was suitable, even walked around in them and confessed they were more comfortable. But he half-defiantly asked to try the others again.

"I'll take these," he started to say, and then saw Grundy's lips compress disapprovingly. "You—you think I ought to take the ones with the broad tips?"

"I do," stated Grundy.

The customer sighed. "Oh, all right. They look lousy, but at least they feel good."

Grundy, wrapping up the package, favored him with his tight end-of-a-sale smile. "That's the important thing, isn't it?"

"I guess so. Well, sure! Why should I pinch my feet into narrow shoes—"

"Where the last is all wrong," Grundy supplied.

"—yeah, just so people'll think I have narrow feet? Hell with them. My comfort comes first," the customer said belligerently, justifying a decision that had been forced on him.

"I'll be damned," Barnes said, standing at the entrance to the stockroom with Mr. Cahill.

"You've seen a master at work, Barnes," said Cahill almost reverently. "Never forget this moment and the lesson you've learned."

But Mr. Cahill had his troubles with Grundy. It was fine, of course, to have a salesman who never missed a day at work, who never came in late, who always kept the floor around his stool tidy—"Put away the shoes as soon as you take them off," Grundy was fond of saying forcefully, "and besides not littering the place, you don't get customers confused about which pair to buy." Grundy was a demon on stock; he hated to see it upset—although "hated" is perhaps too mild a term—he always went into a rigidly controlled rage and let customers wait until he had the stock back in shape again.

That was one thing that upset Mr. Cahill. He believed that the customer always came first. Grundy, on the other hand, argued that disorganized stock ruined a salesman's efficiency.

"How can a man sell if he doesn't know where things are?"

"But there's always time to straighten out the shelves *after* you've finished a sale," Mr. Cahill pointed out.

"I can't work that way."

"Grundy," said Mr. Cahill, more than once, "there's a customer out front. You will please go out and wait on him."

"Is that an order, sir?" Grundy would ask ironically.

"It is."

At first, Grundy used to head uncertainly for the entrance to the stockroom, glance back at the unfinished stock, and then halt, visibly fighting his desire to straighten up and his reluctance to follow that specific command.

"I'll be through in a few minutes," he'd mumble. "You go."

Then there was Grundy's refusal to try on a right shoe first. Every so often, somebody says to the salesman, "My right foot is bigger than the left. I'd like to fit that one first." And salesmen, Mr. Cahill held, should be happy to oblige a customer in so small a matter.

"But the shoes aren't put that way in the box," Grundy obstinately said. "The right shoe is under the tissue paper. It's the left one that comes out first."

"So take a little longer putting them back."

"That is not how I learned to sell shoes, Mr. Cahill: first the left shoe, then the right. I don't mind putting *both* of them on a customer, but I won't go fishing the right one out of the tissue."

He never did, either.

There were many more ways in which Grundy refused to budge, and Mr. Cahill sometimes thought seriously of getting rid of him. But those occasions were only temporary crises, which Grundy always won by sticking to his rigidly set ways, and Mr. Cahill, after cooling off, realized that a salesman of Grundy's caliber should not be fired just because he won't change his methods. If not for Grundy, he had to admit, the store would have trouble meeting its sales quota.

But that was only part of it. Mr. Cahill had studied Grundy over the years, as he felt any good manager should in order to get the best out of his help, and he understood just what was the root of Grundy's trouble.

"I'll drive you home," he said once, when they were locking up for the day. "I want to talk to you about something."

Grundy's sudden distress would have been invisible to anybody else, but not to Mr. Cahill. He said, "But I always go by subway."

"That's what I mean," Mr. Cahill declared. "You always this and you always that, as if there's only one way to do something. Now come on, pile into the car. It's not far out of the way for me."

Grundy looked around as if cops with drawn guns were closing in on him. "No. I mean—no, thanks. I'll take the subway. It's—ah—faster."

"You're not in any hurry." Mr. Cahill held open the door, but Grundy stayed where he was. Ignoring the people passing by, Mr. Cahill said, "I want to help you, Grundy, and I think I can. I've made a study of psychology—that's how I got where I am—and I know what makes a human being tick. You're not ticking, Grundy. You're sticking at half-past."

"I'm not complaining," Grundy replied. "If you're dissatisfied with my work—"

"No, no. It's not that at all. You're—well, you're inflexible. You act as if something awful would happen if you changed your ways."

"Things wouldn't get done right," Grundy said stubbornly.

"They would. Maybe better. You're *afraid* to change. What do you think would happen if you took off the right shoe first, for instance? The customer might die? You might? The floor would cave in? *What?*"

"I'm late," said Grundy. "I have to get home. Things to do—"

He hurried toward the subway. Mr. Cahill, getting moodily into the car, thought he had lost again.

But Grundy was disturbed by Mr. Cahill's shrewd analysis of his fixed behavior pattern. He was no less forceful with customers, yet he wondered if his doing things without variation was merely a question of training. Without even Mr. Cahill being aware of it, Grundy tried a minor experiment—he started lacing a shoe by slipping one end of the lace through alternate holes and then going back to do the same with the other end, instead of painstakingly working one hole at a time from side to side, as he always did. He'd considered it a better, more conservative way, one that did a neater job, but now he wasn't sure and he wanted to be.

He didn't exactly *do* it. He started or, rather, he *thought* about starting. But his hand began to shake and he felt the pressure of terror mount alarmingly in him. Something frightful would occur if he did it—it was as if the walls and the ceiling bulged threateningly at him, daring him to go on.

"If you don't mind, I'm in a hurry," the customer said, and Grundy, relieved to find an excuse, swiftly laced the shoe as he invariably did.

He tried leaving the stock to wait on people; even, when he was asked, to put on the right shoe first; but panic rose in him each time. He knew nothing would happen. He knew it, he knew it, he knew it!

He knew nothing of the sort, only that there was a ghastly sense of fear, a feeling that disaster was daring him to do something differently. He said nothing to Mr. Cahill, but he stopped experimenting. It was much more comfortable. And somehow safer, like taking the match away from a bomb that might blow up himself, the store, customers and Mr. Cahill.

Mr. Cahill, however, neglected to notice Grundy's anxious tries and relieved relapse. A memo had come from Mr. Munson, the president of the company, and Mr. Cahill was worried about it. He knew there would be trouble with Grundy. He attempted to head off the explosion.

"You know," said Mr. Cahill, in what he hoped was a casual tone, as he and Grundy sat at the back of the store after the lunch-hour rush was over, "more than half of the people in the world are women!"

"Anybody who rides in a subway can tell you that," Grundy replied with his usual rancor.

"That's an awful lot of shoes, even figuring one pair each."

"And a lot more selling time. You can wrap up five sales to men in the time it takes to sell a woman."

"Oh, I wouldn't say that," Mr. Cahill objected jocularly. "It takes a little longer, perhaps, but just think how many customers!"

"Somebody else can wait on them. I wouldn't."

Mr. Cahill tried to change Grundy's attitude by breaking it down a little at a time, but he didn't have that long. When Grundy came in on a Monday morning—exactly five minutes early, as always—and went back to the stockroom to put away his jacket, Mr. Cahill stood holding his breath, his entire body stiff, waiting for the blast.

"Mr. Cahill!" Grundy's voice was bigger and more terrifying with indignation than Mr. Cahill remembered ever hearing it before. "May I ask the meaning of this—this *sacrilege*?"

Mr. Cahill filled his lungs and straightened his back and went into the stockroom, where Grundy was glaring at shelves of narrow boxes.

"What's the idea of this, Mr. Cahill?" Grundy demanded. "These are *women's shoes*, aren't they?"

"Why, yes," Mr. Cahill said innocently. "I thought you understood from our conversations that—"

"So that's what you were driving at! Turning Footfitters into a damned female shop!"

"It wasn't my idea," Mr. Cahill said. "Orders from the office."

"Well, they're not going to make me sell women's shoes. As of right here and now, I quit, Mr. Cahill. I'll find another man's shoe-store, and when that one starts selling to women, I'll find another."

He was outside, glowering at the display the window dressers had put in over the weekend and which he'd missed seeing when he came in, probably because the windows were changed so seldom, before Mr. Cahill caught up with him and grabbed his arm.

"Grundy, this isn't fair to Footfitters," Mr. Cahill said in outrage. "You haven't given notice. Are you going to leave Footfitters in the lurch on *opening day*—you, the head salesman, the one we were counting on to put us across?"

"Well—" Grundy began hesitantly, sounding like one of his own former customers.

"Of course you're not! You've been loyal to Footfitters all these years. I can't believe you'd be disloyal at the last moment."

"All right," Grundy capitulated. "I'll help out—but only as far as taking care of men customers goes."

It was Mr. Cahill's first victory and he knew better than to push further. Grundy went back to the stockroom, muttering at the slim boxes, and changed his coat. He stood at the back and watched sourly as women came pouring into the store, eager to buy something and get the free pocketbook or stockings Footfitters was offering. He made no attempt to help the extras, naturally. Mr. Cahill knew he would not go front until a male customer entered, which seemed good enough until the store was mobbed and women were screaming to be waited on.

"Mr. Grundy," said Mr. Cahill tentatively, "I wish you'd jump in just for today. We just can't handle the crowd. And what if Mr. Munson should drop in and see you standing there?"

"Well, what if he should?"

"I know you don't care any more, now that you've decided to leave Footfitters, but think of my career, Mr. Grundy. You know what the office would say—and do."

"That's your affair," Grundy said. "I'm not budging from here until a man customer comes in."

"And you know none will as long as we have all these women here," Mr. Cahill said in a high and despairing wail.

"I know it."

"Then how do you figure you're helping me out?"

Grundy turned his hostile view of the alien invasion of the store to Mr. Cahill. "I'm a man of habit, as you yourself observed. I like routine, in spite of your ideas about why I do things certain ways. I've lived my life the way I was brought up to, doing certain things in certain ways at certain times, and I don't want to change that for you, for Mr. Munson, or for anybody else."

He didn't mention that he had attempted to change his habits and the overwhelming panic he had experienced. He knew better; Mr. Cahill, being an amateur psychoanalyst, would have told him it was because of rivalry with his father or his rebellion against early toilet training or something equally annoying and preposterous.

"That, Grundy, is compulsive behavior," Mr. Cahill said severely. "A compulsive neurotic does what he does because he's afraid of the consequences if he does or doesn't. I mean it's like defying your parents, so to speak, and fearing punishment."

"Nuts," replied Grundy, a word he had previously only thought.

"What do you think would happen if you waited on a woman?"

Grundy's aggressive composure shook slightly. Remembering what he'd suffered in his abortive experiments he had been trying not to think of that. "I don't know," he admitted.

"Then why not find out? You'll see it's not so terrible." Mr. Cahill caught him by the wrist and hauled him toward a seat, where a stout woman was sitting impatiently. "Here is our head salesman, madam. He'll take care of you personally."

"Well, thank goodness *somebody* will," she said in a peevish voice. "Or will he? What's he standing there for, like a *goon*?"

"Go on, Grundy," Mr. Cahill said in an urgent whisper. "She won't eat you."

"I am not afraid of her or anybody else," Grundy said with dignity, but he shook with apprehension and dread—of something he couldn't recognize—as he lowered his rump to the stool.

He stood up immediately, sweating.

"I—can't!"

"Of course you can," Mr. Cahill said persuasively. "Sit down. There, that's a good fellow. Now take off her shoe. Her shoe, Mr. Grundy."

"My right foot's bigger than my left," she said. "That's the one I want fitted."

Grundy goggled at her in horror. "Your—right—foot?"

"You heard the lady," said Mr. Cahill. "The right foot first."

Grundy reached for it, but he drew back. "No!"

"Good Lord," Mr. Cahill exclaimed in exasperation. "The world won't end if you wait on a woman and try on the right shoe first!"

But, of course, it did.

JOURNAL NOTES
Don't Take It To Heart

Theme:
Changing or shucking a compulsion—a habit that has become so deeply grooved that it's an almost unclimbable trench—always produces a feeling of impending doom. Freud and his followers (his opponents, too, for that matter) maintain that this is merely ritualistic thinking. But what if there's an exception?

Possibilities:
Voodoo and other such primitivisms are too blatant; the reader would anticipate the ending right from the start. Must have as ordinary a character as can be found. Spinsters, bookkeepers and kids—it's about time fantasy left them alone, gave them a chance to freshen up through a long rest between stories. Rigid personality needed; can't think of any more unyielding than man I used to work with when I sold shoes. Dogmatic, opinionated, so set in his habits that he sold his way, by God, and no customer or manager could alter it. Good chance also to let the reader in on the trade secrets. Go easy on jargon of the business—takes too much explanation and holds up narrative.

Development:
Character is set, background is set. Whole story depends on strong detail, but keep it short; too long and the punch will either be telegraphed or get as pudgy as a soggy creampuff. Too short, though, and characterization and background will be compressed out of the story. Write first, cut out fat after.

Editorial Comments:
Competent and craftsmanlike, but not one of my personal favorites. That's no criterion, to be sure; authors aren't the best judges of their own work and, like parents, often tend to be fondest of brainchildren that others are indifferent to and vice versa. I'm satisfied with the inside stuff, which I assure you is thoroughly authentic—I was a hotshot shoe dog and could T.I. (talk into) a skig (P.M., which probably means poor or past merchandise, calling for a

bonus ranging from a dime to a dollar), or handle a T.O. (turnover, a hard customer) with the best of them, working everything from schlak (cheap) stores to Fifth Avenue salons while I was learning how to write. After I finished the story, I was worried that the payoff might be obvious. But Editor Howard Browne said no and readers seemed to agree with him. A worrywart, that's me—I used to fret about fit long after customers had left the shop and the unhappy practice is carried over into writing and editing. It's corrosive to the nerves, but produces better work … though sometimes I envy the oblivious joyousness of amateurs. All professionals envy that, while at the same time realizing that what's wrote easy reads hard, as somebody said or should have said.

MAN OF PARTS

THERE WASN'T A TRACE of amnesia or confusion when Major Hugh Savold, of the Fourth Earth Expedition against Vega, opened his eyes in the hospital. He knew exactly who he was, where he was, and how he had gotten there.

His name was Gam Nex Biad.

He was a native of the planet named Dorfel.

He had been killed in a mining accident far underground.

The answers were preposterous and they terrified Major Savold. Had he gone insane? He must have, for his arms were pinned tight in a restraining sheet. And his mouth was full of bits of rock.

Savold screamed and wrenched around on the flat, comfortable boulder on which he had been nibbling. He spat out the rock fragments that tasted—*nutritious*.

Shaking, Savold recoiled from something even more frightful than the wrong name, wrong birthplace, wrong accident, and shockingly wrong food.

A living awal was watching him solicitously. It was as tall as himself, had a pointed spiral drill for a head, three knee-action arms ending in horn spades, two below them with numerous sensitive cilia, a row of socketed bulbs down its front, and it stood on a nervously bouncing bedspring of a leg.

Savold was revolted and tense with panic. He had never in his life seen a creature like this.

It was Surgeon Trink, whom he had known since infancy.

"Do not be distressed," glowed the surgeon's kindly lights. "You are everything you think you are."

"But that's impossible! I'm an Earthman and my name is Major Hugh Savold!"

"Of course."

"Then I can't be Gam Nex Biad, a native of Dorfel!"

"But you are."

"I'm not!" shouted Savold. "I was in a one-man space scout. I sneaked past the Vegan cordon and dropped the spore-bomb, the only one that ever got through. The Vegans burned my fuel and engine sections full of holes. I escaped, but I couldn't make it back to Earth. I found a planet that was pockmarked worse than our moon. I was afraid it had no atmosphere, but it did. I crash-landed." He shuddered. "It was more of a crash than a landing."

Surgeon Trink brightened joyfully. "Excellent! There seems to be no impairment of memory at all."

"No?" Savold yelled in terror. "Then how is it I remember being killed in a mining accident? I was drilling through good hard mineral ore, spinning at a fine rate, my head soothingly warm as it gouged into the tasty rock, my spades pushing back the crushed ore, and I crashed right out into a fault … "

"Soft shale," the surgeon explained, dimming with sympathy. "You were spinning too fast to sense the difference in density ahead of you. It was an unfortunate accident. We were all very sad."

"And I was killed," said Savold, horrified. "*Twice*!"

"Oh, no. Only once. You were badly damaged when your machine crashed, but you were not killed. We were able to repair you."

Savold felt fear swarm through him, driving his ghastly thoughts into a quaking corner. He looked down at his body, knowing he couldn't see it, that it was wrapped tightly in a long sheet. He had never seen material like this.

He recognized it instantly as asbestos cloth.

There was a row of holes down the front. Savold screamed in horror. The socketed bulbs lit up in a deafening glare.

"Please don't be afraid!" The surgeon bounced over concernedly, broke open a large mica capsule, and splashed its contents on Savold's head and face. "I know it's a shock, but there's no cause for alarm. You're not in danger, I assure you."

Savold found himself quieting down, his panic diminishing. No, it wasn't the surgeon's gentle, reassuring glow that was responsible. It was the liquid he was covered with. A sedative of some sort, it eased the constriction of his brain, relaxed his facial muscles, dribbled comfortingly into his mouth. Half of him recognized the heavy odor and the other half identified the taste.

It was lubricating oil.

As a lubricant, it soothed him. But it was also a coolant, for it cooled off his fright and disgust and let him think again.

"Better?" asked Surgeon Trink hopefully.

"Yes, I'm calmer now," Savold said, and noted first that his voice sounded quieter, and second that it wasn't his voice—he was communicating by glows and blinks of his row of bulbs, which, as he talked, gave off a cold light like that of fireflies. "I think I can figure it out. I'm Major Hugh Savold. I crashed and was injured. You gave me the body of a … ” he thought about the name and realized that he didn't know it, yet he found it immediately " … a Dorfellow, didn't you?"

"Not the whole body," the surgeon replied, glimmering with confidence again as his bedside manner returned. "Just the parts that were in need of replacement."

Savold was revolted, but the sedative effect of the lubricating oil kept his feelings under control. He tried to nod in understanding. He couldn't. Either he had an unbelievably stiff neck … or no neck whatever.

"Something like our bone, limb, and organ banks," he said. "How much of me is Gam Nex Biad?"

"Quite a lot, I'm afraid." The surgeon listed the parts, which came through to Savold as if he were listening to a simultaneous translation: from Surgeon Trink to Gam Nex Biad to him. They were all equivalents, of course, but they amounted to a large portion of his brain, skull, chest, internal and reproductive organs, mid-section, and legs.

"Then what's left of me?" Savold cried in dismay.

"Why, part of your brain—a very considerable part, I'm proud to say. Oh, and your arms. Some things weren't badly injured, but it seemed better to make substitutions. The digestive and circulatory system, for instance. Yours were adapted to foods and fluids that aren't available on Dorfel. Now you can get your sustenance directly from the minerals and metals of the planet, just as we do. If I hadn't, your life would have been saved, but you would have starved to death."

"Let me up," said Savold in alarm. "I want to see what I look like."

The surgeon looked worried again. He used another capsule of oil on Savold before removing the sheet.

Savold stared down at himself and felt revulsion trying to rise. But there was nowhere for it to go and it couldn't have gotten past the oil if there had been. He swayed sickly on his bedspring leg, petrified at the sight of himself.

He looked quite handsome, he had to admit—Gam Nex Biad had always been considered one of the most crashing bores on Dorfel, capable of taking an enormous leap on his magnificently wiry leg, landing exactly on the point of his head with a swift spin that would bury him out of sight within instants in even the hardest rock. His knee-action arms were splendidly flinty; he knew they had been repaired with some other miner's remains, and they could whirl him through a self-drilled tunnel with wonderful speed, while the spade hands could shovel back ore as fast as he could dig it out. He was as good as new … except for the disgustingly soft, purposeless arms.

The knowledge of function and custom was there, and the reaction to the human arms, and they made explanation unnecessary, just as understanding of the firefly language had been there without his awareness. But the emotions were Savold's and they drove him to say fiercely, "You didn't have to change me altogether. You could have just saved my life so I could fix my ship and get back … " He paused abruptly and would have gasped if he had been able to. "Good Lord! Earth Command doesn't even know I got the bomb through! If they act fast, they can land without a bit of opposition!" He spread all his arms—the two human ones, the three with knee-action and spades, the two with the sensitive cilia—and stared at them bleakly. "And I have a girl back on Earth … "

Surgeon Trink glowed sympathetically and flashed with pride. "Your mission seems important somehow, though its meaning escapes me. However, we have repaired your machine … "

"You *have*?" Savold interrupted eagerly.

"Indeed, yes. It should work better than before." The surgeon flickered modestly. "We do have some engineering skill, you know."

The Gam Nex Biad of Savold did know. There were the underground ore smelters and the oil refineries and the giant metal awls that drilled out rock food for the manufacturing centers, where miners alone could not keep up with the demand, and the communicators that sent their signals clear around the planet through the substrata of rock, and more, much more. This, insisted Gam Nex Biad proudly, was a *civilization*, and Major Hugh Savold, sharing his knowledge, had to admit that it certainly was.

"I can take right off, then?" Savold flared excitedly.

"There is a problem first," glowed the surgeon in some doubt. "You mention a 'girl' on this place you call 'Earth.' I gather it is a person of the opposite sex."

"As opposite as anybody can get. Or was," Savold added moodily. "But we have limb and organ banks on Earth. The doctors there can do a repair job. It's a damned big one, I know, but they can handle it. I'm not so sure I like carrying Gam Nex Biad around with me for life, though. Maybe they can take him out and … "

"Please," Surgeon Trink cut in with anxious blinkings. "There is a matter to be settled. When you refer to the 'girl,' you do not specify that she is your mate. You have not been selected for each other yet?"

"Selected?" repeated Savold blankly, but Gam Nex Biad supplied the answer—the equivalent of marriage, the mates chosen by experts on genetics, the choice being determined by desired transmittable aptitudes. "No, we were just going together. We were not mates, but we intended to be as soon as I got back. That's the other reason I have to return in a hurry. I appreciate all you've done, but I really must ... "

"Wait," the surgeon ordered.

He drew an asbestos curtain that covered part of a wall. Savold saw an opening in the rock of the hospital, a hole-door through which bounced half a dozen little Dorfellows and one big one ... straight at him. He felt what would have been his heart leap into what would have been his chest if he had had either. But he couldn't even get angry or shocked or nauseated; the lubricating oil cooled off all his emotions.

The little creatures were all afire with childish joy. The big one sparkled happily.

"Father!" blinked the children blindingly.

"Mate!" added Prad Fim Biad in a delighted exclamation point.

"You see," said the surgeon to Savold, who was shrinking back, "you already have a mate and a family."

It was only natural that a board of surgeons should have tried to cope with Savold's violent reaction. He had fought furiously against being saddled with an alien family. Even constant saturation with lubricating oil couldn't keep that rebellion from boiling over.

On Earth, of course, he would have been given immediate psychotherapy, but there wasn't anything of the sort here. Dorfellows were too granitic physically and psychologically to need medical or psychiatric doctors. A job well done and a family well raised—that was the extent of their emotionalism. Savold's feelings, rage and resentment and a violent desire to escape, were completely beyond their understanding. He discovered that as he angrily watched the glittering debate.

The board quickly determined that Surgeon Trink had been correct in adapting Savold to the Dorfel way of life. Savold objected that the adaptation need not have been so thorough, but he had to admit that, since they couldn't have kept him fed any other way, Surgeon Trink had done his best in an emergency.

The surgeon was willing to accept blame for having introduced Savold so bluntly to his family, but the board absolved him—none of them had had any experience in dealing with an Earth mentality. A Dorfellow would have accepted the fact, as others with amnesia caused by accidents had done. Surgeon Trink had had no reason to think Savold would not have done the same. Savold cleared the surgeon entirely by admitting that the memory was there, but, like all the other memories of Gam Nex Biad's, had been activated only when the situation came up. The board had no trouble getting Savold to agree that the memory would have returned sooner or later, no matter how Surgeon Trink handled the introduction, and that the reaction would have been just as violent.

"And now," gleamed the oldest surgeon on the board, "the problem is how to help our new—and restored—brother adjust to life on this world."

"That isn't the problem at all!" Savold flared savagely. "I have to get back to Earth and tell them I dropped the bomb and they can land safely. And there's the girl I mentioned. I want to marry her—become her mate, I mean."

"*You* want to become her mate?" the oldest surgeon blinked in bewilderment. "It is *your* decision?"

"Well, hers, too."

"You mean you did the selecting yourselves? Nobody chose for you?"

Savold attempted to explain, but puzzled glimmmers and Gam Nex Biad's confusion made him state resignedly, "Our customs are different. We choose our own mates." He thought of adding that marriages were arranged in some parts of the world, but that would only have increased their baffled lack of understanding.

"And how many mates can an individual have?" asked a surgeon.

"Where I come from, one."

"The individual's responsibility, then, is to the family he has. Correct?"

"Of course."

"Well," said the oldest surgeon, "the situation is perfectly clear. You have a family—Prad Fim Biad and the children."

"They're not my family," Savold objected. "They're Gam Nex Biad's and he's dead."

"We respect your customs. It is only fair that you respect ours. If you had had a family where you come from, there would have been a question of legality, in view of the fact that you could not care for them simultaneously. But you have none and there is no such question."

"Customs? Legality?" asked Savold, feeling as lost as they had in trying to comprehend an alien society.

"A rebuilt Dorfellow," the oldest surgeon said, "is required to assume the obligations of whatever major parts went into his reconstruction. You are almost entirely made up of the remains of Gam Nex Biad, so it is only right that his mate and children should be yours."

"I won't do it!" Savold protested. "I demand the right to appeal!"

"On what grounds?" asked another surgeon politely.

"That I'm not a Dorfellow!"

"Ninety-four point seven per cent of you is, according to Surgeon Trink's requisition of limbs and organs. How much more of a citizen can any individual be?"

Gam Nex Biad confirmed the ruling and Savold subsided. While the board of surgeons discussed the point it had begun with—how to adapt Savold to life on Dorfel—he thought the situation through. He had no legal or moral recourse. If he was to get out of his predicament, it would have to be through shrewd resourcefulness and he would never have become a major in the space fleet if he hadn't had plenty of that.

Yeah, shrewd resourcefulness, thought Savold bitterly, jouncing unsteadily on his single bedspring leg on a patch of unappealing topsoil a little distance from the settlement. He had counted on something that didn't exist here—the kind of complex approach that Earth doctors and authorities would have used on his sort of problem, from the mitigation of laws to psychological conditioning, all of it complicated and every stage allowing a chance to work his way free.

But the board of surgeons had agreed on a disastrously simple course of treatment for him. He was not to be fed by anybody and he could not sleep in any of the underground rock apartments, including the dormitory for unmated males.

"When he's hungry enough, he'll go back to mining," the oldest surgeon had told the equivalent of a judge, a local teacher who did part-time work passing on legal questions that did not have to be ruled on by the higher courts. "And if he has no place to stay except with Gam Nex Biad's family, which is his own, naturally, he'll go there when he's tired of living out in the open all by himself."

The judge thought highly of the decision and gave it official approval.

Savold did not mind being out in the open, but he was far from being all by himself. Gam Nex Biad was a constant nuisance, nagging at him to get in a good day's drilling and then go home to the wife, kiddies, and their cozy, hollowed-out quarters, with company over to celebrate his return with a lavish supply of capsuled lubricating oil. Savold obstinately refused, though he found himself salivating or something very much like it.

The devil of the situation *was* that he was hungry and there was not a single bit of rock around to munch on. That was the purpose of this fenced-in plot of ground—it was like hard labor in the prisons back on Earth, where the inmates ate only if they broke their quota of rock, except that here the inmates would eat the rock they broke. The only way Savold could get out of the enclosure was by drilling under the high fence. He had already tried to bounce over it and discovered he couldn't.

"Come on," Gam Nex Biad argued in his mind. "Why fight it? We're a miner and there's no life like the life of a miner. The excitement of boring your way through a lode, making a meal out of the rich ore! Miners get the choicest tidbits, you know—that's our compensation for working so hard and taking risks."

"Some compensation," sneered Savold, looking wistfully up at the stars and enviously wishing he were streaking between them in his scout.

"A meal of iron ore would go pretty well right now, wouldn't it?" Gam Nex Biad tempted. "And I know where there are some veins of tin and sulphur. You don't find *them* lying around on the surface, eh? Non-miners get just traces of the rare metals to keep them healthy, but we can stuff ourself all we want … "

"Shut up!"

"And some pools of mercury. Not big ones, I admit, but all we'd want is a refreshing gulp to wash down those ores I was telling you about."

Resisting the thought of the ores was hard enough, for Savold was rattlingly empty, but the temptation of the smooth, cool mercury would have roused the glutton in anyone.

"All right," he growled, "but get this straight—we're not going back to your family. They're your problem, not mine."

"But how could I go back to them if you won't go?"

"That's right. I'm glad you see it my way. Now where are those ores and the pools of mercury?"

"Dive," said Gam Nex Biad. "I'll give you the directions."

Savold took a few bounces to work up speed and spin, then shot into the air and came down on the point of his awl-shaped head, which bit through the soft topsoil as if through—he shuddered—so much water. As a Dorfellow, he had to avoid water; it eroded and corroded and caused deposits of rust in the digestive and circulatory systems. There was a warmth that was wonderfully soothing and he was drilling into rock. He ate some to get his strength back, but left room for the main meal and the dessert.

"Pretty nice, isn't it?" asked Gam Nex Biad as they gouged a comfortable tunnel back toward the settlement. "Non-miners don't know what they're missing."

"Quiet," Savold ordered surlily, but he had to confess to himself that it was pleasant. His three knee-action arms rotated him at a comfortable speed, the horn spades pushing back the loose rock; and he realized why Gam Nex Biad had been upset when Surgeon Trink left Savold's human arms attached. They were in the way and they kept getting scratched. The row of socketed bulbs gave him all the light he needed. That, he decided, had been their original purpose. Using them to communicate with must have been one of the first steps toward civilization.

Savold had been repressing thoughts ever since the meeting of the board of surgeons. Experimentally, he called his inner partner.

"Um?" asked Gam Nex Biad absently.

"Something I wanted to discuss with you," Savold said.

"Later. I sense the feldspar coming up. We head north there."

Savold turned the drilling over to him, then allowed the buried thoughts to emerge. They were thoughts of escape and he had kept them hidden because he was positive that Gam Nex Biad would have betrayed them. He had been trying incessantly, wheedlingly, to sell Savold on mining and returning to the family.

The hell with that, Savold thought grimly now. He was getting back to Earth somehow—Earth Command first, Marge second. No, surgery second, Marge third, he corrected. She wouldn't want him this way ...

"Manganese," said Gam Nex Biad abruptly, and Savold shut off his thinking. "I always did like a few mouthfuls as an appetizer."

The rock had a pleasantly spicy taste, much like a cocktail before dinner. Then they went on, with the Dorfellow giving full concentration to finding his way from deposit to deposit.

The thing to do, Savold reasoned, was to learn where the scout ship was being kept. He had tried to sound out Gam Nex Biad subtly, but it must have been too subtle—the Dorfellow had guessed uninterestedly that the ship would be at one of the metal fabricating centers, and Savold had not dared ask which one. Gam Nex Biad couldn't induce him to become a miner and Dorfellow family man, but that didn't mean he could escape over Gam Nex Biad's opposition.

Savold did not intend to find out. Shrewd resourcefulness, that was the answer. It hadn't done him much good yet, but the day he could not outfox these rock-eaters, he'd turn in his commission. All he had to do was find the ship …

Bloated and tired, Savold found himself in a main tunnel thoroughfare back to the settlement. The various ores, he disgustedly confessed to himself, were as delicious as the best human foods and there was nothing at all like the flavor and texture of pure liquid mercury. He discovered some in his cupped cilia hands.

"To keep around for a snack?" he asked Gam Nex Biad.

"I thought you wouldn't mind letting Prad Fim and the children have some," the Dorfellow said hopefully. "You ought to see them light up whenever I bring it home!"

"Not a chance! We're not going there, so I might as well drop it."

Savold tried to open his cilia hands. They stayed cupped. That was when he realized that he had supposed correctly. Gam Nex Biad *could* prevent him from escaping.

Savold had to get some sleep. He was ready to topple with exhaustion. But the tunnels were unsafe—a Dorfellow traveling through one on an emergency night errand would crash into him hard enough to leave nothing but flinty splinters. And the night air felt chill and hostile, so it was impossible to sleep above ground.

"Please make up your mind," Gam Nex Biad begged. "I can't stay awake much longer and you'll just go blundering around and get into trouble."

"But they've got to put us up somewhere," argued Savold. "How about the hospital? We're still a patient, aren't we?"

"We were discharged as cured. And nobody else is allowed to let us stay in any apartment … except one."

"I know, I know," Savold replied with weary impatience. "Forget it. We're not going there."

"But it's so comfortable there … "

"Forget it, I told you!"

"Oh, all right," Gam Nex Biad said resignedly. "But we're not going to find anything as pleasant and restful as my old sleeping boulder. It's soft limestone, you know, and grooved to fit our body. I'd like to see anybody *not* fall asleep instantly on that good old flat boulder … "

Savold tried to resist, but he was worn out from the operation, hunger, digging, and the search for a place to spend the night.

"Just take a *look* at it, that's all," Gam Nex Biad coaxed. "If you don't like it, we'll sleep anywhere you say. Fair enough?"

"I suppose so," admitted Savold.

The hewn-rock apartment was quiet, at least; everybody was asleep. He'd lie down for a while, just long enough to get some rest, and clear out before the household awoke …

But Prad Fim and the children were clustered around the boulder when he opened his eyes. Each of them had five arms to fight off. And there were Surgeon Trink, the elder of the board of surgeons, and the local teacher-judge all waiting to talk to him when the homecoming was over with.

"The treatment worked!" cried the judge. "He came back!"

"I never doubted it," the elder said complacently.

"You know what this means?" Surgeon Trink eagerly asked Savold.

"No, what?" Savold inquired warily, afraid of the answer.

"You can show us how to operate your machine," declared the judge. "It isn't that we lack engineering ability, you understand. We simply never had a machine as large and complex before. We could have, of course—I'm sure you are aware of that—but the matter just didn't come up. We could work it out by ourselves, but it would be much easier to have you explain it."

"By returning, you've shown that you have regained some degree of stability," added the elder. "We couldn't trust you with the machine while you were so disturbed."

"Did you know this?" Savold silently challenged Gam Nex Biad.

"Well, certainly," came the voiceless answer.

"Then why didn't you tell me? Why did you let me go floundering around instead?"

"Because you bewilder me. This loathing for our body, which I'd always been told was quite attractive, and dislike of mining and living with our own family—wanting to reach this thing you call Earth Command and the creature with the strange name. Marge, isn't it? I could never guess how you would react to anything. It's not easy living with an alien mentality."

"You don't have to explain. I've got the same problem, remember."

"That's true," Gam Nex Biad silently agreed. "But I'm afraid you'll have to take it from here. All I know is mining, not machines or metal fabricating centers."

Savold repressed his elation. The less Gam Nex Biad knew from this point on, the less he could guess—and the smaller chance there was that he could betray Savold.

"We can leave right now," the judge was saying. "The family can follow as soon as you've built a home for them."

"Why should they follow?" Savold demanded. "I thought you said I was going to be allowed to operate the ship."

"Demonstrate and explain it, really," the judge amended. "We're not absolutely certain that you are stable, you see. As for the family, you're bound to get lonesome ... "

Savold stared at Prad Fim and the children. Gam Nex Biad was brimming with affection for them, but Savold saw them only as hideous, ore-crushing monsters. He tried to keep them from saying good-by with embraces, but they came at him with such violent leaps that they chipped bits out of his body with their grotesque pointed awl heads. He was glad to get away, especially with Gam Nex Biad making such a damned slobbering nuisance of himself.

"Let's go!" he blinked frantically at the judge, and dived after him into an express tunnel.

While Gam Nex Biad was busily grieving, Savold stealthily worked out his plans. He would glance casually at the ship, glow some mild compliment at the repair job, make a pretense at explaining how the controls worked—and blast off into space at the first opportunity, even if he had to wait for days. He knew he would never get another chance; they'd keep him away from the ship if that attempt failed. And Gam Nex Biad was a factor, too. Savold had to hit the take-off button before his partner suspected or their body would be paralyzed in the conflict between them.

It was a very careful plan and it called for iron discipline, but that was conditioned into every scout pilot. All Savold had to do was maintain his rigid self-control.

He did—until he saw the ship on the hole-pocked plain. Then his control broke and he bounced with enormous, frantic leaps into the airlock and through the corridors to the pilot room.

"Wait! Wait!" glared the judge, and others from the fabricating center sprang toward the ship.

Savold managed to slam the airlock before Gam Nex Biad began to fight him, asking in frightened confusion, "What are you doing?" and locking their muscles so that Savold was unable to move.

"What am I doing?" glinted Savold venomously. "Getting off your lousy planet and back to a world where people live like people instead of like worms and moles!"

"I don't know what you mean," said the Dorfellow anxiously, "but I can't let you do anything until the authorities say it's all right."

"You can't stop me!" Savold exulted. "You can paralyze everything *except my own arms*!"

And that, of course, was the ultimate secret he had been hiding from Gam Nex Biad.

Savold slammed the take-off button. The power plant roared and the ship lifted swiftly toward the sky.

It began to spin.

Then it flipped over and headed with suicidal velocity toward the ground.

"They did something wrong to the ship!" cried Savold.

"Wrong?" Gam Nex Biad repeated vacantly. "It seems to be working fine."

"But it's supposed to be heading *up*!"

"Oh, no," said Gam Nex Biad. "Our machines never go that way. There's no rock up there."

JOURNAL NOTES
Man Of Parts

Theme:
Herbivores live on vegetation and carnivores live on herbivores, so all Earth life is based on plants. Why not eliminate the middleman, so to speak, and have an extraterrestrial race that lives directly on the metals and minerals of a planets crust?

Possibilities:
Tell from viewpoint of a member of the race? Too alien; the reader can't identify strongly. Viewpoint of human visitors to the planet? Too detached; should experience life there, but contrasting human and alien psychology and society subjectively. Only answer is combining the two in one person, the protagonist—bone and organ bank used to save life of man hurt in crash landing on the planet.

Development:
Using bank to put human and alien identities in one body solves two problems—sharp narrative hook because protagonist has two recollections of who he is (or was) and how he got injured; also eliminates need to learn alien language. But he should be alone to emphasize his reactions. No point killing everybody in a ship except one guy; gory and needless, also too contrived. One-man scout mission, his craft crippled, emergency landing, bang. He's badly damaged, but even better reason for reconstructing him from alien accident victim—he can't survive unless he can get his nourishment same way they do. Give him urgent ties to Earth, such as important assignment in interstellar war and a girl back home. But give his alien body-partner equally vital obligations, such as job he's conditioned to and a family. Then let the two battle. Show what it's like to live on rock and minerals, whole society as seen by human and interpreted by alien. Good twists possible at end—being spared flesh arms is a nuisance when digging, but can be used to break alarmed control of body by alien when ship (repaired now) is reached; ship converted for digging—why would rockeaters want to go into space? No rock there.

Editorial Comments:
A story that can make real an entire alien society, while getting the reader to identify with the protagonist—and all in only 5,000 words—is something to be proud of. Not too many years ago, I'd have needed two or three times this length to get the same data and effects across, which naturally would have diffused the impact. Critic Damon Knight thought I was kicking up literary divots just for the hell of it and Editor Raymond J. Healy considered it the final crushing word on multiple-personality stories. Well, maybe; it's always good to learn afterward what one had in mind, but I was exploring a theme I hadn't encountered elsewhere and trying to get a maximum results with minimum wordage. It demanded careful working out and three drafts before it could be achieved. When Michelangelo said, "Only work can eliminate the traces of work," he wasn't kidding.

LOVE IN THE DARK

BEING LIVY GILROY wasn't easy. It meant having a face a little too long, a figure a little too plump, brown hair brushed and brushed yet always uncurling at the ends. It meant not being able to make herself more than passably attractive. Worse than that, being Livy Gilroy meant being Mrs. Gilroy, the wife of that smug lump asleep in the other bed.

Gilroy wasn't snoring; he was too neat for that. He was always making even stacks of things, or putting them in alphabetical order on shelves, or straightening rugs and pictures, or breathing neatly in the other bed.

Livy closed the bedroom door with a bang. Gilroy didn't stir; he could fall asleep in one infuriating minute, and wake up, eight hours later to the second, in exactly the same unlovely position and disposition. Her high-heeled shoes didn't bother him when she kicked them off, and neither did scraping the chair back against the wall—he hated chair marks on walls—when she sat down to take off her stockings. And Livy Gilroy wanted, venomously, to bother her husband.

Gilroy had married her because he had been made sales manager of the electric battery factory, and he'd had enough of eating in restaurants while he had been a traveling salesman. Besides, it looked better for a man in his position to be married. Livy had accepted him because she was past thirty and nobody else might ask her; besides, she needed someone to support her. So she cooked for him. She cleaned for him. She even tried to keep a budget for him, though that was his idea. He gave her a meager household allowance and nothing else.

Nothing, in this case, must be understood as the complete and humiliating absence of everything. When Livy was particularly incensed about her marriage, which was generally, it was some comfort to know that she could have it easily annulled. And Gilroy couldn't do a thing to stop her. He hadn't, at least, and there was no sign that he intended to, cared to, or even thought of it.

Pulling her slip over her head, Livy wondered about this. She had heard, at least as often as any other girl, that all men were beasts. Gilroy was, of course, a beast in a way—in his special primly exasperating way. But he wasn't a beast in the usual sense. With Livy, anyway. Maybe some woman in a back street hovel thought he was. But that wasn't likely; he would have wedded the lady and saved the cost of this apartment.

What was wrong with Gilroy? It wasn't Livy, because she had known her duty and had been grimly prepared for it, though God knew this tall and pudgy person inspired nothing at all in her.

"Short and pudgy," she thought, reaching around back for the hooks. "Why doesn't somebody put hooks in front where they belong and where a body can get at them, and make a fortune? Short and pudgy is bad enough, but Gilroy's got to be *tall* and pudgy, with a stomach that pulls his shoulders down and caves in his chest. And those black-rimmed glasses—some oculist must have been stuck with them for years. That hair of his—thick, oily, wavy and *yellow*. Like butter starting to melt—"

She looked at him again. What had made her think that marrying him was better than not being married at all? She could have got at least a housekeeper's job somewhere. With the possibility that some man in the household would fall in love with her.

Livy stopped. She crossed her arms over her breasts. It was the oddest sensation.

Somebody was staring at her as she undressed.

Gilroy? It didn't seem possible, but she held her slip in front of her and flipped the switch and looked. He was on his side, one arm under his head, and his back was to her. He never looked at her in the light, so why should he stare at her in the dark?

Livy peered under the window shades. They reached the sills; nobody could see beneath them or around them. She felt like a fool bending to glance under the beds, poking warily among the dresses and suits in the closets, and searching behind the furniture.

The light aroused Gilroy; that was something. He twisted around to face her blurrily.

"What's the matter?" he asked, his thin voice fuzzily peevish.

"Somebody was watching me undress," she said.

"Here?"

She tightened her lips. "I haven't undressed in the street in years," she said. "Of course it was here!"

"You mean somebody's in the room with us?" He reached out for his glasses on the night table. "I don't see anyone."

"I know," she said flatly. "I searched the place. It's empty. Or it might as well be."

He stared at her. He wasn't, of course, looking below her face, though she still had her slip clutched in front of her. He was staring at her face as if she had a smudge on it.

"Do you often have these ideas?" he asked.

"Go on back to sleep," she said. "If you want to act like a psychiatrist, your own case would keep you busy for years."

He was still looking at her face, so she turned off the light. She held the slip until she heard him turn heavily, then grunt as he spread himself in the same position as before.

Livy hung up her slip and began peeling off her girdle. There it was again—hungry eyes peering out of the dark, touching her body with ocular caresses.

It wasn't imagination. It couldn't be. She'd been mentally undressed as often as any other not too attractive girl, and she knew the shrinking, exposed feeling too well to mistake it.

No use turning on the light again. She wouldn't find anyone in the room.

"Let's be reasonable," she thought, fighting an urge to leap into bed and scream. "I'm tired. Pooped, if you want to know. That dreary little Mrs. Hall made a hash out of the bridge game. Why do I always draw town idiots as partners? Is it some curse that was put on my family back in the Middle Ages? That's all I need; it's not enough playing house with this inspecting officer searching for dust under the furniture.

"All right, I'm exhausted and jumpy. I'm normal, or what passes for normal. If anybody mentions Freud to me, I'll start swinging this girdle like a night stick. I'm not losing my mind. I'm not having a wish-fulfillment either, if that's what you're thinking. Livy dear, it's just time I went to bed—and don't go twisting *that* statement around."

Her eyes did ache a bit; all that smoke. Maybe she should cut out cigarettes. Aching eyes could make you see things that weren't there. This wasn't exactly seeing, but maybe it was connected somehow.

Livy closed her eyes experimentally, and the effect was more startling than the skin sensation.

In the dark, with her eyes shut, she could *see* who was staring at her. It gave her a shock until she realized that she could *imagine* it, rather; she couldn't see unless her eyes were open, could she? She tried it and the image disappeared. She closed them again and there it was.

As long as it was her imagination, she studied the imaginary owner of the imaginary eyes. She stared at him just as intently as she imagined he was staring at her.

"Stunning," was her first verdict, and then, "What a build! I must have been peering unconsciously at those physical culture magazines on the newsstands. That long blue hair and those wide blond eyes and cute little straight nose—I always *did* love a man with a cleft in his chin! Heavens, did you ever see such *muscles*? And—wait a minute!"

She opened her eyes quickly. A girl had to have some modesty, even if her imagination didn't. And then something jarred her sense of logic.

Long *blue* hair and wide *blond* eyes? It must have been a twist of her subvocal tongue. She meant long blond hair and wide blue eyes. Of course.

She closed her eyes and rechecked. The hair was blue and the eyes were blond, or close enough to it. That wasn't all, either. It wasn't really hair. It was feathers. Long, very fine, like bird-of-paradise plumage; but feathers. As long as they were sort of combed flat, she could never have guessed. But her stunning imaginary man frowned as she stared at him, and the frown lifted his—well, feathers, into an attractive crest. Very attractive, in fact. She liked the effect much better than hair … .

Peculiar. The dazzling creature was blushing under her stare, and turning his head away shyly. Was it possible to blush a beautiful shocking pink? And to have pointed leprechaun ears much handsomer than the regular male clam-shell variety? And since when does a mental image turn bashful?

"Who cares?" thought Livy. "You're a gorgeous thing, and any psychiatrist cures me of this particular delusion over my dead body! Now go away or I won't get a wink of sleep all night."

With her eyes shut, she saw the unearthly vision walk dutifully toward the bedroom door, open it and close it behind him.

"That you, Livy?" asked Gilroy from his bed.

"Is what me?"

"Opening the door."

"I haven't budged from this spot."

She heard him roll over and sit up again. "I'm a practical man with both feet on the ground," he said. "I don't hear things unless there's something to hear. And I heard the door open and close."

Livy pulled on her nightgown over her head—warm, thick flannel because texture and sheerness didn't matter. "All right, you heard the door open and close," she said, falling back luxuriously on her soft mattress and dragging the heavy blankets up. "You can't get me to argue with you this time of night."

"Something's wrong with you," said Gilroy. "We'll find out what it is tomorrow."

As far as she was concerned, there was nothing whatever wrong with her. Why shouldn't an unhappy woman imagine a handsome, thrilling man admiring her? Maybe there was some hidden and sinister significance in the blue plumage and pointed ears, but she didn't care to know about it.

She knew Gilroy wouldn't risk one of her tempers by waking her up to talk, so she firmly pretended to be sleeping while he dressed, made his own breakfast, and drove away. Then she got out of bed and took off the nightgown.

Sure enough, her flesh shrank. She felt as if she were being spied on.

"Look," she said testily to her subconscious, or libido, or whatever the term was, "not the first thing in the morning. Let me at least brush my teeth and have some of that black mud Gilroy calls coffee."

Anyway, it was ridiculous, right in broad daylight. Phantasms are for the dark. Any decent neurosis ought to know that.

Nevertheless, Livy closed her eyes to test her memory. The exciting dreamboat with the blue plumage, blond eyes and gay ears was exactly the same—staring hungrily at her from somewhere near the vanity. Certainly she saw the vanity; she knew it was there, didn't she? She tried staring back, to see if her imaginary lover boy would blush and turn away again. He didn't, which probably meant that some quirk in her mind had grown bolder, for he grinned becomingly and his blond eyes smiled up and down her body.

"I never would have believed it," she muttered moodily, opening her eyes and proceeding to dress. "Rainy evenings I can understand, but I usually feel so nasty in the morning."

She was washing the dishes after breakfast when she felt the first physical symptoms of her delusion. It was a light, airy kiss on the back of her neck. Goosebumps bloomed, her spine went syrupy, her knees came unhooked.

She swiftly disposed of the thrill by blaming it on a loose end of hair. But she cautiously pinned her thatch all up under a kerchief; another few ethereal kisses there, whether uncurled hair or psychological, and she would climb the wall.

Next time she felt the kiss, it started at her neck and worked down to her shoulder, six distinct and passionate touches of warm, hard lips. Weakly she realized that her hair was still tightly bound and pinned up, and that left only one conclusion to be drawn.

"All right," she said, dizzily happy. "I'm going nutty. Wonder why I never thought of it before."

There were more kisses during the day, enough to keep her glowing. Hallucinations, of course, but wonderful ones, and she resolved to hang grimly onto them. So she left Gilroy his dinner and a note, and then went out to a movie.

In the theater, peculiarly, she felt more alone than she had at home. The picture was nothing to rave about, but she saw it three times to make sure Gilroy would be in bed when she returned.

He was, and breathing. She undressed in no great hurry, finally accustomed to the peeping sensation. But when she was under the covers, she screamed suddenly and scrambled out. Gilroy was awake by the time she turned on the light.

"Now what?" he grumbled.

She goggled at him in alarm. "It wasn't you?" she asked.

"*What* wasn't me?"

She sat tentatively on the edge of the bed and rubbed her arm. "Somebody—I thought it was you—I could feel his fingers on my arm just as plain—"

"Whom," Gilroy asked, confused, "are you talking about?"

She put her chin out. "Somebody tried to get into bed with me."

"M-mm," Gilroy nodded solemnly, acting not at all astonished. He put his plump, white, flat feet into slippers and wrestled into a bathrobe. He said anxiously, "Now don't get alarmed, Livy. We'll see this thing through."

"Don't bother," she said. "As long as I know it wasn't you, I'm satisfied."

"I am not in the habit of *slinking*."

"No," she admitted, looking at him appraisingly. "You haven't the physique. Then again, if you did have, you wouldn't have to slink." She gave her head a shake. "I don't know what to think." And she began to cry.

"Now, none of that," he said. "We'll have you all right in a jiffy."

She stood up, ready to run over the beds, if necessary. "Oh, no, not now, you're not."

"I don't know what you mean," he said, and he went to the telephone extension and called Ben Dashman. He agreed with Ben that it was rather late, but added, "It's urgent, Ben, and you're the only one I can turn to. It's Livy nerves. They've—snapped! You'll have to get your clothes on and come right over."

"Ben Dashman," said Livy scornfully. "Here's one consumer whose resistance that business psychologist can't break down. The two of you will just get to your offices all tired out tomorrow, and for what?"

"When there is a crisis, sleep is a secondary consideration,"

Gilroy said. "Ben and I are men of action. This will not be the first time we've worked through the night."

But Ben, when he arrived, sat on a chair at one side of her bed, and Gilroy sat on his own bed and explained to Ben, over Livy's indignant body, the little he knew of what he referred to as her case. Though the information didn't amount to much, it made her just as embarrassed as the first peeping incident.

If Gilroy was pompous and oratorical, and he was, Ben Dashman could claim the doubtful credit. Gilroy had modeled himself after that successful expert on business psychology, who had read his way up to the vice-presidency-in-charge-of-sales. Ben could quote whose chapters of inspirational and analytical studies, whereas Gilroy had mastered no more than brief sentences and paragraphs. The voice had a lot to do with Ben's sensational rise, however. Gilroy had a slightly petulant voice, about Middle C, while Ben had learned to pitch his a full octave below comfort and to propel his words like strung spitballs.

Physically, Ben was even less appetizing than Gilroy. He had a bigger stomach, wider hips, rounder shoulders, white hair split in the center and stuck damply to his pink head, heavy lips that he loved to pucker thoughtfully, and pince-nez. Gilroy would have paid a lot for a pince-nez that would stay on him, but they either stopped his circulation or fell off.

"Well," said Ben when Gilroy was through. Livy won the bet she had made with herself that that would be his first response; it gave him time to think. "Do you have anything to add, Livy?"

"Sure. Go home, or take Gilroy out to a bar. I want to go to sleep."

"I mean about your—strange feeling," Ben persisted.

"I recommend it to all women," she said. "If I knew how, I'd manufacture and sell these dream admirers on the installment plan, and give them free to the needy. It's made me ten years younger. Now go away. I've a date with my delusion."

"Listen," said Gilroy earnestly. "Ben got out of bed and came over here to help you. We both want to help you. Ben has read all there is to know about mental cases."

"I'm not a mental case," Livy said. "I was until now, but I'm not any more. If you both want to help me, you can develop amnesia and wander out of my life. For good. If I'm sick, it's of you."

Gilroy's face went purple, but Ben pacified him hastily: "Don't answer her, Gilroy. She doesn't know what she's saying. You know how it is with these things."

"The only reason he married me was to save money on a housekeeper," she said in a deliberate tone.

"That's right—" Ben encouraged her, patronizingly.

"Are you agreeing with her?" Gilroy shouted.

"I mean that's right—let her get things off her chest," Ben explained. "It releases tension."

So Livy kept talking and it was wonderful. She said the most insultingly true things about Gilroy and he didn't dare turn them into argument. She didn't know much about psychiatry, but she accused him of all the terms she could remember. It was the first time she had examined out loud the facts of her limitation marriage.

"Come to think of it," she concluded, "I don't know why I stayed here this long. As soon as I can get some money together, or a job, I'll let you know my forwarding address."

Then she went to sleep. Ben assured Gilroy that she seemed to have unburdened her grievances and should have no further disturbances. Her threat to leave he considered mere bravado. He advised rest and a sympathetic attitude.

Taking Ben to the door, Gilroy thanked him abjectly: "I don't know what I would have done without you."

"Forget it," said Ben. "If we didn't all pitch in and help each other when the footing gets rocky, there'd be no cooperation in this world."

"That's right," Gilroy said, brightening. "Wasn't it Emerson who pointed out that cooperation is the foundation of civilization?"

"It's always safe to give Emerson the credit," Ben answered. "Now just don't worry about Livy. If she shows any alarming signs of tension, call me up, day or night, and I'll be glad to do what I can."

It was two months before Livy moved out, actually, and then only because she had no real choice. Finding a job had been harder than she anticipated. She had no experience and the best part of the day to go job-hunting had usually been taken up by cooking, cleaning, shopping, sending out the laundry, and reading. For she had begun consuming psychology books—both normal and abnormal—searching for a parallel to her condition.

She found roughly similar cases, some which were almost identical in unimportant respects. But the really significant symptom, which urged her on in her hunt, she found nowhere.

None of the systematically deluded women had ever had a baby by an imaginary sweetheart. And Livy, her doctor had told her after the usual tests, was indisputably pregnant.

"But that's impossible," she had protested.

"I thought so myself," the doctor, who was Gilroy's physician also, had confessed. "But, you see, the profession is full of surprises."

"That isn't what I mean," Livy said in a panic.

She asked for some aromatic spirits in water. She wanted a chance to rehearse her answer. It sounded absurd even to herself.

She and Gilroy had not changed the basis of her marriage. Gilroy *couldn't* be the father of her child. He wasn't. It was impossible. Under the circumstances, it was absolutely impossible. Yet it was also impossible for her to be pregnant. She had an alibi for every minute of their marriage.

But these days, she realized numbly, when a doctor tells a woman she is going to have a baby, she can start buying a layette.

So she shuffled out of the doctor's office, clutching her list of medical instructions, and that night she told Gilroy.

Gilroy didn't bark or howl; he called Ben Dashman instead. Ben understood the situation instantly.

"Livy's conscience caused those delusions," he said. "She has obviously been having an affair."

"There was nothing obvious about it," Livy said. "It was so *un*obvious, in fact, that I didn't know about it myself."

This time Ben Dashman's presence didn't stop Gilroy from losing his temper. "Are you denying," he yelled, "that you *have* been having an affair?"

"Certainly," said Livy. "I'd know about it, wouldn't I?"

"Well, that's a point, Gilroy," Ben said ponderously. "In the condition Livy's been in lately, she might not have been responsible."

"*I'm* not going to be responsible, and that's for sure," Gilroy said. "We'll find out who the man is if we have to dig clean through her unconscious and down to her pituitary gland!"

Gilroy threw his glasses, the big black-rimmed ones, on the floor and trampled on them. Livy felt a little proud. She had never seen him so angry before. She had never suspected that she could have such an effect on him, or she might have tried it long ago.

"Livy," Ben said gently, "you do know who the man was, don't you?"

"Sure," she said. "It was my dreamboat, my lover boy—the one who ogled me while I was undressing, the one who tried to get into bed with me. I didn't let him until you convinced me he wasn't real. Then I didn't see any reason to be afraid."

"You mean," said Gilroy, terrible in his self-control, "right here in the same room with me?"

"Why not?" she asked reasonably. "It was just a delusion. Do I go around censoring *your* dreams? Though heaven knows they're probably just about selling campaigns and how to make people battery-conscious!"

Ben waved Gilroy to silence. "Then am I to understand," he said, "that your only meetings with your so-called dreamboat have been here in your own bedroom, with your husband asleep in the next bed?"

"That's right," Livy said. "Exactly."

Ben stood up and pointed unpleasantly at Gilroy. "You," he said nastily, "are an ungrateful, inconsiderate, lying scoundrel."

"I am?" Gilroy asked, baffled out of his outrage. "How do you figure that, Ben?"

"Because for some obscure reason you're trying to blacken the name of your wife, when it's perfectly clear that the only man who could be the father is you."

"Oh, no! I can prove it isn't!"

"I'll bet," Livy said, "he could at that. But he doesn't have to, Ben. I'll give him an affidavit that he isn't."

"You see?" Gilroy cried triumphantly.

Ben nodded. "I guess I do. Livy, I respect your gallantry, but it's a mistake to protect the guilty party."

"You don't catch me getting gallant at a time like this," Livy said. "I can't tell you his name, because I don't know it, but I'll be glad to tell you who he is."

She described the phantom who loved her.

"Blue feathers!" yelled Gilroy. "Blond eyes! She isn't crazy, Ben. Oh, no, she thinks *we* are!"

Ben stood up. "Gilroy, I think we need a conference." Gilroy followed him unwillingly and when Livy opened the door carefully, a few moments later, she heard Ben say, "I've read about cases like this. It's a very grave, very deep disturbance—too deep for me to handle, though I'd love to try and I believe I'd do pretty well. But the first thing she needs is protection. From herself and this unscrupulous vandal she imagines has blue plumage and blond eyes."

And Gilroy asked, "Then you think she really believes this nonsense?"

And Ben said, "Of course, poor girl. She's batty. Use your head."

And Gilroy said slowly, "I never thought of that. But why would she claim he's invisible?"

Livy could picture Ben lifting his fat shoulders. "It might take months or years to find out, and the important thing right now is to protect her. That wouldn't hurt you either, Gilroy. Nobody puts any stock in what a patient at a rest home says."

There was more discussion, but Livy didn't stay to hear it. She had climbed out the kitchen window and over the low backyard fence. Finding a taxi took a while, but she got downtown and closed out her savings account.

Now all she had to do was find a place to live. She couldn't go back to Gilroy, of course, and she had some bad moments imagining that her description had been broadcast and that she would be picked up and sent to an asylum. She wasn't worried for herself. But Lover Boy might not find her, and she wouldn't be able to get out and search for him.

Among the classified ads she came across a two-room furnished apartment. It turned out to be across the street from a lumber yard, far enough away from Gilroy to be relatively safe; and the rental was low. She could live on her savings until the baby was born. What would happen after that didn't seem to matter much right now.

When she went to bed, she left strangely alone. It wasn't Gilroy sleeping in the other bed that she missed. She had felt alone in the same room with him up until she thought up Dreamboat. Where was *he*? She squeezed her eyes shut and concentrated. No, he wasn't there. Gilroy's house must have been the special habitat of that particular hallucination.

She disliked facing Gilroy again, and perhaps Ben too, but there apparently was no other way to bring back her blue-plumed, stunning mental phantom. She dressed and called a cab.

There was a light in the bedroom, but she saved investigating that for last. She let herself in with her own key and took off her shoes, then slid through all the other rooms with her eyes firmly shut. Establishing no contact, she opened the bedroom door—and there he was.

His lips were grim, his cleft chin jutted, his blond eyes were savage, and he held his fists in uppercut position as he crouched like a boxer over Gilroy's raging face. He seemed to be rapping out some harsh words, but even Livy couldn't hear him.

"You stinker," she heard Gilroy snarl. "You hit me when I wasn't looking."

And Ben protested, "Don't be an idiot. Your unconscious is punishing you for the way you treated that sweet, troubled girl. I can show you cases just like yours—"

And Gilroy said, "Are you telling me I walked into something?"

Ben told him in a calm voice, "Every psychiatrist knows about the unconscious wish for punishment."

Gilroy yelled, "There's nothing unconscious about my wish to sock you on that fat jaw." And he did.

Lover Boy looked past the battle and saw her in the doorway. His angry face brought forth a slow, unearthly smile, and he walked carefully around the fighting fat men and took her hand. It may have been her imagination, but she *felt* the passionately warm, hard flesh.

She had to open her eyes outside the house and on the way back to her apartment. But she held desperately to his hand.

It was after she came home from the hospital that Ben found her. He told her he had heard of mothers radiating, but that this was the first time he had seen it. She could feel the glow in her face as she showed him the empty crib.

"I know you can't see him," she said, "but I can when I close my eyes. He's a beautiful baby. He has his father's features."

"You caused a little stir at the hospital," Ben said. "That's how I found you."

She laughed. "Oh, you mean the doctor? I thought he'd order himself a straight-jacket."

"Well, delivering an invisible baby is no joke, especially when you're called away from a stag party," Ben said soberly. "He was finally convinced that it was only the liquor, but he hasn't touched a drop since. They never did discover the baby, did they?"

"I had it in my room all the time. They were afraid I'd sue and give them a lot of bad publicity, but I said it was all right." She turned away from the crib. "I don't suppose Gilroy minded the Reno divorce, did he?"

"He knew he was getting off lucky. These kissless-marriage annulments can drive a man to changing his name and moving to another state. But tell me, Livy, how did you arrange the second marriage?"

"By telephone," she said. "I guess you've heard the groom's name and birthplace."

Ben hissed on his glasses, wiped them meticulously. "There was some mention in the newspapers."

"Clrkxsdyl 93J16," she said gaily. "I call him Clark for short. And he comes from Alpha Centauri somewhere. I wouldn't have known that, except he learned to use a typewriter—we don't hear the same frequencies, he says."

Ben's eyes slid away from hers and looked around the shabby apartment. "Well, you do seem happy, I must say."

"There's only one thing that bothers me," she said. "Clark could have picked any woman on Earth. I'm about as average as you can get without being a freak. Why did he want *me*?"

"There's no explaining love," Ben evaded uneasily. He put his pudgy hand in his inside pocket and looked directly at her. "Let's not have any false pride," he said. "You haven't asked Gilroy for a cent, but you have no income and I'd be glad—"

"Oh, we're doing fine," said Livy, shaking her hair, which she had let grow long and straight with no sign of a permanent. "We're getting a raise soon."

"A raise?" Ben was surprised. "From where? For doing what?"

"I'm supposed to be working for Grant's Detective Agency. But it's really Clark who's the operative—private eye, he calls it now, after reading all those mystery stories—and he types up the reports. All I have to do is correct his English now and then. Imagine, he's even learning slang. Grant can't figure out how we get information that's so hard to uncover, but it's easier than pie for Clark."

"Sure," said Ben, going to the door. "But what are you laughing at?"

"Those blue feathers. They tickle!"

Although Ben could have dropped the situation there, there was one thing you could say for him; he was conscientious. He made one more investigation.

"What do you want to know about her for?" Mr. Grant asked coldly and suspiciously.

"I'm a friend of hers," Ben explained, handing Grant his business card. "I just want to make sure she's earning a good living. She divorced a—well, somebody I used to know, and she wouldn't take any alimony. I offered to help out, but she said she's doing all right working for you."

Grant's professionally slitted eyes developed a glint of smug possession. "Oh, I was afraid you might want to hire her away from me," he said. "That girl is the best operative I ever had. She could shadow a nervous sparrow. Why, she's got methods—"

"Good, huh?"

"Good?" repeated Grant. "You'd think she was invisible!"

JOURNAL NOTES
Love In The Dark

Theme:
Why hasn't the succubus idea been given a thoroughly modern treatment? Every version I recall is nineteenth-century Gothic and straight fantasy. Putting it into everyday terms should be much more effective; making the invisible lover an extraterrestrial instead of a supernatural visitation ought to introduce fresh problems and complications.

Possibilities:
There are three—viewpoint of man, woman or extraterrestrial. Man's viewpoint is liable to sound like something out of Spicy Science Fiction. Woman's angle has some nice potentialities. Alien slant has been done too often.

Development:
Unhappy woman needed. Not overly attractive, or admiration, whether from extraterrestrial or human, wouldn't be unusual. Single? Not enough conflict. But how can she be married and have love affair without outraging editor, publisher, reader, post office, etc.? "Kissless marriage" euphemism tabloids are so addicted to? Good—reader is on her side, especially if her husband is noteworthily unlovable. Both need strong characterization, much stronger than the alien, who handsome and striking, just sharpens their antipathy and finally explodes it. Hold down when dealing with husband, or the marriage would be totally incredible; small, highly unpleasant, *nagging* traits are better—prim sleeper, irritatingly neat, pompous but not grotesquely so, married her to get home-cooked meals *and* because a married man is a sounder business proposition. She can't be ordinary female, embittered, shrewish, and so forth, griping about her fate. Must be given brittle wit so she looks good in comparison and is amusing even when furious. Ad-agency gal transplanted to suburbs, in other words, but only the brittleness, not the chic or blasé. Blue hair and blond eyes for the invisible extraterrestrial; nice small

shock. Everything has to be made legal—annulment, naturally; telephone marriage to the lover (lots of that during World War II); invisible baby that turns hospital upside down. Use alien's invisibility in practical money-making way. What could be better than an invisible detective?

Editorial Comments:
Livy is one of my favorite characters. She really comes to life. That's a big private triumph—I had to give up writing confessions because, when I tried to capture female emotions, I squashed them in my knobby fist. The technical trick that stands out here is the relative directness of the plot versus the intricate deviousness of the intra- and interpersonal relationships; it's like ping-pong doubles on a fast train. I fretted considerably about the switch in viewpoint at the end, realized there was no other way to condense the story.

THE MAN WITH ENGLISH

LYING IN THE HOSPITAL, Edgar Stone added up his misfortunes as another might count blessings. There were enough to infuriate the most temperate man, which Stone notoriously was not. He smashed his fist down, accidentally hitting the metal side of the bed, and was astonished by the pleasant feeling. It enraged him even more. The really maddening thing was how simply he had goaded himself into the hospital.

He'd locked up his drygoods store and driven home for lunch. Nothing unusual about that; he did it every day. With his miserable digestion, he couldn't stand the restaurant food in town. He pulled into the driveway, rode over a collection of metal shapes his son Arnold had left lying around, and punctured a tire.

"Rita!" he yelled. "This is going too damned far! Where is that brat?"

"In here," she called truculently from the kitchen.

He kicked open the screen door. His foot went through the mesh.

"A ripped tire and a torn screen!" he shouted at Arnold who was sprawled in angular adolescence over a blueprint on the' kitchen table. "You'll pay for them, by God! They're coming out of your allowance!"

"I'm sorry, Pop," the boy said.

"Sorry, my left foot," Mrs. Stone shrieked. She whirled on her husband. "You could have watched where you were going. He promised to clean up his things from the driveway right after lunch. And it's about time you stopped kicking open the door every time you're mad."

"Mad? Who wouldn't be mad? Me hoping he'd get out of school and come into the store, and he wants to be an engineer. An engineer—and he can't even make change when he—hah!—helps me out in the store!"

"He'll be whatever he wants to be," she screamed in the conversational tone of the Stone household.

"Please," said Arnold. "I can't concentrate on this plan."

Edgar Stone was never one to restrain an angry impulse. He tore up the blueprint and flung the pieces down on the table.

"Aw, Pop!" Arnold protested.

"Don't say 'Aw, Pop' to me. You're not going to waste a summer vacation on junk like this. You'll eat your lunch and come down to the store. And you'll do it every day for the rest of the summer!"

"Oh, he will, will he?" demanded Mrs. Stone. "He'll catch up on his studies. And as for you, you can go back and eat in a restaurant."

"You know I can't stand that slop!"

"You'll eat it because you're not having lunch here any more. I've got enough to do without making three meals a day."

"But I can't drive back with that tire—"

He did, though not with the tire-he took a cab. It cost a dollar plus tip, lunch was a dollar and a half plus tip, bicarb at Rite Drug Store a few doors away and in a great hurry came to another fifteen cents—only it didn't work.

And then Miss Ellis came in for some material. Miss Ellis could round-out any miserable day. She was fifty, tall, skinny and had thin, disapproving lips. She had a sliver of cloth clipped very meagerly off a hem that she intended to use as a sample.

"The arms of the slipcover on my reading chair wore through," she informed him. "I bought the material here, if you remember."

Stone didn't have to look at the fragmentary swatch. "That was about seven years ago—"

"Six-and-a-half," she corrected. "I paid enough for it. You'd expect anything that expensive to last."

"The style was discontinued. I have something here that—"

"I do not want to make an entire slipcover, Mr. Stone. All I want is enough to make new panels for the arms. Two yards should do very nicely."

Stone smothered a bilious hiccup. "Two yards, Miss Ellis?"

"At the most."

"I sold the last of that material years ago." He pulled a bolt off a shelf and partly unrolled it for her. "Why not use a different pattern as a kind of contrast?"

"I want this same pattern," she said, her thin lips getting even thinner and more obstinate.

"Then I'll have to order it and hope one of my wholesalers still has some of it in stock."

"Not without looking for it first right here, you won't order it for me. You can't know *all* these materials you have on these shelves."

Stone felt all the familiar symptoms of fury—the sudden pulsing of the temples, the lurch and bump of his heart as adrenalin came surging in like the tide at the Firth of Forth, the quivering of his hands, the angry shout pulsing at his vocal cords from below.

"I'll take a look, Miss Ellis," he said.

She was president of the Ladies' Cultural Society and dominated it so thoroughly that the members would go clear to the next town for their dry goods, rather than deal with him, if he offended this sour stick of stubbornness.

If Stone's life insurance salesman had been there, he would have tried to keep Stone from climbing the ladder that ran around the three walls of the store. He probably wouldn't have been in time. Stone stamped up the ladder to reach the highest shelves, where there were scraps of bolts. One of them might have been the remnant of the material Miss Ellis had bought six-and-a-half years ago. But Stone never found out.

He snatched one, glaring down meanwhile at the top of Miss Ellis's head, and the ladder skidded out from under him. He felt his skull collide with the counter. He didn't feel it hit the floor.

"God damn it!" Stone yelled. "You could at least turn on the lights."

"There, there, Edgar. Everything's fine, just fine."

It was his wife's voice and the tone was so uncommonly soft and soothing that it scared him into a panic.

"What's wrong with me?" he asked piteously. "Am I blind?"

"How many fingers am I holding up?" a man wanted to know.

Stone was peering into the blackness. All he could see before his eyes was a vague blot against a darker blot.

"None," he bleated. "Who are you?"

"Dr. Rankin. That was a nasty fall you had, Mr. Stone— concussion, of course, and a splinter of bone driven into the brain. I had to operate to remove it."

"Then you cut out a nerve!" Stone said. "You did something to my eyes!"

The doctor's voice sounded puzzled. "There doesn't seem to be anything wrong with them. I'll take a look, though, and see."

"You'll be all right, dear," Mrs. Stone said reassuringly, but she didn't sound as if she believed it.

"Sure you will, Pop," said Arnold.

"Is that young stinker here?" Stone demanded. "He's the cause of all this!"

"Temper, temper," the doctor said. "Accidents happen." Stone heard him lower the Venetian blinds. As if they had been a switch, light sprang up and everything in the hospital became brightly visible.

"Well!" said Stone. "That's more like it. It's night and you're trying to save electricity, hey?"

"It's broad daylight, Edgar dear," his wife protested. "All Dr. Rankin did was lower the blinds and—"

"Please," the doctor said. "If you don't mind, I'd rather take care of any explanations that have to be made."

He came at Stone with an ophthalmoscope. When he flashed it into Stone's eyes, everything went black and Stone let him know it vociferously.

"Black?" Dr. Rankin repeated blankly. "Are you positive? Not a sudden glare?"

"Black," insisted Stone. "And what's the idea of putting me in a bed filled with bread crumbs?"

"It was freshly made—"

"Crumbs. You heard me. And the pillow has rocks in it."

"What else is bothering you?" asked the doctor worriedly.

"It's freezing in here." Stone felt the terror rise in him again. "It was summer when I fell off the ladder. Don't tell me I've been unconscious clear through till winter!"

"No, Pop," said Arnold. "That was yesterday—"

"I'll take care of this," Dr. Rankin said firmly. "I'm afraid you and your son will have to leave, Mrs. Stone. I have to do a few tests on your husband."

"Will he be all right?" she appealed.

"Of course, of course," he said inattentively, peering with a frown at the shivering patient. "Shock, you know," he added vaguely.

"Gosh, Pop," said Arnold. "I'm sorry this happened. I got the driveway all cleaned up."

"And we'll take care of the store till you're better," Mrs. Stone promised.

"Don't you dare!" yelled Stone. "You'll put me out of business!"

The doctor hastily shut the door on them and came back to the bed. Stone was clutching the light summer blanket around himself. He felt colder than he'd ever been in his life.

"Can't you get me more blankets?" he begged. "You don't want me to die of pneumonia, do you?"

Dr. Rankin opened the blinds and asked, "What's this like?"

"Night," chattered Stone. "A new idea to save electricity—hooking up the blinds to the light switch?"

The doctor closed the blinds and sat down beside the bed. He was sweating as he reached for the signal button and pressed it. A nurse came in, blinking in their direction.

"Why don't you turn on the light?" she asked.

"Huh?" said Stone. "They are."

"Nurse, I'm Dr. Rankin. Get me a piece of sandpaper, some cotton swabs, an ice cube and Mr. Stone's lunch."

"Is there anything he shouldn't eat?"

"That's what I want to find out. Hurry, please."

"And some blankets," Stone put in, shaking with the chill.

"Blankets, Doctor?" she asked, startled.

"Half a dozen will do," he said. "I think."

It took her ten minutes to return with all the items. Stone wanted them to keep adding blankets until all seven were on him. He still felt cold.

"Maybe some hot coffee?" he suggested.

The doctor nodded and the nurse poured a cup, added the spoon and a half of sugar he requested, and he took a mouthful. He sprayed it out violently.

"Ice cold!" he yelped. "And who put salt in it?"

"Salt?" She fumbled around on the tray. "It's so dark here—"

"I'll attend to it," Dr. Rankin said hurriedly. "Thank you."

She walked cautiously to the door and went out.

"Try this," said the doctor, after filling another cup.

"Well, that's better!" Stone exclaimed. "Damned practical joker. They shouldn't be allowed to work in hospitals."

"And now, if you don't mind," said the doctor, "I'd like to try several tests."

Stone was still angry at the trick played on him, but be cooperated willingly.

Dr. Rankin finally sagged back in the chair. The sweat ran down his face and into his collar, and his expression was so dazed that Stone was alarmed.

"What's wrong, Doctor? Am I going to—going to—"

"No, no. It's not that. No danger. At least, I don't believe there is. But I can't even be sure of that any more."

"You can't be sure if I'll live or die?"

"Look." Dr. Rankin grimly pulled the chair closer. "It's broad daylight and yet you can't see until I darken the room. The coffee was hot and sweet, but it was cold and salty to you, so I added an ice cube and a spoonful of salt and it tasted fine, you said. This is one of the hottest days on record and you're freezing. You told me the sandpaper felt smooth and satiny, then yelled that somebody had put pins in the cotton swabs, when there weren't any, of course. I've tried you out with different colors around the room and you saw violet when you should have seen yellow, green for red, orange for blue, and so on. Now do you understand?"

"No," said Stone frightenedly. "What's wrong?"

"All I can do is guess. I had to remove that sliver of bone from your brain. It apparently shorted your sensory nerves."

"And what happened?"

"Every one of your senses has been reversed. You feel cold for heat, heat for cold, smooth for rough, rough for smooth, sour for sweet, sweet for sour, and so forth. And you see colors backward."

Stone sat up. "Murderer! Thief! You've ruined me!"

The doctor sprang for a hypodermic and sedative. Just in time, he changed his mind and took a bottle of stimulant instead. It worked fine, though injecting it into his screaming, thrashing patient took more strength than he'd known he owned. Stone fell asleep immediately.

There were nine blankets on Stone and he had a bag of cement for a pillow when he had his lawyer, Manny Lubin, in to hear the charges he wanted brought against Dr. Rankin. The doctor was there to defend himself. Mrs. Stone was present in spite of her husband's objections—"She always takes everybody's side against me," he explained in a roar.

"I'll be honest with you, Mr. Lubin," the doctor said, after Stone had finished on a note of shrill frustration. "I've hunted for cases like this in medical history and this is the first one ever to be reported. Except," he amended quickly, "that I haven't reported it yet. I'm hoping it reverses itself. That sometimes happens, you know."

"And what am I supposed to do in the meantime?" raged Stone. "I'll have to go out wearing an overcoat in the summer and shorts in the winter—people will think I'm a maniac. And they'll be *sure* of it because I'll have to keep the store closed during the day and open at night—I can't see except in the dark. And matching materials! I can't stand the feel of smooth cloth and I see colors backward!" He glared at the doctor before turning back to Lubin. "How would you. like to have to put sugar on your food and salt in your coffee?"

"But we'll work it out, Edgar dear," his wife soothed. "Arnold and I can take care of the store. You always wanted him to come into the business, so that ought to please you—"

"As long as I'm there to watch him!"

"And Dr. Rankin said maybe things will straighten out."

"What about that, Doctor?" asked Lubin. "What are the chances?"

Dr. Rankin looked uncomfortable. "I don't know. This has never happened before. All we can do is hope."

"Hope, nothing!" Stone stormed. "I want to sue him. He had no right to go meddling around and turn me upside down. Any jury would give me a quarter of a million!"

"I'm no millionaire, Mr. Stone," said the doctor.

"But the hospital has money. We'll sue him and the trustees." There was a pause while the attorney thought. "I'm afraid we wouldn't have a case, Mr. Stone." He went on more rapidly as Stone sat up, shivering, to argue loudly. "It was an emergency operation. Any surgeon would have had to operate. Am I right, Dr. Rankin?"

The doctor explained what would have happened if he had not removed the pressure on the brain, resulting from the concussion, and the danger that the bone splinter, if not extracted, might have gone on traveling and caused possible paralysis or death.

"That would be better than this," said Stone.

"But medical ethics couldn't allow him to let you die," Lubin objected. "He was doing his duty. That's point one."

"Mr. Lubin is absolutely right, Edgar," said Mrs. Stone.

"There, you see?" screamed her husband. "Everybody's right but me! Will you get her out of here before I have a stroke?"

"Her interests are also involved," Lubin pointed out. "Point two is that the emergency came first; the after-effects couldn't be known or considered."

Dr. Rankin brightened. "Any operation involves risk, even the excising of a corn. I had to take those risks."

"You had to take them?" Stone scoffed. "All right, what are you leading up to, Lubin?"

"We'd lose," said the attorney.

Stone subsided, but only for a moment. "So we'll lose. But if we sue, the publicity would ruin him. I want to sue!"

"For what, Edgar dear?" his wife persisted. "We'll have a hard enough time managing. Why throw good money after bad?"

"Why didn't I marry a woman who'd take my side, even when I'm wrong?" moaned Stone. "Revenge, that's what. And he won't be able to practice, so he'll have time to find out if there's a cure ... and at no charge, either! I won't pay him another cent!"

The doctor stood up eagerly. "But I'm willing to see what can be done right now. And it wouldn't cost you anything, naturally."

"What do you mean?" Stone challenged suspiciously.

"If I were to perform another operation, I'll be able to see which nerves were involved. There's no need to go into the technical side right now, but it is possible to connect nerves. Of course, there are a good many, which complicates matters, especially since the splinter went through several layers—" Lubin pointed a lawyer's impaling finger at him. "Are you offering to attempt to correct the injury—gratis?"

"Certainly. I mean to say, I'll do my absolute best. But keep in mind, please, that there is no medical precedent."

The attorney, however, was already questioning Stone and his wife. "In view of the fact that we have no legal grounds whatever for suit, does this offer of settlement satisfy your claim against him?"

"Oh, yes!" Mrs. Stone cried.

Her husband hesitated for a while, clearly tempted to take the opposite position out of habit. "I guess so," he reluctantly agreed.

"Well, then, it's in your hands, Doctor," said Lubin.

Dr. Rankin buzzed excitedly for the nurse. "I'll have him prepared for surgery right away."

"It better work this time," warned Stone, clutching a handful of ice cubes to warm his fingers.

Stone came to foggily. He didn't know it, but he had given the anesthetist a bewildering problem, which finally had been solved by using fumes of aromatic spirits of ammonia. The four blurred figures around the bed seemed to be leaning precariously toward him.

"Pop!" said Arnold. "Look, he's coming out of it! Pop!"

"Speak to me, Edgar dear," Mrs. Stone beseeched.

Lubin said, "See how he is, Doctor."

"He's fine," the doctor insisted heartily, his usual bedside manner evidently having returned. "He must be—the blinds are open and he's not complaining that it's dark or that he's cold." He leaned over the bed. "How are we feeling, Mr. Stone?"

It took a minute or two for Stone to move his swollen tongue enough to answer. He wrinkled his nose in disgust.

"What smells purple?" he demanded.

JOURNAL NOTES
The Man with English

Theme:
What would it be like to have one's senses completely reversed? Damned nasty, no doubt, but let's get specific—what would happen, how great would the confusion and frustration be, how (if at all) can it be coped with?

Possibilities:
No need to hunt for setups; put an ordinary guy into the situation-but make sure he needs at least some senses acutely developed to make a living—and treat the problem with intense realism. Nothing to be gained by moving the situation out of the present; keep it right here and right now. The more immediately recognizable the background and character, the greater the reader identification.

Development:
An artist, who depends so much on his senses, is the most obvious protagonist. Therefore, discard. Good everyday job, yet one that demands sense of touch and eye for color—owner of a small yard-goods store. The reversal of senses would most likely be caused by accident. so he should be hot-tempered enough to create his own accident. First argument with wife and son (wants son to help out in store during summer vacation; wife objects; also refuses to feed him three times a day because—he's dyspeptic and can't eat restaurant food); nuisance of a customer he has to be polite to because she's a power with the upper crust in town; use ladder that runs on rails around store—I almost fell off enough of them; emergency operation, discovery of reversed senses, distraught doctor, no legal case, doctor offers to operate again—can't guarantee success, naturally—and howler of a kicker when the senses are switched even further.

Editorial Comment:
Editor Frederik Pohl gave me part of a weekend and an exact wordage to meet. By limiting writing time and length, though, he

eliminated some aggravating self-imposed difficulties. I had figured on examining—in detail—just how the protagonist would live with his reversed senses, increase his frustration until another operation would be necessary, and then use this kicker, which is probably the most explosive one I've ever invented. (Funny Thing Dept.: The British can't understand the title; they have another term for putting "English"—backspin—on a ball. I found that out when Author Arthur C. Clarke asked baffledly what the blazes the title meant. I told him. "Oh!" he exclaimed. "You mean—" And I forget the expression he used.)

THE BIOGRAPHY PROJECT

THERE WAS SOMETHING TREMENDOUSLY EXCITING about the opening of the Biofilm Institute. Even a hardened Sunday supplement writer like Wellman Zatz felt it.

Arlington Prescott, a wiper in a contact-eyeglass factory, while searching for a time machine, had invented the Biotime Camera, a standard movie camera—minus sound, of course—that projected a temporal beam, re-accumulated it, and focused it on a temporal-light-sensitized film. When he discovered that he had to be satisfied with merely photographing the past, not physically visiting it, Prescott had quit doing research and become principal of a nursery school.

But, Zatz explained, dictating his notes by persfone to a vox-typer in the telenews office, the Biofilm Institute was based on Prescott's repudiated invention. A huge, massive building, mostly below ground, in the 23rd century style, and equipped with 1,000 Biotime Cameras, it was the gift of Humboldt Maxwell, wealthy manufacturer of Snack Capsules. There were 1,000 teams of biographers, military analysts, historians, etc., to begin recording history as it actually happened—with special attention, according to Maxwell's grant, to past leaders of industry, politics, science, and the arts, in the order named.

Going through the Biofilm Institute, Wellman Zatz gained mostly curt or snarled interviews with the Bioteams; fishing through time for incidents or persons was a nervous job, and they resented interruptions.

He settled finally on a team that seemed slightly friendlier. They were watching what looked like a scene from Elizabethan England on the monitor screen.

"Sir Isaac Newton," Kelvin Burns, the science biographer, grunted in reply to Zatz's question. "Great man. We want to find out why he went off the beam."

Zatz knew about that, of course. Sunday feature articles for centuries had used the case of Sir Isaac to support arguments for psychic phenomena. After making all his astonishing discoveries by the age of 25, the great 17th century scientist had spent the rest of his long life in a hunt for precognition, the philosopher's stone, and other such paraphernalia of mysticism.

"My guess," said Mowbray Glass, the psychiatrist, "is paranoia caused by feelings of rejection in childhood."

But the screen showed a happy boy in what seemed to be a normal 17th century home and school environment. Glass grew puzzled as Sir Isaac eventually produced his binomial theorem, differential and integral calculus, and went to work on gravity—all without evidencing any symptoms of emotional imbalance.

"The most unbelievable demonstrative and deductive powers I've encountered," said Pinero Schmidt, the science integrator. "I can't believe such a man could go mystical."

"But he did," Glass said, and tensed. "Look!"

Alone in a dark, cumbersomely furnished study, the man on the screen, wearing a satin coat, stock and breeches, glanced up sharply. He looked directly into the temporal beam for a moment, and then stared into the shadows of the room. He grabbed up a silver candlestick and searched the corners, holding the heavy candlestick like a weapon.

"He's mumbling something," reported Gonzalez Carson, the lip-reader. "Spies. He thinks somebody's after his discoveries."

Burns looked puzzled. "That's the first sign we've seen of breakdown. But what caused it?"

"I'm damned if I know," admitted Glass.

"Heredity?" Zatz suggested.

"No," Glass said positively. "It's been checked."

The Bioteam spent hours prying further. When the scientist was in his thirties, he developed a continuing habit of looking up and smiling secretly. On his deathbed, forty years later, he moved his lips happily, without fear.

"'My guardian angel,'" Carson interpreted for them. "'You've watched over me all my life. I am content to meet you now.'"

Glass started. He went to one Bioteam after another, asking a brief question of each. When he came back, he was trembling.

"What's the answer, Doc?" Zatz asked eagerly.

"We can't use the Biotime Camera any more," Glass said, looking sick. "My colleagues have been investigating the psychoses of Robert Schumann, Marcel Proust and others, who all eventually developed delusions of persecution."

"Yeah, but why?" Zatz persisted.

"Because they thought they were being spied upon. And they were, of course. By us!"

JOURNAL NOTES
The Biography Project

Theme:
One time paradox I've never seen is changing history through invisible observation. That is, if it's not possible to travel through time physically, only via camera or some such, wouldn't the sense of being watched change the lives of those being spied upon?

Possibilities:
Big-scale historical treatment comes to mind first, of course. Maybe this is why first Napoleon and then Hitler didn't invade British Isles. Negative—something that militarily *should* have been done wasn't done. Dig deeper; active shadowing can produce dramatic tension as the victim is hounded to desperation, but this is an unverified and unverifiable haunted feeling and it can't be directional, as in shadowing. That indicates emphasis of the psychological. Can't build on the sense of being watched, so it should be used as a snapper. Use characters of the past who went nuts, blame it on the device. (No trite time paradox—history is changed, but the change is part of history.)

Development:
Isaac Newton is a fine—because otherwise baffling—subject. But other areas are needed to substantiate the payoff. Can't handle them one after another or even simultaneously; too stretched out. Besides, the longer a surprise punch line is delayed, the greater the chance of being outguessed by the reader. A project subsidized by tycoon. (Mild satirical opportunities.) Touch on inventor; disappointed because it's only a way to view instead of visit the past. Keep him out of story—his chagrin would complicate unnecessarily.) Could have member of one of the project teams as central character, but danger of exaggerating technical stuff and emotional reactions. Best protagonist would be a newsman assigned to cover story—wouldn't be too hep or personally involved and can report on project better.

Editorial Comments:
I'd been holding this idea for some time when a hole appeared in *Galaxy*; two pages had to be filled. I hunted through manuscripts and called agents, but the stories were either telegraphed (the commonest fault in short-shorts) or overlong. So I set the margins on my typewriter and wrote *The Biography Project* to fit. I'd have preferred another few hundred words to move around in, but they couldn't be had, which meant heroic compression. If you check the length, you'll find it's almost exactly 800 words! The technical feat here was to shoehorn needed detail into a plot that couldn't be boiled down so drastically that it made no sense, and to let go of the snapper at the right moment, which, in short-shorts, always means before the reader sees it coming. The whole thing was the sort of challenge that's supposed to be good for one, and definitely is in the development of skill—but it's hell on the nerves.

AT THE POST

WHEN GILROY CAME into the Blue Ribbon, on 49th Street west of Broadway, he saw that nobody had told Doc Hawkins about his misfortune. Doc, a pub-crawling, non-practicing general practitioner who wrote a daily medical column for a local tabloid, was celebrating his release from the alcoholic ward, but his guests at the rear table of the restaurant weren't in any mood for celebration.

"What's the matter with you—have you suddenly become immune to liquor?" Clocker heard Doc ask irritably, while Clocker was passing the gem merchants, who, because they needed natural daylight to do business, were traditionally accorded the tables nearest the windows. "I said the drinks were on me, didn't I?" Doc insisted. "Now let us have some bright laughter and sparkling wit, or must we wait until Clocker shows up before there is levity in the house?"

Seeing the others glance toward the door, Doc turned and looked at Clocker. His mouth fell open silently, for the first time in Clocker's memory.

"Good Lord!" he said after a moment. "Clocker's become a *character*!"

Clocker felt embarrassed. He still wasn't used to wearing a business suit of subdued gray, and black oxfords, instead of his usual brilliant sports jacket, slacks and two-tone suede shoes; a tie with timid little figures, whereas he had formerly been an authority on hand-painted cravats; and a plain wristwatch in place of his spectacular chronograph.

By all Broadway standards, he knew, Doc was correct—he'd become strange and eccentric, a character.

"It was Zelda's idea," Clocker explained somberly, sitting down and shaking his head at the waiter who ambled over. "She wanted to make a gentleman out of me."

"*Wanted to*?" Doc reported, bewildered. "You two kids got married just before they took my snakes away. Don't tell me you phhtt already!"

Clocker looked appealingly at the others. They became busy with drinks and paper napkins.

Naturally, Doc Hawkins knew the background: That Clocker was a race handicapper—publisher, if you could call it that, of a tiny tip sheet—for Doc, in need of drinking money, had often consulted him professionally. Also that Clocker had married Zelda, the noted 52nd Street stripteuse, who had social aspirations. What remained to be told had occurred during Doc's inevitably temporary cure.

"Isn't anybody going to tell me?" Doc demanded.

"It was right after you tried to take the warts off a fire hydrant and they came and got you," said Clocker, "that Zelda started hearing voices. It got real bad."

"How bad?"

"She's at Glendale Center in an upholstered room. I just came back from visiting her."

Doc gulped his entire drink, a positive sign that he was upset, or happy, or not feeling anything in particular. Now, however, he was noticeably upset.

"Did the psychiatrists give you a diagnosis?" he asked.

"I got it memorized. Catatonia. Dementia praecox, what they used to call, one of the brain vets told me, and he said it's hopeless."

"Rough," said Doc. "Very rough. The outlook is never good in such cases."

"Maybe they can't help her," Clocker said harshly, "but I will."

"People are not horses," Doc reminded him.

"I've noticed that," said Handy Sam, the armless wonder at the flea circus, drinking beer because he had an ingrown toenail and couldn't hold a shot glass. Now that Clocker had told the grim story, he felt free to talk, which he did enthusiastically. "Clocker's got a giant brain, Doc. Who was it said Warlock'd turn into a dog in his third year? Clocker, the only dopester in the racket. And that's just one—"

"Zelda was my best flesh act," interrupted Arnold Wilson Wyle, a ten-percenter whom video had saved from alimony jail. "A solid boffola in the bop basements. Nobody regrets her sad condition more than me, Clocker, but it's a sure flop, what you got in mind. Think of your public. For instance, what's good at Hialeah? My bar bill is about to be foreclosed and I can use a long shot."

Clocker bounced his fist on the moist table. "Those couch artists don't know what's wrong with Zelda. I do."

"You do?" Doc asked, startled.

"Well, almost. I'm so close, I can hear the finish-line camera clicking."

Buttonhole grasped Doc's lapel and hung on with characteristic avidity; he was perhaps Clocker's most pious subscriber. "Doping races is a science. Clocker maybe never doped the human race, but I got nine to five he can do it. Go on, tell him, Clocker."

Doc Hawkins ran together the rings he had been making with the wet bottom of his tumbler. "I shall be most interested," he said with tabloid irony, clearly feeling that immediate disillusionment was the most humane thing for Clocker. "Perhaps we can collaborate on an article for the psychiatric journals."

"All right, look." Clocker pulled out charts resembling those he worked with when making turf selections. "Zelda's got catatonia, which is the last heat in the schizophrenia parlay. She used to be a hoofer before she started undressing for dough, and now she does time-steps all day."

Doc nodded into a fresh glass that the waiter had put before him. "Stereotyped movements are typical of catatonia. They derive from thwarted or repressed instinctual drive; in most instances, the residue of childhood frustrations."

"She dance all day, huh, Clocker?" asked Oil Pocket, the Oklahoma Cherokee who, with the income of several wells, was famed for angeling bareback shows. He had a glass of tequila in one hand, the salted half of a lemon in the other. "She dance good?"

"That's just it," Clocker said. "She does these time-steps, the first thing you learn in hoofing, over and over, ten-fifteen hours a day. And she keeps talking like she's giving lessons to some jerk kid who can't get it straight. And she was the babe with the hot routines, remember."

"The hottest," agreed Arnold Wilson Wyle. "Zelda doing time-steps is like Heifetz fiddling at weddings."

"I still like to put her in show," Oil Pocket grunted. "She stacked like brick tepee. Don't have to dance good."

"You'll have a long wait," observed Doc sympathetically, "in spite of what our young friend here says. Continue, young friend."

Clocker spread his charts. He needed the whole table. The others removed their drinks, Handy Sam putting his on the floor so he could reach it more easily.

"This is what I got out of checking all the screwball factories I could reach personal and by mail," Clocker said. "I went around and talked to the doctors and watched the patients in the places near here, and wrote to the places I couldn't get to. Then I broke everything down like it was a stud and track record."

Buttonhole tugged Doc's lapel. "That ain't scientific, I suppose," he challenged.

"Duplication of effort," Doc replied, patiently allowing Buttonhole to retain his grip. "It was all done in an organized fashion over a period of more than half a century. But let us hear the rest."

"First," said Clocker, "there are more male bats than fillies."

"Females are inherently more stable, perhaps because they have a more balanced chromosome arrangement."

"There are more nuts in the brain rackets than labor chumps."

"Intellectual activity increases the area of conflict."

"There are less in the sticks than in the cities, and practically none among the savages. I mean real savages," Clocker told Handy Sam, "not marks for con merchants."

"I was wondering," Handy Sam admitted.

"Complex civilization creates psychic insecurity," said Doc.

"When these catatonics pull out, they don't remember much or maybe nothing," Clocker went on, referring to his charts.

Doc nodded his shaggy white head. "Protective amnesia."

"I seen hundreds of these mental gimps. They work harder and longer at what they're doing, even just laying down and doing nothing, than they ever did when they were regular citizens."

"Concentration of psychic energy, of course."

"And they don' t get a damn cent for it."

Doc hesitated, put down his half-filled tumbler. "I beg your pardon?"

"I say they're getting stiffed," Clocker stated. "Anybody who works that hard ought to get paid. I don't mean it's got to be money, although that's the only kind of pay Zelda'd work for. Right, Arnold?"

"Well, sure," said Arnold Wilson Wyle wonderingly. "I never thought of it like that. Zelda doing time-steps for nothing ten-fifteen hours a day—that ain't Zelda."

"If you ask me, she *likes* her job," Clocker said. "Same with the other catatonics I seen. But for no pay?"

Doc surprisingly pushed his drink away, something that only a serious medical puzzle could ever accomplish. "I don't understand what you're getting at."

"I don't know these other cata-characters, but I do know Zelda," said Arnold Wilson Wyle. "She's got to get something out of all that work. Clocker says it's the same with the others and I take his word. What are they knocking theirself out for if it's for free?"

"They gain some obscure form of emotional release or repetitive gratification," Doc explained.

"Zelda?" exploded Clocker. "You offer her a deal like that for a club date and she'd get ruptured laughing."

"I tell her top billing," Oil Pocket agreed, "plenty ads, plenty publicity, whole show built around her. Wampum, she says; save money on ads and publicity, give it to her. Zelda don't count coups."

Doc Hawkins called over the waiter, ordered five fingers instead of his customary three. "Let us not bicker," he told Clocker. "Continue."

Clocker looked at his charts again. "There ain't a line that ain't represented, even the heavy rackets and short grifts. It's a regular human steeplechase. And these sour apples do mostly whatever they did for a living—draw pictures, sell shoes, do lab experiments, sew clothes, Zelda with her time-steps. By the hour! In the air!"

"In the air?" Handy Sam repeated. "Flying?"

"Imaginary functioning," Doc elaborated for him. "They have nothing in their hands. Pure hallucination. Systematic delusion."

"Sign language?" Oil Pocket suggested.

"That," said Clocker, before Doc Hawkins could reject the notion, "is on the schnoz, Injun. Buttonhole says I'm like doping races. He's right. I'm working out what some numbers-runner tells me is probabilities. I got it all here," he rapped the charts, "and it's the same thing all these flop-ears got in common. Not their age, not their jobs, not their—you should pardon the expression—sex. They're *teaching*."

Buttonhole looked baffled. He almost let go of Doc's lapel.

Handy Sam scratched the back of his neck thoughtfully with a big toe. "Teaching, Clocker? Who? You said they're kept in solitary."

"They are. I don't know who. I'm working on that now."

Doc shoved the charts aside belligerently to make room for his beefy elbows. He leaned forward and glowered at Clocker. "Your theory belongs in the Sunday supplement of the alleged newspaper I write for. Not all catatonics work, as you call it. What about those who stand rigid and those who lie in bed all the time?"

"I guess you think that's easy," Clocker retorted. "You try it sometime. I did. It's work, I tell you." He folded his charts and put them back into the inside pocket of his conservative jacket. He looked sick with longing and loneliness. "Damn, I miss that mouse. I got to save her, Doc! Don't you get that?"

Doc Hawkins put a chunky hand gently on Clocker's arm. "Of course, boy. But how can you succeed when trained men can't?"

"Well, take Zelda. She did time-steps when she was maybe five and going to dancing school—"

"Time-steps have some symbolic significance to her," Doc said with more than his usual tact. "My theory is that she was compelled to go against her will, and this is a form of unconscious rebellion."

"They don't have no significance to her," Clocker argued doggedly. "She can do time-steps blindfolded and on her knees with both ankles tied behind her back." He pried Buttonhole's hand off Doc's lapel, and took hold of both of them himself. "I tell you she's teaching, explaining, breaking in some dummy who can't get the hang of it!"

"But who?" Doc objected. "Psychiatrists? Nurses? You? Admit it, Clocker—she goes on doing time-steps whether she's alone or not. In fact, she never knows if anybody is with her. Isn't that so?"

"Yeah," Clocker said grudgingly. "That's what has me boxed."

Oil Pocket grunted tentatively, "White men not believe in spirits. Injuns do. Maybe Zelda talk to spirits."

"I been thinking of that," confessed Clocker, looking at the red angel unhappily. "Spirits is all I can figure. Ghosts. Spooks. But if Zelda and these other catatonics are teaching ghosts, these ghosts are the dumbest jerks anywhere. They make her and the rest go through time-steps or sewing or selling shoes again and again. If they had half a brain, they'd get it in no time."

"Maybe spirits not hear good," Oil Pocket offered, encouraged by Clocker's wilingness to consider the hypothesis.

"Could be," Clocker said with partial conviction. "If we can't see them, it may be just as hard for them to see or hear us."

Oil Pocket anxiously hitched his chair closer. "Old squaw name Dry Ground Never Rainy Season—what you call old maid—hear spirits all the time. She keep telling us what they say. Nobody listen."

"How come?" asked Clocker interestedly.

"She deaf, blind. Not hear thunder. Walk into cactus, yell like hell. She hardly see us, not hear us at all, how come she see and hear spirits? Just talk, talk, talk all the time."

Clocker frowned, thinking. "These catatonics don't see or hear us, but they sure as Citation hear and see *something*."

Doc Hawkins stood up with dignity, hardly weaving, and handed a bill to the waiter. "I was hoping to get a private racing tip from you, Clocker. Freshly sprung from the alcoholic ward, I can use some money. But I see that your objectivity is impaired by emotional considerations. I wouldn't risk a dime on your advice even after a race is run."

"I didn't expect you to believe me," said Clocker despairingly. "None of you pill-pushers ever do."

"I can't say about your psycho-doping," declared Arnold Wilson Wyle, also rising. "But I got faith in your handicapping. I'd still like a long shot at Hialeah if you happen to have one."

"I been too busy trying to help Zelda," Clocker said in apology.

They left, Doc Hawkins pausing at the bar to pick up a credit bottle to see him through his overdue medical column.

Handy Sam slipped on his shoes to go. "Stick with it, Clocker. I said you was a scientist—"

"*I* said it," contradicted Buttonhole, lifting himself out of the chair on Handy Sam's lapels. "If anybody can lick this caper, Clocker can."

Oil Pocket glumly watched them leave. "Doctors not think spirits real," he said. "I get sick, go to Reservation doctor. He give me medicine. I get sicker. Medicine man see evil spirits make me sick. Shakes rattle. Dances. Evil spirits go. I get better."

"I don't know what in hell to think," confided Clocker, miserable and confused. "If it would help Zelda, I'd cut my throat from head to foot so I could become a spirit and get the others to lay off her."

"Then you spirit, she alive. Making love not very practical."

"Then what do I do—hire a medium?"

"Get medicine man from Reservation. He drive out evil spirits."

Clocker pushed away from the table. "So help me, I'll do it if I can't come up with something cheaper than paying freight from Oklahoma."

"Get Zelda out, I pay and put her in show."

"Then if I haul the guy here and it don't work, I'm in hock to you. Thanks, Oil Pocket, but I'll try my way first."

Back in his hotel room, waiting for the next day so he could visit Zelda, Clocker was like an addict at the track with every cent on a hunch. After weeks of neglecting his tip sheet to study catatonia, he felt close to the payoff.

He spent most of the night smoking and walking around the room, trying not to look at the jars and hairbrushes on the bureau. He missed the bobbypins on the floor, the nylons drying across the shower rack, the toothpaste tubes squeezed from the top. He'd put her perfumes in a drawer, but the smell was so pervasively haunting that it was like having her stand invisibly behind him.

As soon as the sun came up, he hurried out and took a cab. He'd have to wait until visiting hours, but he couldn't stand the slowness of the train. Just being in the same building with her would—almost—be enough.

When he finally was allowed into Zelda's room, he spent all his time watching her silently, taking in every intently mumbled word and movement. Her movements, in spite of their gratingly basic monotony, were particularly something to watch, for Zelda had blue-black hair down to her shapely shoulders, wide-apart blue eyes, sulky mouth, and an astonishing body. She used all her physical equipment with unconscious provocativeness, except her eyes, which were blankly distant.

Clocker stood it as long as he could and then burst out, "Damn it, Zelda, how long can they take to learn a time-step?"

She didn't answer. She didn't see him, hear him, or feel him. Even when he kissed her on the back of the neck, her special place, she did not twist her shoulder up with the sudden thrill.

He took out the portable phonograph he'd had permission to bring in, and hopefully played three of her old numbers—a ballet tap, a soft shoe, and, most potent of all, her favorite slinky strip tune. Ordinarily, the beat would have thrown her off, but not any more.

"Dead to this world," muttered Clocker dejectedly.

He shook Zelda. Even when she was off-balance, her feet tapped out the elementary routine.

"Look, kid," he said, his voice tense and angry, "I don't know who these squares are that you're working for, but tell them if they got you, they got to take me, too."

Whatever he expected—ghostly figures to materialize or a chill wind from nowhere—nothing happened. She went on tapping.

He sat down on her bed. *They* picked people the way he picked horses, except he picked to win and they picked to show. To show? Of course. Zelda was showing them how to dance and also, probably, teaching them about the entertainment business. The others had obviously been selected for what they knew, which they went about doing as single-mindedly as she did.

He had a scheme that he hadn't told Doc because he knew it was crazy. At any rate, he hoped it was. The weeks without her had been a hell of loneliness—for him, not for her; she wasn't even aware of the awful loss. He'd settle for that, but even better would be freeing her somehow. The only way he could do it would be to find out who controlled her and what they were after. Even with that information, he couldn't be sure of succeeding, and there was a good chance that he might also be caught, but that didn't matter.

The idea was to interest *them* in what he knew so they would want to have him explain all he knew about racing. After that—well, he'd make his plans when he knew the setup.

Clocker came close to the automatic time-step machine that had been his wife. He began talking to her, very loudly, about the detailed knowledge needed to select winners, based on stud records, past performances of mounts and jockeys, condition of track and the influence of the weather—always, however, leaving out the data that would make sense of the whole complicated industry. It was like roping a patsy and holding back the buzzer until the dough was down. He knew he risked being cold-decked, but it was worth the gamble. His only worry was that hoarseness would stop him before he hooked *their* interest.

An orderly, passing in the corridor, heard his voice, opened the door and asked with ponderous humor, "What you doing, Clocker—trying to take out a membership card in this country club?"

Clocker leaped slightly. "Uh, working on a private theory," he said, collected his things with a little more haste than he would have liked to show, kissed Zelda without getting any response whatever, and left for the day.

But he kept coming back every morning. He was about to give up when the first feelings of unreality dazed and dazzled him. He carefully suppressed his excitement and talked more loudly about racing. The world seemed to be slipping away from him. He could have hung onto it if he had wanted. He didn't. He let the voices come, vague and far away, distorted, not quite meaningless, but not adding up to much, either.

And then, one day, he didn't notice the orderly come in to tell him that visiting hours were over. Clocker was explaining the fundamentals of horse racing ... meticulously, with immense patience, over and over and over ... and didn't hear him.

It had been so easy that Clocker was disappointed. The first voices had argued gently and reasonably over him, each claiming priority for one reason or another, until one either was assigned or pulled rank. That was the voice that Clocker eventually kept hearing—a quiet, calm voice that constantly faded and grew stronger, as if it came from a great distance and had trouble with static. Clocker remembered the crystal set his father had bought when radio was still a toy. It was like that.

Then the unreality vanished and was replaced by a dramatic new reality. He was somewhere far away. He knew it wasn't on Earth, for this was like nothing except, perhaps, a World's Fair.

The buildings were low and attractively designed, impressive in spite of their softly blended spectrum of pastel colors. He was in a huge square that was grass-covered and tree-shaded and decorated with classical sculpture. Hundreds of people stood with him, and they all looked shaken and scared. Clocker felt nothing but elation; he'd arrived. It made no difference that he didn't know where he was or anything about the setup. He was where Zelda was.

"How did I get here?" asked a little man with bifocals and a vest that had pins and threaded needles stuck in it. "I can't take time for pleasure trips. Mrs. Jacobs is coming in for her fitting tomorrow and she'll positively murder me if her dress ain't ready."

"She can't," Clocker said. "Not any more."

"You mean we're dead?" someone else asked, awed. It was a softly pudgy woman with excessively blonde hair, a greasily red-lipped smile and a flowered housecoat. She looked around with great approval. "Hey, this ain't bad! Like I always said, either I'm no worse than anybody else or they're no better'n me. How about that, dearie?"

"Don't ask me," Clocker evaded. "I think somebody's going to get an earful, but you ain't dead. That much I can tell you."

The woman looked disappointed.

Some people in the crowd were complaining that they had families to take care of while others were worried about leaving their businesses. They all grew silent, however, when a man climbed up on a sort of marble rostrum in front of them. He was very tall and dignified and wore formal clothes and had a white beard parted in the center.

"Please feel at ease," he said in a big, deep, soothing voice, like a radio announcer for a symphony broadcast. "You are not in any danger. No harm will come to you."

"You *sure* we ain't dead, sweetie?" the woman in the flowered housecoat asked Clocker. "Isn't that—"

"No," said Clocker. "He'd have a halo, wouldn't he?"

"Yeah, I guess so," she agreed doubtfully.

The white-bearded man went on, "If you will listen carefully to this orientation lecture, you will know where you are and why. May I introduce Gerald W. Harding? Dr. Harding is in charge of this reception center. Ladies and gentlemen, Dr. Harding."

A number of people applauded out of habit ... probably lecture fans or semi-pro TV studio audiences. The rest, including Clocker, waited as an aging man in a white lab smock, heavy-rimmed eyeglasses and smooth pink cheeks, looking like a benevolent doctor in a mouthwash ad, stood up and faced the crowd. He put his hands behind his back, rocked on his toes a few times, and smiled benevolently.

"Thank you, Mr. Calhoun," he said to the bearded man who was seating himself on a marble bench. "Friends—and I trust you will soon regard us *as* your friends—I know you are puzzled at all this." He waved a white hand at the buildings around them. "Let me explain. You have been chosen—yes, carefully screened and selected—to help see that you are asking yourselves why you were selected and what this cause is. I shall describe it briefly. You'll learn more about it as we work together in this vast and noble experiment."

The woman in the flowered housecoat looked enormously flattered. The little tailor was nodding to show he understood the points covered thus far. Glancing at the rest of the crowd, Crocker realized that he was the only one who had this speech pegged. It was a pitch. These men were out for something.

He wished Doc Hawkins and Oil Pocket were there. Doc doubtless would have searched his unconscious for symbols of childhood traumas to explain the whole thing; he would never have accepted it as some kind of reality. Oil Pocket, on the other hand, would somehow have tried to equate the substantial Mr. Calhoun and Dr. Harding with tribal spirits. Of the two, Clocker felt that Oil Pocket would have been closer.

Or maybe he was in his own corner of psychosis, while Oil Pocket would have been in another, more suited to Indians. Spirits or figments? Whatever they were, they looked as real as anybody he'd ever known, but perhaps that was the naturalness of the supernatural or the logic of insanity.

Clocker shivered, aware that he had to wait for the answer. The one thing he did know, as an authority on cons, was that this had the smell of one, supernatural or otherwise. He watched and listened like a detective shadowing an escape artist.

"This may be something of a shock," Dr. Harding continued with a humorous, sympathetic smile. "I hope it will not be for long. Let me state it in its simplest terms. You know that there are billions of stars in the Universe, and that stars have planets as naturally as cats have kittens. A good many of these planets are inhabited. Some life-forms are intelligent, very much so, while others are not. In almost all instances, the dominant form of life is quite different from—yours."

Unable to see the direction of the con, Clocker felt irritated.

"Why do I say *yours*, not *ours*?" asked Dr. Harding. "Because, dear friends, Mr. Calhoun and I are not of your planet or solar system. No commotion, please!" he urged, raising his hands as the crowd stirred bewilderedly. "Our names are not Calhoun and Harding; we adopted those because our own are so alien that you would be unable to pronounce them. We are not formed as you see us, but this is how we might look if we were human beings, which, of course, we are not. Our true appearance seems to be—ah—rather confusing to human eyes."

Nuts, Clocker thought irreverently. Get to the point.

"I don't think this is the time for detailed explanations," Dr. Harding hurried on before there were any questions. "We are friendly, even altruistic inhabitants of a planet 10,000 light-years from Earth. Quite a distance, you are thinking; how did we get here? The truth is that we are not 'here' and neither are you. 'Here' is a projection of thought, a hypothetical point in space, a place that exists only by mental force. Our physical appearances and yours are telepathic representations. Actually, our bodies are on our own respective planets."

"Very confusing," complained a man who looked like a banker. "Do you have any idea of what he's trying to tell us?"

"Not yet," Clocker replied with patient cynicism. "He'll give us the convincer after the buildup."

The man who looked like a banker stared sharply at Clocker and moved away. Clocker shrugged. He was more concerned with why he didn't feel tired or bored just standing there and listening. There was not even an overpowering sense of urgency and annoyance, although he wanted to find Zelda and this lecture was keeping him from looking for her. It was as if his emotions were somehow being reduced in intensity. They existed, but lacked the strength they should have had.

So he stood almost patiently and listened to Dr. Harding say, "Our civilization is considerably older than yours. For many of your centuries, we have explored the Universe, both physically and telepathically. During this exploration, we discovered your planet. We tried to establish communication, but there were grave difficulties. It was the time of your Dark Ages, and I'm sorry to report that those people we made contact with were generally burned at the stake." He shook his head regretfully. "Although your civilization has made many advances in some ways, communication is still hampered—as much by false knowledge as by real ignorance. You'll see in a moment why it is very unfortunate."

"Here it comes," Clocker said to those around him. "He's getting ready finally to slip us the sting."

The woman in the housecoat looked indignant. "The nerve of a crumb like you making a crack about such a fine, decent gentleman!"

"A blind man could see he's sincere," argued the tailor. "Just think of it—*me*, in a big experiment! Will Molly be surprised when she finds out!"

"She won't find out and I'll bet she's surprised right now," Clocker assured him.

"The human body is an unbelievably complicated organism," Dr. Harding was saying. The statement halted the private discussion and seemed to please his listeners for some reason. "We learned that when we tried to assume control of individuals for the purpose of communication. Billions of neural relays, thousands of unvolitional functions—it is no exaggeration to compare our efforts with those of a monkey in a power plant. At our direction, for example, several writers produced books that were fearfully garbled. Our attempts with artists were no more successful. The static of interstellar space was partly responsible, but mostly it was the fact that we simply couldn't work our way through the maze that is the human mind and body."

The crowd was sympathetic. Clocker was neither weary nor bored, merely longing for Zelda and, as a student of grifts, dimly irritated. Why hold back when the chumps were set up?

"I don't want to make a long story of our problems," smiled Dr. Harding. "If we could visit your planet in person, there would be no difficulty. But 10,000 light-years is an impossible barrier to all except thought waves, which, of course, travel at infinite speed. And this, as I said before, is very unfortunate, because the human race is doomed."

The tailor stiffened. "Doomed? Molly? My kids? All my customers?"

"*Your* customers?" yelped the woman in the housecoat. "How about mine? What's gonna happen, the world should be doomed?"

Clocker found admiration for Dr. Harding's approach. It was a line tried habitually by politicians, but they didn't have the same kind of captive audience, the control, the contrived background. A cosmic pitch like this could bring a galactic payoff, whatever it might be. But it didn't take his mind off Zelda.

"I see you are somewhat aghast," Dr. Harding observed. "But is my statement *really* so unexpected? You know the history of your own race—a record of incessant war, each more devastating than the last. Now, finally, Man has achieved the power of worldwide destruction. The next war, or the one after that, will unquestionably be the end not only of civilization, but of humanity—perhaps even your entire planet. Our peaceful, altruistic civilization might help avert catastrophe, but that would require our physical landing on Earth, which is not possible. Even if it were, there is not enough time. Armageddon draws near.

"Then why have we brought you here?" asked Dr. Harding. "Because Man, in spite of his suicidal blunders, is a magnificent race. He must not vanish without leaving a *complete record* of his achievements."

The crowd nodded soberly. Clocker wished he had a cigarette and his wife. In her right mind, Zelda was unswervingly practical and she would have had some noteworthy comments to make.

"This is the task we must work together on," said Dr. Harding forcefully. "Each of you has a skill, a talent, a special knowledge we need for the immense record we are compiling. Every area of human society must be covered. We need you—urgently! Your data will become part of an imperishable social document that shall exist untold eons after mankind has perished."

Visibly, the woman in the housecoat was stunned. "They want to put down what *I* can tell them?"

"And tailoring?" asked the little man with the pin-cushion vest. "How to make buttonholes and press clothes?"

The man who looked like a banker had his chin up and a pleased expression on his pudgy face.

"I always knew I'd be appreciated some day," he stated smugly. "I can tell them things about finance that those idiots in the main office can't even guess at."

Mr. Calhoun stood up beside Dr. Harding on the rostrum. He seemed infinitely benign as he raised his hands and his deep voice.

"Friends, we need *your* help, *your* knowledge. I know you don't want the human race to vanish without a *trace*, as though it had never existed. I'm *sure* it thrills you to realize that some researcher, *far* in the *future*, will one day use the very knowledge that *you* gave. Think what it means to leave *your* personal imprint indelibly on cosmic history!" He paused and leaned forward. "Will you help us?"

The faces glowed, the hands went up, the voices cried that they would.

Dazzled by the success of the sell, Clocker watched the people happily and flatteredly follow their frock-coated guides toward the various buildings, which appeared to have been laid out according to very broad categories of human occupation.

He found himself impelled along with the chattering, excited woman in the housecoat toward a cerise structure marked Sports and Rackets. It seemed that she had been angry at not having been interviewed for a recent epic survey, and this was her chance to decant the experiences of twenty years.

Clocker stopped listening to her gabble and looked for the building that Zelda would probably be in. He saw Arts and Entertainment, but when he tried to go there, he felt some compulsion keep him heading toward his own destination.

Looking back helplessly, he went inside.

He found that he was in a cubicle with a fatherly kind of man who had thin gray hair, kindly eyes and a firm jaw, and who introduced himself as Eric Barnes. He took Clocker's name, age, specific trade, and gave him a serial number which, he explained, would go on file at the central archives on his home planet, cross-indexed in multiple ways for instant reference.

"Now," said Barnes, "here is our problem, Mr. Locke. We are making two kinds of perpetual records. One is written; more precisely, microscribed. The other is a wonderfully exact duplicate of your cerebral pattern—in more durable material than brain matter, of course."

"Of course," Clocker said, nodding like an obedient patsy.

"The verbal record is difficult enough, since much of the data you give us must be, by its nature, foreign to us. The duplication of your cerebral pattern, however, is even more troublesome. Besides the inevitable distortion caused by a distance of 10,000 light-years and the fields of gravitation and radiation of all types intervening, the substance we use in place of brain cells absorbs memory quite slowly." Barnes smiled reassuringly. "But you'll be happy to know that the impression, once made, can *never* be lost or erased!"

"Delighted," Clocker said flatly. "Tickled to pieces."

"I knew you would be. Well, let us proceed. First, a basic description of horse racing."

Clocker began to give it. Barnes held him down to a single sentence— "To check reception and retention," he said.

The communication box on the desk lit up when Clocker repeated the sentence a few times, and a voice from the box said, "Increase output. Initial impression weak. Also wave distortion. Correct and continue."

Barnes carefully adjusted the dials and Clocker went on repeating the sentence, slowing down to the speed Barnes requested. He did it automatically after a while, which gave him a chance to think.

He had no plan to get Zelda out of here; he was improvising and he didn't like it. The setup still had him puzzled. He knew he wasn't dreaming all this, for there were details his imagination could never have supplied, and the notion of spirits with scientific devices would baffle even Oil Pocket.

Everybody else appeared to accept these men as the aliens they claimed to be, but Clocker, fearing a con he couldn't understand, refused to. He had no other explanation, though, no evidence of any kind except deep suspicion of any noble-sounding enterprise. In his harsh experience, they always had a profit angle hidden somewhere.

Until he knew more, he had to go along with the routine, hoping he would eventually find a way out for Zelda and himself. While he was repeating his monotonous sentence, he wondered what his body was doing back on Earth. Lying in a bed, probably, since he wasn't being asked to perform any physical jobs like Zelda's endless time-step.

That reminded him of Doc Hawkins and the psychiatrists. There must be some here; he wished vengefully that he could meet them and see what they thought of their theories now.

Then came the end of what was apparently the work day. "We're making splendid progress," Barnes told him. "I know how tiresome it is to keep saying the same thing over and over, but the distance is such a *great* obstacle. I think it's amazing that we can even *bridge* it, don't you? Just imagine—the light that's reaching Earth at this very minute left our star when mammoths were roaming your western states and mankind lived in caves! And yet, with our thought-wave boosters, we are in instantaneous communication!"

The soap, Clocker thought, to make him feel he was doing something important.

"Well, you are doing something important," Barnes said, as though Clocker had spoken.

Clocker would have turned red if he had been able to. As it was, he felt dismay and embarrassment.

"Do you realize the size and value of this project?" Barnes went on. "We have a more detailed record of human society than Man himself ever had! There will be not even the most insignificant corner of your civilization left unrecorded! Your life, my life—the life of this Zelda whom you came here to rescue—all are trivial, for we must die eventually, but the project will last eternally!"

Clocker stood up, his eyes hard and worried. "You're telling me you know what I'm here for?"

"To secure the return of your wife. I would naturally be aware that you had submitted yourself to our control voluntarily. It was in your file, which was sent to me by Admissions."

"Then why did you let me in?"

"Because, my dear friend—"

"Leave out the 'friend' pitch. I'm here on business."

Barnes shrugged. "As you wish. We let you in, as you express it, because you have knowledge that we should include in our archives. We hoped you would recognize the merit and scope of our undertaking. Most people do, once they are told."

"Zelda, too?"

"Oh, yes," Barnes said emphatically. "I had that checked by Statistics. She is extremely cooperative, quite convinced—"

"Don't hand me that!"

Barnes rose. Straightening the papers on his desk, he said, "You want to speak to her and see for yourself? Fair enough."

He led Clocker out of the building. They crossed the great square to a vast, low structure that Barnes referred to as the Education and Recreation Center.

"Unless there are special problems," Barnes said, "our human associates work twelve or fourteen of your hours, and the rest of the time is their own. Sleep isn't necessary to the psychic projection, of course, though it is to the body on Earth. And what, Mr. Locke, would you imagine they choose as their main amusements?"

"Pinball machines?" Clocker suggested ironically. "Crap games?"

"Lectures," said Barnes with pride. "They are eager to learn everything possible about our project. We've actually had the director himself address them! Oh, it was inspiring. Mr. Locke—color films in three dimensions, showing the great extent of our archives, the many millions of synthetic brains, each with indestructible memories of skills and crafts and professions and experiences that soon will be no more—"

"Save it. Find Zelda for me and then blow. I want to talk to her alone."

Barnes checked with the equivalent of a box office at the Center, where, he told Clocker, members of the audience and staff were required to report before entering, in case of emergency.

"Like what?" Clocker asked.

"You have a suspicious mind," said Barnes patiently. "Faulty neuron circuit in a synthetic duplicate brain, for example, Photon storms interfering with reception. Things of that sort."

"So where's the emergency?"

"We have so little time. We ask the human associate in question to record again whatever was not received. The percentage of refusal is actually *zero*! Isn't that splendid?"

"Best third degree I ever heard of," Clocker admitted through clamped teeth. "The cops on Earth would sell out every guy they get graft from to buy a thing like this."

They found Zelda in a small lecture hall, where a matronly woman from the other planet was urging her listeners to conceal nothing, however intimate, while recording—"Because," she said, "this must be a psychological as well as a cultural and sociological history."

Seeing Zelda, Clocker rushed to her chair, hauled her upright, kissed her, squeezed her.

"Baby!" he said, more choked up than he thought his control would allow. "Let's get out of here!"

She looked at him without surprise. "Oh, hello, Clocker. Later, I want to hear the rest of this lecture."

"Ain't you glad to see me?" he asked, hurt. "I spend months and shoot every dime I got just to find you—"

"Sure I'm glad to see you, hon," she said, trying to look past him at the speaker. "But this is so important—"

Barnes came up, bowed politely. "If you don't mind, Miss Zelda, I think you ought to talk to your husband."

"But what about the lecture?" asked Zelda anxiously.

"I can get a transcription for you to study later."

"Well, all right," she agreed reluctantly.

Barnes left them on a strangely warm stone bench in the great square, after asking them to report back to work at the usual time. Zelda, instead of looking at Clocker, watched Barnes walk away. Her eyes were bright; she almost radiated.

"Isn't he wonderful, Clocker?" she said. "Aren't they all wonderful? Regular scientists, every one of them, devoting their whole life to this terrific cause!"

"What's so wonderful about that?" he all but snarled.

She turned and gazed at him in mild astonishment. "They could let the Earth go boom. It wouldn't mean a thing to them. Everybody wiped out just like there never were any people. Not even as much record of us as the dinosaurs! Wouldn't that make you feel simply awful?"

"I wouldn't feel a thing." He took her unresponsive hand. "All I'm worried about is us, baby. Who cares about the rest of the world doing a disappearing act?"

"I do. And so do they. They aren't selfish like some people I could mention."

"Selfish? You're damned right I am!"

He pulled her to him, kissed her neck in her favorite place. It got a reaction—restrained annoyance.

"I'm selfish," he said, "because I got a wife I'm nuts about and I want her back. They got you wrapped, baby. Can't you see that? You belong with me in some fancy apartment, the minute I can afford it, like one I saw over on Riverside Drive—seven big rooms, three baths, one of them with a stall shower like you always wanted, the Hudson River and Jersey for our front lawn—"

"That's all in the past, hon," she said with quiet dignity. "I have to help out on this project. It's the least I can do for history."

"The hell with history! What did history ever do for us?" He put his mouth near her ear, breathing gently in the way that once used to make her squirm in his arms like a tickled doe. "Go turn in your time-card, baby. Tell them you got a date with me back on Earth."

She pulled away and jumped up. "No! This is my job as much as theirs. More, even. They don't keep anybody here against their will. I'm staying because I want to, Clocker."

Furious, he snatched her off her feet. "I say you're coming back with me! If you don't want to, I'll drag you, see?"

"How?" she asked calmly.

He put her down again slowly, frustratedly. "Ask them to let you go, baby. Oil Pocket said he'd put you in a musical. You always did want to hit the big time—"

"Not any more." She smoothed down her dress and patted up her hair. "Well, I want to catch the rest of that lecture, hon. See you around if you decide to stay."

He sat down morosely and watched her snake-hip toward the Center, realizing that her seductive walk was no more than professional conditioning. She had grown in some mysterious way, become more serene—at peace.

He had wondered what catatonics got for their work. He knew now—the slickest job of hypnotic flattery ever invented. That was *their* pay.

But what did the pitchmen get in return?

Clocker put in a call for Barnes at the box office of the Center. Barnes left a lecture for researchers from his planet and joined Clocker with no more than polite curiosity on his paternal face. Clocker told him briefly and bitterly about his talk with Zelda, and asked bluntly what was in it for the aliens.

"I think you can answer that," said Barnes. "You're a scientist of a sort. You determine the probable performance of a group of horses by their heredity, previous races and other factors. A very laborious computation, calling for considerable aptitude and skill. With that same expenditure of energy, couldn't you earn more in other fields?"

"I guess so," Clocker said. "But I like the track."

"Well, there you are. The only human form of gain we share is desire for knowledge. You devote your skill to predicting a race that is about to be run; we devote ours to recording a race that is about to destroy itself."

Clocker grabbed the alien's coat, pushed his face grimly close. "There, that's the hook! Take away the doom push and this racket folds."

Barnes looked bewildered. "I don't comprehend—"

"Listen, suppose everything's square. Let's say you guys really are leveling, these marks aren't being roped, you're knocking yourself out because your guess is that we're going to commit suicide."

"Oh." Barnes nodded somberly. "Is there any doubt of it? Do you honestly believe the holocaust can be averted?"

"I think it can be stopped, yeah. But you birds act like you don't want it to be. You're just laying back, letting us bunch up, collecting the insurance before the spill happens."

"What else can we do? We're scientists, not politicians. Besides, we've tried repeatedly to spread the warning and never once succeeded in transmitting it.

Clocker released his grip on the front of Barne's jacket. "You take me to the president or commissioner or whoever runs this club. Maybe we can work something out."

"We have a board of directors," Barnes said doubtfully. "But I can't see—"

"Don't rupture yourself trying. Just take me there and let me do the talking."

Barnes moved his shoulders resignedly. He led Clocker to the Administration Building and inside to a large room with paneled walls, a long, solid table and heavy, carved chairs. The men who sat around the table appeared as solid and respectable as the furniture. Clocker's guess was that they had been chosen deliberately, along with the decorations, to inspire confidence in the customer. He had been in rigged horse parlors and bond stores and he knew the approach.

Mr. Calhoun, the character with the white beard, was chairman of the board. He looked unhappily at Clocker.

"I was afraid there would be trouble," he said. "I voted against accepting you, you know. My colleagues, however, thought that you, as our first voluntary associate, might indicate new methods, but I fear my judgment has been vindicated."

"Still, if he knows how extinction can be prevented—" began Dr. Hardin, the one who had given the orientation lecture.

"He knows no such thing," a man with several chins said in an emphatic basso voice. "Man is the most destructive dominant race we have ever encountered. He despoiled his own planet, exterminated lower species that were important to his own existence, oppressed, suppressed, brutalized, corrupted—it's the saddest chronicle in the Universe."

"Therefore his achievements," said Dr. Harding, "deserve all the more recognition!"

Clocker broke in: "If you'll lay off the gab, I'd like to get my bet down."

"Sorry," said Mr. Calhoun. "Please proceed, Mr. Locke."

Clocker rested his knuckles on the table and leaned over them. "I have to take your word you ain't human, but you don't have to take mine. I never worried about anybody but Zelda and myself; that makes me human. All I want is to get along and not hurt anybody if I can help it; that makes me what some people call the common man. Some of my best friends are common men. Come to think of it, they all are. They wouldn't want to get extinct. If we do, it won't be our fault."

Several of the men nodded sympathetic agreement.

"I don't read much except the sport sheets, but I got an idea what's coming up," Clocker continued, "and it's a long shot that any country can finish in the money. We'd like to stop war for good, all of us. Little guys who do the fighting and the dying. Yeah, and lots of big guys, too. But we can't do it alone."

"That's precisely our point," said Calhoun.

"I mean us back on Earth. People are afraid, but they just don't know for sure that we can knock ourself off. Between these catatonics and me, we could tell them what it's all about. I notice you got people from all over the world here, all getting along fine because they have a job to do and no time to hate each other. Well, it could be like that on Earth. You let us go back and you'll see a selling job on making it like up here like you never saw before."

Mr. Calhoun and Dr. Harding looked at each other and around the table. Nobody seemed willing to answer.

Mr. Calhoun finally sighed and got out of this big chair. "Mr. Locke, besides striving for international understanding, we have experimented in the manner you suggest. We released many of our human associates to tell what our science predicts on the basis of probability. A human psychological mechanism defeated us."

"Yeah?" Clocker asked warily. "What was that?"

"Protective amnesia. They completely and absolutely forgot everything they had learned here."

Clocker slumped a bit. "I know. I talked to some of these 'cured' catatonics—people you probably sprung because you got all you wanted from them. They didn't remember anything." He braced again. "Look, there has to be a way out. Maybe if you snatch these politicians in all the countries, yank them up here, they couldn't stumble us into a war."

"Examine your history," said Dr. Harding sadly, "and you will find that we have done this experimentally. It doesn't work. There are always others, often more unthinking, ignorant, stupid or vicious, ready to take their places."

Clocker looked challengingly at every member of the board of directors before demanding, "What are the odds on me remembering?"

"You are our first volunteer," said a little man at the side of the table. "Any answer we give would be a guess."

"All right, guess."

"We have a theory that your psychic censor might not operate. Of course, you realize that's only a theory—"

"That ain't all I don't realize. What's it mean?"

"Our control, regrettably, is a wrench to the mind. Lifting it results in amnesia, which is a psychological defense against disturbing memories."

"I walked into this, don't forget," Clocker reminded him. "I didn't know what I was getting into, but I was ready to take anything."

"That," said the little man, "is the unknown factor. Yes, you did submit voluntarily and you were ready to take anything—but were you psychologically prepared for this? We don't know. We *think* there may be no characteristic wrench—"

"Meaning I won't have amnesia?"

"Meaning that you *may* not. We cannot be certain until a test has been made."

"Then," said Clocker, "I want a deal. It's Zelda I want; you know that, at any rate. You say you're after a record of us in case we bump ourself off, but you also say you'd like us not to. I'll buy that. I don't want us to, either, and there's a chance that we can stop it together."

"An extremely remote one," Mr. Calhoun stated.

"Maybe, but a chance. Now if you let me out and I'm the first case that don't get amnesia, I can tell the world about all this. I might be able to steer other guys, scientists and decent politicians, into coming here to get the dope straighter than I could. Maybe that'd give Earth a chance to cop a pardon on getting extinct. Even if it don't work, it's better than hanging around the radio waiting for the results."

Dr. Harding hissed on his glasses and wiped them thoughtfully, an adopted mannerism, obviously, because he seemed to see as well without them. "You have a point, Mr. Locke, but it would mean losing your contribution to our archives."

"Well, which is more important?" Clocker argued. "Would you rather have *any* record than have us save ourself?"

"Both," said Mr. Calhoun. "We see very little hope of your success, while we regard your knowledge as having important sociological significance. A very desirable contribution."

The others agreed.

"Look, I'll come back if I lame out," Clocker desperately offered. "You can pick me up any time you want. But if I make headway, you got to let Zelda go, too."

"A reasonable proposition," said Dr. Harding. "I call for a vote."

They took one. The best Clocker could get was a compromise.

"We will lift our control," Mr. Calhoun said, "for a suitable time. If you can arouse a measurable opposition to racial suicide—*measurable*, mind you; we're not requiring that you reverse the lemming march alone—we agree to release your wife and revise our policy completely. If, on the other hand, as seems more likely —"

"I come back here and go on giving you the inside on racing," Clocker finished for him. "How much time do I get?"

Dr. Harding turned his hands palm up on the table. "We do not wish to be arbitrary. We earnestly hope you gain your objective and we shall give you every opportunity to do so. If you fail, you will know it. So shall we."

"You're pretty sure I'll get scratched, aren't you?" Clocker asked angrily. "It's like me telling a jockey he don't stand a chance—he's whammied before he even gets to the paddock. Anybody'd think do-gooders like you claim you are would wish me luck."

"But we do!" exclaimed Mr. Calhoun. He shook Clocker's hand warmly and sincerely. "Haven't we consented to release you? Doesn't this prove our honest concern? If releasing *all* our human associates would save humanity, we would do so instantly. But we have tried again and again. And so, to use your own professional terminology, we are hedging our bets by continuing to make our anthropological record until you demonstrate another method … if you do."

"Good enough," approved Clocker. "Thanks for the kind word."

The other board members followed and shook Clocker's hand and wished him well.

Barnes, being last, did the same and added, "You may see your wife, if you care to, before you leave."

"If I care to?" Clocker repeated. "What in hell do you think I came here for in the first place?"

Zelda was brought to him and they were left alone in a pleasant reading room. Soft music came from the walls, which glowed with enough light to read by. Zelda's lovely face was warm with emotion when she sat down beside him and put her hands in his.

"They tell me you're leaving, hon," she said.

"I made a deal, baby. If it works—well, it'll be like it was before, only better."

"I hate to see you leave. Not just for me," she added as he lit up hopefully. "I still love you, hon, but it's different now. I used to want you near me every minute. Now it's loving you without starving for you. You know what I mean?"

"That's just the control they got on you. It's like that with me, too, only I know what it is and you don't."

"But the big thing is the project. Why, we're footnotes in history! Stay here, hon. I'd feel so much better knowing you were here, making your contribution like they say."

He kissed her lips. They were soft and warm and clinging, and so were her arms around his neck. This was more like the Zelda he had been missing.

"They gave you a hypo, sweetheart," he told her. "You're hooked; I'm not. Maybe being a footnote is more important than doing something to save our skin, but I don't think so. If I can do anything about it, I want to do it."

"Like what?"

"I don't know," he admitted. "I'm hoping I get an idea when I'm paroled."

She nuzzled under his chin. "Hon, I want you and me to be footnotes. I want it awful bad."

"That's not what really counts, baby. Don't you see that? It's having you and stopping us humans from being just a bunch of old footnotes. Once we do that, we can always come back here and make the record, if it means that much to you."

"Oh, it does!"

He stood and drew her up so he could hold her more tightly. "You do want to go on being my wife, don't you, baby?"

"Of course! Only I was hoping it could be here."

"Well, it can't. But that's all I wanted to know. The rest is just details."

He kissed her again, including the side of her neck, which produced a subdued wriggle of pleasure, and then he went back to the Administration Building for his release.

Awakening was no more complicated than opening his eyes, except for a bit of fogginess and fatigue that wore off quickly, and Clocker saw he was in a white room with a doctor, a nurse and an orderly around his bed.

"Reflexes normal," the doctor said. He told Clocker, "You see and hear us. You know what I'm saying."

"Sure," Clocker replied. "Why shouldn't I?"

"That's right," the doctor evaded. "How do you feel?"

Clocker thought about it. He was a little thirsty and the idea of a steak interested him, but otherwise he felt no pain or confusion. He remembered that he had not been hungry or thirsty for a long time, and that made him recall going over the border after Zelda.

There were no gaps in his recollection.

He didn't have protective amnesia.

"You know what it's like there?" he asked the doctor eagerly. "A big place where everybody from all over the world tell these aliens about their job or racket." He frowned. "I just remembered something funny. Wonder why I didn't notice it at the time. Everybody talks the same language. Maybe that's because there's only one language for thinking." He shrugged off the problem. "The guys who run the shop take it all down as a record for whoever wants to know about us a zillion years from now. That's on account of us humans are about to close down the track and go home."

The doctor bent close intently. "Is that what you believe *now* or—while you were—disturbed?"

Clocker's impulse to blurt the whole story was stopped at the gate. The doctor was staring too studiously at him. He didn't have his story set yet; he needed time to think, and that meant getting out of this hospital and talking it over with himself.

"You kidding?" he asked, using the same grin that he met complainers with when his turf predictions went sour. "While my head was out of the stirrups, of course."

The doctor, the nurse and the orderly relaxed.

"I ought to write a book," Clocker went on, being doggedly humorous. "What screwball ideas I got! How'd I act?"

"Not bad," said the orderly. "When I found you yakking in your wife's room, I thought maybe it was catching and I'd better go find another job. But Doc here told me I was too stable to go psychotic."

"I wasn't any trouble?"

"Nah. All you did was talk about how to handicap races. I got quite a few pointers. Hell, you went over them often enough for anybody to get them straight!"

"I'm glad somebody made a profit," said Clocker. He asked the doctor, "When do I get out of here?"

"We'll have to give you a few tests first."

"Bring them on," Clocker said confidently.

They were clever tests, designed to trip him into revealing whether he still believed in his delusions. But once he realized that, he meticulously joked about them.

"Well?" he asked when the tests were finished.

"You're all right," said the doctor. "Just try not to worry about your wife, avoid overworking, get plenty of rest—"

Before Clocker left, he went to see Zelda. She had evidently recorded the time-step satisfactorily, because she was on a soft-shoe routine that she must have had down pat by the time she'd been ten.

He kissed her unresponsive mouth, knowing that she was far away in space and could not feel, see or hear him. But that didn't matter. He felt his own good, honest, genuine longing for her, unchecked by the aliens' control of emotions.

"I'll spring you yet, baby," he said. "And what I told you about that big apartment on Riverside Drive still goes. We'll have a time together that ought to be a footnote in history all by itself. I'll see you ... after I get the real job done."

He heard the soft-shoe rhythm all the way down the corridor, out of the hospital, and clear back to the city.

Clocker's bank balance was sick, the circulation of his tip sheet gone. But he didn't worry about it; there were bigger problems.

He studied the newspapers before even giving himself time to think. The news was as bad as usual. He could feel the heat of fission, close his eyes and see all the cities and farms in the world going up in a blinding cloud. As far as he was concerned, Barnes and Harding and the rest weren't working fast enough; he could see doom sprinting in half a field ahead of the completion of the record.

The first thing he could have done was recapture the circulation of the tip sheet. The first thing he actually did do was write the story of his experience just as it had happened, and send it to a magazine.

When he finally went to work on his sheet, it was to cut down the racing data to a few columns and fill the rest of it with warnings.

"This is what you want?" the typesetter asked, staring at the copy Clocker turned in. "You *sure* this is what you want?"

"Sure I'm sure. Set it and let's get the edition out early. I'm doubling the print order."

"Doubling?"

"You heard me."

When the issue was out, Clocker waited around the main newsstands on Broadway. He watched the customers buy, study unbelievingly, and wander off looking as if all the tracks in the country had burned down simultaneously.

Doc Hawkins found him there.

"Clocker, my boy! You have no idea how anxious we were about you. But you're looking fit, I'm glad to say."

"Thanks," Clocker said abstractedly. "I wish I could say the same about you and the rest of the world."

Doc laughed. "No need to worry about us. We'll muddle along somehow."

"You think so, huh?"

"Well, if the end is approaching, let us greet it at the Blue Ribbon. I believe we can still find the lads there."

They were, and they greeted Clocker with gladness and drinks. Diplomatically, they made only the most delicate references to the revamping job Clocker had done on his tip sheet.

"It's just like opening night, that's all," comforted Arnold Wilson Wyle. "You'll get back into your routine pretty soon."

"I don't want to," said Clocker pugnaciously. "Handicapping is only a way to get people to read what I *really* want to tell them."

"Took me many minutes to find horses," Oil Pocket put in. "See one I want to bet on, but rest of paper make me too worried to bother betting. Okay with Injun, though—horse lost. And soon you get happy again, stick to handicapping, let others worry about world."

Buttonhole tightened his grip on Clocker's lapel. "Sure, boy. As long as the bobtails run, who cares what happens to anything else?"

"Maybe I went too easy," said Clocker tensely. "I didn't print the whole thing, just a little part of it. Here's the rest."

They were silent while he talked, seeming stunned with the terrible significance of his story.

"Did you explain all this to the doctors?" Doc Hawkins asked.

"You think I'm crazy?" Clocker retorted. "They'd have kept me packed away and I'd never get a crack at telling anybody."

"Don't let it trouble you," said Doc. "Some vestiges of delusion can be expected to persist for a while, but you'll get rid of them. I have faith in your ability to distinguish between the real and unreal."

"But it all *happened*! If you guys don't believe me, who will? And you've *got* to so I can get Zelda back!"

"Of course, of course," said Doc hastily. "We'll discuss it further some other time. Right now I really must start putting my medical column together for the paper."

"What about you, Handy Sam?" Clocker challenged.

Handy Sam, with one foot up on the table and a pencil between his toes, was doodling self-consciously on a paper napkin. "We all get these ideas, Clocker. I used to dream about having arms and I'd wake up still thinking so, till I didn't know if I did or didn't. But like Doc says, then you figure out what's real and it don't mix you up any more."

"All right," Clocker said belligerently to Oil Pocket. "You think my story's batty, too?"

"Can savvy evil spirits, good spirits," Oil Pocket replied with stolid tact. "Injun spirits, though, not white ones."

"But I keep telling you they ain't spirits. They ain't even human. They're from some world way across the Universe—"

Oil Pocket shook his head. "Can savvy Injun spirits, Clocker. No spirits, no savvy."

"Look, you see the ones we're all in, don't you?" Clocker appealed to the whole group. "Do you mean to tell me you can't feel we're getting set to blow the joint? Wouldn't you want to stop it?"

"If we could, my boy, gladly," Doc said. "However, there's not much that any individual or group of individuals can do."

"But how in hell does anything get started? With one guy, two guys—before you know it, you got a crowd, a political party, a country—"

"What about the other countries, though?" asked Buttonhole. "So we're sold on your story in America, let's say. What do we do—let the rest of the world walk in and take us over?"

"We educate them," Clocker explained despairingly. "We start it here and it spreads to there. It doesn't have to be everybody. Mr. Calhoun said I just have to convince a few people and that'll show them it can be done and then I get Zelda back."

Doc stood up and glanced around the table. "I believe I speak for all of us, Clocker, when I state that we shall do all within our power to aid you."

"Like telling other people?" Clocker asked eagerly.

"Well, that's going pretty—"

"Forget it, then. Go write your column. I'll see you chumps around—around ten miles up, shaped like a mushroom."

He stamped out, so angry that he untypically let the others settle his bill.

Clocker's experiment with the newspaper failed so badly that it was not worth the expense of putting it out; people refused to buy. Clocker had three-sheets printed and hired sandwich men to parade them through the city. He made violent speeches in Columbus Circle, where he lost his audience to revivalist orators; Union Square, where he was told heatedly to bring his message to Wall Street; and Times Square, where the police made him more along so he wouldn't block traffic. He obeyed, shouting his message as he walked, until he remembered how amusedly he used to listen to those who cried that Doomsday was near. He wondered if they were catatonics under imperfect control. It didn't matter; nobody paid serious attention to his or their warnings.

The next step, logically, was a barrage of letters to the heads of nations, to the U.N., to editors of newspapers. Only a few of his letters were printed. The ones in Doc's tabloid did best, drawing such comments as:

"Who does this jerk think he is, telling us everybody's going to get killed off? Maybe they will, but not in Brooklyn!"

"When I was a young girl, some fifty years ago, I had a similar experience to Mr. Locke's. But my explanation is quite simple. The persons I saw proved to be my ancestors. Mr. Locke's new-found friends will, I am sure, prove to be the same. The World Beyond knows all and tells all, and my Control, with whom I am in daily communication Over There, assures me that mankind is in no danger whatever, except from the evil effects of tobacco and alcohol and the disrespect of youth for their elders."

"The guy's nuts! He ought to go back to Russia. He's nothing but a nut or a Communist and in my book that's the same thing."

"He isn't telling us anything new. We all know who the enemy is. The only way to protect ourselves is to build TWO GUNS FOR ONE!"

"Is this Locke character selling us the idea that we all ought to go batty to save the world?"

Saddened and defeated, Clocker went through his accumulated mail. There were politely non-commital acknowledgements from embassies and the U.N. There was also a check for his article from the magazine he'd sent it to; the amount was astonishingly large.

He used part of it to buy radio time, the balance for ads in rural newspapers and magazines. City people, he figured, were hardened by publicity gags, and he might stir up the less suspicious and sophisticated hinterland. The replies he received, though, advised him to buy some farmland and let the metropolises be destroyed, which, he was assured, would be a mighty good thing all around.

The magazine came out the same day he tried to get into the U.N. to shout a speech from the balcony. He was quietly surrounded by a uniformed guard and moved, rather than forced, outside.

He went dejectedly to his hotel. He stayed there for several days, dialing numbers he selected randomly from the telephone book, and getting the brushoff from business offices, housewives and maids. They were all very busy or the boss wasn't in or they expected important calls.

That was when he was warmly invited by letter to see the editor of the magazine that had bought his article.

Elated for actually the first time since his discharge from the hospital, Clocker took a cab to a handsome building, showed his invitation to a pretty and courteous receptionist, and was escorted into an elaborate office where a smiling man came around a wide bleached-mahogany desk and shook hands with him.

"Mr. Locke," said the editor, "I'm happy to tell you that we've had a wonderful response to your story."

"Article," Clocker corrected.

The editor smiled. "Do you produce so much that you can't remember what you sold us? It was about—"

"I know," Clocker cut in. "But it wasn't a story. It was an article. It really—"

"Now, now. The first thing a writer must learn is not to take his ideas too seriously. Very dangerous, especially in a piece of fiction like yours."

"But the whole thing is true!"

"Certainly—while you were writing it." The editor shoved a pile of mail across the desk toward him. "Here are some of the comments that have come in. I think you'll enjoy seeing the reaction."

Clocker went through them, hoping anxiously for no more than a single note that would show his message had come through to somebody. He finished and looked up blankly.

"You see?" the editor asked proudly. "You're a find."

"The new Mark Twain or Jonathan Swift. A comic."

"A satirist," the editor amended. He leaned across the desk on his crossed forearms. "A mail response like this indicates a talent worth developing. We would like to discuss a series of stories—"

"Articles."

"Whatever you choose to call them. We're prepared to—"

"You ever been off your rocket?" Clocker asked abruptly.

The editor sat back, smiling with polite puzzlement. "Why, no."

"You ought to try it some time." Clocker lifted himself out of the chair and went to the door. "That's what I want, what I was trying to sell in my article. We all ought to go to hospitals and get ourself let in and have these aliens take over and show us where we're going."

"You think that would be an improvement?"

"What wouldn't?" asked Clocker, opening the door.

"But about the series—"

"I've got your name and address. I'll let you know if anything turns up."

Clocker closed the door behind him, went out of the handsome building and called a taxi. All through the long ride, he stared at the thinning out of the city, the huddled suburban communities, the stretches of grass and well-behaved woods that were permitted to survive.

He climbed out at Glendale Center Hospital, paid the hackie, and went to the admitting desk. The nurse gave him a smile.

"We were wondering when you'd come visit your wife," she said. "Been away?"

"Sort of," he answered, with as little emotion as he had felt while he was being controlled. "I'll be seeing plenty of her from now on. I want my old room back."

"But you're perfectly normal!"

"That depends on how you look at it. Give me ten minutes alone and any brain vet will be glad to give me a cushioned stall."

Hands in his pockets, Clocker went into the elevator, walked down the corridor to his old room without pausing to visit Zelda. It was the live Zelda he wanted to see, not the tapping automaton.

He went in and shut the door.

"Okay, you were right and I was wrong," Clocker told the board of directors. "Turn me over to Barnes and I'll give him the rest of the dope on racing. Just let me see Zelda once in a while and you won't have any trouble with me."

"Then you are convinced that you have failed," said Mr. Calhoun.

"I'm no dummy. I know when I'm licked. I also pay anything I owe."

Mr. Calhoun leaned back. "And so do we, Mr. Locke. Naturally, you have no way of detecting the effect you've had. We do. The result is that, because of your experiment, we are gladly revising our policy."

"Huh?" Clocker looked around at the comfortable aliens in their comfortable chairs. Solid and respectable, every one of them. "Is this a rib?"

"Visits to catatonics have increased considerably," explained Dr. Harding. "When the visitors are alone with our human associates, they tentatively follow the directions you gave in your article. Not all do, to be sure; only those who feel as strongly about being with their loved ones as you do about your wife."

"We have accepted four voluntary applicants," said Mr. Calhoun.

Clocker's mouth seemed to be filled with cracker crumbs that wouldn't go down and allow him to speak.

"And now," Dr. Harding went on, "we are setting up an Information Section to teach the applicants what you have learned and make the same arrangement we made with you. We are certain that we shall, before long, have to increase our staff as the number of voluntary applicants increases geometrically, after we release the first few to continue the work you have so admirably begun."

"You mean I *made* it?" Clocker croaked unbelievingly.

"Perhaps this will prove it to you," said Mr. Calhoun.

He motioned and the door opened and Zelda came in.

"Hello, hon," she said. "I'm glad you're back. I missed you."

"Not like I missed you, baby! There wasn't anybody controlling my feelings."

Mr. Calhoun put his hands on their shoulders. "Whenever you care to, Mr. Locke, you and your wife are free to leave."

Clocker held Zelda's hands and her calmly fond gaze. "We owe these guys plenty, baby," he said to her. "We'll help make the record before we take off. Ain't that what you want?"

"Oh, it is, hon! And then I want you."

"Then let's get started," he said. "The quicker we do, the quicker we get back."

JOURNAL NOTES
At The Post

Theme:
Maybe psychiatrists are wrong about the symbolism behind the stereotyped movements in catatonia—darned if they don't look like communication and/or instruction!

Possibilities:
Several problems. The movements seem to be repeated endlessly, yet this might be only relative; over a long span, changes can be noted. Why so long, though? Difficulty of communication would be the answer. Obviously not communicating with anyone around, unless handled as a fantasy—why bring in the supernatural? Must be connected with whoever would be far enough away to make communication tough (like the static in short-wave transmission) and yet have a solid motive for wanting the data. Aliens? Could be seizing minds to get information for invasion, but that's pure extract of corn; forget it. Questing because we're heading for space and they want to know what to expect—not much improvement and it doesn't explain pre-rocketry catatonia. Altruistic aliens, too far away to avert Alphabet-bomb doom, but want to make a permanent record of the human race before it extinguishes itself? That accounts for prior catatonia—wars of increasing ferocity plus zooming technology make for single-end extrapolation—and interstellar distances (and radiation) would explain interference; also semantic difficulties.

Development:
A frightening theme, so characterization and treatment must be extra-entertaining to offset the revulsion. Risk of Runyonesquerie, but can be avoided because powerful emotion required. Payoff should be hopeful (for a gladsome change), but no guarantee that doom is averted. Biblical solution: find-one-honest-man kind of thing.

Editorial Comments:
Finding the right characters took days of selection; each had to be

light and likable, yet make important contributions to plot advancement. Explaining catatonia without halting the story was a high hurdle; more days consumed before I came upon the device of having Clocker and Doc Hawkins do a duet, with a chorus effect from the other characters. There's an immense amount of Fortean reasoning: what the catatonics are doing, why they don't rebel, burning of witches in Middle Ages, gibberish books and paintings, crackpot prophets of holocaust, etc. The original version ended with Clocker going back in defeat, hopeless. Dissatisfied, I kept the story around for weeks, hoping to find a Biblical solution. I finally did. Financially, the story was disastrous; in satisfaction, it was worth every minute.

HERO

JOE LYONS SHOULD HAVE BEEN GLAD to be so close to home. The Earth turned ponderously on his right, and the moon lay stolidly before him—and behind him was the red pinpoint Mars.

It had been three years since he had seen that sight, but he had no nostalgic lump in his throat, picturing himself home at last with his mother and brother. Lyons had the important problem of approaching Earth at the correct angle, distance and speed.

His automatic distance-finder triangulated his position in space. The integrator figured his position in relation to Earth at his present speed, and the angle at which he would approach it.

He made the slight changes the figures called for, blasting his bow tubes once at full speed, then at quarter capacity, and correcting his course by an eighth stern port blast that brought the ship pointing a degree over to the left of the moon. Earth was blowing up to an enormous, shining globe. At the right moment—

Nine times he circled the world, his speed gradually falling from miles a second to miles a minute; and then the air was screaming around the hull. He was over Africa. He turned the bow north, until he flew over the Pacific.

He overtook California, the Rockies, the middle west; and in the distance he could see the Atlantic seaboard. Only then did he close the radio circuit, for instructions from the home port.

"Hello, Lyons!" an excited voice broke out. "Ronkonkoma calling Lyons. If you hear me, please answer—"

The sound shocked him into dumbness. After three years of hearing no Earthly voice ...

Experimentally, he cleared his throat to test the quality of the sound it produced.

"Lyons speaking," he said uncertainly.

"Anything wrong, Lyons?" the voice rushed out in anxiety. "We spotted you four hours ago—been trying to get you ever since. Anything wrong?"

"N-nothing wrong," he said in a careful monotone, though he was not sure his voice would not crack, squeak or stop altogether.

"Fine!" the announcer cried. "It sure is great to hear you, Lyons!" Then, suddenly businesslike: "Cut your speed, Lyons.

Pittsburgh just reported sighting you flashing overhead at a rate that'll shoot you right past us."

"Okay," Lyons said.

He held down the bow studs until he could feel the ship sinking slightly with the loss of momentum. He leaned forward and stared at the keel visi-plate. Low, broad buildings, nonc more than forty stories tall; an unscientific hodgepodge of narrow and wide streets, less than half of them mechanized, in spite of the three years he had been away.

"Isn't that Philadelphia under me?" he asked.

"Yeah. You should be here in about ten minutes. Brake when you cross Long Island City."

"Are you all clear down there?" Lyons asked.

The announcer's next words mystified him. "Boy, are we! You're the only ship coming in here today, Lyons. Everybody else is rerouted over to Ashokan."

"What's the idea?"

"Don't ask questions, pal. Just keep a'coming, fast as you can. You can't get here too fast to suit us. But be careful, will you?"

Ronkonkoma, set aside just for his small ship? Ashokan would be mobbed, swamped with all the ships that usually landed and took off in both ports. It was senseless. They would jam themselves up with an unnecessary snarl of rocket traffic— "Making repairs down there?" he asked puzzledly. "Nope. The place was never in better shape. How does it feel to be back, pal?"

"Not bad," Lyons said abstractedly.

"That all?" the announcer shouted.

But Lyons was busy with his controls. The gigantic buildings, square-roofed for helicopter landings; web-bridged; levels of mechanized ways and traffic streets; the air lanes swarming.

Manhattan, and danger of collision. He nosed up, out of the air lanes, over the East River, free now of bridges, and across Queens. Steadily, he checked his rushing speed. The long oval of Lake Ronkonkoma lay directly ahead.

Lyons was not stolidly unemotional. He had a job of landing to do, and he had to do it efficiently. Any other Globe-Circler rocket pilot would have behaved the same way. The important thing was get your ship down safely—it represented an enormous investment.

Thinking of nothing but the job at hand, Lyons kicked the stern, braked until the ship's bow fluttered over the hangars and angled down in a long dive, straight for the water.

Blackness, the tumbling, hissing, swooping blackness of water drowned all of his visi-plates, smashing along the hull with deafening roar.

Suddenly the water glowed yellow. He headed directly for the lights. The ship faltered, sagged heavily, its last momentum swiftly dying. It sank unevenly to the bottom.

Something gripped it and dragged it across the bed of the lake and up, until it burst into the light and over the shore, between the passenger and freight platforms of the tremendous rocket station.

"Okay, Lyons," the announcer cried eagerly. "Come on out!"

But Lyons sat numbly in his oil pressure chair, scared stiff.

"I—I can't!" he stammered. "All those people—"

They were packed densely on both platforms. Nervously he began to understand why all rocket traffic had been rerouted from Ronkonkoma. He could not hear the noise of the crowd, though he could see mouths open widely, arms wave hysterically, noisemakers whirring.

"I—d-don't want t-to come out," he whispered.

Through the double hull he heard faint pounding.

"Come on, Lyons!" the announcer pleaded. "Get it over with. You can't stay in there all day."

So many people to face, Lyons thought frantically. Even a few would make him self-conscious. Alone so long in the silence, no one to speak to—he wasn't even sure he could talk sense any more. There had been long months of dreadful, absolute, vacuum silence, alone in a cramped ship with even the nearest planets remote points of light. And there had been no one to tell him whether his gabblings were coherent.

"I can't face them," he muttered, cowering in his seat.

"Stop that nonsense, Lyons!" the announcer rapped sternly. "If they have to, they'll cut their way in. You might as well open the door."

Lyons stood up shakily, trying desperately not to look at the visi-plates, so frighteningly crowded with people. Holding on to the high, thick back of the control seat, he moved to the door. His feet were ton weights, his knees sagged miserably under the unaccustomed drag of gravity.

The pounding on the hull was growing louder. If he didn't open the port, they would cut their way in and drag him out. Then he'd get a bawling out from headquarters for letting his ship be scuttled.

It wouldn't last long, he told himself anxiously. He could make some excuse and break away. Landsickness—fever— maybe he could get the authorities to rush him to a hospital, and quiet. He stumbled through the hold corridor he had walked along so many times in the past three years that he knew every weld seam and rivet, every plate in the floor. He walked on past the stairwell that led down to the ground level gang hole. Reluctant to leave the ship that had been his sole home and companion for three years, he clung to the wheel of the airlock. Conscious of the pounding so close to him now, he backed away from the inner airlock, staring at it. He could leave it at lock position. He could slink behind the fuel hoses and hide there if they cut their way in. He would be out of the noise and swarm just that much longer.

But he couldn't, of course. His mother, his brother, his friends—were they still alive? Somehow he had to get past that mob and find then. That, suddenly, became his most overwhelming apprehension.

He whirled the airlock wheel until it came to rest, shot the bolts out of their holes. Air rushed in to fill the partial vacuum that in nearly a year of space travel had been caused by the slow leakage through the great outside washer.

The noise was closer. If they would only give him a chance to get used to the sound of human voices and the press of crowds! Normally he was not afraid of people. But this was so sudden—the change from silence to deafening clamor.

His hands shook so that he could scarcely make them grip the outer airlock wheel. That one he turned very slowly, reluctantly. He clutched the lever that drew in the safety bolts, listening intently for sounds to come through the thick, insulated door. There was dead silence, almost as if he were still out in space. He could no longer hear the terrifying din, and that gave him courage.

He threw the lever. Abruptly, he leaped back. The outer lock crashed in, forced by the weight that had been pressing against it.

A mob! Rushing in to snatch at him!

He could not close the inner airlock. It was too late. Men and women were surrounding him, pawing at him, shouting at him. Men and women dressed in formal red skin-tight spun glass suits with flowing green capes of synthetic fur and narrow brimmed or brimless toques.

"Commander Lyons!" a red-faced, portly man boomed, grabbing his limp hand. "I am Abner Connaught, elected President of the World-State in your absence. In the name of the peoples of Earth, I welcome you."

"Commander Lyons?" the space aviator stammered. "Why, I'm just a regular rocket pilot."

He flushed when the crowd laughed. The word passed along to

those at the distant ends of the platforms; then the entire rocket station, packed with people, howled with laughter.

He hung back, ashamed, angry.

The men and women who ringed him were evidently politicians and officials, for when they urged him out of the airlock and onto the platform, the crowd respectfully surged away.

He found himself at a battery of microphones, facing another battery of television scanners, inside a circle of armed police. Beyond, the mob milled, trying to get him—yelling, waving arms.

President Connaught drew him before the microphones. Unwinking, the giant television eyes stared at him.

"Fellow citizens of the World-State," the President's voice boomed again, "three years ago we watched Commander Lyons flash away from Earth, out into space—an intrepid explorer flying through the uncharted wastes of nothingness toward Mars, there to solve the mystery of its possible commercial value.

"For three years we have watched and prayed for his safe return. Now, at last, he returns to us, modest as ever, unchanged by the acid test he has gone through. We are grateful for his safe return and—"

On and on and on, in the changeless formula of politicians since the world began. Lyons had to stand uneasily while the blank-eyed scanners stared at him and the mob behind glowered at the police guard; but at least they were silent now.

He shifted from one foot to the other. His hands hung down clumsily; he could find nothing to do with them. And, all the while, the blank, terrifying stares that he could not avoid.

Nervously, he turned his head. Outside of the ring of officials, two faces leaped into his sight—immobile, remote faces that smiled at him almost as if he were a stranger.

"Mom!" he cried. "Sid!"

Simultaneously, their faces grew pale and distressed. They pursed their lips behind their forefingers warningly, to hush him.

For President Connaught had wheeled about, gripped his shoulder, and was saying: "Now, Commander, tell us what you found on Mars. Remember, my lad, the entire world is listening reverently for your first words."

Lyons gazed in frozen fascination at the microphones. His mind refused to think of two words that could possibly be connected. He stood trembling, unable to speak, as the crowd became restless. The President glanced at him curiously.

"I—I can't talk to—to them," he stammered.

His nerve broke suddenly; he stumbled to his mother, threw his arms around her.

"—I can't talk to—to them," he stammered. "Please, Joseph," she whispered, "for my sake." He drew away from her. "Joseph?" he asked. "Not Joey any more?"

Gently, his brother Sid caught his arm and led him toward the microphones.

"I know how you feel," he said in a low, tense voice. "That's why a speech was written for you. Just read off that paper they gave you."

Lyons looked at the paper, glanced around pleadingly. Sid and his mother motioned him forward. The President smiled encouragingly and put him before the frightening array of broadcasting equipment.

He began to read. The words were meaningless to him, and he read in a flat, hurried, rattling voice, without pause or inflection, glad he did not have to think of what to say. It was all there on the paper, whatever it meant.

He scarcely realized he had finished until President Connaught patted him on the back and said:

"Thank you, Commander. That was splendidly put. And now, fellow citizens, let us wait patiently until Commander Lyons is rested and his Martian films developed, when we shall hear more from him. I am sure our patience will be rewarded."

A detachment of police surrounded Lyons and his family and made a way through the crowd to a long, sleek car outside the rocket station. Two men sat in the rear. Lyons stopped uncertainly when he saw them smiling at him. "It's all right, Joseph," his mother said soothingly. "They're Mr. Morrison and Mr. Bentley. You know them, don't you?"

The president and the treasurer of Globe-Circlers! "Hello," Lyons murmured respectfully. "It's nice of you to be here."

"Modest as ever," Morrison said, and laughed. "Eh, Bentley?"

The treasurer grinned. All at once, the car was in motion and swooped into the tunnel highway toward New York. Sid and his mother sat nervously facing young Lyons, their mouths tight in humorless, formal smiles.

"Is my old room ready for me, Mom?" he asked, desperately trying to make conversation.

His mother looked embarrassed.

"I don't know how to say this, Commander," Bentley said, at last. "I think you'll prefer having us be frank with you."

"Certainly," Lyons replied.

"Well, you must give up ideas of going back to your old life. No more small apartments or flying. You're a world hero, you know."

"Sure," Sid added brightly. "You're on top of the heap, Joe."

"A world hero?" Lyons asked quizzically. "What's that?"

"It's an old word we rediscovered," Morrison volunteered.

"It seems that in our prosaic civilization, until now, there was not sufficient public interest in a single man to make him a hero. In your case, the situation got somewhat out of hand. The newscasters made so much of your flight that the public elevated you to the position of hero. To capitalize on your fame, you must live up to it."

Lyons felt uncomfortable. "I don't understand—"

"Through you," Bentley said, "the world can advance centuries at a leap. Interplanetary travel, on schedule—the riches of the other planets—"

Lyons nodded. "But how do I do all that?"

"All the planets are open to our exploration," Morrison explained. "Globe-Circlers has built two interplanetary ships—yours and a newer, larger one—the first of what will eventually be a great fleet of space liners. Obviously, a single group of stockholders hasn't the money to build all that are needed. Therefore, we put up you, Commander Lyons, in whom the public has enormous confidence; the public puts up the money to build the ships; and we call the fleet the Lyons Line."

"It's the grandest opportunity in the world for you, Joseph," his mother put in.

Sid shook his arm excitedly. "You'll be president of the new company, Joe! And they're going to give me a big job too!"

"And I'd like to help all I can," Lyons admitted. "Only I don't see how I fit in as president of the company. I'm just a pilot."

His mother said: "Don't worry about it, Joseph. Mr. Morrison and Mr. Bentley will tell you what you have to do and when to do it."

"It'll be an irresistible combination," Morrison declared, tapping Lyons' knee, "your reputation, our commercial experience and the money we shall allow the public to invest. Just leave everything to us, Commander, and we'll be top men in this little old world!"

They rushed through the tunnel without encountering any traffic, which had been rerouted to the surface highways. When they came up into an upper city street level the driver swung the car uptown, then under a building that Lyons recognized as the Grand American Hotel—Earth's largest and most expensive.

"Well, Commander," Bentley said expansively, as they went toward the glittering elevator, "here's where you're going to live. In the Grand American Hotel!"

Lyons blinked. "It's nice, but I wouldn't feel right in a place like this. I wish you'd let me stay in my old room at home."

"Now, Joseph," his mother protested, "Mr. Morrison and Mr. Bentley hired an entire floor of the hotel for you. Beside I gave up our little flat. It was no place for us."

"I liked it," Lyons said wistfully.

He let himself be guided up to a lavish suite of rooms. In the huge foyer he hesitated, confused. A staff of servants—it seemed like hundreds to him—was lined up for his inspection. They all bowed low.

Embarrassed, Joe Lyons sidled around them into a lavishly furnished living room. He could see through the doors into other rooms, carpeted with gorgeous, thick-napped rugs, furnished extravagantly.

"I'd never get used to it," he mumbled. "It scares me."

"Nonsense, my boy," Morrison said. "In no time you'll be striding around as if you were born here. Anyhow, the public expects the president of the Lyons Line to live in a place that fits his position."

"I guess so." Lyons' space-tanned brow creased. "But it still doesn't seem right. You built a space ship and I flew it. I've been handling G-C rockets for the last ten years and according to the tests I was the fittest pilot. That's all it was."

"But if the people want you to be president of the company, Joseph," his mother said, "that's all there is to it."

"Sure, if it means giving space travel a boost. That's my ambition."

"Quite right, Commander," Bentley approved, putting a sheaf of papers and a pen in his hand. "Would you mind signing at the bottom, please?"

Obligingly, Lyons scrawled his signature.

"What does it say?" he asked.

"These are the Lyons Line incorporation documents. You have accepted the presidency of the company."

Morrison folded the papers, and put them in his pocket. He shook Lyons' hand. "We'll leave you now, my boy. Get some sleep. We'll see you tomorrow."

His mother kissed him, and left with his brother Sid.

A butler entered. "Dinner is served, sir. If you wish to sleep, your bedroom is ready."

He was hungry and tired. He managed to eat, though a crew of servants kept slipping plates under his nose. He could hardly wait to sleep in a soft bed with cool white sheets.

In the bedroom he began zipping down the talon fastener of his trim blue jacket, then paused. His forearm had touched a bulge in the breast pocket. He had been so confused he had forgotten it, which he had never thought possible. From his pocket he drew out a statuette.

A photo-statue, made of developer plastic, in natural color. Anyone would have recognized it as a product of a sculptor-camera; but the statue itself would have caused amazement.

"Lehli," he whispered to it.

The sadly smiling little face did not change. In his imagination he could see the red iron-oxide sand of Mars beneath her tiny sandaled feet, just as it had been when he had taken the picture. The shining black hair was only printed on smooth plastic, but he could imagine its silky wealth, could vision the lovely, delicate, sensitive features; the slim body in its flowing white toga.

"Cahm bahk sssoon, Joyeee," he heard the sweet, sibilant voice echo.

"Gosh, I wish I could, Lehli," he whispered. "But it looks like I won't be able to do it for quite awhile. But sooner or later I'll be back with you, Lehli, darling, when I'm not needed around here."

He placed the statuette gently on the night table and undressed. On the return from Mars, he had thought expectantly of invigorating showers, for lack of gravity did not allow them on shipboard.—But he was too exhausted to do anything but fall into bed. Funny, he thought unhappily, how Sid and his mother had changed; no warmth at all. Nothing like Lehli who had been so generously affectionate.

A hand, shaking his shoulder, roused him out of his slumber. He opened his eyes and saw Sid bending over him. His mother smiled at him from the foot of the bed.

"My goodness!" she said. "You certainly must have been tired. You've been asleep almost twenty-four hours."

He yawned and stretched, threw the covers off and stood on the floor.

"Boy, I sure feel better. I bet I could've slept a week if you'd let me."

"Sorry, Joe," Sid apologized. "We had to wake you. There's going to be a big blow-out for you tonight—official reception and all that stuff, and you're supposed to make the first announcement of the new company."

"Well, gosh, Sid," Lyons complained. "I was sort of hoping I'd have a day to myself. I wanted to look up some of old pilot buddies—"

"Some of them'll be at the reception," Sid broke in abruptly. "But, Joe, you've got to think of yourself last, the way we've learned to. You're the biggest public figure in the world today. Everything depends on you, and it all has to work out!"

"What do you mean?"

"Well, tonight's the official reception. You make the announcement and the public gets interested. Tomorrow you inspect the space ship that's going to take off in the afternoon. The public buys our stocks, see?"

"Space ship?" Lyons asked. "For where?"

"Your recording instruments and films and all that scientific stuff is being analyzed by our scientists. They'll be finished in time to make any changes in the equipment that'll be necessary.

"The ship's going to Mars?" Lyons asked eagerly.

"Yep, the first of the Lyons Line."

"Boy, if I could only be on her!" Lyons exclaimed.

It was impossible, of course. He had his duty to do first. "What is this, Joseph?" his mother was demanding. She was holding the photo-statue. "Who is she?"

"Lehli, a Martian girl," he said. "I—I'm going to marry her."

"Marry her? With that horrible coppery skin? Oh, Joseph, the girls on Earth are much nicer!"

"That's protective coloration," he protested. "Cuts off actinic rays."

"But a Martian! Maybe she isn't even human!"

"Yes, she is. Her folks escaped from Earth before one of the ice ages."

Sid grinned knowingly. "One of those savages, eh, Joe?"

Lehli, descendant of the gentle, cultured Martian race, a savage? Lyons' face went white and his hands clenched.

"You'll give her up for my sake?" his mother pleaded.

"But, Mom—"

They heard the elevator door slide open.

"That's Morrison and Bentley, Mom," Sid said quickly. "Go out and talk to them. I'll help Joe get dressed. When she had left, he said to his brother: "Don't worry Mom like that, Joe. You know you can't go back and marry that Martian girl. Your place is here, advancing interplanetary travel. Besides, you know how she worries about us—Dad killed in a crack-up, either of us liable to do the same. Morrison is going to marry her if this deal goes through, and she likes him a lot. It'll be a great break for all of us."

"Yeah, I know," Lyons said doubtfully. "I'll do what I'm supposed to, but after that's finished there's no reason why I can't go back to Mars."

Sid didn't answer but his face was grimly abstracted. Lyons allowed himself to be put into a formal red spun-glass suit, clasped the green cape around his throat and donned a brimless toque. In spite of his discomfort in civilian clothes, he was handsome and dashing.

The butler was standing outside the door with a tray in his hands. Lyons took the single glass it contained and drank the vitalizing breakfast cocktail. Then he followed Sid into the sitting room. Morrison, Bentley, his mother were there—and a beautiful girl. They shook hands with him.

"What a change in you, Commander," Morrison said. "Nothing like a good sleep to put you on your feet." He led the girl forward. "This is Mona Trent—our most famous and glamorous studio star."

"How do you do, Miss Trent?" Lyons murmured.

"Not Miss Trent. Call her Mona, and please be very attentive to her," Bentley adjured. "Think of the publicity—pairing off the two most popular young people in the world today!"

Mona smiled charmingly and took his arm as they entered the elevator. But descending to the main floor and walking through corridors to the vast ballroom, packed with people and audio-casting equipment, Lyons was wondering how interplanetary travel could be advanced by his being attentive to a beautiful audio actress.

People jumped to their feet when they entered. Lyons felt his nervousness coming back. Hands were shoved out at him to be shaken. He shook them obediently. A paper was put in his limp grip and he was brought before the battery of audio microphones and scanners. By staring at the paper and thinking of nothing else, he was able to read off his speech without too much trouble.

Then they ate; speeches were blasted at him; and Mona sat at his right, gazing adoringly at him and angrily demanding that he be more attentive, when no one could hear. Passively, he listened when she whispered meaningless nonsense at him, apparently just to make him look at her.

"Don't be so stupid," she breathed, while her eyes were melting at him. "Smile. Laugh. It's for the effect."

He tried to, but whispering idiotic gabble at her was something beyond him. He was straightforward, as were most rocket pilots. He could see the strategy in being courteous to investors who could advance rocketry; but he couldn't understand the need for acting as if he loved a popular audio star.

She finally demanded that he dance with her. He swept around the floor with her in his arms. Embarrassingly, everybody got off the dance floor as soon as he stepped on it; but she refused to let him stop.

He saw the crowd in confusion. In the compact rows of faces he saw—old buddies of his!

He halted abruptly and walked eagerly toward them, his hand out in greeting. They jumped up and took his hand, grinning a little uncomfortably.

"Gosh, it's great to see part of the old gang again," he enthused. "How about coming up to my place when this brawl's over?"

"Well, we'd sure like to, Commander," Sam Martin, one of them said. "But, hell, roughneck pilots like us can't be seen with a hero like you."

"Quit your kidding, fellers," Lyons said, and laughed.

He introduced Mona. Curiously, their discomfort increased. He sat down and tried to draw them out in conversation. They spoke only when he addressed them, and then in the most deadening respectful tones. Gradually, he was growing more puzzled, defeated and lonely, when Mona led him back to the floor.

Why was everybody so cold and remote? Not only his old buddies, but even his mother and Sid. Despite his loyalty, he was forced to admit that. Mona Trent did not baffle him. She only regarded him as another leading man.

But everybody else—why weren't they as friendly as they used to be? Why didn't they give him the companionship he craved?

Lehli was not like that. Lehli was warm, generous, affectionate—and understanding ...

The next day, standing inside the space ship, waiting for the portable audiocasting equipment to be assembled so he could address the entire world as if he were the greatest expert on rocketry, he felt like the last fool in creation. All this—simply because he had been lucky enough not to have his own ship smashed either by a meteor or by an error in landing.

Mona Trent hung on his arm; Morrison and Bentley were close by; Sid and his mother, of course, could only look on at a distance at a launching exhibition.

"What do you think of her?" Morrison boasted. "First of the fleet!"

"She's a beauty," Lyons admitted.

"If we play our cards right, my boy," Morrison whispered in his ear, "we'll be billionaires! The public's already hollering to buy!"

"I wasn't thinking about making a lot of money," Lyons said. "All I want to do is help out all I can, and go back—"

"Hold it, Commander," Bentley interrupted. "The audios are ready."

Joe Lyons began walking through the ship, praising it into the microphones. In this he was sincere; she was the finest, most modern, most completely equipped space ship he had even thought possible.

He spoke simply and effectively. Then he took a prepared speech out of his pocket and began reading it. It was mostly a repetition of what he had already said two or three times—the profit possibilities of space travel, the commercial value of the other planets, civilization reaching upward.

His eyes were traveling slightly ahead of his voice when he saw a paragraph that shocked him speechless. It read:

I hesitate to bring my personal affairs into a momentous occasion like this; but I am sure you will all be happy to hear of my engagement to the most beautiful girl in the Universe—Mona Trent! Fat three years we have been separated ... .

He glared furiously at Morrison and Bentley. They looked anxious as they gestured him to read on. Grimly his mouth tightened. He walked swiftly away from the audiocasters. Morrison had to jump in and take over.

Bentley and Mona tried to follow Lyons. He slammed a door on them and strode alone through the magnificent control cabin, the living quarters, the laboratory, the cargo hold. There he paused and put his hand into an open crate.

Damn them all, he swore, let them use him all they wanted to, let them make billionaires of themselves—he didn't care, if rocketry could be helped only in that way. But they'd made a damn hero out of him, cut him off from his friends, turned Sid and his mother into schemers—and now were trying to force him into marrying a girl he didn't love!

Sid or his mother must have told Morrison and Bentley about Lehli, and to prevent—

He stalked back, stiff-legged and ominous. Sam Martin, the same old buddy he had seen the night before, stepped forward and saluted.

"We leave in ten minutes, sir!"

Lyons was supposed to shake hands with the crew and wish them luck, and he did. But when the audiocasters left and Mona angrily followed them, Lyons stood stubbornly still.

"Come on, Commander," Bentley urged. "They're going to take off."

Lyons folded his arms. Anxiously, they tried to hurry him. He shook them off savagely.

"What's wrong, my boy?" Morrison asked, surprised. "I picked up a ray-gun in the hold—" Lyons began meaningly.

"Stop talking nonsense and come along," Bentley said, annoyed.

There was a gun in Lyons' hand.

"Out of here, you two," he snapped at Bentley and Morrison. "As for the rest of you, I'll blast my way to the controls if I have to!"

Bentley and Morrison did not resist when he jabbed his gun into their backs and forced them to the airlock.

"Walk out of here naturally," he grated, "or you'll have a sweet scandal on your hands. So long!"

Their faces were pale, but somehow they managed to walk out. The crowd burst into cheers—which were abruptly shut off. Lyons closed the outer airlock, whirled the wheel, shot the bolts; did the same with the inner port. He thrust his gun at the crew.

"Get to your stations," he ordered coldly. "I'm going along on this ride!" His chin set. "Go on—get!"

One moment more they hesitated, then grins crossed their faces.

"Sure," Sam Martin said. "What the hell're we to stop you? Nothing but a bunch of Globe-Circlers, not a hero among us."

Lyons searched their faces for irony that was not there.

"Cut it out, boys!" he begged. "You guys have known me for years. I'm still the same Joe Lyons! No hero, either!"

The ship started to move along the mechanized ways to the take-off gun.

"Don't wanna contradict, Commander," Sam Martin said seriously, "but flying between Earth and Mars, alone, does leave a mark on a guy. Either he cracks or he comes out a hero. You're a hero—even if you don't wanna be one. We're all together now, though, depending on each other—and on you!"

In the same ship with four of his oldest Mends!

Perhaps on Mars he'd be only a human being again—not a lonely hero.

Smiling, Lyons pressed his forearm against Lehli's statuette inside his jacket, and then he turned his head away. It wasn't right for men to see tears in a hero's eyes.

JOURNAL NOTES
Hero

THEMES:
The first spaceman inevitably will be *the* hero of heroes—and heroism is an exploitable commodity.

POSSIBILITIES:
A loudmouth makes the first trip to Mars, capitalizes offensively on it and what a great guy he is, embarrasses governnmentand serious supporters of space flight, yet they can't discredit him because that would hurt their cause; get rid of him by sweet-talking him (through his oversize ego) into taking ship way the hell off to the moons of Jupiter—won't have to worry about him for years and meanwhile can use his success story to get public support. Editor Weisinger says no—make him sympathetic character.

DEVELOPMENT:
Pilot, just doing a job, returns froms Mars, is steamrollered by adulation. In love with a Martian girl, but returned out of sense of duty. Hero-worship is ruthlessly being used by heads of company (and mother and brother) to whip up backing for development of space flight. Pilot is astonished to find he's made president of company—figurehead, of course; the top men will tell him what to say and do. Yet all he wants is to be one of the boys and that's impossible now. He takes this cynicism as long as he can retain his ideas, but goes (at gunpoint) along on next flight, back to his Martian girl friend. Yet he *still* isn't just one of the boys to the crew. Maybe on Mars he'd be only a human being again instead of a lonely hero.

EDITORIAL COMMENT:
I still think the original development had better story potential, but a sale was a sale, especially in the financially bleak days of 1939, when this was written. In terms of the science fiction of that time, Editor Weisinger was justified in asking for a complete reversal of slant—strong emotion was a particularly hard quality to find in stories. I wasn't wholly successful here—there are clear signs of

strain on a still insecure technique. If I were doing the story now, it would be smoother and under greater control, but I'm not sure it would be as effective; that desperate sincerity, like the appeal of handicrafts, can't be duplicated by know-how alone. I *hated* the big shots, was *exasperated* with the mother and brother, and was *angry* and *bewildered* and *yearning* right along with the Hero ... and that Martian girl was the most wonderful creature ever, to *me*. Nevertheless, I can't help wondering how good that other story would have been.

AND THREE TO GET READY . . .

USUALLY, PEOPLE GET COMMITTED to the psycho ward by their families or courts, but this guy came alone and said he wanted to be put away because he was deadly dangerous. Miss Nelson, the dragon at the reception desk, put in a call for Dr. Schatz and he took me along just in case. I'm a psycho-ward orderly, which means I'm big and know gentle judo to put these poor characters into pretzel shapes that don't hurt them, but keep them from hurting themselves or somebody else.

He was sitting there, hunched together as if he was afraid that he'd make a move that might kill anyone nearby, and about as dangerous-looking as a wilted carnation. Not much bigger than one, either. Maybe five-four, 125 pounds, slender shoulders, slender hands, little feet, the kind of delicate face no guy would ever pick for himself, but a complexion you'd switch with if you've got a beard of Brillo like mine that needs shaving every damned day.

"Do you have this gentleman's history, Miss Nelson?" asked Dr. Schatz, before talking to the patient.

Her prim lips got even tighter. "I'm afraid not, Doctor. He ... says it would be like committing suicide to give it to me."

The little fellow nodded miserably.

"But we must have at least your name—" Dr. Schatz began.

He skittered clear over to the end of the bench and huddled there, shaking. "But that's exactly what I can't give you! Not only mine—*anybody's*!"

One thing you've got to say for these psychiatrists: they may feel surprised, but they never show it. Tell them you can't eat soup with anything except an egg-beater and they'll even manage to look as if they do that, too. I guess it's something you learn. I'm getting pretty good at it myself, but not when I come up against something as new as this twitch's line. I couldn't keep my eyebrows down.

Dr. Schatz, though, nodded and gave him a little smile and suggested going up to the mental hygiene office, where there wouldn't be so many people around. The little guy got up and came right along. They went into Schatz's office and I went to the room adjoining, with just a thin door I could hear through and open in a hurry if anything happened. You'd be surprised how seldom anything does happen, but it doesn't pay to take chances.

"Now, suppose you tell me what's bothering you," I heard Dr. Schatz say quietly. "Or isn't that possible, either?"

"Oh, I can tell you *that*," the little guy said. "I just can't tell you my—my name. Or yours, if I knew it. Or anyone else's."

"Why?"

The little guy was silent for a minute. I could hear him breathing hard and I knew he was pushing the words up to his mouth, trying to make them come out.

"When I say somebody's name three times," he whispered, "the person dies."

"I see." You can't throw Dr. Schatz that easy. "Only persons?"

"Well—. ." The little guy hitched his chair closer; I heard it shriek and grate on the cement floor. "Look, I'm here because it's driving me nuts, Doc. You think I am already, so I've got to convince you I'm not. I have to give you proof that I'm right."

The doctor waited. They always do at times like that; it kind of forces the patients to say things they maybe didn't want to.

"The first one was Willard Greenwood," said the little guy in a slow, tense voice. "You remember him—the Undersecretary down in Washington. A healthy man, right? Good career ahead of him. I see his name in the papers. Willard Greenwood. It has a … a *round* sound to it. I find myself saying it. I say it three times. Right out loud while I'm looking at his picture. So what happens?"

"Greenwood committed suicide last week," Dr. Schatz said. "He'd evidently had psychological difficulty for some time."

"Yes. I didn't think much about it. A coincidence, like. But then I see a newsreel of this submarine launching a few days ago. *The Barnacle*. I say the name out loud three times, same as anybody else might. You've done that yourself sometimes, haven't you? Haven't you?"

"Of course. Names occasionally have a fascination."

"Sure. So *The Barnacle* runs into something and sinks. I began to suspect what was going on; so, like an experiment, you might say, I picked another name out of the papers. I figured it ought to be somebody who isn't psycho, like Greenwood turned out to be, or old and sick, or a submarine which might be expected to run into danger. It had to be somebody young and healthy. I picked the name out of the school news. A girl named Clara Newland. Graduating from Emanuel High. Seventeen."

"She died?"

The little guy gave a kind of sob. "Automobile crash. She was the only one who was killed. The others all only got hurt. Last Sunday."

"Those could be coincidences, you know," Dr. Schatz said very gently. "Perhaps you said other names aloud and nothing happened, but you remember those because something did."

The guy kicked his chair back; I could hear it slide. He probably got up and leaned over the desk; they do that when they're all excited. I put my hand on the knob and got ready.

"As soon as I knew what was going on," he said, "I stopped saying names three times. I didn't dare say them even *once*, because that might make me say them again and then again—and you know what the payoff would be. But then last night . .

"Yes?" Dr. Schatz said, prompting him when he halted.

"A bar got held up. It was when the customers had left and the bartender was getting ready to lock the place. Two guys. There was a scuffle and the bartender was killed. The cops came. One of the crooks was shot; the other got away. The crook who was shot was—"

I opened the door a slit and looked in. He was showing a clipping to Schatz, with his finger pointing shakily at one place.

"Paul Michaels," said the doctor.

"Don't say it!" the little guy yelled. I was ready'to race in, but Dr. Schatz made a warning motion that the guy wouldn't notice that told me I wasn't needed. "I don't want to say it! If I do, it'll be three times and he'll die!"

"I think I understand," Schatz said. "You're afraid to mention names three times because of the result, and—well, what do you want us to do?"

"Keep me here. Stop me from saying names three times. Save God knows how many people from me. Because I'm deadly!"

Schatz said we'd do our best, and he got the guy committed for observation. It wasn't easy, because he still wouldn't give his name, and Dr. Merriman, the head of the psychiatric department, almost had another heart attack fighting about it.

We got together, Dr. Schatz and I, after the little guy had his pajamas and stuff issued and a bed assigned to him.

"That's a hell of a thing to carry around," I said, "thinking people die when you say their names three times. It would drive anybody batty."

"A vestige of childhood," he told me, and explained how kids unconsciously believe their wishes can do anything. I could remember some of that from my own childhood—my old man was a holy terror with the strap and many's the time I wished he was dead—and then got scared that maybe he would die and it would all be my fault. But I outgrew it, which Schatz said most people do. Only there are some who don't, like our little nameless friend, and they often get themselves twisted up like this.

"But that Paul Michaels," I said. "The crook who got shot. He's in the critical ward right here in this hospital."

"It's a city hospital," he answered, lighting a butt and looking tired. "Everything the private hospitals won't touch, we get. That's why we have this patient, too."

"Any special instructions?" I asked.

"I don't think so. This kind of case is seldom either suicidal or homicidal, unless the guilt feelings get out of hand. Keep him calm, that's all. Sedation if he needs it."

I had plenty to do around the mental hygiene ward without the little guy to worry about, but he wasn't much trouble. Until about an hour or two after supper, that is. I had some beds to move around and a tough customer to get into the hydrotherapy room, so I didn't pay much attention to the little guy and his restless eyes.

He came up to *me*, twitchy as hell, and grabbed my arm with both his hands.

"I keep thinking about that—that name," he babbled. "I keep wanting to say it. *Do* something! Don't let me say it!"

"Who?" I asked, blank for a minute, and then I remembered. "You mean this crook Paul Michaels—"

He got white and jumped up and tried to stop my mouth, but I'd already said it. I tried to calm him down and finally had the nurse give him some phenobarb, all the time explaining that the name had slipped out and I was sorry. You know, soothing him.

He said, trembling, "Now I know I'm going to say it. I just know I will." And he shuffled over to the window and sat there holding his head, looking sick.

I got to bed about midnight, still wondering about the poor little guy who thought he could kill people that easy. I had the next morning off, but I didn't take it. There were cops all over the place and Dr. Schatz looked real worried.

"I don't know how our new patient is going to take this," he said, shaking his head. "That Paul Michaels we had here—"

"Had?" I repeated. "What do you mean, had? He transferred to a prison hospital or something?"

"He's dead," Schatz said.

I closed my mouth after a few seconds. "Aw, nuts," I grumbled, disgusted with myself. "I was almost believing the little guy did it. Michaels was shot up bad. Hell, he was on the critical list."

"That's right. There'd be nothing remarkable if he died… from the bullet wound. But his throat was slit."

"And the little guy?"

"We have him full of Nembutal. He was shouting that he had said Michael's name three times and that Michael, would have to die and he would be responsible."

"You haven't told him yet," I said.

"Naturally not. It would really put him into a spin."

It was a solid mess from top floor to basement, so I had to give up my morning off. The patients, except the little guy who was in isolation, all found out about Michaels somehow—you can't stop things like that from spreading—and I had a time handling them. In between, though, I learned how the case was developlng.

There was this old cop Slattery we generally have for cases like Michaels sitting outside the critical ward, watching who went in and out. There had been somebody with Michaels on the stick-up, see, who made it while Michaels was plugged, and the cops don't take chances that maybe the accomplice or someone from the underworld might want to get at the patient when he's helpless. They always put a guard on.

Well, Slattery is all right, but he maybe isn't so alert any more, and somebody slipped past him late at night, cut Michaels' neck with probably a razor blade, and then got out again without Slattery noticing. The other patients were all doped up or asleep, so they were no help. Slattery, though, swore nobody except nurses on duty in the ward or on the floor went past him. He claimed he didn't fall asleep once during the night, and the funny thing is the nurses said the same. Or maybe it's not so funny; they like the old man and might do a little lying to help him off a rough spot.

Well, that put the girls on an even worse spot. If they were telling the truth, that Slattery had been awake the whole night, then one of them must have done it. Because Slattery had said that only the nurses went in and out of the ward. Capt. Warren, the Homicide man, jumped on that fast and got the girls to line up in front of Slattery.

"Well, Slattery?" Warren said. "One of these nurses must have been the killer. Do you recognize one who went in there with no business to? Or did one of them act suspicious, and which was it?"

Slattery looked unhappy as he went down the line and stared at the girls' faces. He shook his head figuring, I guess, that he was in for some real trouble now.

"It was pretty dim in the ward," he mumbled. "All they keep on is a little night light—just enough so the girls can find their way around without tripping, but not bright enough to keep the patients awake. I can't even be sure which nurses went in and out."

"Nothing suspicious?" Slattery demanded.

"Search me. They were nurses and my job is to keep anybody else out. As long as they were nurses and it was so dim there, one of them could have had an army rifle under her uniform and I wouldn't know."

Capt. Warren questioned the girls, got nowhere, and had them all checked to see if one didn't know Michael, well enough to want to knock him off.

I got all that from Sally Norton, one of the homely babes in the mental hygiene ward, when she came back from the grilling to go on duty. She went to her locker to change and then ran back, yipping, and grabbed Dr. Schatz. She had her uniform held up in front of her, like a shield, kind of, and she was shaking it angrily.

"Just take a look at this, Doctor!" she said. "Came back clean from the laundry yesterday and I haven't even worn it yet, and look at it now!"

"If there's anything wrong with the laundry, take it up with them," he said, annoyed. "I'm having enough trouble keeping my patients quiet with all this racket going on over Michaels."

"But that's just it. I wouldn't be surprised if it has something to do with Michaels." And she showed him the sleeve, where there were red spots down near the wrist.

Schatz called in Capt. Warren and Dr. Merriman, the head of the mental hygiene department. Merriman looked sicker than usual; he kept his hand inside his jacket, over his heart. All this excitement wasn't doing him any more good than it was doing the patients.

Warren was interested, all right. Being there in the hospital, it was easy to run a test and prove the spots were blood, human, Type B—which happened to be Michaels' blood type. He wasn't the only one in the hospital with that type, of course, but it isn't so common that Capt. Warren could disregard it.

Warren started to give Sally a bad time, but Dr. Merriman cut in and told him about the little guy and the story about saying names three times.

"What in hell kind of nonsense is this?" Warren asked. "I'm looking for evidence, not a screwball fairy tale some nut thought up."

"Exactly," Dr. Schatz said fast; he'd been trying to head off Dr. Merriman, but hadn't dared to interrupt. "It's a fairly typical delusion with no more basis in fact than witches or goblins. I can't sanction questioning a disturbed patient because of it."

"You don't have to bother," said Warren. "I've got more important things—"

"The point," Dr. Merriman went on, "is that this man claimed he was afraid to mention—specifically, mind you—the name of Paul Michaels. That was why he wanted to be committed, in fact."

Warren looked baffled. "You mean you think he said Michaels' name three times and Michaels died because of that?"

"Certainly not," Merriman said stiffly. "It's a remarkable coincidence that deserves investigation, that's all. Or perhaps my idea of police work differs from yours."

I don't know how Schatz managed it, but he let Capt. Warren know that Dr. Merriman was getting on in years and ought to be humored. So I went along with them to the little guy's bed, where he was just coming out of the sedative. He was still groggy, but he saw us coming and ducked his left hand under the blanket.

Well, that's all you have to do to get a cop suspicious, make a sudden move like running out of a bank at high noon or ducking one hand under a blanket. Warren hauled it out, with the little guy resisting and trying to hide his pinky in his palm. The cop straightened out the pinky. It was colored red under the fingernail.

"Blood?" I asked, confused, and then got busy because the little guy was trying to pull away while Capt. Warren took some scapings.

It wasn't blood. It was lipstick, according to the lab test.

"There," said Dr. Schatz, satisfied, "you see? You've upset my patient, and for what?"

"Plenty," Warren said between his teeth, "and I'm going to upset him some more."

He had me hold the little guy down—I didn't want to until Dr. Merriman overrode Schatz's objections and ordered me to—while two cops put the little guy into Sally Norton's stained uniform and painted his mouth with lipstick.

You know, with that slender build of his and the cap on, he didn't look bad. Better than Sally, if you want to know, but who doesn't?

"All right," Schatz said, "he could have gotten past Slattery in that dim light. Admitted. But what makes you think he did? And why should he have done so?"

"The lipstick on the pinky," said Warren. "If you want to do a decent job, you don't just slap it on—you shape it with your little finger. Why? That depends. If the guy's psycho, he could have done Michaels in just because. But suppose he's the guy who was with

Michaels, on the job—Michaels was the only one who could have identified him. But Michaels was in a coma. So this character had to get into the hospital somehow and slit Michaels' throat to keep him from talking. Either way, it figures."

Dr. Merriman nodded. "That was my own opinion, Captain.

"You're lying! You're lying!" the little guy screamed. "I said his name three times and he died! They always die! It's the curse I have to bear!"

"We'll see," said Dr. Merriman. "Say *my* name three times." The little guy cowered away. "I—I can't. I have enough deaths on my conscience now."

"You heard me!" Dr. Merriman shouted, turning a dangerous red in the face. "Say my name three times!"

The little guy looked appealingly at Dr. Schatz, who said soothingly, "Go ahead. I know you're convinced it works, but it's completely contrary to logic. Wishes *can't* kill. This may prove it to you."

The little guy said Dr. Merriman's name three times, pale and shaking and looking about ready to throw up with fear.

Warren put Slattery—*and* another guard—on the psycho ward, and started a check on the little guy's fingerprints.

When I got to work the next day, the ward was a tomb. It might as well have been. Sally Norton was crying and Dr. Schatz was all pinch-faced and the little guy was running around the room yelling that he shouldn't have been forced to do it.

"Do what?" I wanted to know.

"Dr. Merriman died last night," Schatz said. I looked at the little guy in horror. "Him?"

"No, no, of course not," said Schatz, but it was in a flat voice, not the impatient way he would have told me a day ago. "Dr. Merriman had a cardiac lesion. He could have gone at any time. There may even have been a deep unconscious wish to escape the pain and fear, and this patient's delusion could have given Dr. Merriman a psychological escape. It's the principle behind voodooism. The victim wills himself to death; the hexer merely supplies the suggestion."

It was pretty bad for a while, until Capt. Warren showed up with a big grin on his face. It soured when he heard that Dr. Merriman had died, but he threw out the idea that the little guy had done it.

Matter of fact, he had the cops put the arm on him and said, "Arnold Roach, I arrest you for complicity in the murder—" And so forth and so on.

The little guy, whose name turned out to be what Warren said, had been unlucky enough to leave some fingerprints around. They had him, sure enough, except that he stuck to this whammy story and hired a good psychiatrist, who got him an insanity plea. So we have him back in the ward here. And if you think he's given up and started mentioning people's names even once, let alone three times, you're battier than he is. He screams whenever somebody mentions *any* name. It's a hell of a job remembering not to call the patients by name when he's around.

"Look, what do you think?" I asked Dr. Schatz. "Is the guy psychotic or did he cop a lucky plea?"

Dr. Schatz ran his hand across his mouth and talked through his fingers. "I think he's psychotic. There's never any proof of that, of course, but his behavior bears me out. It's definitely psychotic."

"And what about this story of his about saying names three times? All right, maybe he made up those items before he showed up here—after all, they were dead already and nobody could say he had or hadn't said their names three times before they died. And Michaels—the little guy helped him shuffle out with a razor across the throat. But what about Dr. Merriman?"

"I've already told you," Schatz said tiredly. "Cardiac lesion and hypothetical death wish triggered by suggestion.

I put the mop back in the bucket and began wringing it after a fast swab at the floor. I didn't feel happy and I showed it.

"That's a guess," I answered. "What if the little guy is right and people *do* die when he says their names three times?"

"Why don't you try it and see?" he asked.

I almost upset the pail. "Me? You're the psychiatrist. Why don't you?"

"Because I know it's purely a childish delusion. I don't need any proof."

"That," I said, leaning on the mop, "is not a scientific attitude, Doctor."

"The devil with it," he grunted in annoyance. "If it's bothering you that much, I'll do it."

But he always seems to have something else to do whenever I remind him.

JOURNAL NOTES
And Three to Get Ready . . .

THEME:
One of the most persistent remnants of childhood is the belief in the power of the wish. But what if somebody actually *could* wish others to death?

POSSIBILITIES:
Editor Howard Browne specifically asks for take-your-pick payoff. In other words, plenty of evidence that it's a deliberate trick ... and doubt that *all* of it is. That takes tight mystery plotting.

DEVELOPMENT:
A motive is needed. Frighten somebody, as in voodoo? Corn. Series of contrived disasters for some gain? Overused. Theme indicates psychotic condition if carried to necessary extremes. Good enough—guy *pretends* he's cursed. But why? Not for safety; no movement and it calls for bang-bang conclusion. He's using it to get into a hospital with a psycho word. He talks his way into the psycho ward. but his prey is in another part of the hospital. Wants to know where the loot is? Strictly for the comics. Wants to shut him up? Better. The two were in a murder holdup, the other guy was plugged and is on critical list, he wants to knock him off before being identified either in delirium or questioning. Police regulations call for a guard, only nurses and doctors allowed in. Could disguise himself as a doctor, but too transparent—make him small and slight so he can pass as a nurse. Narrator *not* a doctor; the nagging doubt would be subjective—uh-uh. An orderly. Payoff is that doctor won't let the killer wish him to death, which raises question in reader's mind—is the name-three-times pure trickery or partly real?

EDITORIAL COMMENT:
This was written to order and with a strict deadline. In spite of that, Editor Browne and Agent Harry Altshuler, plus many readers, opined that if *The Lady or The Tiger*? had not been written, this would have been the definitive example of the take-your-pick

category. It's a workmanlike story, I know, with a barbed narrative hook and a fast interlocking plot and exactly the kind of ending that was asked for. But as good as they claim? I'm actually more interested in the point it makes, if they're right: Art is an accidental by-product of a job that has to be done; you don't achieve it by deciding that's what you are going to do. The attitude sounds crass, but it isn't. Unless a writer works for *and reaches* an audience, and can see his things in print so he can learn and progress, the odds are that he's in a state of creative stasis. It's a competent story, which is all I was aiming to produce.

PROBLEM IN MURDER

GILROY SPREAD THE OFFICE COPY of the *Morning Post* over the editor's desk and stared glumly at the black streamer. The editor was picking at his inky cuticles without looking at them; he was watching Gilroy's face.

"Twelfth ax victim found in Bronx," Gilroy grumbled. "Twelve in two weeks—and not a single clue."

The editor drew in his breath with a pained hiss and yanked out a handkerchief to dab at a bleeding finger. Gilroy raised his gaunt head, annoyed.

"Why don't you get a manicure, chief?" he pleaded. "That nail-picking of yours is getting me too used to blood."

The editor wrapped the handkerchief around his finger and said, "I'm taking you off the torso story, Gilroy. What's the difference who goes down to headquarters and gets the police handout? Admit it yourself—outside of the padding, your stories are the same as any of the other papers'. Why should I keep an expensive man on the job when a cub can do as well? There are other stories waiting for you to tackle them."

Gilroy sighed and sat down. He sighed again and stood up, going behind the editor's desk to the window that looked over the dark river to the lights in Jersey. His long, hewn face twisted thoughtfully at them.

"You're right, of course, chief. But, hell!" He turned around. "Do we *have* to get our handouts from the cops? How about *us* doing some detective work? Chief—will you leave that finger alone?"

The editor looked up hastily, although his thumb continued to caress the bleeding cuticle. "Our own detecting?" he repeated. "How? You—and no other reporter, either—ever got close enough to the victims to give an eyewitness description of what they looked like. The cops won't even let you take a peek. They find an arm or a leg, all wrapped up in brown grocery bags; but did you ever see them? All night long they've got radio cars riding up and down the Bronx, yet nearly every morning they find arms or legs."

"I know, but—"

"What can you do when the cops can't stop the murders?"

"Get a look at the chopped off limbs," Gilroy said doggedly, coming around slowly to the front of the desk, his hands in his pockets. his head down, and his wide mouth pursed. "That's the main thing." He looked up angrily. "Why don't the cops let us take a fast look? There'd be more chance of identification. Not much more, maybe, but more."

The editor shrugged and went back to his cuticles. "You keep saying that. Do you have any concrete ideas?"

"Sure," Gilroy said slowly. "If we use our heads, we *can* see one of those limbs."

"How?" the editor asked, mildly skeptical.

"The bulldog edition's just hitting the stands. The final hasn't been put to bed yet. Suppose we insert a reward for finding one of the arms, legs, or whatever the next one will be, and bringing it here. Tell me *that* wouldn't get results."

"It might," the editor admitted. He rolled a sheet of paper into his typewriter. "How much should I make it for—two hundred and fifty? I can clear it with the board of directors ... especially if there are any results."

"*Two-fifty*?" Gilroy exclaimed. "Do you know you can get people killed in this town for a hundred? Make it about fifty—seventy-five tops. But they have to bring the thing here and let us take care of the cops."

The editor nodded and typed. "Seventy-five," he said, "and I have a good spot for it. I'm dropping the subhead on the ax yarn and this goes there in a box. How's that?"

"Great." Gilroy grinned and rubbed his bony hands together. "Now if the interns don't send us samples from the hospitals, we can grab off an exclusive. Anyhow, I'm going up to the Bronx and look around myself."

The editor leaped out of his chair and grabbed Gilroy's lapel. "The hell you are! I've kept my men out of there so far, and they're staying out till the terror is over. How would you like to find yourself hacked to pieces, and all the cops can find is an arm or a leg? You're not going, Gilroy. That's final!"

"All right, chief," Gilroy said with a mournful expression. "You don't want me to go, I don't go."

"And I'm not kidding. I'm not yellow—you know that; but that's the one place we stay out of. The cops up there are scared witless. If the maniac doesn't get you, they will, with a couple of wild shots. Don't go. I mean it!"

Gilroy got off the subway at 174th Street, on the Grand Concourse, and walked south along the wide, bright highway. Traffic sped north, south and east, but none of it turned west into the terror district. He met no pedestrians. The police had been taken off their beats along the Concourse to patrol the dark side streets.

Riding up to the eastern boundary of the danger area, Gilroy had decided approximately where he would spend the night. Dismembered limbs had been found as far north as Tremont Avenue, as far south as 170th Street, west to just short of University Avenue, and east almost to the Concourse. The geographical center of the area, therefore, would be a few blocks west of the elevated station at 176th Street and Jerome Avenue, but Gilroy knew it was too well patrolled for the murderer to be found there.

He entered an apartment house on the Concourse, which at that point is about forty feet above the surrounding streets. He took the self-service elevator down five stories to the street level and walked boldly toward Jerome Avenue. His hands were out of his pockets, ready to snap over his head if a policeman challenged him. But if anyone in civilian clothes were to approach, his long, lean legs were tense to sprint an erratic course, to dodge knives or axes.

Several times he crouched in shallow doorways or behind boulders in vacant lots when he caught sight of policemen traveling in pairs. He realized how helpless they were against the crafty killer, and why, in spite of their tense vigil, murders had been committed at the rate of one a night, excepting Sundays, for the past two weeks. He, a reporter, not particularly adroit in skulking, found no difficulty in getting through the police cordon to Jerome Avenue and 176th Street!

He looked carefully before crossing under the elevated; when he saw that the road was completely deserted, he raced from post to post, across to a used-car lot. While he was still on the run, he chose a car slightly to the front of the first row, flung open the door, and crouched down on the floor. From that position, with his eyes just above the dashboard, he had a relatively clear view of the avenue for blocks each way. He made himself comfortable by resting against the panel. From time to time he cautiously smoked a cigarette, blowing the smoke through the hood ventilator. He was not impatient or in a hurry—the odds were that spending the night in the car would be fruitless; only by an off-chance might the murderer happen to pass. But even so, it was better than merely waiting for the official police bulletins, and there was always the hope that perhaps the maniac *would* slink by him.

Gilroy relaxed; his eyes did not. They automatically peered back and forth along the empty, shadowy avenue.

He wondered where the murderer got his victims. All through the terror area, only policemen were out at night, and then in pairs. House doors were locked. Stores were closed. People getting off late from work stayed at downtown hotels rather than go home through the dark with horror in lockstep behind them. After the first murders, taxi drivers could be bribed to enter the area; now they refused fantastic tips without regret. The elevator trains carried no passengers getting off here.

Even Gilroy, deadened to violence, could sense the cloyed atmosphere, the oppression of lurking horror in ambush. Through those streets, where terror hid and struck, paired policemen walked too quickly and nervously, afraid of somehow being separated—hundreds of patrolmen, every available man in the city—watchful as only deathly frightened men can be.

Yet in the morning, for all their watchfulness, another victim would be found somewhere within the borders of the danger area—only a limb or part of a limb; the rest of the body would never be found nor identified.

That was another point that puzzled Gilroy. Obviously the slayer had some superperfect method of disposing of the bodies. Then why did he casually leave a limb where it could be easily found after each murder? Bravado? It must have been, for those dismembered limbs could have been disposed of even more easily than the rest of the bodies. If not for that apparent egomaniacal quirk, the crimes could have been committed indefinitely, without detection.

It was long after midnight. Gilroy fished a cigarette out of an open pack in his pocket. For only an instant, he bent under the dash to hide the match's flare. When he straightened up—

A man was walking north along the avenue! A man in a top coat too big for him, a hat that shadowed his face, a small package in his left hand.

A small package!

He halted. Gilroy could have sworn that the halt was absentminded. The man raised the package and looked at it as if he had just remembered it. Then he dropped it neatly in a box of rubbish. He walked on at no more than a stroll.

Gilroy clutched the door handle. Cursing, he stopped turning it before it opened; a white-roofed police car was slowly cruising by. Gilroy knew that the passenger cop rode with his gun resting alertly out the open window.

For a moment Gilroy calculated his chance of dashing across the avenue, scooping up the bundle and following the murderer before he escaped. There was no chance. It would be suicidal.

The elevated pillars hid his view of the corner toward which the killer had strolled. When he did not cross, Gilroy knew that he had turned up that street.

At that point the police car drew abreast, and Gilroy saw the men inside stare at every doorway, every shadow behind the posts, the dark lot he was hiding in— And then they rode past without seeing him. When they reached the corner, Gilroy clutched the door handle, waiting for them to whip suddenly off the avenue and up that street. They didn't. The murderer must have vanished somehow.

Gilroy slid out of the car, crouched and scuttled to the nearest pillar, like a soldier running under fire. He stood there until he was certain that no one had seen him. Then he darted from post to post, to the one that stood opposite the rubbish box.

In the next instant, he had snatched up the bundle, on the run, and huddled against a wall, hugging the revoltingly shaped parcel under his arm. He edged swiftly along the building to the corner where the maniac had disappeared.

Nobody was there, of course. But he broke into a limber sprint, stuffing the bundle into his belt under the loose jacket, where it could not be seen. At the corner he slowed to an unsuspicious walk.

He picked a lucky moment to do it. Two policemen in the middle of the northwest block shouted for him to halt, came running with drawn guns—

He stopped and waited, his hands ostentatiously above his head. They reached him, covering him from both sides.

"Who the hell are you?" one demanded with angry panic. "Why are you out?"

"Gilroy, reporter on the *Morning Post*. You'll find my identification papers in my inside breast pocket. I'm unarmed."

Brutally, to cover his fear, the cop at his left tore the wallet out and held the papers to the street light. He blew out his breath without shame and handed the wallet to his partner.

"All right," the second growled, relieved but still shaking. "You can put them down, you lousy jerk. You know how close you came to getting plugged?"

"We got all we can do to keep from shooting each other when we pass another beat," the first patrolman said. "You stinking reporters don't have a heart."

Gilroy grinned. "Now, now, boys, it's only your nerves. All you have to worry about is a maniac. I need a story!"

"You'll get a story," the first cop said, viciously quiet. "We'll boot you onto the El and report your paper to the commissioner. That will give you something to cover."

"With both hands," said the other policeman.

They expected him to cringe before this threat. It would mean being denied the official police bulletins. But as they strode grimly toward the elevated station, Gilroy's forearm pressed reassuringly against the brown paper bundle inside the top of his pants. Official bulletins—*huh*!

At five after nine the next morning, Gilroy and the night editor were roused from their respective beds and ordered to see the police commissioner immediately. They met outside his office.

"What's up?" Gilroy asked cheerily.

"*You* should ask," the editor grumbled. "Your idea snapped back."

"Come on, you two," a police clerk said. "Get inside."

"Here it comes," the editor said resignedly, opening the door that led to Police Commissioner Major Green.

The major was a retired army officer, a short, wide, stiff man with a belligerent mustache. He sat upright and walked square and his voice was loud enough to make the wings of his mustache flutter—always in indignation. He ran the police department like a military post, and the jails like stockades, and he had an extremely vague idea of civil rights.

Major Green pushed back from his desk and stabbed them with a hostile glare. "You're from the *Morning Post*, eh?" he barked in clipped military tones. "I'm being easy with you. Your paper campaigned for my party. Take that reward offer out and put in a complete retraction. I won't press for suspension of publication."

The editor opened his mouth to speak. But Gilroy cut in sharply: "That sounds like censorship." He fished out a cigarette and lit it.

"Damn right it does," Major Green snapped. "That's just what it is, and the censorship is going to stay clamped on tight just as long as that maniac in the Bronx keeps our citizens terrified. And put out that cigarette before you get thrown out."

"We don't want to fight you, commish," Gilroy said, speaking with deadly deliberation around the cigarette that dangled uncharacteristically from the corner of his mouth. "If we have to, of course, we're in a much better position to fight than you are. Our newspapers'll take on only self-imposed censorship— when they think it's to the public's advantage."

Green's cold eyes bulged out of his stern face. Rage flushed every burly inch. Independently of his tense arms, his fingers clawed the desk.

"Why don't you shut up, Gilroy?" the editor hissed viciously. "Gilroy, eh? That's the rat who sneaked inside the cordon—" "Why should I shut up?" Gilroy broke in, ignoring the commissioner. "Ask him what he's done these last two weeks. Don't. I'll tell you.

"He's the only one in the police department who's allowed to make statements to the press. Reporters can't interview cops or captains; they can't even get inside the danger area at night—unless they try. He forces retractions on papers that step out of line.

"Well, what good has it done? He hasn't identified a single victim. He can't find the rest of the bodies. He doesn't know who the murderer is, or where he is, or what he looks like. And the murders're still going on, every night except Sunday!"

"Don't pay any attention to him, sir," the editor begged.

"I expect an arrest in twenty-four hours," Green said hoarsely.

"Sure." Gilroy's clear baritone drowned out his chief's frightened plea. "For the last two weeks you've been expecting arrests every twenty-four hours. How about giving us one? And I don't mean some poor vag picked up on suspicion.

"I'll give you a better proposition. You've been feeding us that line of goo because you don't have anything else to say. Most of the papers didn't even bother printing it after the first week.

"First of all, let us say anything we want to. We're not going to tip off the maniac. We do our own censoring, and we do it pretty well. Then, let us inside the danger zone with official recognition. We get inside anyhow, one way or another; but there's always the danger of being plugged by your hysterical cops. Finally, let us see the dismembered limbs and photograph them if we want to. Isn't that simple? And you'll get a lot further than you are so far."

Trembling, Major Green stood up, his craggy face shrunken into angles and creases of fury. He pushed his chair away blindly. It toppled and crashed, but he did not hear its clatter.

He caught up the telephone. "I'm—" He strangled and paused to clear his clogged throat. "I'm handling this my own way. I live up in the terror area with my wife and three kids. I'll tell you frankly—every night I'm afraid I'll go home and find one of them missing. I'm scared stiff! Not for myself. For them. You'd be, too, in my place.

"Here's my answer, damn you!" The telephone clicked and they heard a shrill metallic voice. "Get me Albany—the governor!"

Gilroy avoided the editor's worried eyes. He was too concerned with Major Green's reason for calling Albany.

"This is Major Green, sir, police commissioner of New York City. I respectfully urge you to declare martial law in the Bronx danger district. The situation is getting out of hand. With the mayor's permission, I request the national guard for patrol duty. The confirmatory telegram will be sent immediately... . Thank you, sir. I appreciate your sympathy—"

He clapped down the receiver and turned to them grimly. "Now see if you can squeeze past the militia sentries on every corner in the territory. There'll be a sundown curfew—everyone indoors for the rest of the night.

"Martial law—that's the only answer to a maniac! I should have had it declared long ago. Now we'll see how soon the murders'll stop!

"And," he stated menacingly, "I still want that retraction, or I'll get out an injunction. Fall out!"

In utter gloom, the editor went through the outer office. "Pretty bad, chief," Gilroy said grudgingly. "We could slip past the police cordon. Napoleon couldn't patrol every street before, but the militia can put a sentry on every corner. It doesn't matter, anyhow, so I guess you'd better print a retraction."

The editor glared. "Really think so?" he asked with curt sarcasm.

Gilroy did not reply. In silence they walked out of the office.

"Well, let's not take it so hard," the editor said finally. "He was going to declare martial law anyhow. He was just looking for an excuse. It wasn't our fault. But, just the same, that nipplehead—"

"Lousy nipplehead is the term, chief," Gilroy amended. When they reached the elevator, the switchboard operator called out: "You from the *Morning Post*? They want you down there right away."

They stepped into the elevator. The editor hunched himself into his topcoat collar. "The louse must have called up the board," he said hollowly. "Here's where we get hell from the other side."

Defeated, he hailed a taxi, though he was not in a hurry. Gilroy gave his Greenwich Village address. The editor looked up in surprise.

"Aren't you coming with me?" he asked anxiously.

"Sure, chief. I want to get something first."

At the apartment house, the editor waited in the taxi. Gilroy went upstairs. He took the brown grocery bag out of the refrigerator and made a telephone call.

"Willis, please." He held the wire until he was connected. "Hello. Gilroy speaking. Anything yet, Willis? ... No? .

O. K. I'll call later."

He went down with the package in his pocket. As they rode downtown to the newspaper building, Gilroy said, for the first time with concern on his face:

"If declaring martial law'd help, I wouldn't mind, even though it means giving that stiff-necked ape credit for brains. But this ax murderer'll only be scared off the streets; and when martial law'll be lifted, he'll go right back to work again. Green won't get him that way. He's got to be outfoxed. And he's plenty sly."

The editor remained silent. From his set, dazed expression, Gilroy knew he was thinking of a terse note in his pay envelope. Gilroy did not have to worry about his job; he might have to take less than he was getting at the moment, but he could always manage to get on a paper. The editor, though, would have to start again as a legman, and that would completely demoralize him.

"Aw, don't let it get you down, chief," Gilroy said as they stepped out of the taxi at the *Morning Post* building. "If I have to, I'll take the whole rap. I'll say I forged your initials to the print order. Anyhow, they're only going to warn us. You know—A newspaper can't afford to antagonize its sources of information. Make an immediate retraction and don't let it happen again.

The editor nodded, unconvinced. Under board orders, Major Green had been the *Morning Post's* pet appointee in the election campaign.

The day shift in the newsroom greeted them much too heartily. Gilroy recognized the ominous symptom. He had often discovered himself being overcordial to reporters about to be fired.

They entered the city editor's office. When he saw them, the city editor shook his head pityingly.

"You boys certainly started something. The board's sore as hell. They're holding a special meeting right now—"

The night editor stuffed his hands into his pockets and turned away.

"Sit down, boys. It might take some time before they cool off enough to be able to speak distinctly."

"Cut out the funeral march, boss," Gilroy said sharply. "You and the chief can soothe them. And even if Green cuts us off the official bulletin, we still can get along. Take a look at this!"

He had taken the parcel out of his pocket and put it on the desk. He ripped off the brown grocery bag.

"It's a foot!" the city editor cried.

"A *woman's* foot!" the night editor added, horrified. "Cut off at the ankle. *Ugh*!"

The city editor yanked the telephone toward him. Gilroy held down the receiver grimly. "I'm not calling the cops," the editor explained. "I'm sending for a photog."

"Not yet," Gilroy stated flatly. "It's not as simple as that. Take a look at the foot first." He picked it up callously and showed them its sole. "See what I see? The skin is perfectly even—unthickened even at the pressure points. Not a corn or callus, toe joints straight—"

"So what?" the city editor demanded. "She could've worn made-to-order shoes. Maybe she was perfectly fitted all her life."

"Shoes aren't made that way," Gilroy retorted. "They've got to prevent the foot from spreading somewhat or else they won't stay on, so there are always points of contact that cause callus. Even if she'd walked barefoot on rugs all her life, there'd still be a tiny thickening."

The city editor pursed his mouth and stared. He had not imagined so much trouble from a simple ax murder. The night editor looked fascinatedly at the foot, picking blindly at his cuticles.

"Suppose she was a cripple or a paralytic," the city editor said. "The muscles aren't atrophied. But for some reason or other, this foot never walked."

He removed the telephone from the city editor's unconscious grasp and called Willis again. When he had finished speaking, his face was grave. He picked up the foot again and pointed to an incision.

"I cut out a piece of muscle in the heel with a safety razor," he said, "and brought it to the chemist at Memorial Hospital. I made the incision because I knew she wasn't a paralytic. Muscles contain glycogen and glucose, the sugar derived from the glycogen. When you move a muscle, the energy to do it comes from burning the glucose, which turns to lactic acid. Even if she'd been a complete paralytic—hadn't moved in years—there'd still've been a minute quantity of lactic acid."

"What'd he find?" the night editor asked.

"Not a trace of lactic acid! Chief—get Green on the telephone and find out what time the national guard'll be at their posts."

The night editor was accustomed to Gilroy's unexplained hunches. He quickly got an outside wire. "Major Green? ... *Morning Post.* What time will the militia be in the Bronx? ... Five o'clock? ... Quick work... . Thanks."

"Wow!" Gilroy shouted. "Stay here, chief. I've got to find him before Green clamps down his martial law, or he'll be shot or arrested!"

In half the number of strides it would take a normal man in a normal state of mind, he was at the elevator, ringing furiously.

The city editor could not keep up with Gilroy's mental pace. "What the hell was he talking about? Who'll be shot or arrested—the maniac?"

"I guess so," the night editor replied, unworried, absolutely confident in Gilroy. "Who else could he mean? I guess he's going up to the Bronx to find him."

But Gilroy did not go to the Bronx. His first stop was at the Forty-second Street Library. Rapidly, yet carefully, he flipped through the index files on every subject that might be a clue. He eliminated hundreds of titles; even so he had to write out dozens of slips.

The man at the pneumatic tube was not astonished by the bundle of slips shoved viciously at him. "Another case, Mr. Gilroy?" he asked.

"Yeah," the tall reporter growled. "A pip."

In the south hall he appropriated an entire table on which he spread his books as quickly as they came up from the stacks. He scanned the contents pages, occasionally going through a chapter for more detailed information; wherever necessary, he looked through the indices of books that seemed to hold the key. A long sheet of foolscap swiftly became crowded with names.

He groaned at the clock. It was almost noon when he requested the city directory and a map of the Bronx. It was not very recent, but he was certain that the man he sought had lived in the same house for some time. With his ponderous equipment, he would have to, Gilroy reasoned.

He went through the enormous Bronx directory, eliminating every one of his references who did not live in the danger area. When he had finished, it was twenty to one, and there was not a single name left for him to investigate. He bad eliminated all of them; not one lived in the district where terror reigned.

And he had only four hours and twenty minutes before that area would be under martial law—when it would be too late!

The two editors listened sympathetically, but they had no plan to offer. Gilroy scarcely heard them tell how they had soothed the board of directors. He was too frantically engaged in thinking.

How do you track down one man out of a city of nearly eight million? You don't know his name, what he looks like, where he came from, what he did before, who knew him. You only know that he lives in a mile-square territory, containing perhaps a hundred thousand people.

Gilroy did not have to ignore the city editor's persistent questioning. The night editor had quieted him to a glowering sulk by telling him that Gilroy would explain when there was no danger of being made a fool by a wild intuition.

"If we had block spies, like they have in Europe," Gilroy muttered, "we'd have had him long ago. But then he'd have been executed for doing something he didn't do. Well, three and a half hours to save the poor lug. How do I go about finding him?"

If he could interview every person in that mile-square district, he could easily find the man. Gilroy dismissed the idea. It was fantastic. But suddenly his eyes sparkled and he grinned at the night editor.

"Chief, I've got to make a canvass of the danger area. Will you back me? I've never let you down so far. Where do we get the dough to hire Peck, the ad distributors?"

The night editor writhed in his chair. He picked at his cuticles and his foot tapped nervously. "Special requisition," he said dully.

"Oh, no!" the city editor stated flatly. "I'm not writing it!"

"You don't have to. I'll do it."

Gilroy and the city editor realized the anguish that the night editor had gone through in making his resolution to back Gilroy. The business staff looked cockeyed at every expenditure, even routine ones; and this requisition, based on an unexplained hunch, they could not justify, even to themselves.

"O.K.," Gilroy said in a low, respectful voice. "I'll call Peck and ask for their rates." Reverently, in a manner befitting the night editor's gallant sacrifice—possibly of his job—Gilroy made a ritual of dialing. "Peck? ... *Morning Post*. Can you interview everyone in the territory between the Grand Concourse and University Avenue, from 170th Street to Tremont Avenue, in an hour and a half? ... Good. How much will it cost? ... Cheap enough. I'll be right down with a check and a questionnare."

He waited until the night editor wrote out the requisition, watching sympathetically the whitened, trembling fingers as they scrawled out the numerals. At each figure Gilroy knew that those fingers were trying to rebel against their violation of conditioning.

Gilroy squirmed impatiently in the squad captain's car. It was too much for him to sit by and merely watch the men going in and out of buildings. All over the danger area Peck investigators were ringing doorbells and calming down the terrified inhabitants enough to open their doors.

"I can't sit here," Gilroy protested. He opened the door. "I'm going to cover a few streets myself."

The squad captain restrained him politely. "Please, Mr. Gilroy. The whole territory has been mapped out. Each man's beat dovetails with the next one's. You'll only throw them off their stride."

Gilroy subsided, grumbling furiously. He knew that the men were working with maximum efficiency, yet he could not help feeling that his own efforts would speed them up, perhaps inspire them.

Each investigator had a hard-cover notebook in which to write the answers he received. The books were divided into sections—four-fifths for "ignorance," one-tenth for "no," and the other tenth for "yes."

Gilroy's facile imagination could picture the astonishment his men's questions could cause: "I don't know what you're talkin' about, mister." "Sorry. We don't want any." "*Hah*?"

For a short while he amused himself with various fancied interviews; then he went back to cursing the men's slowness. In spite of his pessimism, the job was finished in the specified hour and a half, and the crew met at the squad captain's car, parked in the center of the district.

Gilroy eagerly collected the filled notebooks. "Send them home now," he said to the squad captain. "But there's ten bucks in it for you if you drive me around to these addresses."

He had been amazed to find so many affirmative answers. With the captain's help he organized the addresses into a route. As they rode to the first, Gilroy saw evidence of the terror that part of the Bronx lived in. Normally, children played noisily in the street, women sat on folding chairs on the sidewalks, delivery men made their rounds. But all was silent, deserted; frightened faces peered through drawn curtains.

At the first he rang cheerfully. A young man cautiously opened the door, which was held by a newly installed chain.

"An investigator was here a short while ago," Gilroy said, speaking through the narrow crack. "You answered his question affirmatively."

The youth suddenly brightened. "That's right. I've been interested in the problem ever since I began reading science fiction. I think—"

It was a matter of some minutes before Gilroy could escape and go to the next address. There he had less trouble escaping; but after several stops he lost his temper.

"These damned science-fiction fans!" he snarled at the startled squad captain. "The place swarms with them. They've got to explain everything they know about the subject and ask what you think and why you're going around getting opinions. I've got about a hundred and fifty addresses to investigate, all in less than an hour-and probably a hundred and forty-nine of them are science-fiction readers!"

At the seventeenth name he stopped abruptly. "This isn't getting me anywhere. Lay out the rest of these addresses in a spiral, starting from the middle of this territory."

The squad captain reorganized the route. They sped to the center of the danger area; and once again Gilroy began ringing doorbells, this time with a growing lack of cheerfulness as he eliminated one science-fiction fan after another. They were all scared to death of opening their doors; they made him wait until they did; and then he couldn't get away.

He came to a street of private houses. Immediately his enthusiasm returned. Inventors and experimenters are more likely to live in their own homes than in apartment houses. Landlords are not very hospitable to the idea of explosions, which, in their minds, are invariably connected with laboratory equipment. Then again, apartment houses hold room space at a premium, and scientists need elbow room.

He had only one address to investigate in this entire Street of ultra-respectable, faintly smug one-family houses, each identical with the one next door, each nursing its few pitiful square yards of lawn.

But Gilroy felt exceedingly hopeful when he stopped at the proper house and looked up at the dingy curtains, unwashed windows, and the tiny lawn, absolutely untouched in all the years it had been there. Only a scientist, he felt, could be so utterly neglectful. Gilroy was so certain he had come to the end of the trail that, before he left the car, he paid the squad captain and waited until he drove off.

Almost jauntily, then, he rang the bell. When there was no answer, he rapped and waited. He rang a trifle more insistently.

Suddenly children, no longer whitefaced and terrified, came dashing happily out of houses for blocks around. Gilroy wheeled in alarm. They were screaming: "Sojers! A parade—*yay*!"

In panic, Gilroy glanced at his watch. It was a quarter to five, and from Jerome Avenue detachments of militia marched along the street, pausing at street corners to post armed guards. When they fell into step and approached Gilroy, the street crossing had four bayoneted sentries.

Gilroy stopped his polite ringing and tapping. His left thumb jabbed at the bell and stayed there; his right fist battered away at the door. And the militia marched closer, more swiftly than Gilroy had ever suspected heavily armed men could walk. The officer stared directly at him.

Just then the door opened and a small, wrinkled, old face peered up at him. The watery eyes behind their thick glasses gazed into his with infinite patience and lack of suspicion.

"Professor Leeds?" Gilroy snapped out. The old man nodded, the webs around his weak eyes wrinkling expectantly, utterly trustful. Gilroy did not look back over his shoulder. He could hear that the guard was nearly abreast now. "May I come in?" he demanded abruptly.

His tall form blocked the soldiers from Professor Leeds' view. The old man said, "Of course," and held the door wide. Gilroy hastily barged into a small dark space between the outer and inner doors. Leeds was saying apologetically: "I'm sorry I was so late answering the door; my servant is ill and I had to come up from my laboratory in the cellar."

"An investigator was here today," Gilroy broke in. "He asked you a question. You answered in the affirmative."

For the first time the old man's eyes clouded, in bewilderment, not suspicion. "That's true. I wanted to discuss the problem with him, but he merely wrote something in a notebook and went away. I thought it was very odd. How do you suppose he knew?"

Without answering or waiting for an invitation, Gilroy strode through the hall to the front room, with the professor pattering behind.

Another old man, considerably more ancient than Leeds, sat at the window in a wheel chair. He turned at their approach. Gilroy suddenly felt uncomfortable under his keen, distrustful scrutiny.

But Leeds still asked, gently persistent: "How do you suppose he knew that I was experimenting with synthetic life?"

"Shut up, perfessor!" the old man in the wheel chair shrieked. "Don't you go blabbin' everythin' you know to no international spy like him. That's what he is, a-snoopin' and a-pryin' into your affairs!"

"Nonsense, Abner." Leeds faced Gilroy. "Don't pay any attention to him. You're not a spy, are you, Mr.… . uh—"

"Gilroy. No. I came here—"

"He brought me up from a child. I know he doesn't like to hear this, but his mind isn't what it used to be. He's a nasty-minded old crank."

Abner drew in his creased lips with a hiss of pain. Then he rasped: "No spy, huh? Why's he bustin' in with them sojers on his heels?"

"That's the point, boys," Gilroy said. He shoved his battered hat off his angular brow and sat on a plush sofa that was red only in isolated spots. Most of the nap had come off on countless pants, dust had turned it to a hideous purple, and a number of its springs coiled uselessly into the air. "Sit down, please, professor."

Leeds sat in the depths of a huge chair and folded his hands.

"You *are* trying to synthesize life, aren't you?"

The professor nodded eagerly. "And I almost have, Mr. Gilroy!"

Gilroy leaned forward with his elbows on his high knees. "Do you read newspapers, professor? … I mean, lately?"

"I have so much to do," Leeds stammered, his lined, transparent skin flushing. "Abner neglected his diabetic diet— gangrene set in— and his leg had to be amputated. I have to do all the cleaning, cooking, shopping, buy my material and equipment, take care of him—"

"I know," Gilroy interrupted. "I figured you didn't read the—"

He stopped in amazement. The professor had creaked to his feet and rushed to Abner's side, where he stood patting the old servant on the shoulder. Tears were squeezing out of Abner's eyes.

"Ain't it bad enough I can't do nothin'," the old man wailed, "and I gotta let you take care of me? You're plumb mean, talkin' 'bout it!"

"I'm sorry, Abner. You know I don't mind taking care of you. It's only right that I should. Wouldn't you do it for me?"

Abner wiped his nose on his sleeve and grinned up brokenly. "That's so," he admitted. "Reckon I must be gittin' into my second childhood."

Leeds returned to his seat, confident that Abner was pacified, and looked expectantly at Gilroy. "You were saying—"

"I don't want to scare you, professor. I'm here to help you."

"Fine," Leeds smiled, with absolute trust.

"You watch that there slicker," Abner whispered hoarsely.

"You made several limbs and at least one foot, didn't you?" Gilroy asked. "You weren't satisfied with them, so you threw them away."

"Oh, they were no good at all, complete failures," Leeds confided.

"Let's leave that until later. No doubt you had good reasons for discarding the limbs. But you just threw them away in the street, and people found them. Now the people up here're afraid of being murdered and hacked to pieces. They think those limbs were chopped off corpses!"

"Really?" Leeds smiled tolerantly. "Isn't that silly? A few simple tests would prove that they never lived."

"I made a couple of those tests," Gilroy said. "That's how I found out that they were synthetic limbs. But you won't convince the cops and these people up here that they were. So now there's martial law in this part of the Bronx, with soldiers posted on every corner."

Leeds stood up; he shuffled back and forth, his hands twisting anxiously behind his back. "Oh, dear," he gasped. "My goodness! I had no idea I would cause so much trouble. You understand, don't you, Mr. Gilroy? I was experimenting with limbs, studying them, before I felt I was ready to construct an entire synthetic human being. The limbs were highly imperfect. I had to dispose of them somehow. So, when I went out for walks at night, I wrapped them up and threw them away. They seemed so imperfect to me. They scarcely looked human, I thought—"

Abner's mouth had dropped open in astonishment. He compressed it grimly and said: "You gotta clear yourself, perfessor. You're the first Leeds that anybody ever called a murderer! Go out and tell them!"

"Precisely." Leeds walked purposefully toward his topcoat, draped over a sagging grand piano. "Dear me—I had no idea! I know just how the people feel. They must think I'm just a common Jack the Ripper. Please help me with my coat, Mr. Gilroy. I'll go right down and explain to the authorities that it was all a terrible mistake; and I'll bring a synthetic limb with me as proof. That will clear everything up."

Abner bounced excitedly in his chair. "Atta boy, perfessor!"

"Wait a minute," Gilroy said sharply, before the situation could get out of hand. He snatched the coat and held it tightly under his arm. "You'll be stopped by the sentries. They'll search you. Most of them're green kids out on what they think is a dangerous job—getting a bloodthirsty maniac. If they find a synthetic limb on you, bullets're liable to start flying—plain nervousness, you know, but in the line of duty."

"Heavens!" Leeds cried. "They wouldn't actually *shoot* me!"

"They might. But suppose they let you through—"

"You'd come up against a police commissioner who hates to have anyone prove he's a fool. He's drawn hundreds of cops off their regular beats to patrol this section. Luckily he didn't catch you. So he had to have martial law declared. The papers've been giving him hell, demanding the maniac's arrest. He's jittery. His reputation's at stake.

"Then you come in telling him that the limbs were synthetic, that there weren't any murders. Why, he'd perjure himself and line up hundreds of witnesses to prove that, you were the murderer. He'd take your own confession and twist it to prove that you were cutting people up to study them. Don't you see? ... He's got to solve these murders, but he's got to solve them the right way: with someone in the electric chair!"

Leeds dropped into a chair. His watery eyes clung to Gilroy's, frankly terrified. "What shall I do?" he begged in scared bewilderment.

The reporter had to escape that pleading, frightened stare. He gazed down at the charred fireplace. "Damned if I know. Anything but explaining to Major Green. Anything but that!"

"He's right, perfessor," Abner chattered, fearful for his master's life. "I know them durned coppers. Don't care who they send to the chair, long's they got somebody to send there so's they get the credit."

At that point Leeds broke down. Babbling in honor, he shuffled swiftly out of the room. Gilroy leaped after him, along the hall and down to the cellar.

He heard sobbing in the basement laboratory. He clattered down the steps. He was surrounded by shelves of canned and bottled chemicals that clung to the raw cement walls and had been gathering dust for the good part of a century. A broad bench was constructed in two parts, one on each side of a twin, broad-bellied sink that had originally been meant for laundry. A furnace squatted stolidly in the midst of the apparatus.

Then he saw Leeds, half concealed by the furnace, crouching protectively over a deep zinc tank like a bathtub.

"When will they come to arrest me?" he moaned. "I'd hoped to finish my experiment—I'm so close to the solution!"

Gilroy was touched. "They're not coming to arrest you," he said gently. "So far the cops don't know who did it."

"They don't?" Leeds brightened. "But *you* found out."

"The cops never know anything. Only—" He hesitated, then blurted his single fear: "There's the chance that Major Green might become panicky that his maniac's slipping out of his fingers. He might have the militia search the houses!"

The old man trembled with redoubled fear. "If they did that—"

"This's what they'd find," Gilroy said, looking into the clear bath that filled the high, sharply square tank. In his career he had seen disgusting sights, but the human skeleton at the bottom of the chemical bath, with shreds of muscle, wisps of fatty nerves and an embryonic tracery of veins and arteries adhering to the almost exposed bones, made his hobnailed heart shrink. It took an effort to realize that the tattered remains were not remains but beginnings. The naked skull bore only the revolting fundamentals of what would eventually become features. "They'd think you were dissolving a body in acid!"

Leeds stared at the corpse in fascinated horror. "It *does* look like a dissolving body, doesn't it?" he quavered. "But it won't when it's complete—"

"When'll that be?" Gilroy demanded hopefully.

"In about twenty-four hours." The old man looked up at Gilroy's abstracted face. "Do you think that will be enough time?"

"God knows. I certainly don't."

The situation definitely held a concrete danger. Gilroy knew that high positions often twisted the morality of men who had them. Most men in Major Green's place would unscrupulously sacrifice a single life for the good will of eight million, and perhaps a national reputation. Major Green, in particular, had been conditioned to think very little of individuals. If the militia searched the house, Leeds was almost in the chair.

They climbed up to the front room. Abner still sat at the window; he seemed to be fascinated by the militiamen standing at ease on the four street corners within his vision.

"Huh—young whippersnappers!" he hissed at the boys standing guard. "If I had my leg back, I'd get past them fast enough, you betcha!"

Leeds' characteristic optimism had ebbed away, sapped by the knowledge of the chaos his lifework had caused. He sat huddled in a chair as far away from the window as the wall would permit, his terrified mind absolutely useless to Gilroy.

The tall reporter saw only one hope. He felt his analysis of Green had been correct, but—he did not have to convince the commissioner! He had only to convince the public. Green would be washed up as a public figure; on the other hand, Leeds would be saved from being railroaded to the electric chair, and the chief's expense account would be cleared by a scoop! For any single item, he would gladly sacrifice Major Green.

He gripped the professor's thin arm in a hand like a tree root.

"I'll get you out of this," he promised.

"Can you really?" Leeds asked breathlessly. "You don't know how I—"

"Don't step out of the house until I come back. In a couple of minutes it'll be curfew. Chances are I won't be back before morning—"

Leeds followed him to the door in a panic. "But please don't leave me, Mr. Gilroy! Please—"

"You'll be all right. Abner's here with you."

"Sure," Abner croaked from the front room. "You got nothin' to fret about with me here. But ain't it time for my mush and milk, perfessor?"

"I'll get it for you immediately," Leeds quavered; then Gilroy was out in the darkening street, wondering how he was going to get past the alert sentries, who had already turned to watch his long body glooming up uncertainly toward them.

On the other side of the Concourse, out of the martial-law district, Gilroy crowded himself into an inadequate telephone booth and dialed the office. Getting past the sentries had been ridiculously easy; he had only had to show them his Guild card and explain that he worked on the night shift, and they had let him pass.

The night editor answered, rather tiredly.

"Gilroy, chief. Listen carefully. I found the guy. That thing I showed you today wasn't real. It was synthetic. The others were, too. I've got to clear him. He's working on a whole one— you know what I mean. If it's found, he's cooked."

"What do you want me to do?"

Gilroy put his mouth against the transmitter and said in a low tone: "I can clear him and grab off a scoop. That'd fix up that special-requisition business for you. He's got an entire one that's about half done. Send me down a photog with plenty of film. We'll take pix of the thing developing, slap it on the front page, and Nappie can go fly a kite!"

"Nothing doing, Gilroy," the editor said decisively. "This'd fix my job more than the special req. The board has big plans for Nappie. They're making eyes at Albany; after that it's only a step to the White House. Nope. This'd knife him. It'd mean my job for sure."

"Wouldn't it be worth it?"

"Look, Gilroy—I'm taking enough of a chance as it is, backing you. I can't go sticking my chin out at the board any more than that. Just be a good boy and figure out some other way of saving your pal. You can do it. I'll back you all you want. But get a beat if you can."

"O.K., chief," Gilroy said fatalistically. "I'll go home and grab some sleep. Leave me a blank signed req. I'll dope something out."

Long before dawn, Gilroy's mind came awake. He did not open his eyes, for, through his shut lids, he could see that the sun had not yet risen. He lay quietly, thinking. His blanket, which, of course, was too short when spread the usual way, covered him in a diamond shape, one end caught tightly beneath his feet and the other high on his bony neck. His knees were drawn up, soles pressed against the baseboard.

Ever since attaining full growth, he had been forced to sleep that way; but his adaptive nature did not rebel against conforming to beds that were too small, telephones in booths that reached his solar plexus unless he shoehorned himself down, or bus seats that scraped his sensitive knees.

In some way, he was thinking, he had to stop the reign of terror in the Bronx; prevent suspicion from being focused on Professor Leeds; and, at the same time, cover the night editor's expense account—which meant getting a beat that would not smash Major Green's reputation.

But, to keep the police commissioner's record clean, he needed a victim. Gilroy knew enough about public pressure to realize that a sacrifice was absolutely vital. Left to himself, Green would find himself one—anybody it could be pinned on. The public would be satisfied, and the strutting martinet would again be a hero.

Gilroy's duty was plain: he would have to find a victim for Green.

At that point Gilroy's eyes almost snapped open. By sheer will power he kept them shut, and contented himself with grinning into the dark. What a cinch! he exulted. He'd get a victim, and a good one! All at one shot—end the terror, clear the professor, get a scoop and save the chief's job! Incidentally, he would also give Napoleon a lush boost, but that was only because it worked out that way.

Gilroy pulled his knees higher, kicking the blanket smooth without even thinking about it, and turned over to go back to sleep. There were a few trifling details, but they could be settled in the morning.

The city editor had scarcely glanced at the memos left on his desk when Gilroy strode in.

"Morning,, boss," the reporter greeted cheerily. "Did the chief leave a requisition?"

"Yeah, a blank one, signed. Fill in the amount. I don't know—he must be going soft, leaving himself wide open like that."

Gilroy waved his hand confidently. "He's got nothing to worry about. Tonight we'll have an exclusive that'll burn up the other rags.

"But, first of all, do you know a good, reliable undertaker, and how much will he charge?"

"Oh, go to hell," the editor growled, puttering about among the papers on his desk. Then his mouth fell open. "An *undertaker*?"

Instead of answering, Gilroy had dialed a number. "Gilroy ... How's he coming along? ... No, not Abner; the other one... . Good... . Is there any way of speeding it up? ... Well, even a few hours'll help. I'll be up as soon as I fix everything down here... . Oh, you don't have to get panicky. Just stick in the house until I get there."

"Who was that?" the editor demanded. "And why the undertaker?"

"Never mind; I'll take care of it myself. I want your gun. I'll get a hammer and cold chisel off the super. Write a req for the gun—the paper'll take care of it. Let's see, anything else? Oh, yeah—"

Gravely, he took the gun from the astounded city editor. As he sat down at the typewriter and began tapping at the keys, he was completely aware of the city editor's stare. But he went on typing.

Within a few minutes he yanked the paper out of the machine and disappeared into the elevator. In the basement he borrowed the hammer and cold chisel from the apathetic superintendent. For nearly an hour he pounded, hidden away behind the vast heating system. When he put the gun into his back pocket, the serial numbers had been crudely chiseled off.

Then he took a taxi and made a tour of undertaking establishments. Curiously, he seemed less interested in prices, caskets and the luxuriousness of the hearses than he was in the condition of the owners' businesses and the character of the drivers.

He found the midtown funeral parlors too flourishing for his satisfaction. He drove to a Tenth Avenue frame-house establishment.

"Rotten," the owner grumbled in reply to Gilroy's question. "The city's taking over these here tenements. Nobody lives here, so how can they be kicking off? I'll have to get out soon, myself."

Gilroy approved of the driver, who had evidently seen plenty of shady funerals. He offered the owner a flat sum for a full day's rental of the hearse and chauffeur. He was extremely pleased to see the gloating light in the owner's sad eyes. There would be no questions asked and no answers given here, he thought shrewdly.

Finally he called the city editor and told him bluntly to have two photographers waiting for his call, ready to meet him anywhere in the city. He slammed down the receiver before the editor began cursing.

It was merely another experience in a reporter's life to be driving uptown in a hearse. At 125th Street he suddenly remembered something very important. He had the driver stop, walked two blocks toward the Third Avenue El. When he returned twenty minutes later, he carried a bundle, which he threw into the long wicker basket inside the hearse.

He had not anticipated any difficulty in passing the militiamen. He knew that mailmen, street cleaners, telegraph boys, doctors, and hearses would be able to move around freely within the martial-law area.

They rode, unchallenged, directly to Professor Leeds' door.

There he and the driver slid the basket out and carried it into the house. The sentries were scarcely aware of their actions.

"I'm so happy to see you again, Mr. Gilroy!" the professor cried. Then he gaped at the basket. "What is your plan?" he asked anxiously.

From the front room came Abner's querulous voice: "They ain't here for me, are they, perfessor?"

"No, Abner," Gilroy called out assuringly. "Stay here, driver."

He led the professor down to the basement laboratory.

Gilroy nodded in a satisfied way at the body in the tank.

"Another two hours and it will be finished," Leeds said.

The epidermis was almost completely formed. Only in isolated spots could the glaring red muscle be seen where the skin bad not quite joined. Its fingers and toes had no nails; and, excepting the lack of hair, eyebrows and lashes, its features were distinctly human and complete.

"I'm just waiting for the hair to grow. That's the final stage. The skin will be whole in a few minutes. Then the nails—"

Gilroy heard wheels rumbling over the ceiling. The cellar door flung open and Abner shouted down, in terror: "Perfessor! Hey—them durn sojers're goin' through all the houses on this here Street!"

Gilroy leaped up the stairs and dashed through the hall to the front windows. At each end of the block he saw eight soldiers; four stood in the gutter, facing opposite sides of the street with leveled guns. The other four paired off and entered houses with fixed bayonets.

"They can't do that 'thout a warrant," Abner protested.

"Can't they?" Gilroy snorted. "They can, and they're doing it. Sit here by the window, Abner, and warn us when they're getting close. They still have half a block to go before they reach us. Come on, prof—"

He removed the bundle from the long wicker basket and raced down to the cellar. While he ripped off the paper, he ordered the professor to take the body out of the chemical bath and dry it.

Leeds cried out: "He isn't complete yet!" But he removed the body, in spite of his complaints, dragged it to the floor and dried it. "It isn't alive!" he suddenly wailed, his hand shaking against its chest. "It should be—it's perfect!"

Gilroy shook out an entire outfit of clothing, a pair of old shoes and a filthy hat that closely resembled his own. "If he isn't alive, all the better," he said. "Anyhow, I always thought it was too much to expect him to live. Take fish, for instance. Put them in the same kind of water they always lived in—temperature just right, plenty of oxygen, plenty of food—and what do they do? They die. You make a body that's identical to a living one, all the necessary organs, all the chemical ingredients for life—and it just doesn't live. Otherwise it's perfect.

"Here, lift up his legs so I can slip these pants on him.

"You're on the wrong track, prof. when it comes to making synthetic human beings. You can give them everything but the life force. But there is one thing you can do. You can grow limbs on people who don't have 'em. Give Abner a leg. His life force can vitalize the synthetic leg."

They pulled a shirt on the body and tucked it inside the trousers. Gilroy spent a mad few minutes trying to knot a tie in reverse, until he knelt and tied it from behind. While he forced its arms into a vest and jacket, Leeds squeezed its flabby, yielding feet into shoes.

Then Abner croaked: "They're only two houses away, perfessor!"

Leeds grew too jittery to tie the laces. Gilroy did it, crammed the battered hat into the body's coat pocket, and roared for the hearse driver to bring down the basket. It was the work of a moment to load the corpse into it and strap on the cover. Almost at a run, he and the driver carried it up the cellar stairs to the front door. They dropped it while Gilroy made a hurried telephone call:

"Boss? Gilroy. Send the two photogs to 188th and Triboro Bridge. Right before the entrance. I'll pick them up in a hearse. Be there with the chief if you can get him to wake up.

He paused a moment to pat Abner on the back encouragingly. He said: "You're all clear, prof. Look in the *Morning Post* tonight. Drain the tank. If they ask about it, say you used to bathe a dog in it. So long!"

They carried the wicker basket to the hearse at a slow, fitting pace, just as the militiamen were leaving the next house. At the same funereal rate of speed they cruised through the martial-law area, which was being thoroughly searched, until they came to the Grand Concourse.

"Open it up!" Gilroy rapped out suddenly.

They streaked through traffic, turned east. At the bridge they had to wait fifteen minutes before the photographers arrived in taxis.

Gilroy dismissed the cabs, paid off his hearse driver, and ordered the photographers to help him with the basket. A scant three minutes later another taxi drew up at the hearse and the city and night editors scrambled out excitedly. They sent their cabs away.

"What the hell is this?" the city editor demanded. "Robbing graves?"

"Just give us a hand and keep quiet," Gilroy said calmly.

They carted the heavy basket to a deserted dumping ground behind two vacant furniture warehouses that had been condemned by the city for the new bridge approach. He removed the basket cover and ordered the photographers to help him take the body out and hold it erect.

"Now watch this," he grinned.

While the editors and photographers watched in horrified amazement, Gilroy backed off ten feet and fired the gun at the corpse's heart. He quietly wiped his fingerprints off the butt, removed the body from the photographers' inert hands, and laid it gently on its back, crooking its right hand around the gun. He placed the cap on the ground beside the naked, hairless head. Then he crumpled a sheet of paper in his hand and just as deliberately smoothed it.

"Snap the body from a few angles. Wind up with a shot of this note."

The two editors snatched at the note in a single wild grab. They read it swiftly.

"Holy smoke!" the night editor shouted. "'I am the torso murderer. I realize that I have been insane for some time, and, during my lapse from sanity, I kidnapped and hacked to death a number of people. But the cordon of soldiers hounded me from one place to another, until I am finally driven to suicide in order to prevent my being captured. My name I shall take to the grave with me, that my former friends be spared the horror of knowing that once they loved this murderous maniac. God save my soul!'"

The four men grinned admiringly at Gilroy. But the towering reporter dismissed their admiration with a modest wave of his astoundingly long, incredibly bony arm.

"The only thing I regret is that this's a gorgeous build.up for Major Green—the lousy nipplehead!" he said mournfully. "The autopsy'll show a thousand proofs that this thing never lived, but a fat lot Nappie'll care. And to think that I'll probably be the cause of making him governor!"

He insisted on holding the creased suicide note for the photographers to aim at, claiming that it required a certain artistic touch.

JOURNAL NOTES
Problem In Murder

Theme:
Let's turn the *corpus delicti* situation upside down—suppose there's a mutilated corpse without a murder?

Possibilities:
There are many fantastic ways to get an unmurdered mutilated corpse, but all demand identification with him and end with the death and not a tense mystery. The idea is to *start* with the corpse and work up to the discovery that there has been no murder. In science fiction, this means that the corpse was never alive and so couldn't have been killed.

Development:
Impossible to have a scientist protagonist; reader would have to be told the setup almost immediately. A detective *might* figure it out, but for him to sell the answer to his superiors would take a stupefying amount of gab. Ordinary citizen wouldn't be believable; he'd have to have a damned convincing reason to stick his nose where it might get sliced off by a murderer or bashed in by a police club. Finding slayer of somebody close might do it, but not if the corpse had never been alive. A reporter with a flair for detection? He has the Big Picture, an incentive for plugging away at the case, the facilities to do so *and* irritating (and therefore suspense-building) handicaps. No, not a whole corpse; would inevitably be autopsied and the answer found bafflingly but quickly. "Torso" murders so loved by tabloids—an arm here, a leg there, *then* one single corpse to be used for ironical twist in which protagonist knows and reader knows, but not the cops or general public, because the corpse has to be used to get the "killer" off the hook.

Editorial Comment:
The story was written in 1939 and what happened nearly a decade and a half later is downright funny. I was asked to submit several of my stories for radio adaptation. This one was selected and I

read it over before doing the script. Not having read it in all these years, I was intensely unhappy with a number of things. The characters were mainly overdrawn. The action inclined toward shrillness and a dead run. I'd certainly have cut out the references toward science fiction because I feel that it strains the willing suspension of disbelief, like the fictional private eye who declares scornfully that he's not like those private eyes you read about in fiction. All the same, I found myself trying to guess the way the story would turn out—I'd forgotten everything but the theme! (With about 5,000,000 words published and broadcast in between the writing and the reading, that's understandable.) And damned if the payoff didn't surprise me! When a writer outfoxes himself, he's performed a Neatest Trick of the Week.

GOLD ON GOLD*

Before I tell you how I came to do what I did, I have to tell you how I affected the world from birth on.

I was born the year World War I started, graduated the year Roosevelt and Hitler came to power, got married the day World War II began, had a son 20 days after Pearl Harbor, founded *Galaxy* Magazine just minutes ahead of the Korean War, got divorced the year of Sputnick, remarried the year of the Gulf of Tonkin Resolution.

In other words, I'm a historical Typhoid Mary and should be paid a dollar by every man, woman and child on Earth—a lousy buck apiece—not to make any major moves any more.

While I'm waiting for that, let me tell you some lesser details of how I came to do what I did.

I discovered science fiction when I was 13—a magazine with monstrous ants and a spastic man looking up at a girl in a bronze bra and filmy skirt being tenderly held in the mandibles of one of the bugs. It was beautiful, so beautiful that I decided right then to become an sf writer. As for not deciding to become an sf artist, how could a 13-year-old kid—or anyone else, for that matter—compete with the peerless Frank R. Paul?

So I studied English and the sciences as hard as I could and wrote stories for the school magazines. After that, I wrote and wrote—thousands and thousands of words that—well, I'd walk to the post office to mail my stories and come back to find a rejection slip waiting for me at home. I never could figure out how the editors did that.

Then I started bringing manuscripts to the editors instead of mailing them. I got them back even faster that way. But I persevered—and one day I brought a story to a wonderful old man named T. O'Conor Sloane. He got dangerously excited about it for a man of 82—but he said it was much too good for *Amazing Stories*. So he took it and me upstairs to the editor of the company's prestige magazine, the *Delineator*, and demanded that it be read. I got it back when I

---

returned home. I think it arrived before I did. Next month, the *Delineator* folded. I immediately saw the connection but I wanted to sell that story and brought it back to Dr. Sloane. He maintained that it was too good for his magazine and refused to buy it.

So I never sold that story because *Amazing* was the only sf magazine at that time, and I lost the story somehow. I can't tell you if it was all that good, but maybe you can judge by what I remember of it. In it, I manfully exposed the miscreants who were exploiting the slave labor in the mines of Venus, and told of the revolt that freed the poor Earthlings.

Now if that story was too good for *Amazing*, maybe it accounted for the dreadful stories Dr. Sloane bought. But can you imagine what the *rejects* were like?

Well, I was 18 then and not too easily discouraged. I went on writing. My parents were vociferously against it. How, they wanted to know, could anyone make a living putting black marks on white paper? So I wrote and worked at any job I could find, and there weren't many, because this was at the bottom of the Great Depression. I remember being a bus boy in a fancy place called Roadside Rest. I was interviewed by three Rumanian brothers, who owned it, and though I didn't know it, I was hired because there was nobody else around. So I worked from 10 in the morning to 2 the next morning—and then had to walk home because the buses stopped running at midnight. It was a 7-mile walk and I was pooped. But I was there at 10 the next morning, ready to put in another 16-hour day. Did I mention that I worked for the waiters, seven of them, and each gave a quarter, or a grand total of $1.75?

But the brothers were there already and I was told to come into the office, where they unanimously told me I couldn't work there any more. But why, I asked. Because, they said, you are a writer, an artist, and we couldn't stand the thought of a writer being a bus boy. But you're not paying me, I argued, the waiters are—and besides, I've never sold a story—so how can I be called a writer? They were Rumanianly adamant, though I begged, pleaded, cajoled. I went home in despair—and found a letter from someone named Desmond Hall awaiting me. It was on Street & Smith stationery—and it said that he was happy to inform me that my latest story had been accepted for *Astounding Stories*! A check would be arriving soon!

I showed my parents the letter. They were unconvinced. After all, how much could a story bring? I didn't know. The letter didn't say, only that Mr. Hall was cutting 1,500 words from it. I told my parents that brought the wordage to 19,500—and if they paid a cent a word, it would be $195, or $97.50 for half a cent. They scoffed. But the check arrived in a week or so—and it was for an astounding $195! I suddenly became a big man in my family's eyes, a 20-year-old writer!

I went to meet Mr. Hall, who immediately put me on a first-name basis, and said he wanted to buy more material from me. So I moved from Far Rockaway, a seashore resort that was mobbed in the summer and abandoned in winter, a dismal place to live, to Greenwich Village, just ten minutes' walk from Street & Smith. It was wonderful. I sold half a dozen stories to Des in pretty short order. He told me it was impossible to make a living writing science fiction and urged me to diversify. But first, I didn't know how, and second, it was sf I wanted to write.

Meanwhile, my first story was published and appeared on the stands. More important than my being immortal for a month was that Hitler and Mussolini promptly launched an attack on the Rhineland, and Ethiopia.

Now *Astounding* was nominally edited by F. Orlin Tremaine, but Des Hall was the actual editor. And one day Des was promoted to editor of *Mademoiselle*; he had won first prize for the name, though Tremaine became its first editor. Tremaine had done such a lousy job that Street & Smith put out a second Volume I, Number I. So Tremaine had been demoted and found himself with 3 million words to read for *Astounding* over a weekend. Instead of going through the manuscripts, however, he hurried to the Tombs to get an astrological reading from an imprisoned fortune teller named Evangeline Adams, the leading astrologist of the day. He had to wait while Wall Street men crowded into her cell. I don't know what she told him, but—here it gets a little complicated.

I was writing under the name of Clyde Crane Campbell. The other Campbell, John W. Jr., wasn't well enough known at the time to make it seem a less than likely name for me. The reason? Nazism's anti-Semitism had spread all through the world and it permeated Street & Smith, so I knew better than to write under my own name. When Des was promoted, he recommended me as his successor on *Astounding*. I was turned down because of my religion. If you think I was angry, you should have heard and seen Des! And I never sold a word to Tremaine.

That's not entirely Tremaine's fault. I had run out of good sf ideas and he didn't know and cared even less how to get them out of me, as Hall had. So I became book reviewer for *Mlle*. at a fat $15 a month—and couldn't get review books from the publishers—they told me to come back when *Mlle*. was established! I consequently had to rewrite reviews from the *New York Times* and *Herald-Tribune,* which turned out to be a bad notion and my column was dropped. I wrote one story for *Mlle*., under the name of Julian Graey (I had tried Grey, then Gray, and finally combined them and sold one single story). It was cockeyed comedy in the vein of the wild humor of the Thirties. And that was that.

I returned home when I had no choice. I sold shoes Saturdays for $4 a day and would have worked more had there been enough business to warrant it. Come summer, I became a professional drowner. The city was threatening to lay off lifeguards on stretches of beach that were officially safe—where nobody drowned or had to be rescued. So I would swim out beyond the ropes and thrash around until the guard on the beach saved me. I had to be carried to the nearest first-aid station and revived. Thinking up a new name and address for each drowning took some doing, but it wasn't that that ended my career. The last guard had dived to rescue me—and laid his head open on the catamaran and I had to pull him in. I couldn't go from hero to victim again, and that was the end of my easy $1.50 per drowning.

Three years passed, years of hunting for work, finding very little, and trying to write over my family's renewed objections. I can't blame them. It was terribly discouraging.

And then came John W. Campbell Jr., new editor of *Astounding*. I got a splendid letter from him about a story I had dispiritedly written and submitted. It was a lackluster creation about a man and dog getting their identities switched and their attempts to get the villain, a surgeon, to switch them back again. The *real* problem, wrote Campbell, was communication—how could the man in the dog's body convey his predicament to someone who could help him? I spent two months on the story—but Campbell bought it, retitled it "A Matter of Form" and ran it as his first *Nova* story. It was disastrous finally, but it went over so well that I followed with the same reporter-detective hero in "Problem in Murder," the search for the mass murderer who left legs and arms in garbage cans every day but Sunday; the limbs turned out to have never been alive—yet, to satisfy the bullying police commissioner and the panicked public, a murderer had to be found. The hero took the last experiment, an almost but not quite complete body from the vat, dressed it, took it through the cordon in a hearse, wrote a suicide note for the corpse that had never lived, shot it, and the resulting scoop built up the commissioner for a shoo-in as governor.

Funny how awful an sf story sounds when condensed. I remember being backed into describing one at a party: "There are these giant brains in glassite domes in the Arctic, and they belong to aliens who know the entire history of the Earth because they're immortal—" The process was so embarrassing that I never did write that story.

I was shuffling through the rain one day toward Street & Smith without an idea in my head except a subvocal song about walking...No, wait a minute. I have to tell you how come I started writing under my own name. After my turndown for Des Hall's job, along came a man named Stanley G. Weinbaum, with the most marvelously invented yarns about the most lovable Martians and things that readers loved so much that S&S had to drop its anti-Semitism. John Campbell also put me on a first-name basis and told me to use my name, which I very thankfully did.

So, as I was saying, I was shuffling through the rain and there was this song I was subvocalizing about walking between the raindrops...hey, how about that for a story! I had it half worked out by the time I reached John's office—only, after I hit him with it, he vetoed inverted ionization as the reason water wouldn't touch my hero. He wanted a pure fantasy with maybe a water gnome to put a curse on the protagonist. Now why would he want a fantasy when he's putting out an sf magazine. Well, that was his business, not mine. All right, a supernatural curse. But why? And how is it gotten rid of?

I wrote it, finally, as "Trouble With Water" and found myself famous. But why did Campbell want fantasy? Because he needed stories for his new magazine, *Unknown*, and I was in the first issue!

You can't imagine the impact *Unknown* had on writers. I, for one, dropped science fiction and joyfully turned out fantasies—nothing but fantasies—for the next two years. They included "Warm, Dark Places," "Day Off" and the biggest hit of all, a novel called "None But Lucifer."

Well, I finally wrote a short sf story in between fantasies and tried it out on John. He wanted fantasies from me. So I gave it to Mort Weisinger, editor of *Thrilling Wonder*. It was about the first man to land on Mars, such a complete heel and opportunist, wanting to turn his fame into money, that the equivalent of NASA fired him off to Mars again, to get rid of him. Mort, never one to leave well enough alone, wanted it turned into a tear-jerker, so I wrote a four-handkerchief story called, simply enough, "Hero." It was a stinker, a real bummer, but it sold—and it got Mort to sell me to the publisher of *Thrilling Wonder Stories* as Mort's assistant. My fist editorial job! How about that?

I'll tell you how about that. It paid $30 a week, which wasn't quite enough to support a wife, and 20 days after Pearl Harbor, a child, and it was so mechanical that two years of it destroyed the pleasure of editing. I had come to it with the most exalted feeling of exultation, and left it with style and pride completely gone.

I went next to setting up, as managing editor, a pair of true detective magazines, then resigned to write a million words a year for these and other such magazines. It got so I couldn't look at another rape victim's face. So I turned to comic books, writing as many a four scripts a week. Now THAT paid! And so did radio. By that time, I'd teamed up with Ken Crossen and we were on our way to the top—and I got drafted.

I spent a couple of years in the Pacific as a combat engineer, and when I got out, the markets we had developed together were gone, and he left his wife and three children to escape to the West Coast, disguised with a beard and dark glasses, and with a girl of 21.

That was the last I saw of Ken. It was 1946, and I still had the same wife and son, and I couldn't get back to writing. So I had to find something else. It turned out to be exporting rebuilt bookbinding machinery. I knew as little about them as I had engineering, which was zero, except for pushing and pulling and hauling pieces of bridges together, and road grading—from the position of D-handle shovel operator. Even the infantry had pitied us. I made lots of money in the bookbinding business before it dried up.

By that time, I was ready to go back to writing. But what? *Unknown* had folded, and I didn't want to go back to sf for the very reason Des Hall had spelled out—it was too much work for too little dough. So I turned again to the comic books and soon worked my way up to the highest-paid writer in the field—and collapsed. I did, not the field.

I was doing my best to recover when a girl who had worked for Ken and me called me in to present a publishing program to a French-Italian publishing firm, named, in translation, World Editions.

It seems they had a big slick magazine in France and Italy that was selling two or three million copies a week. A cross between beautifully executed comics and confession stories, less beautifully executed, it was dubbed *Fascination* and set loose on the American public with a huge advertising program. There were five issues—the last sold 5% of its print order of several hundred thousand, or was it a million? I forget. Anyhow, they were too stubborn to get out of the American market with such a beating, and so I was asked to submit a publishing program.

I surveyed the entire magazine market. It was early 1950, and everywhere I looked, magazines were in deep trouble. As soon as paper rationing had ended in 1946, everyone who could read—or could hire someone to read—was putting out everything from comics to fashion magazines. The one exception was science fiction.

On the basis of experience, I should have submitted anything but an sf magazine, a fantasy magazine projected for later, once the sf one was established, and a series of paperback sf novels. But I saw that *Astounding* was going off into one cult after another—John Campbell was rushing up dead ends, the latest being *Dianetics*, in his search for a meaningful universe—and *Fantasy & Science Fiction* was brand new, and flying in the face of the single immutable law of those fields: that readers don't like fantasy in their sf, or sf in their fantasy. A very high-grade sf magazine could fit right between them. And thus I offered my publishing program to the Italian representative World Editions, a great guy named Lombi. He offered it to the publisher who lived on the Riviera, who must have flipped a coin, because neither he nor Lombi knew anything at all about sf or fantasy, and it came up yes.

I gave them a choice between *Galaxy* and *If*. I liked both titles, but I left the decision to Lombi and his boss on the Riviera. They, in turn, didn't know what a galaxy was, and *If* seemed to them too short, and they left the choice to me. So I and our art director, Washington Irving van der Poel (Van for short), talked over possible cover layouts—and my present wife's (Nicky's) first husband, a great calligrapher, designed the lettering. Harry Harrison lent us his apartment to display the many variations of both *Galaxy* and *If*, which a large number of people, including writers, artists, and readers, were asked to vote on.

Curiously, almost all wrote on their secret ballots that they personally liked *Galaxy* and an inverted-L layout, but each thought nobody else would. That was good enough for us—*Galaxy* it was and the inverted-L layout won. So did Crome-Kote, the closest printing paper to photographic glossies, which I had asked for pretty urgently for our cover stock. Despite its high cost and difficulty of handling I got what I asked for.

The fact is that I got every single thing I wanted, from word rates to rights. The going rate was a top of two cents a word—I got the price up to three cents minimum, four cents or more for steady contributors, plus $100 for short-shorts. And we bought first-serial rights only.

Suddenly, writers and artists offered us everything they were turning out, and many of the greats came out of retirement to join us. It was a wonderful time to be alive and editing *Galaxy*. And in the unbelievable space of five issues, *Galaxy* was in the black!

Just in case you think I'm paranoid about being a historical Typhoid Mary, consider this—only months after *Galaxy* was born, the Korean War started.

And paper became impossible to buy at any price. Our printer had set us up with a contract with a mill—or so we thought. It turned out he had the contract, not us, and we were forced to look elsewhere. I went through the yellow pages and called every printer I found, asking if we could hook up with them. The only one who said yes was a printing broker named Robert M. Guinn, who had followed *Galaxy*'s astonishing rise toward first place with considerable awe.

The paper was more like blotter than newsprint, but we missed only one issue in switching printers. And we came to be great friends with Bob Guinn, of which more later.

Now back to Lombi. He was in the U.S. on a visitor's visa, not allowed to work here or be paid by *Galaxy*. One day he was called down to Washington by the Immigration Dept. and shown all of a letter but the signature—which stated that he was a dirty Italian communistic fascist who ought to be sent back where he came from. Affidavits and appeals failed. He was sent back to Italy, his visa withdrawn.

I still don't know who sent that letter, but it's no coincidence that as soon as Lombi was out of the country, internal warfare developed between the American, French and Italian offices of World Editions. We had hired an ex-music publisher as president of the American office, who had been hired just about as he was to lock his door and declare bankruptcy, and a circulation director. I had told Lombi at the onset to call in all unsold copies of *Galaxy*'s first year—and the president and the circulation director got hold of them and stuffed their garages with these soon-to-be-priceless copies of the magazine. Then strange things happened to our sales. Readers wrote in that they couldn't find it on any newsstand anywhere.

The upshot was that the Riviera guy sent the head of the French office to New York to find out what went wrong. To make a short story of all this, the Frenchman cabled back to the Riviera that the magazine was a dud and should immediately be sold—to the American president and the circulation director, and their price was $3,000. I got in touch hurriedly with Lombi and told him of this. The time in Rome was 4:30 A.M., but Lombi got up and raced to the Riviera. The publisher instantly sent a cable stopping negotiations and followed up with another visit by Lombi to take care of the matter.

I was told by the two American scoundrels that I was part of the deal, but I wasn't having any. Lombi arrived by plane and we began looking for a better buyer. A number of outfits here were interested, but, as I said, we were becoming great friends with the printing broker, Bob Guinn, and I got him to make a bid. I don't know how much, but Lombi made the sale with the Riviera man's blessing—and no sooner had Guinn bought it than the inside job became clear to Lombi. The distribution pattern had been deliberately loused up—by shipping *Galaxy* all over the South, where there was practically nobody interested in sf, and into hamlets all over the North and West.

Lombi called his boss and told him of this sabotage, and the boss told Lombi to buy back the magazine from Guinn. Guinn gave him his price. Lombi was aghast—but this is four times as much as we paid! Guinn grinned and told him he, Guinn, knew what he was buying, whereas World Editions hadn't known what they were selling. Lombi went home, but not in dishonor. I hated to see him go. We'd had a fine relationship.

But Guinn was equally good to work for. He left policies, decisions and rates up to me, and involved me in distribution and advertising problems. I mention advertising because World Editions had, over my protests, run a back cover ad for a book called "Confessions of a French Chambermaid"—and we'd lost 10,000 readers for each of the three months of the contract. *Galaxy* went to the top of the field after that, never to lose ground.

And then came *Beyond Fantasy Fiction*. It was beautiful—for 10 wonderful issues. By then we had learned that there wasn't a big enough audience to support a fantasy magazine, so it died just as *Unknown* had, a decade before, of financial malnutrition. If *Beyond* had come first, I think it would have had the same effect and the same misty memories as *Unknown*.

After we had vacated the title *If* in 1950, Jim Quinn put it out, but couldn't keep it going. And so I got both titles to edit. This was more than an extra job for me—it enabled me to buy stories that weren't *Galaxy* standard and thus keep writers happy, as well as giving me the chance I'd never before had of bringing new ones up to Galaxy.

As for the *Galaxy* novel reprints—they weren't handled right as packages, being more like numbered magazines than paperbacks. I got that go-ahead just as the paperback market broke, but it was too late.

All this was from 1950 to 1961, eleven memorable years. What happened to me then? I had been in a disastrous car crash that finally wore me down to 126 pounds and eventually into the hospital with a poor chance of my ever being able to walk again. I was there for a long time, till my weight was back to normal and the crippling cured.

So, if you remember, I remarried and the big buildup came to South Vietnam. I'm not ecstatically happy about being retired, but there is nothing I can do about it. I surface with an occasional story. The rest of the time I count my blessings—and there are many—a wonderful, beautiful wife and a beautiful, wonderful stepdaughter, a fine son and daughter-in-law and four splendid grandchildren, and your friendship.

Would I go back to editing? Never, for two reasons. I haven't the vigor to entice and coax the best stories out of the best writers against the damnable deadlines. Second, I think the day of magazines is coming to an end, science fiction in particular. They can't compete with all the series anthologies there are for two more reasons. The anthologies pay better rates and, in addition, royalties. Second, they can be left on the newsstands indefinitely and in more places than magazines, including supermarkets.

But I wouldn't take a million cruzeiros for the memories I have of being about as good an editor in those 11 years as John Campbell was in his great years from 1938 to 1941. That took some doing. And nothing could induce me to do it again.

It wouldn't be safe for the world, would it?

Dear Retro SF Reader:

The inquiry into uncharted domains of the outer and inner human cosmos has been a central issue of the best in science fiction literature for over fifty years! Besides being of eminent metaphysical interest, many of the science fiction classics of the golden and silver age are veritable gems of prose fiction. Gateways Retro Science Fiction is dedicated to the preservation of the very best writings of the pioneers of this genre of American literature. We plan to re-issue novels and novellas from those earlier days as well as the RETRO VISIONS anthology series.

For current information and a catalog of Retro SF, you may contact us through any of the following means:

Gateways Retro SF

P.O. Box 370
Nevada City, CA 95959-0370
USA
phone: (530) 271-2239
(800) 869-0658
email : retrosf@gatewaysbooksandtapes.com
websites :
www.retrosf.com
www.gatewaysbooksandtapes.com
www.sciencefictionmuseum.com
www.sfradiotheater.com

Thanks for your interest and enthusiasm !

Gateways Books and Retro SF Staff